**"But let's make sure we understand each other.
This alliance between the Order and the werewolves
is a fragile thing. If we screw this up, you could
wind up being hunted again."**

I slapped the SUV. "This SUV is red."

Simon waited for me to expand on that point.

"It's cold outside," I said.

Simon still stared at me.

"You're kind of acting like a dick," I tried.

"What are you doing?" Simon demanded.

"Oh, I'm sorry. I thought we were playing some weird game where we made completely obvious statements," I explained.

"According to your file, you're almost a century old." Simon turned and went back to the front seat. "Maybe it's time you grew up."

He probably had a point. On the other hand, I am pretty old, and one thing that's a constant is that when people tell you to grow up, what they usually mean is that you should do what's expected of you. If I was any good at that, I'd have died a long time ago.

Praise for the Pax Arcana series:

"The Pax Arcana books are seriously good reads. Action, humor, and heart with unexpected twists and turns. If you are (like me) waiting for the next Butcher or Hearne—pick up Elliot James. Then you can bite your nails waiting for the next James, too."

—*New York Times* bestselling author Patricia Briggs

"Loved it! *Charming* is a giant gift basket of mythology and lore delivered by a brilliant new voice in urban fantasy. Elliott James tells stories that are action-packed, often amusing, and always entertaining."

—*New York Times* bestselling author Kevin Hearne

"I loved this book from start to finish. Exciting and innovative, *Charming* is a great introduction to a world I look forward to spending a lot more time in."

—*New York Times* bestselling author
Seanan McGuire

"Grab some snacks and settle back as splendid debut author James serves up a Prince Charming tale yanked sideways. John Charming comes from a prominent line of dragon slayers, witch-finders and killers trained by the Knights Templar, but now he has a problem: He has become what they hunt. James's reluctant hero faces threats and danger with a smart-ass attitude that keeps the narrative fast-paced, edgy and amusing. Mark this name down—you will undoubtedly be seeing more from James!"
—*RT Book Reviews*

IN SHINING ARMOR

PAX ARCANA: BOOK 4

ELLIOTT JAMES

www.orbitbooks.net

Copyright © 2016 by Elliott James LLC
Excerpt from *Legend Has It* copyright © 2016 by Elliott James LCC
Excerpt from *Chasing Embers* copyright © 2016 by James Bennett

Cover design by Wendy Chan
Cover photograph © James Wragg/Trevillion Images
Cover copyright © 2016 by Hachette Book Group, Inc.

Orbit
Hachette Book Group
1290 Avenue of the Americas, New York, NY 10104
www.orbitbooks.net

Printed in the United States of America

RRD-C

First Edition: April 2016

10 9 8 7 6 5 4 3 2 1

Orbit is an imprint of Hachette Book Group, Inc. The Orbit name and logo are trademarks of Little, Brown Book Group Limited.

The Hachette Speakers Bureau provides a wide range of authors for speaking events. To find out more, go to www.hachettespeakersbureau.com or call (866) 376-6591.

The publisher is not responsible for websites (or their content) that are not owned by the publisher.

Library of Congress Cataloging-in-Publication Data

Names: James, Elliott, author.
Title: In shining armor / Elliott James.
Description: First Edition. | New York : Orbit, 2016. | Series: Pax Arcana ; Book 4
Identifiers: LCCN 2015043779 | ISBN 9780316302333 (paperback)
Subjects: | BISAC: FICTION / Fantasy / Contemporary. | FICTION / Fantasy / Paranormal. | FICTION / Action & Adventure. | FICTION / Fantasy / Urban Life. | GSAFD: Fantasy fiction.
Classification: LCC PS3610.A4334 I5 2016 | DDC 813/.6—dc23 LC record available at http://lccn.loc.gov/2015043779

To my mother. These aren't your kind of books, but if I'm doing my own thing it's because I know you'll love me anyway, and that is the most precious gift any parent can give.

Why should I be dismayed
Though flame had burned the whole
World, as it were a coal,
Now I have seen it weighed
Against a soul?

—From "A Friend's Illness" by W. B. Yeats

PART THE FIRST

Baby Come Back

Prologue

BOSTON: 1965

It was four thirty in the morning, and Tess Arbiter was up and had breakfast cooking when I went to pick up my partner, Nick. Red-haired, pale-skinned, medium-sized with a bit of heft to her after six kids, Tess was swathed in a thick, soft-looking light blue nightgown. She didn't even try to get me to sit down at the dining room table, just shoved a paper plate with a toasted ham-and-egg sandwich, two potato cakes, and some sausage links into my hand. I took off the top slice of bread and began to add the sausage and the potato cakes to the sandwich.

"I hate it when you do that," Tess grumbled while she poured me a cup of coffee. "It's like you just want to get the meal over with as fast as possible."

"If I don't have a hand free, your husband will want to drive," I explained. "Assuming he ever finishes his constitutional." That's what the Arbiters called it when Nick spent a lot of time on the can: his constitutional.

"Nick's not that bad a driver," Tess said loyally, but she was smiling while she said it.

"That's right!" Nick exclaimed as he swaggered downstairs. He didn't make any attempt to move quietly or lower his voice, but all of the Arbiter kids could probably sleep through earthquakes or thunderstorms after growing up in a house that had five siblings and Nick

*in it. My partner was a tall, burly guy with bushy hair and a boom-
ing voice and a big beard. Nick's midlife crisis was taking him to
some strange places, and he was wearing a shirt that was supposed
to be multicolored but mostly had varying shades of tan and brown
swirling around. The shirt also had wide-open flaring collar flaps
and two buttons undone to expose Nick's hairy chest. "All those speed-
ing tickets prove it. If I was a bad driver, I'd have wrecked by now."*

*"That's like saying someone can't have a drinking problem
because he's put so many beers away," I said.*

*Nick raised his palms up and spoke to the sky theatrically. "Jesus,
how did I wind up with two mothers? And how is one of them male
and thirteen years younger than me? That's got to be some kind of
miracle, right? Maybe not an immaculate conception, but something."*

*"Don't take the Lord's name in vain!" Tess scolded as she brought
Nick a thick black all-weather coat. "You need God on your side."*

*"That wasn't swearing; that was a sincere question to the
divine," Nick said equably as he shrugged into the coat. "Geez,
Tess, this coat is a little warm for this time of year, isn't it?"*

*"She's trying to hide that shirt from the eyes of man," I mumbled
through a mouthful of sandwich.*

"Shut it," Nick advised.

*"Do you want another sandwich like Johnny's before you go,
Nicholas?" Tess asked.*

*"Tess, relax," Nick told her. "We're just going to check out the
North End Tunnels again. Unusual rat activity."*

*Tess looked like she wanted to swear. The North End Tunnels
were a constant problem. They ran under a large section of Boston,
and nobody seemed to know who had really built them. The tunnels
seemed to attract ghosts and undead and cult activity like some kind
of freak magnet too. Every couple of years, we had to send coordi-
nated teams in to clean the place out when too many high school kids
or vagrants started hearing weird things or going missing. But Tess*

was a knight's wife, and she focused on the essentials. "What kind of unusual activity? Are rats coming out of the place or going into it?"

"Turcopolier Crockett didn't say," I answered. A turcopolier was one of three men in the Order who functioned as both leader and liaison, coordinating between the various chapters and incorporating outsiders as needed. Sometimes, these outsiders were mercenaries and outlaws hired to do a limited, specific task without knowing why or who they were working for. Sometimes, they were lay sergeants, men who had failed out of knight training but were still useful in a limited combat capacity, or people who weren't of the blood but who had stumbled into our world and were very capable fighters. Sometimes, they were lay servants, people of the blood who weren't suited for any kind of combat but were still compelled to serve, or ordinary people who had learned about our world and were permitted to live in exchange for being useful in more passive ways. "Which would make you feel better?"

Tess aimed a clout at me for some reason, then noticed that I had finished my sandwich. "You're done already? Do you want another sandwich? I've got plenty left over here."

"Tess, leave it," Nick grumbled. "I've already got seven mouths to feed without pouring food down the human garbage disposal here."

I topped off my coffee while they squabbled. One way or another, the topic of food wound up taking up about seventy percent of all the Arbiters' conversations, or at least their public ones. It was the socially acceptable outlet through which Tess expressed both love and anxiety, and she had too much of both for such a limited medium. When we were finally ready to leave, Tess gave me a hug that silently asked me to take care of her husband, and I gave her a back pat that said I'd do my best.

Nick and I walked out onto the dark street where I had my Mustang parked. It was early fall, and the morning air was chill and damp with last night's rain, the kind of insidious cold that clings and seeps.

We were supposed to be insurance investigators, and Nick's neighbors were used to him coming or going at weird hours and leaving for days or weeks at a time. They certainly didn't suspect that we were Knights Templar, or that we hunted any and all monsters who broke the ancient truce that kept the world of magic a secret from mankind.

I turned on the radio, and the Seekers' "I'll Never Find Another You" came on. I had mixed feelings about rock and roll—it seemed like a distilled version of swing to me, and some of it was catchy and some of it was powerful and some of it just seemed like drug-soaked morons who couldn't carry a tune, screaming into a microphone because they badly needed an ass-kicking.

"Let's get some news." Nick reached over for a radio dial, and I slapped his hand away.

"Here's some breaking news." I put on my best radio announcer's voice. "Early this morning, John Charming told his partner Nick Arbiter to keep his big fat paws off Charming's radio."

"That's not news," Nick grumbled sourly. "I already knew you were uptight."

"Nope. I'm calm, and I'd like to stay that way," I replied. "Listening to you bellyache and come up with conspiracy theories takes me out of my center." Lately, it seemed like all of the news was about assassinations, riots, blackouts, Soviet aggressions, and US escalations that nobody wanted to call a war even though we'd officially sent marines to Vietnam. Like the rest of the country, Nick and I couldn't seem to agree on what it all meant.

"Stay in your center? Jesus, you sound like the beatniks," Nick complained. To Nick, all protestors were beatniks no matter what they called themselves nowadays. "What do I care about your center? I've got six kids! I haven't been able to focus for twenty years."

"You went through the same meditation training I did." It was a fascination with Eastern arts and philosophies that had originally gotten the Knights Templar branded as heretics and forced them

to go underground in the first place, and our chapter in particular emphasized martial arts and meditation.

"Yeah, but I was smart enough not to take it too seriously," Nick took a piece of foil-wrapped gum out of his chest pocket. "Is that why this car smells like incense? Have you been meditating in here?"

I didn't respond.

Nick laughed. "You still shagging those college girls?"

"They say they're liberating their sexuality," I said mildly. "I'm just trying to help." The truth was, the whole free love thing was starting to feel a little empty.

"Uh-huh." Nick smacked his gum noisily. Beneath all of his bluster and tough talk, Nick was a family man. I wasn't, and I wasn't ever going to be. "Listen, John, you got a bad deal. I know that. What with the vasectomy and all."

I was a monster hunter whose mother had been bitten by a werewolf while she was still pregnant with me. I had never shown any sign of werewolf taint as a child, but the Knights Templar had made me get a vasectomy at the age of twelve anyhow, just in case. It was one of their many conditions for letting me live.

"Me and Tess have been thinking about this," Nick said seriously. "You're getting up in years, man. And it's not like there aren't all kinds of orphans with knights' blood in them. You know what our orphanages are like."

I did. Intimately. "What are you getting at, Nick?"

"You're what? Twenty-seven? Twenty-eight?" Nick asked. "You can't have kids. So what? Get married and adopt! There are all kinds of women who'd go for you. Even some with knight's blood now. That whole malaria thing proved you don't have any werewolf in you."

I kept quiet. The malaria that had almost killed me, the same malaria that Nick took as proof that I was entirely human, had actually woken up something latent during my body's last-ditch efforts to save itself. I had never changed shape during a full moon, but ever since that brush with death, my senses had been getting sharper, my muscles stronger, and my ability to heal faster. In a few years, I would find out if I aged normally or not, and if I didn't, I was going to have some big decisions to make.

"Maybe you could find a bug hugger," Nick sounded uncharacteristically awkward. "Bug Huggers" was slang for a small, much-mocked chapter of the Knights Templar who believed that the Order was going to have to focus more on working with the supernatural world instead of just policing it. "None of their women would give a flip about... you know."

"Thanks, Dad," I said. The Righteous Brothers' "Unchained Melody" came on, and I turned up the radio.

"Hey, man," Nick said uncomfortably. "We're partners."

"I'll think about what you're saying," I promised, and we pulled into the construction site where our chapter's turcopolier had called the meeting. The large abandoned brick building was set off by aluminum fencing and a network of orange girders with panel-board walkways between them. The place had been a small factory that manufactured explosives during both world wars, but a decrease in demand and an increase in safety regulations had put it out of business. Now it would be cheaper to build a new factory than upgrade this place to modern standards. I didn't know what Templar-owned business had bought the place or for what reason, and didn't care.

I stopped in front of the gate and waited for someone to identify my car and come out to let us in. Nick stared at the old factory with subdued interest. "It would be hard to become an architect after all this."

"What?" I asked.

Nick gestured vaguely at the building. "Don't you ever wonder what you'd have done if you hadn't been born into this life? Or if you hadn't made it through knight training? I would have liked to build things."

I didn't say anything. All knights were bound by a magical pact our ancestors entered into with the Fae centuries ago. The geas *hummed in our blood and vibrated in our bones. Whatever we could do to keep the existence of the supernatural a secret, we did. There wasn't much point complaining about it.*

A big grey block of a man in a construction helmet emerged from shadow and unlocked the gate. He was accompanied by a guard dog and carrying a transistor radio, but the radio was really just to make sure that no strange magic was operating in the area. Any spell strong enough to matter would interfere with radio reception. The guard checked our licenses, inspected our thumbs to make sure the fingerprints had been burnt off, and shone a light into our eyes. Then we both made a secret sign, but Nick knew the guy and whatever I was, it wasn't enough to set dogs barking, and it was all pretty perfunctory.

It wasn't that the guard was being sloppy exactly. When members of our chapter were six years old, they attended a ceremony where they had to hold a brooch shaped like a beetle. It was a haunted brooch, and any normal person who wasn't protected from outside mental influences by a knight's geas would imagine the brooch coming to life and burrowing into their skin. Any normal person who didn't fling the brooch away died from a heart attack or embolism within half a minute. It was the Order's way of making sure no cuckoo birds somehow wound up in a knight's nest; the geas that bound us to our duty was the tightest security there was. We couldn't betray the Order if we wanted to.

Nick introduced us, and the guard, Tom, was polite enough, but he was from an older generation, and I saw something flicker behind his eyes when he heard my name. We drove on to what was probably consecrated ground. Other cars were already in the lot, and we parked and made our way through the gutted carcass of the building. At the bottom of a concrete stairwell was a storage area that had been converted into a bomb shelter in the '50s. Ten knights were already down there, as well as my chapter's quartermaster, three priests, and Turcopolier Crockett.

"You're late," said our turcopolier.

Nick ostentatiously checked his watch. "We're five minutes early."

"For a knight, that's late," the turcopolier said flatly, and he had a point. Left to my own devices, I would have shown up earlier and canvassed the place more carefully before entering, but I wasn't about to make Nick look bad by saying as much. If Nick wasn't burned out, he was definitely getting a little toasty. I just had to keep him alive until he couldn't pass the physicals any longer, and then the Templars would put Nick to work in some other capacity, maybe even give him a desk job at the insurance company that we supposedly worked for, one of the many businesses that the Order owned and ran as a legitimate front. Nick could spend the rest of his middle age sifting through insurance claims, looking for signs of unusual activity.

The room was large, about the size of a small gym, and the walls were covered with the more traditional weapons of monster hunting that would work under any magical conditions. There were swords and crossbows and longbows and silver steel knives and axes and pikes and flasks of holy water along with kerosene lamps and torches and stakes. We exchanged some terse greetings with a few other knights, but the quartermaster was standing in front of the open door to a weapons storage room, and he called Nick over to where he had a flamethrower set aside. "Arbiter, come here. You're operating your team's flamethrower."

Nick already knew the safety procedures—the big guys always got the flamethrowers and the bulky suits and tanks that went with them—but he listened patiently while the quartermaster reviewed the basics of flamethrower use. I drifted behind him. Cleaning out the North End Tunnels always required weapons that were too dangerous or specialized or unconventional for knights to keep in private homes or car trunks. I would probably wind up handling incendiary or poison gases, or low-grade explosives, or flasks of flammable moonshine whose stills had been primed with holy water.

Except . . . something was wrong. I caught a whiff of the

quartermaster's scent with the enhanced senses that I wasn't supposed to have, and the thing talking to Nick smelled like the quartermaster, but... it also didn't smell like the quartermaster. The quartermaster—or whatever was pretending to be him—smelled wrong in other ways too. He was leaking hate and rage into the air though he was acting calm and professional.

What was going on? Knights couldn't be possessed, and the quartermaster's appearance couldn't be an illusion. The same magical blood oath that bound us knights to our duty kept any other kind of mind magic from affecting us. A doppelganger or a nix wouldn't smell like the quartermaster, and a fetch would never have made it past the building's wards. Was this some kind of cunning person who had come up with a spell that actually combined them with the quartermaster? Could something be animating the quartermaster's corpse?

I hadn't had my new senses long, and I still didn't entirely trust them. So, I looked at the thing's eyes—a lot of times, odd glints or dilations or even inverted reflections in the pupils will give shapechangers away, but the move was a mistake. The thing looked up. Its eyes met mine, and we both knew instantly. It knew I knew it wasn't the real quartermaster. I knew it knew. I can't explain how. I was looking at some completely different person, some cold and alien and hate-filled thing peering out at me from the husk of the quartermaster's body. The skin it was wearing was completely irrelevant. The skin it was wearing. A name popped into my head: skinwalker. It was the last coherent thought I had.

The thing reached for a sawed-off shotgun that it was wearing holstered in a hip sheath like a handgun. I was faster than it was, but Nick was between us, and he'd sensed some movement or tension from me even though I was behind him. My partner was in the middle of pulling on a lot of bulky gear, and when he started to turn, he forced me to move even farther to get around him. The skinwalker tilted the shotgun in its straps and pulled the trigger while I was pushing Nick out of the way of the blast. There was an impossibly loud sound and a searing hot pain in my gut, and then I was somewhere propped against something and unable to move.

A massive pounding, rushing sound filled my head, like my head was inside a giant seashell, or a giant seashell was in my head. I still saw bullets tear holes in the skinwalker's clothes without puncturing its skin. Or more to the point, without puncturing its skin suit. The skinwalker fired another shot with its shotgun and then reached for the handgun holstered at its other side, drawing and firing while it moved back toward the machine guns.

A silver steel knife flew straight between the skinwalker's eyes, but the tip of the blade skidded over flesh that was not the skinwalker's flesh, as if the point was sliding on ice.

That was the last thing I saw. There was no enclosing field of darkness. I was just gone.

The sound of muffled screams and the smell of burning flesh woke me, and I came to under a pile of bodies. Nick's eyes were staring at me emptily from a blood-covered face. I shifted and saw the skinwalker with his back to me, standing there three yards away in his natural form. He was a wiry male with all of his hair shaved off. His naked body was covered in sigils and symbols made out of fresh blood. The suit he had made out of our quartermaster's skin was carefully laid out on the floor by his feet like a suit of Sunday clothes.

Turcopolier Crockett was the one screaming through a gag, and in a moment I saw why. The skinwalker was cooking the turcopolier's right foot in a portable camp stove, doing some kind of dance around the flames while he chanted in a language I didn't know.

Skinwalkers weren't illusionists. They had the ability to literally assume someone else's form. The neutral ones could do this by looking in another person's eyes, and claimed that their gift came from the Great Spirit, but the evil ones learned to duplicate that

power through unnatural means. They mimicked another creature's form only after making a suit out of that being's skin, a suit
that they wore like a pelt. This skinwalker obviously planned to
make a suit out of the turcopolier. Maybe it was working its way
up the Knights Templar's chain of command.

From a purely tactical standpoint, that probably saved my life.

The most dangerous thing about the evil skinwalkers was that
their magical disguises were also a form of magical armor. The skin
suits redistributed energy down their length and into the fourth
dimension where they were anchored, like a chain that conducts
electricity and disperses it into the ground. The magical disguises
worked that way with all energy. Heat. Impact. Whatever.

But the skinwalker wasn't wearing one of his magical skin suits now.

I erupted from beneath the bodies of my brothers. The skinwalker was moving at the normal human speed that I had left
behind, and I broke his neck with a forearm hammer before he
had half turned around.

The skinwalker collapsed, and I stared at Turcopolier Crockett.
He lay there bound, broken-limbed, and bleeding.

He had seen me take a shotgun blast to the stomach. He had
seen too much.

"Do it," the turcopolier rasped. "And to hell with you."

I unstrapped my belt and began to make a tourniquet around
his right leg. "I'm not that kind of a monster," I told him.

At least I would have a head start. The turcopolier's gaze told
me everything I needed to know. A skinwalker had just killed four-
teen of his men. A skinwalker, the worst kind of cunning man there
was, even worse than necromancers, and that wasn't an exaggera-
tion. Before skinwalkers could leave their original human forms
behind, they had to kill one of their parents or siblings or children.
Skinwalkers had to commit incest, or sleep with a corpse, or practice cannibalism. Some said that skinwalkers had to do all of those

things. It was only when skinwalkers had symbolically destroyed all of their ties to their own humanity and individual identity that they were able to assume someone else's.

And the turcopolier was staring at me, the man who was trying to save his life, as if I were more of an abomination than the thing I had saved him from. And then it wasn't the turcopolier staring at me like that. It was me. It was me who lay there bound and bleeding, staring back at me—at myself—with loathing.

"This will work out in the end," I assured the me that was lying there. "The knights will have to stop hunting you eventually. You're the one who's going to end a knight/werewolf war in the twenty-first century. The knights are going to start working with a pack of good werewolves calling themselves the Round Table. You'll find a woman named Sig, a valkyrie, and she's not going to blame you for any of this."

Wait. What?

I woke up fully alert, missing Nick and Tess and their kids, Maggie and Robert and Brian and Marie and Kevin and John, as if I'd just lost them. But then an awareness of the present began rushing into me like the tide filling a hole in the sand, and the pain began to fade. Not go away but integrate with the experiences of the last half-century. I just lay there, careful not to wake up Sig, who was half draped over me. Her head was nested on my shoulder. Her long cool hair trailed over my naked stomach, and her left leg was curled over mine.

That hadn't felt like a normal dream. I had relived that memory before, while a prisoner of the Knights Templar. Was I experiencing some kind of posttraumatic symptom from holding the Sword of Truth? I'd had some weird experiences with dreams while hanging out with a cunning woman named Sarah White too, and she'd as much as told me that I'd opened a door that didn't close. Was the dream just a dream? Are they ever?

I listened to Sig's breathing until I fell back to sleep.

1

OOOH BABY

Once Upon a Time, I was too happy. I know that's not rational, but there's still a part of me that blames everything that happened afterward on that one simple fact. Something bad had to happen. I was having one of the most perfect days of my life, and I allowed myself to be too happy.

It had snowed while Sig Norresdotter and I were camping in the Cascades, one of those early April snows that have been becoming more common in southwest Virginia in recent years. Our heaviest snows have begun in February, and from March onward, the mountain weather seems to fluctuate forty degrees every three days, going from snow to T-shirt weather back to snow again, as if the weather were bipolar.

In any case, there's something about getting naked and keeping warm in an insulated tent while the world around you is frozen that adds a layer of intensity to the experience. Sig had kept up a running joke about how the weekend wasn't exactly the kind of date with Prince Charming that most women pictured—she would make proclamations about needing the Royal Roll of Toilet Paper before going off into the woods, or start yelling for footmen to come make us s'mores while we were entangled in our sleeping bag—but she was cracking jokes because she doesn't like getting mushy, not because she was being passive-aggressive.

I suppose I could have found the Prince Charming references slightly annoying—my name may be John Charming, but I'm not royalty, and nobody in my family ever was—but Sig and I were in that physical-intoxication phase of a new relationship where every word, gesture, and glance is saturated in a hormonal nimbus. I wanted to fill my hands and mouth and heart with her. Her skin felt like it should be glowing, and she smelled like home. Honestly, she could have belched loudly and called my mother a whore, and I would have had to struggle not to view it as some kind of delightful postmodern irony.

The hike back down the mountains had been magical too, like traveling through a series of paintings. The Freezing-Your-Ass-Off collection, maybe, but still beautiful. Then we'd decided to bypass the interstate and wound up getting lost in a little nowhere Appalachian town called Eccleston about twenty minutes outside Blacksburg, Virginia. We stopped at this brick building that looked like an old-fashioned general store, and discovered that it was a restaurant called the Palisades. It was like finding a diamond in a plug of tobacco.

Warm air gusted through antique grates in the wooden floor while we drank hot cider and thawed out. I was trying not to release obscene-sounding sighs when the waitress brought out some of the best focaccia I'd ever had in my life. The outer crust of the bread was lightly dusted with spices, and when my teeth broke through that crisp surface, they sank into soft warmth lightly infused with cheese.

"Sweet mother of all that's good and crunchy," I said reverently. "Forget the pizza. I just want six more of these appetizers."

"I can't believe you ordered pizza anyway." Sig had refused to give up the menu even after she ordered, and she was still studying it intently as if trying to make sure that it wasn't some kind of trick. "You can get a pizza anywhere. How many places around here have food like this?" Sig had ordered quail that was stuffed with chestnuts and Italian sausage and then covered with some kind of cranberry glaze, and I could see her point.

"I ordered before I tasted this appetizer," I said. "This place doesn't look all that swanky, and it's hard for anybody to screw up a pizza so badly that I can't get behind it."

"It's not like we look all that fancy ourselves," Sig observed. "I haven't showered in two days."

"Don't worry." I reached over and got her to put her menu down by taking her hand and planting a lingering kiss on the back of her wrist while I lightly stroked her pulse. We made eye contact, and I promised, "When I get you into a shower, I'll clean you thoroughly."

Sig cleared her throat. Her voice was a little huskier than usual. "You do realize that *thoroughly* means focusing on more than two places, right?"

"Those areas behind the elbows and knees are very impor-tant," I said virtuously.

Sig laughed and released my hand. "Oh, please. Whoever said cleanliness is next to godliness never showered with you."

That made me smile. "You know, you're joking around a lot more these days."

"I'm happy." She confessed this as if it were a character flaw. After a moment's reflection, she added, "You're joking around less. Or at least not in the same way."

"I'm happy too," I told her, meaning it.

That's when her cell phone rang. See what I mean? It was like the universe was speaking.

17

We both froze. We'd had a no-cell-phone agreement for the weekend.

"Shit," Sig swore as the phone rang a second time, then confessed. "I checked my messages while you were in the restroom. I forgot to turn it back off."

I nodded. "You'd better answer it." It might not be logical, but if something bad occurred while Sig and I had our cell phones turned off for the weekend, that's just the way it was. But if we ignored an active cell phone ringing and later found out that something bad had happened...

Sig answered the cell phone. My hearing is sharper than a normal human's, so I didn't have to wonder why her face went blank. The voice on the other end was Ben Lafontaine, and he sounded urgent and grim. "Hey, Sig, this is Ben. Is John with you?"

Ben Lafontaine is in charge of the somewhat whimsically named Round Table, the alliance of werewolf packs who have made a treaty with the Knights Templar. Ben is also technically my leader, a fact that we both skirt around because of my authority issues and the fact that neither of us is sure who would win in a fight. I'm pretty sure Ben would gladly let me lead the Round Table if I wanted the job and wouldn't be a complete disaster at it. In practice, Ben is somewhere between a mentor and a qualified ally and a friend, and I would pretty much do anything he asked me to do anyhow as long as he was asking. I owe Ben a lot. Sig handed the phone over to me wordlessly.

I didn't waste any time. "What is it?"

"It's Constance," he said. "Our goddaughter has been kidnapped."

∿2∿

THE TRUTH, THE HOLE IN THE TRUTH, AND SOMETHING LIKE THE TRUTH

As soon as Sig and I got off the commuter plane, we were greeted by Ben and an impossibly handsome blond-haired man. The private airstrip was disguised as a straight patch of road between two vast stretches of cornfields in the middle of nowhere, Massachusetts. It was dark and bitterly cold, but I already said it was Massachusetts, so at least one of those three facts is probably redundant.

"This is Simon Travers," Ben said, handing me a large white paper bag full of thick, greasy hamburgers. I was carrying a guitar case that had a couple of interesting items beneath the false bottom and wearing the backpack from my hiking trip, so I had to make some minor adjustments. "He's your Grandmaster's fixer."

My Grandmaster?

Ben was a large Chippewa slab of craggy, big-boned muscle, and the scowl on his face was fairly ominous. Ben smelled bad too, and I don't mean he stank in any conventional sense; Ben was dumping rage pheromones into the air like toxic waste.

Constance wasn't even a year old, and I don't think Ben had spent much more face-to-face time with her than I had, but our goddaughter's abduction was still hitting him on some primal level. Ben had lost a child at some point way back in his long life, maybe a century ago, maybe more, and that's all I knew about it. Maybe that's all I'll ever know about it. But I occasionally catch glimpses of how that loss has defined him.

And that wasn't even taking his wolf instincts into account.

"I won't say it's a pleasure, Mr. Charming, but I've heard a lot about you." The blond man offered me a brief handshake and a tight smile. He was so good-looking that he was almost pretty, but if he was Emil Lamplighter's number one fixer, this Simon was a dangerous man. He turned his attention to Sig, and his smile became less perfunctory. He took her hand and held it rather than shook it. "And I've heard about you as well, Miss Norresdotter. I've never met a Valkyrie before."

Something about the way he said it made it clear that he meant he'd never slept with a Valkyrie before. This Simon was a charming fuck, dressed in some vaguely European-looking black outdoor jacket that was thin but well insulated. His teeth were white and straight but not too perfect. His eyes were green and bright and clever and cold. The two weapons that I could spot barely made bulges.

"Let go of my hand," Sig said pleasantly.

"Oh, right." Simon smiled a smile that somehow managed to be both sheepish and dazzling, and released her hand as if suddenly realizing that he had become entranced. Which was bullshit. This guy didn't do anything by accident. "I'm sorry."

"That's not what your mom says," Sig said.

He looked at her puzzled. "Is that some kind of *yo mama* joke?"

"Valkyrie talk to the dead," Sig reminded him. "Your mother says you're not sorry. In fact, she says you're a complete shit toward women. I don't think her spirit is going to find peace until you grow up, settle down, and stay faithful to one woman."

Simon Travers paled. He somehow managed to physically recoil from Sig without taking a step backward.

"Let's fucking get on with this." Ben rarely cusses, and I checked off a mental box that said *uh-oh*.

"Right, I'll get the car." Simon hightailed it for a nearby barn before we could offer to walk with him.

"Did you really see his mother's ghost?" I asked Sig conversationally.

"No." Her tone was matter-of-fact. "But I can tell that he doesn't have any living family. Some people carry that around with them. And men like him always have mommy issues."

Ben didn't give a shit. "The knights think Constance's abduction is an inside job, John. They think there's a werewolf traitor."

I doubled down on that *uh-oh*. "They would."

"Here's what I don't understand." Sig hadn't been thrilled to discover that I had a goddaughter I'd never told her about, and her voice was taut. In my defense, I had been trying to honor a promise. Constance Lamplighter is the last surviving family member of the Templar's Grandmaster; she's got knight's blood and a werewolf strain just like me, and Ben and I had agreed to become her secret godfathers as part of the treaty between the werewolves and the knights. "If you have a goddaughter, why haven't you been a more active part of her life?"

"Believe it or not, some people think I'm better at finding trouble than preventing it," I said dryly. Sig made a sound that was half a sigh and half a snort.

"Exactly," I agreed. "Ben and I decided that it would be safer if I kept my distance while so many knights and werewolves still blame me for upsetting the old status quo. He's Constance's protector. I'm her insurance policy."

"And I did a great job," Ben said stonily.

Sig reached over and put an arm on his shoulder. "We'll find her, Ben."

Valkyries have ways of finding out things that nobody has any business finding out, and I have a knight's training and a werewolf's innate tracking abilities. Modesty has its place, but if Sig and I couldn't find Constance...no, screw that. We were going to find Constance. But I have a hard time making promises I can't really guarantee, so I said, "Whoever did this did it to make trouble, Ben. They want us to lose hope or control."

Ben took a deep breath, and when he let it back out, his shoulders shifted as if adjusting to weight. "Yeah, I know." And then he walked off a few steps and stared in the direction Simon had gone. The gesture was purely symbolic. We would be able to hear anything the other said for a lot farther off than that, but I respected his request for a little space.

There was a brief lull. I heard a car door open and close, but the vehicle must have been soundproof, because it didn't move and I didn't hear any sounds coming from inside it. Simon was probably taking the opportunity to have a few last-minute words with whatever knights he'd brought along, I decided, or making the last private phone call he would have for a while. Sig decided to take the opportunity to start another conversation. "I'm not happy that you've been keeping secrets from me, John."

"I know," I admitted. "I don't blame you."

"And I'm not happy that we don't have time to really talk about it either," Sig said.

We'd had a few hours in the plane, and Sig had barely said anything except to intermittently ask me questions about Constance. But I didn't bring that up. I actually appreciated that Sig hadn't said much while I was struggling with some serious rage and she was primed to say the wrong thing. So, I kept it simple. "Thanks for coming anyway."

She smiled faintly for the first time since we'd left Virginia. "Thanks for not trying to stop me."

I grimaced, and after a moment, Sig bumped her shoulder against mine. "You know I've got your back, right?"

I had difficulty swallowing for a moment. It had been a long time since I'd had someone who really knew me and who I could still count on. "Yeah."

"That doesn't mean I'm not going to make you pay for this later," she clarified.

Ben turned slightly and started to smile, but the expression turned into a spasm and twitched out. "We've got to get to later first."

Some kind of Nissan family vehicle began pulling up. At a guess, the SUV would blend in better wherever we were going than an Aston Martin. Simon was in the shotgun seat, and the big man driving was broad-shouldered and flat-skulled, his hair shaved down to stubble. Two empty seats were by windows in the middle of the vehicle, and the space between them led to a back row where a thin older man and a young woman somewhere in her late twenties were sitting. The silver-haired man seemed like the kind of person you would call a gentleman, wearing an expensive beige suit, a grey overcoat, a maroon scarf, and a faint smile that just barely peeked out of his neatly trimmed beard. The woman had her pink hair done up in a ponytail and was wearing a Blink 182 T-shirt beneath an open blue parka. Her skin was pale and her makeup was vivid to accentuate that fact. She was a solidly built, fit woman with bright, curious eyes and strong cheekbones.

"The two in the back are Nathan Weber and Dawn Jenkins," Ben grunted. "They're merlins."

"Merlins?" Sig asked.

"The knights' magical researchers and psychics," I explained. "Knights don't like to call them cunning folk. When I was a knight, they were sort of a dirty little secret that wasn't really a secret. Like America's electoral college."

Ben still wasn't inclined to chat. "Times are changing. The driver's name is Tom something. He doesn't talk much."

Simon stepped out of the car and opened the trunk, a hatchback. Sig and I threw our stuff in the back while Ben went ahead and got in.

"That was a cute stunt, bringing up my mother." Simon spoke to me, completely ignoring Sig. She loves that. "But let's make sure we understand each other. This alliance between the Order and the werewolves is a fragile thing. If we screw this up, you could wind up being hunted again."

I slapped the SUV. "This SUV is red."

Simon waited for me to expand on that point.

"It's cold outside," I said.

Simon still stared at me.

"You're kind of acting like a dick," I tried.

"What are you doing?" Simon demanded.

"Oh, I'm sorry. I thought we were playing some weird game where we made completely obvious statements," I explained.

"According to your file, you're almost a century old," Simon turned and went back to the front seat. "Maybe it's time you grew up."

He probably had a point. On the other hand, I am pretty old, and one thing that's a constant is that when people tell you to grow up, what they usually mean is that you should do what's expected of you. If I was any good at that, I'd have died a long time ago.

Ben had already sat between the two merlins by the time Sig and

I piled in, so we took the middle seats. You can often tell a lot about a person by the inside of their vehicle, but the SUV we were in was so clean and impersonal that I wondered if our hosts had left any fingerprints on it. It smelled like gun oil and dark chocolate.

Sig tensed and stared at the woman, Dawn. "You smell like death."

Dawn stared back. "Umm...I use deodorant?"

Sig didn't laugh. "I don't mean a literal smell. Death is clinging to you like an odor. It's weird."

The woman's expression cleared, but it was the older merlin who spoke up. "Dawn has been walking in the shadows of the dead."

"What does that mean, exactly?" Sig asked. Her stillness was kind of like a dog's when it's heard something it can't quite identify.

"I've been psychically retracing people's last moments, trying to figure out why they got killed," Dawn explained. "I can't read knights when they're alive, but once they're dead, I can pick up some of the psychic impressions they left behind. It's kind of like being a medium, I guess. I'm echoing the thoughts of people who aren't alive any longer. But they are just echoes, not active presences."

Sig nodded slowly, so I picked up the slack. "Why are there dead knights? Somebody tell me about Constance's kidnapping." I went ahead and took a burger out of the bag Ben had given me. It was cold, but werewolves burn a lot of calories. I offered one to Sig, but she made a face and declined.

"There's not much to tell yet," Simon said. "Constance lived with four people: two retired knights pretending to be her grandparents, a werewolf pretending to be her mother, and an active knight pretending to be her father—"

"Wait a minute," Sig interrupted. "Why was a werewolf with the knights?"

"Mr. Lafontaine insisted that there be a werewolf involved in protecting Constance too," Simon explained, his face and tone still expressionless. "She's been acting as Constance's nanny."

"It's Tula," Ben told Sig.

"Tula," Sig repeated blankly. Tula had been one of my claw back when I was doing my own version of *Dances with Wolves* back in Wisconsin, and that had been my first reaction too. Tula was a natural killer long before she became a werewolf. She likes to fight, and Tula had come to America specifically because there was a war going on between werewolves and the Knights Templar at the time. In fact, the only reason Tula left the Finnish military was because they wouldn't let her into sniper school.

"I thought it would be good for her," Ben explained.

When Tula had first become a werewolf, she had left a human child behind in her old life because she thought it was safer for the child that way. That decision still haunted her. Ben was doing his subtle-leader thing—providing one of his most competent and trustworthy wolves for security and helping her deal with some of her issues at the same time.

"The werewolf claims that Constance was up all night the night before, and that might be why the werewolf fell asleep on the couch downstairs," Simon informed me. "She woke up because the lights were flickering, and then they went out. The werewolf says she heard a bedroom door open upstairs, and then there was a strange sound. She described it as a noise like you'd hear sitting next to a window on an airplane. Then the door closed and the sound stopped. The werewolf says she ran upstairs and pounded on Constance's door. No one answered. She says she couldn't hear anyone moving in the house, and there was a funny smell in the air—"

"Marshlike, I believe she said," Nathan interjected.

Simon frowned impatiently at the interruption. "—so she kicked down the door. And the room was empty. She searched the rest of the house, and she found the bodies of the knights pretending to be Constance's grandparents. They had been poisoned. The knight, Austin, and Constance were gone."

I didn't like the way Simon kept saying *she says*, with a subtle emphasis on the *says*. I didn't like the way he wouldn't use Tula's name either. But I understood his suspicions. "So, you or somebody like you showed up," I said. "And Tula is saying that maybe this Austin kidnapped Constance and killed two other knights and disappeared down a magic rabbit hole. And she has no proof. Is that about it?"

"No," Simon said. "Tula wasn't alone. Somebody like me showed up, and Constance was missing and there were a bunch of werewolves in the house."

"Tula called me first," Ben said. Well, yeah. Of course she did. And of course Ben took steps to make sure she didn't wind up getting disappeared. But what a hot mess. The knights blaming the werewolves. The werewolves blaming the knights.

"Dogs and cats, living together," I commented. "Mass hysteria!" Nobody laughed. Well, it was a lot funnier when Bill Murray said it.

"Do you realize what this means, John?" Sig asked.

"I think that's pretty obvious," I said cautiously. "Constance is missing, and we need to figure out who did it."

"It means the werewolves and the knights have a difference of opinion they can't resolve," Sig said gently. "And they want you to be the diplomatic mediator."

Oh my God.

"Look, help walk me through this a little slower," I said to the car in general. "Does the house have a security camera setup?"

"It does, but it's not internet-accessible," Simon said. "That would be as big a security weakness as it would be a defense. The cameras show the grandparents going to their room and falling asleep. They show the werewolf lying down on the couch. Austin picked Constance up in his arms and walked her around in circles in front of the stairwell. And then the cameras stopped functioning."

Magic will do that. "Was Austin walking Constance around in circles like he was trying to put her to sleep, or like he was doing some kind of ritual?" I asked.

"And I would know that how?" Simon asked.

Okay. "Were there any other signs of magic?"

"Constance and Austin's scent trail ends at the bedroom," Ben said grimly. "But I don't pick up any other funny smells around it."

"And I didn't pick up any signs of runes or sigils etched into the door," Nathan added. "No traces of smoke, powder, paint, or chalk. No scratched engravings."

"I didn't get any weird psychic impressions off the door either," Dawn added. "As far as I can tell, it's just an ordinary door."

"We all know how to confuse scents," I said. "This Austin could have backtracked."

"We've been over every inch of that house. There aren't any secret doors that we don't know about," Simon said. "I didn't just check the surfaces; I measured the dimensions of every room, hallway, and ceiling, and checked them against the rest of the house."

Yeah, well, there are dimensions and there are dimensions.

"I'm guessing the place is warded to keep outside magic from getting in," I said dryly.

"I did the defenses myself." Dawn had an accent straight from South Boston. "That place is sealed up tighter than a nun's butt."

At a guess, Dawn hadn't enjoyed being a female with magical proclivities raised in a Catholic order.

"So, how did magic get in?" Sig somehow made the question sound idle.

"If there was magic, it would have had to be initiated by someone inside the house." Nathan sounded like he regretted that fact, speaking softly and calmly.

"Tula doesn't know magic," I pointed out.

"Neither does Austin," Simon replied tightly. "I went to the same training center that he did. We became knights together."

Great. So, it was personal for everybody.

"Tula's not in a good place now," Ben added, as if I'd made that last observation out loud. "And these people are acting like she's a traitor."

"Where is she?" I tried not to growl it.

"She's not being tortured," Simon didn't say that like the possibility was absurd. He said it like he regretted the fact. "She's in lockdown."

"I seem to recall the Knights Templar having a sword that can compel people to tell the truth," I said tartly. I'd held the sword myself, and it wasn't one of my fondest memories. Grasping that hilt was like giving your soul an enema. "It should be pretty easy to clear her."

"I don't think you understand how tight the security is around the Sword of Truth. Claimh Solais is one of the four great treasures of the Tuatha De Danaan." Simon's voice was equally tense. "We can't just check it out of its location like a library book, not if we don't want to draw attention to it. Constance's existence is a secret."

"Apparently it isn't," I snapped, but then I tried to tone it down a little. Thinking about my own issues with the Knights Templar and interrogations and captivity wasn't good for my cool.

"I see what you're saying, though." I saw what he wasn't saying too. If the sword was that important, somebody might have even kidnapped Constance because they wanted the sword, and this might be a ploy to draw the sword out of its safe place. We would get all the facts we could through traditional methods first.

Nathan seemed to pick up on something in my body language or my silence. His voice was soothing. "No one is chained up in a dungeon. There's a secret basement level beneath the house, but it was made to provide extra living quarters."

I struggled to refocus. "What about toxicology? Somebody said the two grandparent stand-ins were poisoned. Did anybody work up a lab on Tula? If she was poisoned, it might explain why she fell asleep. Most poisons wouldn't kill a werewolf, but they might knock them out."

"We're still working on that," Nathan replied. "This all happened relatively recently. Mr. Lafontaine brought along a lot of werewolves who were good at fighting, but he didn't bring a mobile lab."

The driver spoke for the first time. He had a soft voice for such a big man, but every word still sounded like an accusation. "If Austin had poisoned the bitch, he would have used wolfsbane."

Simon interceded, speaking with an undertone of menace that was more effective for being casual. "Tom, shut up. If I wanted your opinion, I'd cut it out of you." And this Tom shut up. Fast.

Nathan spoke up again. "You're assuming anyone who poisoned Tula would have wanted to kill her, Thomas. But that's a faulty assumption. The one thing we can be sure of is that whoever kidnapped Constance did it to cause trouble between werewolves and knights, and the best way to do that was to leave Tula alive. If she was dead, she wouldn't be causing friction right now. We would all be united, looking for Austin or whoever kidnapped him."

I liked this guy. Not only did Nathan use Tula's name, but he seemed to be a voice of reason. Perversely, this meant he was somebody I had to keep an eye on. If I were pulling strings and playing people against each other, that's exactly how I would act. Everybody thought Iago was a good guy too.

"What about this walking-in-the-shadow-of death business?" Sig asked. I couldn't tell if she was being healthily skeptical or territorial. Communicating with the dead was her job. "What did you find out, Dawn?"

"Not much. Did you ever see that show, *Star Trek: The Next Generation?*"

When no one responded, I cleared my throat. "I'm more of a *Firefly* fan myself."

"Fine, I'm a geek," Dawn said. "The show had this character who was an empath, Deanna Troi. She could sense emotions, but all she ever did was say useful things like *This alien who's trying to kill us is hostile, Captain.* Or *This person who's crying hysterically is very sad.* That's me right now. I can tell you that Beth and David didn't suspect anything before they were poisoned. I can tell you that Tula is very angry and sad and feels guilty and is barely holding it together. But she could be that way because she feels like she failed Constance, or because she feels bad about betraying us."

"And you can't read Austin's psychic impressions because his geas keeps anyone from picking him up on any kind of psychic radar," Sig finished. "But doesn't that mean he's still alive?"

Simon clearly didn't like all the implications of that. "The other aspect of Austin's geas is that it would have kept him from betraying the Grandmaster."

Ben grunted. "Can I talk freely without getting any of you killed?"

I couldn't see it, but there was a smile in Dawn's voice. "That is so sweet! Thank you."

"We're all fairly high in the Grandmaster's confidence," Simon said cautiously. "That's why we're here."

"Then you know all that stuff about knights not being able to be traitors is horse dung," Ben growled. "If some Templar loon decided kidnapping Constance was the best way to keep magic a secret for some crazy reason that only made sense to him, his magical oath wouldn't have done squat."

Sig became more alert. This was another thing about the bargain Ben and I had made with Emil Lamplighter that she didn't know about. I had only told one other person Emil Lamplighter's secret, and that was because Akihiko Watanabe had already deduced most of it, and I had needed to gain his provisional trust in order to kill him.

"Yes, but less than twelve people in the world know that," Simon said carefully. "And half of us are in this car."

"Perhaps you'd better make that eleven," Nathan said matter-of-factly. "The Valkyrie doesn't know what we're talking about, Simon."

I could feel Sig tighten next to me. All of her. I had kept another secret from her, and now that fact was being rubbed in her face in front of a bunch of strangers.

I looked at Sig sheepishly. "You complete me?"

Sig's face was rocky soil. No expression was growing there.

Simon glanced over his shoulder at Sig. "Do you really not know?"

"I promised I'd keep Emil's secrets," I responded for her. I know, I know, she doesn't like that either. "And the only way to keep a secret is not to tell it."

Sig didn't look like she was impressed by my integrity or my reasoning. "You might as well tell me what's going on now," she said to the car in general. "You're going to need my help, and I want to know how mad at John I am."

Urrrgggh.

I opened my mouth.

"Shut it," Sig advised me, and after a few seconds, I decided to take that advice. It was better than having a knock-down drag-out argument with her in the middle of all of these people and keeping any of us from focusing on the issue at hand.

"You know that we descendants of the original Knights Templar are bound by a spell, correct?" Nathan verified. "We have to keep the existence of magic a secret from the outside world. It's in our DNA, like a command in a computer's operating system."

"Yes, I know about your geas," Sig said shortly. Her last relationship had left her with some serious trust issues. "John told me that much."

Nathan chuckled. "That part's horrible, but it is also fairly simple. Where it gets complicated and..."

He paused for the right words, and Dawn supplied them. "Fucked-up."

Nathan grimaced slightly. "It gets complicated and messy the same way that most things get complicated and messy. Someone told a lie, and we are still going to increasingly convoluted extremes trying to cover up that lie."

"What lie?" Sig asked guardedly.

"We knights are taught from birth that our geas involves all sorts of other boundaries," Nathan answered. "For example, we are told that our geas forces us to stay loyal to the Knights Templar. We are told that it prevents us from killing other knights. That it compels us to have many children and train those children to fight and be otherwise useful."

Sig's mouth tightened. "That sounds like a lot of lies to me."

I sighed. "They're all tangled together in one big lie, Sig. Our geas compels us to keep the existence of the supernatural a secret, period. It doesn't specify how."

Sig is quick, but it was a lot to take in. "I don't understand. Wouldn't the knights...I mean, you know...figure it out sooner or later? Kids are told that Santa exists too."

Nathan plugged back in. "But Santa is not a consistent and culturally reinforced lie throughout a person's lifetime."

"Here's another thing," Dawn added. "Most of the things tacked on to the geas like constitutional amendments are common sense. If you're of the bloodline, and you're compelled to keep the supernatural a secret from the world, it doesn't take long to figure out that you can't do it by yourself. And since you know this, the geas really does compel you to do what you can to keep the Knights Templar together."

Sig's voice was thoughtful. "So, because you have to keep the secret, and you know you need the Templars to help you keep the secret, the geas forces you to stay in the Templars just like you're told it will?"

Isn't that what Dawn had just said? I decided not to ask that out loud.

"If these made-up provisos are the kind of thing that the geas naturally kicks in and enforces anyhow, why make up a lie in the first place?" Sig asked.

I couldn't see Simon's face, but he sounded like he was sneering slightly. "Because not all humans have common sense."

"And some people are just flat-out insane too," I added. "A sociopath knight might seriously believe the best way to keep the supernatural a secret is to start assassinating his superiors so that he can take control. In that case, his geas wouldn't kick in naturally. Hell, it might actually make him go through with the idea."

"And this big lie prevents that?" Sig demanded skeptically.

"It does!" Nathan's enthusiasm came back. "Belief is the most powerful force there is. This hypothetical sociopath John's talking about doesn't even think about shooting his superior, because he knows he can't. Just like I wouldn't walk into a desert if I grew up being told it had high levels of radiation from being used for atomic bomb testing, and I'd had friends who'd died from wandering into the area. It would never even occur to me. This hypothetical sociopath would start to get a panic attack if he even thought about shooting another knight seriously, and then he would be convinced the geas was causing it."

Seeing Sig's doubt, I backed Nathan up. "It's true. In World War II, a nurse ran out of pain-killers and told a burn victim that a sugar pill was morphine. The soldier had seen other wounded soldiers relax and go to sleep after taking a pill, so he ate that sugar pill and didn't feel the pain from his third degree burns anymore. His mind shut his pain centers completely down. That experiment's been duplicated hundreds of times under lab conditions. It's called the placebo effect."

"And belief works in negative ways too," Nathan chimed in. "There are documented cases of people who died because they thought they'd been bitten by a poisonous snake and hadn't been. People who have died just because a houngan or witch doctor pointed at them and told them to, and I can tell you for a fact that magic doesn't work that way."

Sig sighed unhappily. "So, basically, you knights are all brainwashed from birth."

It was Dawn who responded to that. "Exactly."

"I can see why the Templar bigwigs want to keep this Big Lie going," Sig admitted. "But some knights still must figure out the truth."

"Sure," I said. "And then knights like Simon here eliminate them for the greater good."

"Or recruit them," Nathan amended. "That's how I met Dawn. But Dawn is one in a million."

I glanced over my shoulder. It was dark, but something

about Dawn's expression made me think she was blushing. "A lot of us merlins have the sight."

Ben had been waiting patiently for his moment, and he took it: "You say less than twelve people know the truth, Simon. But that's what you hope, not what you know."

If there had ever been any real emotion in Simon's voice, it had died somewhere during the conversation. "Even if Austin has gone rogue, and I don't think he has, we have to act like that isn't even possible."

"While you hunt him down and eliminate him, you mean," I clarified.

"If it comes to that," Simon agreed. "Not raising too many of the wrong kinds of questions is as important to the Grandmaster as Constance's safety."

"To him, maybe." Ben's voice was stark. "I promised Emil Lamplighter I wouldn't tell his secrets, but I also told him that I'm not sacrificing any of my people for his games. If Constance is alive, I'm bringing her home."

Nathan tried another approach. "No offense, Mr. Lafontaine, but how is you being convinced that a knight is a traitor any better than Simon wanting to believe your werewolf is responsible?"

"Because there were three knights and one werewolf." Ben's voice was cold. "The odds are on my side."

It seemed to me that somebody should say something. Then it seemed to me that the somebody was probably me. Then it seemed to me that my mind should shut up and mind its own mind business, but it was too late. "He's right, Ben," I said reluctantly. "All these agendas are just getting in the way. Maybe there is no traitor. For all we know, an intruder could have figured some way to get past the defenses and abduct Austin while he was walking Constance to her bedroom, or impersonate him. I saw something like that happen with a skinwalker once."

Was this situation what that weird dream had been about? Was there a skinwalker involved, or some other kind of magic impersonator, and was a skinwalker the closest metaphor that my mind could grasp? Hopefully not. I'd once had a dream where I was in a restaurant and saw my name on the list of pizza toppings too. The last thing I needed was supernaturally significant dreams bringing more magic weirdness into my life.

"I read about that incident while I was researching you." Simon's voice dropped below zero degrees. "But that was half a century ago."

Sig forgot that she was mad at me for a moment. "John's just saying that we need to keep our minds open. For example, Tula wasn't protected by a geas. She could have been possessed by something. Or one of you knights in this car could be an insane traitor, since you know how the geas really works."

None of the Templars were offended when Sig mentioned that last possibility. They didn't even have an awkward moment. That's a knight thing.

"If Constance is—" Ben started, but then the satellite radio that Simon had on low in the background stuttered off, and we all fell silent for a second.

It could have just been bad reception, but we were already paranoid and keyed up, so the first thing that occurred to everyone in the vehicle was that there was magic in the atmosphere disrupting the wireless, ungrounded technology. We were on a mountain road at this point, going around a curve, and our headlights illuminated a large fallen tree lying across the road. The driver, Tom, started to instinctively hit the brakes, but Simon's reactions were faster. He lunged his foot over Tom's side and stepped on the gas, grabbing the steering wheel and turning the SUV off the road, over a steep embankment.

∾3∾

ANNNNNND...ACTION!

Simon's actions weren't as suicidal as they seemed. The bank was only moderately steep, not a sheer drop-off, and he was a professional paranoid. His mind instantly added up "magic" and "tree blockade" and came up with "ambush." And since somebody wanted to make our vehicle stop right in front of that tree, Simon wanted the opposite. The trees were fairly dense but not impossibly so, and Tom began to aim us for a patch where there were a good two hundred feet of relatively clear ground. He angled us just enough to slow our descent down the bank but not cause us to tip over. The SUV scraped and rebounded off one tree and completely shattered a smaller one that got in the way. Tom's airbag triggered, but Simon already had a gun in his right hand by that point, and he instantly fired a bullet through the inflating air bag and out the front windshield while grabbing the steering wheel with his left hand again. Tom regained visibility and control in a few seconds.

Yeah, Simon was Emil's go-to fixer for a reason.

So, going over the bank was a desperate move, but it turned out to be the best option we had. After a startled pause, someone—actually a lot of someones—from the road up above started firing at us with high-powered rifles. Most of the shots smacked into trees or went over our heads. Firing at a moving target on a slope is difficult under the best of circumstances, much less at night among a lot of tree cover. But the back window of the SUV still shattered, and bits of brain and bone blew out over my shoulder.

Bits of Nathan Weber's brain and bones. Dawn began screaming.

A moment later, the window next to me shattered, and I actually felt the air from the bullet's passage like an icy slice against my cheek as it kept going and made another puncture wound in the front windshield.

A man—it was dark and the SUV was vibrating and bumping and shaking painfully, and I only got a brief impression of a Caucasian in a red stocking cap with a large brown moustache—appeared in our high beams, running at us on Sig's side of the vehicle from the woods below. He paused to bring up a shotgun, but Sig had reached around the front seat and removed a large handgun from the driver's holster by this point, and she shot at the attacker three or four times before the SUV passed. She didn't bother to roll down her window, and I heard glass shattering through the loud rumble of the SUV and the man's roars. And make no mistake, he was roaring. It was an animal challenge that I recognized immediately.

He was a werewolf.

I was hearing all of this, not seeing it, because a lot of things were happening fast and simultaneously, and while Sig had been removing her gun, I had been removing my seat belt. At the same time that she was firing, I was opening my door and throwing myself out of the vehicle. It wasn't a well-thought-out plan. It just seemed like the SUV wasn't going to end well, and there were going to be attackers coming after us; I wanted to put myself between them and Sig. I mean, between them and the others. I hit the ground rolling and didn't break anything doing so.

The SUV took the light with it, but the optic nerves beneath my retinas were shifting and twisting as my infravision kicked in. The man Sig had shot was still a reddish blur rather than an outline, but I heard him gargling some twelve feet away from me, and then I heard something else: the howls of wolves. At least some of our attackers must have been waiting to pounce on us in wolf form. They hadn't had time to tear off their clothes and shift. Hell, I didn't have time to tear off my clothes and shift.

My guitar case was in the SUV, and all I had was my silver steel knife. I always have my silver steel knife. It was in my hand before I even thought about it. The knife wasn't enough to deal with several shifted werewolves, though, so I ran for the guy Sig had shot. He'd had a weapon, and the odds were pretty good that the shotgun shells were loaded with silver fragments. If the werewolves had known where to ambush us, they'd also known who and what they were ambushing.

Sig had shot the man twice in the chest, and the gun she'd taken from the driver must have had werewolf-killers in it. Of course it had. I anchored my knife in the trunk of a nearby small tree so that I could pick the shotgun up, then swiveled. The werewolves weren't howling anymore; they were moving silently and fast. I had a brief impression of three dark silhouettes coming in fast and discharged one barrel of the shotgun, then the other.

It was a large-bore shotgun, and it really must have been loaded with silver shot. I dropped two wolves. Unfortunately, the shotgun also couldn't hold more than two shells at a time, and another wolf was almost on me. I dropped the shotgun and yanked my knife out of the tree trunk, and only the fact that the wolf was approaching fast from a higher elevation saved me. Instead of coming in low, it leaped for me, hoping to barrel me over and find my throat.

Instead, I swiveled, and the wolf's momentum carried it past me. Its teeth tore off part of my left ear and its claws tore furrows down my chest through my jacket, but nothing that would kill me. When the wolf landed several feet away, my knife was anchored in the base of its skull at an angle.

The SUV wasn't hurtling through the woods anymore. I hadn't registered any large crashing sounds while I was fighting for my life, but somewhere below me, the SUV's headlight beams were still, and its wheels were making spinning sounds. Vague heat blurs were moving down from the road, but they weren't coming down on top of me. These were attackers who had been positioned behind the felled tree, and they were running down the bank toward the SUV at an angle that would carry them below and past me. There were at least a dozen of them, and they were moving on two legs.

Some kind of cross-country motorcycle—I never did read a logo—came down the bank at me then. I had the warning of its motor gunning to life and saw the headlight beams lipping over the side of the bank, and I whirled around a tree for cover. Even with the tree between us, I saw the bike's headlight beam drop lower and grow larger. There was a low-hanging branch next to my shoulder, and I brought my weight down on the frozen wood hard with slightly greater-than-human strength and a whole lot of adrenaline. The branch snapped off with a sharp crack.

I didn't have time to be smooth. The motorcycle came fast, and when I went back around the tree, I didn't swing the branch like a baseball bat. I couldn't. It was maybe eight feet long, and its tip was slender and spreading out into narrow twigs. I charged the rider and used the branch like a springy jousting lance. He tried to swerve, but that actually made the bike slide out from beneath him even before I shoved the branch into his shoulder.

The bike went shuddering and thudding past me on its side and the rider went down flat on his back and kept skidding toward me, but he wasn't stunned. I dropped the branch and tried to knee-drop the wind out of him, but the asshole moved to his side and started grappling with me before my weight even came fully down. I got my fingers around the edge of his motorcycle helmet, and it was strapped tight, thank God. I threw my weight violently to the side, off of him, and his muscles tensed to resist me, his weight anchoring him. It was his first instinct and his last mistake. His neck broke.

Weapon. Weapon. Weapon. I found a handgun holstered by his side. I couldn't see what kind it was in the dark, but it had a magazine and the heft of a Colt .45, the kind that used to be a standard military-issue sidearm. A lot of Colt .45s wound up in a lot of black markets and gun shows and pawn shops when most of the armed forces stopped using them. All those supply sergeants had to pay for their kids' colleges somehow. I removed the magazine and checked the top bullet. The metal hummed against my fingertips in a way that was unmistakable. Silver. Good. There was gunfire in the woods below me, and a heat outline coming from the side where another of the attackers had broken off from the main group.

A voice called out, "Joe?" This werewolf could only see an infrared outline, and I guess he wanted to verify that I wasn't his friend or brother or lover or whatever this Joe was to him before he fired. That was so sweet. I rewarded his concern by putting two bullets in his center mass. People who have tender feelings shouldn't kidnap my goddaughter. I could tell from the hot trails his blood made in the cold dark air that he wasn't wearing a bulletproof vest. I left the bike rider paralyzed so that we could ask him questions later. If there was a later.

Time time time time time. The remaining attackers were firing continuously somewhere down the bank, their bullets smacking into and off of metal. It sounded like they had pinned the survivors in the SUV down while they were still recovering from whatever had stopped the vehicle. There was no way to call for help even if I knew who to call, not with so much shapeshifting filling the air with ambient magic. I had to do something big and stupid and fast.

The first crazy thing that might work flitted through my brain, and I went with it, took a handkerchief out of my back pocket, and ran toward the motorbike. The gas tank had a screw-on cap, and I found a stick and jammed it into the middle of the handkerchief, then stuffed the handkerchief partway down the opening. When I pulled the cloth out, it was soaked in gasoline. I managed to screw the cap partially back on over the handkerchief, with half the handkerchief in the motorbike's tank and half sticking out. There was no time to think of all the reasons what I was about to do wouldn't work, so I pulled the bike up, kick-started it, and took off down the bank, aiming for the larger concentration of heat outlines.

Ironically, it was someone from the SUV who fired on me, shooting out my bike's headlight and taking a chunk out of my left thigh. The werewolves who had set up the ambush couldn't immediately tell if I was the original motorbike rider back on task or not, and they hesitated long enough for me to get within striking distance. I had some matches—I always have matches—but I couldn't light them and carry a gun and steer a bike at the same time, so I lowered the handgun until it was right next to the gas-soaked handkerchief and fired through it into the ground. Nothing happened, so I fired again, and this time, the handkerchief ignited.

I didn't wait, not for a second. I pulled the handlebars up into a wheelie and aimed the motorbike in the ambushers' general direction, and dropped off the back. The bike actually went a lot farther on one wheel than I thought it would, the handkerchief burning from its side. The bike might have gone all the way past the concentration of trees that the ambushers were firing from if the gas tank hadn't exploded. But it did.

The blast wasn't like the movies. The motorbike didn't become a huge bomb that would have taken out half a city block. In fact, I don't think any of the werewolves got hit by shrapnel, or seriously hit anyway, though two trees and a lot of fallen leaves caught on fire. But the gunfire stopped, and I lurched to my feet and staggered toward the ambushers, still holding on to my gun. The werewolves had been staring at the bike with infravision, and their heat-sensitive eyes were temporarily blind from the burst of fire and light. They couldn't orient on me with their hearing because their acute ears were temporarily deaf from the loud explosion of sound. They couldn't smell me because the air was full of the smell of burning gasoline.

And I walked straight into and around their tree cover and murdered those blind, deaf bastards until my bullets ran out, firing head shots off into disoriented opponents from close up. I tried to move from tree to tree and maintain some cover, but something impossibly heavy hit me in the chest and took me down anyway. I don't know who shot me.

I had some limited vision because of the flames caused by the bike. A werewolf ran up to me and leveled a high-powered hunting rifle at me, but then a large fallen branch literally took his head off. The branch flew straight through the air like a spear the size of a small battering ram and removed his head from his shoulders. Sig's work. A large grey wolf bounded over me and surged toward the remaining attackers—Ben, alive—and I heard someone scream. One of the knights from the SUV was firing continuously, evenly spaced, unhurried shots. Another wolf came at me, but then Sig was there, picking the wolf up by the throat with one hand and stabbing it through the chest with a silver knife that she'd picked up from some fallen knight.

I guess I figured it was safe to pass out then. Or I had no choice. My last conscious thought was that I was wearing the jacket Sig had gotten me for Christmas. It was ruined.

∾4∾

SHE'S A HEARTBREAKER,
ALL RIGHT

I wasn't out long. I heard voices before I even realized how hard it was to open my eyes, two conversations going on at once.

Simon, far off: "Do you still think our traitor isn't a werewolf?"

Dawn, close up: "I can't tell if he's alive or not."

Ben's voice, distant and tight: "So, who told these mutts we'd be coming down this road tonight?"

Sig, angry and scared, right over me: "I'd know it if he was dead."

Simon: "That's the question isn't it? Are these werewolves part of your alliance?"

Ben: "Yeah, but only kind of. This is the Dogtown bunch. Biggest bunch of troublemakers in the Round Table."

Sig: "It's got to be silver. But this is a bullet wound, not shot."

Simon: "Then let's question their leader."

Ben: "We can't. He's dead."

For some reason, in the state I was in, I thought Ben was talking about me. I shuddered. My chest was cold and heavy.

Someone had cut my shirt open, and icy hands were probing around my breastbone. It hurt. When I opened my eyes, I saw Sig's outline. I tried to say something, and spit blood out of my windpipe. "Uhlph."

"John?" She sounded frantic.

"I love you," I gasped. It seemed very important to say that. I never had.

"Fuck you!" she snarled. And her fingers drove through my chest like a spear.

When I woke up again, I was in the backseat of a car that smelled like werewolves. Werewolves I didn't know. I was lying down with my head in Sig's lap. I opened my eyes and saw the back of Dawn's head. She was driving the car.

"Hey, there," Sig said. "Welcome back." She sounded a lot happier than I felt.

I put a hand over my chest and rubbed to make sure it was still there. Or had come back.

"Here," Sig said, and handed me a bottle of water and some beef jerky strips left over from our hiking trip. "You need to eat."

I wasn't hungry. I felt like I wanted to go back to sleep, and I was afraid to go back to sleep, because part of me was afraid I wouldn't wake up again. I forced myself to eat the damn beef jerky. My mouth was dry, and I drained half the bottle of water just getting the first mouthful down. My throat didn't want to swallow.

"Where are we going?" I croaked.

"To Constance's house," Sig said. "Remember?" I braced myself on my left palm to straighten up and almost screamed. But I managed it. "Where's everybody else?"

"Nathan and Tom are dead." Dawn didn't sound too lively

herself. "Simon is trying to clean up the mess we made back there."

I groaned. "How?" All that gunfire, the explosion…

"The Grandmaster moved Constance here for a reason," Dawn said. "The town below is a small retirement community for Templars. The whole police force is made up of retired knights or people from our bloodline who failed out of squire training."

"What about Ben?" I croaked.

"He's organizing werewolves he trusts to go after whatever's left of this Dogtown pack." Sig's voice held a certain cold satisfaction. "The three we left alive back there don't seem to know anything about who tipped their leaders off about us."

"Uhhmn," I grunted.

"Who is this Dogtown bunch?" Sig asked. "I thought werewolves didn't like to refer to themselves as dogs."

"Dogtown was an old Massachusetts settlement," Dawn said from the driver's seat. "A bunch of witches and werewolves tried to take it over and turn it into a supernatural community. When the place started getting a reputation, the knights went in and ended it hard. To werewolves who don't like knights, Dogtown is like their Alamo."

Sig stroked my forehead. "So, why did this bunch stick around when John's pack changed its name to the Round Table and started working with the Templars?"

"Probably because they could be a bigger pain in the ass that way," I gasped.

Sig digested that. "I guess Ben couldn't just toss them out when he was trying to convince a lot of Bernard's old followers that he wasn't holding grudges."

"Yeah, but if somebody told their leader that Ben was on their territory without much protection, in secret…" I stopped because even as out of it as I was, a thought came to me with a certain cold clarity. If we had all disappeared on top of Constance's abduction…oh, hell. The werewolves would have blamed the knights for Ben's death and the knights would have blamed the werewolves for Simon's, and both sides would have been convinced that there were survivors who had planned the whole thing and had gone into hiding. Somebody really was trying hard to start up another werewolf/knight war.

"Maybe I could—" I started, and Sig put a hand on my upper thigh and squeezed. Fortunately, it wasn't the part of my thigh that had been shot off.

"Somebody was trying to stop us from investigating the house," she said. "So, let's do that."

Yeah, okay. That made sense. I rubbed my chest.

"I had to force my hand up through your breastbone to pull that silver bullet out," she said tightly.

"Huh," I said a little weakly. "Listen, when I said there was something I wanted to get off my chest…"

It was a pretty lame attempt at a joke, but Sig started giggling, way too loud, and it just grew louder. She couldn't seem to stop. Soon, she was gasping and convulsing. "Shut up," she wheezed.

"It's good to see you too," I told her quietly.

Sig leaned over and kissed me, and I could tell that her cheeks were wet. But what she whispered was, "You're still going to pay for not telling me about Constance."

"I know," I said.

∽5∾

COULD WE GET THAT ON TAPE?

It was a long driveway that led to Constance Lamplighter's house. I hadn't seen the place from below because it was on a small plateau on the side of the mountain, and a series of tall trees lined up in front of it like a pike wall. There was a clear field of fire between these trees and the house, and on the other side of the thicket was at least half a mile of barren slope. A big man with thinning brown hair was waiting for us in the yard, flanked by three wolves who weren't really trained dogs and however many knights and werewolves were hidden in the surrounding trees. He was wearing brown cords and a long, dark winter coat.

"That's Bob." Dawn's voice was full of tension. "He's in charge of investigating Constance's disappearance on-site."

"Are you all right?" Sig asked her.

"No." Dawn didn't even think about it. "I'm really pissed. Not just at you. I'm pissed at everything right now. But you too."

She smelled like it. "That's understandable," I told her.

"No, it's not," she countered angrily. "I shouldn't be mad at you. You didn't kill Nathan."

"I didn't say you were right," I replied. "I said it was understandable. You have to be mad at something—that's how the mind works." *Or doesn't work*, but I decided not to add that. The first time I had met Molly Newman, maybe my favorite person in the whole world, I had taken some of my baggage out on her. I both wished Molly were there and was glad she wasn't. Molly was still healing from burns she'd gotten the last time she'd worked with me and Sig.

"People like me, born into the knights' bloodline with the sight? We were condemned long before you came along with your little werewolf problem," she said.

That seemed a bit of a non sequitur. And *little* werewolf problem? But all I said was "Okay."

"They called us witches. Now even the Crusaders have a few psychics, but they call them prophets and don't let them research magic."

"Okay," I repeated.

"I'm just saying, if anybody should know better than to blame somebody for something that's not their fault, it's me," she explained.

"Uhm," I grunted. I just wasn't up for much soul-searching or barely coherent conversation.

We got out of the car. The wolves smelled Sig and me, but none of them changed to human form to greet us. When Dawn was closer to Bob, she asked, "Have you found anything yet?"

Bob was solid and strong-looking but not in a gym-monkey kind of a way. He appeared to be in his forties, and his big-boned face looked like it hadn't smiled in years. "Nothing new."

"That means you haven't found anything at all!" Dawn snapped. I was starting to wonder how close she and Nathan had been.

Bob looked like he wanted to snap back, but after a tense

moment, he nodded and looked at me. "So, you're the werewolf knight we've been waiting for? You look kind of pale."

"I've been writing a lot of poetry about how nothing but death lasts forever," I explained. I was a little tense myself. "Can we see the bedroom where Constance disappeared?"

"Sure," Bob agreed. "I want to see you work some miracles."

The house itself was big but not quite a mansion, a pleasant-looking brick building in three parts. The large middle section was two stories high and held the bedrooms on the second floor, the adjoining sections one story and spread out like wings. There was a series of hedges with gravel pathways and statues and sitting benches to the left of the structure, and the back deck was the length of the entire house. White boards with strange designs drawn on them were hanging beneath the rain gutters, which is one of the good things about being in New England: you can display hex wards openly and everyone will just think you're old or being kitschy or ironic.

"Every window is bulletproof," Bob informed us. "And the brick walls are actually double-thick, with armor plating between the layers. Just about every part of the house has been blessed by a priest too, and there are salt rings and warding stones beneath our feet."

"Good," I said, since Bob seemed to want me to say something, and then I followed him into the house, watching him carefully just in case pressing the doorbell the wrong way dropped visitors into a shark tank or something.

Constance's forest-green bedroom was covered with thick, soft carpeting and colorful pictures of trees and woodland animals. There was a bookcase full of small children's books, at least half of them made of soft puffy plastic material. A plush brown beanbag chair was against the far wall, surrounded by toys with things that Constance could spin or honk or ring or pull on with her developing fingers. In the east corner, a modern white plastic changing table was loaded down with wipes and baby powder and diapers, set across from an old-fashioned wooden crib. It would have been a nice picture if the room had had any windows, or if I hadn't been looking at it through a shattered doorway. One of the hinges was still loose where the door had been kicked in, and the strips of wood where the lock guard used to be were splintered and frayed. Precise little squares of plaster were missing where someone had cut chunks out of the wall beside the doorframe to see if there was anything unusual built into it.

I looked over the scene and tried to be dispassionate. "I'm going to need a pint of ice cream, a loaf of bread, and lots of meat and cheese."

"Why?" Bob demanded.

"Because I'm hungry," I said reasonably. I was still a little woozy, but at least my appetite was coming back.

"John's healing," Sig told Bob. "He got shot up with silver bullets on the way up here."

"Simon didn't really go into a lot of detail about that," Bob observed.

"And he's the one who should," I pointed out. "I really do need food."

"I could use a bite too," Sig added pleasantly.

Bob reluctantly pulled out a cell phone and called somebody downstairs, just in case I was trying to get him out of the way for some nefarious purpose. I didn't take it personally.

"Where's the door?" I asked Dawn.

"I had them take it to the basement," Dawn said. "Nathan set up a small lab down there."

"Good." I put my nose next to the thin wooden strips lining the doorway. First the base, then up its length, inhaling deeply.

"Are you looking for something specific?" Bob asked.

"No." I kept tracing the outline of the doorframe with my nose. "What about you, Sig? Are you picking up anything?"

"No," she said curtly. "All those wards outside are keeping any spirits away."

It was when I got to the part of the door where the frame was splintered that I smelled something odd and froze. "Have you tested to see what kind of wood this is?" I asked Bob.

"Constance has been missing for less than a day," Bob said with a hint of asperity. "I gave Simon a splinter to send to the nearest lab, but we haven't gotten it back yet. But Mr. Lafontaine smelled all this too, and he didn't pick up anything unusual."

"He wouldn't unless he's been to Southeast Asia," I said while I shaved a small strip of wood off the paneling.

"John, stop being cryptic!" Sig reprimanded. "What's going on?"

"I have no idea." That was nothing but the truth. "This wood is from a balete tree. Why would a doorway in Massachusetts be lined with wood strips from a tree that grows in the Philippines?"

The main cellar looked like your standard ranch house foundation, but there was a secret door behind a removable panel board covered with tools. Once through, I found myself in an underground complex made out of smooth concrete that had been designed to function with or without power. Old-fashioned torch holders were built into the walls side by side with modern motion detectors and wind chimes. Every door was solid steel and looked like it was built to withstand mortar fire.

Wireless signals couldn't reach us, but Dawn's lab had a computer wired in with cable connections, and for once, the

Internet was directly useful. Doing a Boolean search on balete trees and magic led me almost immediately to Philippine mythology and dalaketnons, a supernatural species who live in multiple dimensions simultaneously. According to the stories, dalaketnons go back and forth from their home world to ours by walking through holes in large magical dalakit trees. I'd actually known that. I hadn't known that *dalakit* was another name for balete trees.

"Sweet Sophia," Dawn breathed. She was looking at her own printed-off article, and she read out loud from a passage. It described how baletes were a cousin of banyan trees, and how the seeds of both are spread by birds who eat the trees' figs. The birds drop the seeds on other trees, and then the seeds become parasites, growing over the host trees and strangling them, sometimes becoming so massive that a balete tree will form over the top of the host tree and swallow it whole.

"Gross," Sig commented. "But so what?"

"Symbolism is really important in magic," I said. I probably should have let Dawn explain, but I had other things on my mind than manners. "The balete tree sounds like it's symbolically perfect for making a dimensional portal. You plant one thing from someplace else on top of another thing, and it grows around the host until both things are intertwined in the same space."

"But even if these dalaketnon things do have a spell for making magical doors out of balete trees, why would some Philippine monster want to kidnap Constance?" Bob demanded. "And how—"

I cut him off. "One thing at a time."

I was on my hands and knees, smelling the fragments of Constance's bedroom door, when I said, "I've found something else," or made some sounds that approximated those words anyhow. I was chewing on a cold leftover steak.

"What is it?" Bob demanded.

"There's an adhesive patch right here that got left behind when some tape got pulled off." I pointed at a place on the door.

"We already know that." Bob's expression was puzzled and defensive and a little pissed. "There's a couple of places like that on the door. I picked them up with fluorescent lighting. They're where some pictures were taped up. Look." He pointed at the ripped posters that had been set aside on the lab floor. One was of a rainbow with woodland creatures running over it. The other had brightly smiling dancing people in different costumes doing a jig with their arms linked.

"I've been going over those posters to see if there are any designs or sigils hidden in them," Dawn added. "I haven't found anything like that."

"Look closer." I got a blown-up picture of Constance's door, taken from the security cameras right before magic knocked the house's power off line. I handed the blow-up to Bob so that he could look at it, then picked up Constance's posters off the floor. I smelled the places where the posters had traces of adhesive or fragments of tape still on them, then matched those places and laid them over the areas where tape had left a scent trace on the door. There was one spot left over.

"Put your finger here," I told Bob, and I put my index finger next to the remaining patch, right beside the corner of a poster but not quite on it.

He did, and his face tightened as he felt a residue of stickiness with the tip of his index finger.

"The posters have six places where tape left a smell," I said. "The door has seven."

Bob looked at the picture. He looked at his index finger. "So, someone taped something to the door and removed it. It could have been weeks ago."

I tore another chunk off the steak. I had to work at it because my mouth was dry. "I don't think so. I think I know what happened."

It took a bit to track down a roll of tape, but when I did, I led Dawn and Bob and Sig back to the stairwell across from Constance's door. The roll of tape I was holding was an inch and a half wide, basically white paper on one side and adhesive on the other. I pointed at the stairwell bannister. "There's another adhesive smell where someone stuck some tape to the far side of the stairway rail right here."

Bob nodded cautiously. Curiosity and hope seemed to have won out over the defensive-animosity thing he had going. I pulled some tape free and anchored it on the inside of the bannister rail, then pulled the tape roll until a nine-inch strip was bared and extended. "You've been trying to figure out how Austin could have done a spell without leaving any symbols carved or drawn in the door, or saying any words that Tula would have heard. Suppose Austin had a spell written on a tape roll like this one?" I said conversationally. "Not a complete spell, but almost. Maybe just missing one rune or sigil."

Nobody said anything.

"We're standing in a blind spot where the cameras don't cover," I continued. "And Austin knew it. So, imagine Austin took out a marker and finished the spell right here." I pantomimed drawing something on the tape.

"That's when the lights started going on and off and the cameras went offline!" Dawn exclaimed, shaking off a little of the distracted agitation that had been clinging to her like a layer of tar since the ambush.

"But the spell wasn't complete yet, so Austin removed the

tape and walked up to the door." I demonstrated walking to the bedroom with a roughly nine-inch strip of tape pulled free from the main roll. There was no door, so I anchored the end of the tape on the wall next to the doorframe. I had to use about an inch of the tape's surface, but when I was done, the tape roll was dangling from the wall like a Christmas stocking. "He attached the runes to the door. When they touched the balete wood, it completed the spell, like connecting a circuit or something. Then Austin opened the door. Presto Amazo, it's a door to another world. That's when Tula heard a weird air-pressure suction sound."

"Runes don't work like that!" Dawn protested. "They have to be etched or carved or scratched into a surface. Their molecules have to be a part of the object they're transforming into a vehicle."

I shrugged. 'Maybe they only work this way on balete wood. The trees are symbolic of one thing attaching and growing on top of something else, using it for its own purposes."

Dawn became thoughtful. "I wish Nathan were here. He lived for stuff like this."

I didn't want to disrespect her grief, but I didn't want to indulge it either. "He certainly gave that impression." I stepped halfway between the doorway and ripped the tape off before continuing. "When the portal was open, Austin removed the tape. Once he closed the door, the magic portal was sealed behind him, and there was no sign of whatever runes or sigils he used."

"Except for that one place on the door that smelled like tape adhesive," Sig added thoughtfully.

"Sure," I said. "But Tula came upstairs and kicked the door in. The posters came loose and nobody thought to count the number of adhesive patches on the posters and the number on the door."

Dawn looked like her mind had gone someplace else. Bob was concentrating on the roll of tape so hard and so angrily that I half expected it to burst into flame. I wondered if Simon was going to want to kill Bob to make sure nobody figured out that Austin was a traitor. Sig was smiling at me with the corner of her mouth quirked upwards slightly. But still, nobody said anything until Bob shook his head and said, "You son of a bitch."

That's actually a no-no phrase around werewolves, but I didn't react. "What?"

Bob checked his watch. Like most people familiar with the supernatural, he wore the old-fashioned wind-up kind that wouldn't be affected by surges of magical energy. "You've been here thirty-two minutes."

I stood up and gave him a wry grin, but then I got dizzy and had to steady myself against a stairway railing.

"You don't just need food," Sig informed me. "You need rest."

"I'm not being stubborn," I said. "The first forty-eight hours after somebody goes missing are the most important. That works for mankind or magickind."

"I understand," Sig replied, and the nice thing about Sig was that she really did. "But you don't want to be a complete wreck when it's time to go after her either."

I nodded. "You're right. But I'm not done here yet."

∾6∾

BY DAWN'S EARLY LIGHT

We broke up into individual tasks. Bob had to walk far enough away from the lingering magic in the atmosphere to use his cell phone, staying in contact with Simon and trying to track down any of the house's contractors who might have installed that balete door frame. Dawn was trying to work out a way to follow Constance, using a combination of books that Nathan had brought along and intuitive techniques involving trances and dream states. Sig was walking the outer boundaries of Dawn's wards with a knight escort. She wanted to see if she could find any helpful spirits in the woods who might have useful information for her, like whether anyone strange had been prowling in the woods around the house or was watching the house now.

For my part, I was drinking a large mug of coffee and interviewing Tula. Tula is big-boned and strong-looking, a five foot seven Finnish woman with wide hips, hard fat, and brownish-blond hair. Or blondish-brown hair. Tula is also one of the toughest people I know and usually a pretty cold customer; of all of us, I had expected Tula to be the angriest and most vengeful, but she was drained and shell-shocked and devastated. She hadn't slept, and her voice and face were empty. Tula reminded me of one of those dried-out husks that look like an actual insect until you pick it up, and then it crumbles and collapses in your fingers. After the tenth or twelfth one-word response I'd gotten from her, I just asked point-blank, "Can you tell me anything that might help me, Tula?"

She wiped her cheek as if there were tears there. There weren't, but I think that's only because she was dehydrated. "I can tell you she's sweet. I can tell you she's innocent. I can't tell you how much. I don't have the words. I'm an alien here."

I think Tula said that because she was Finnish and speaking a non-native language, not because she was a werewolf.

"Tula—" I said.

"I held her right here." She touched her left shoulder. "I rubbed her back and she blended into me and I could feel her. We were connected. And I told her I would love her and keep her safe and she believed me. She was so sweet. She was so fucking perfect."

"I think Constance is in another dimension," I said. "If we can get there, I might need you to help me find her. If you're bonded with her."

I don't really believe that wolves can always locate their mates or packs or pups with some sixth sense. If that were true, they wouldn't need to howl. But wolves are plugged into some group awareness on a level far more primal than any human would be comfortable acknowledging, and if there's one fundamental law of the universe, it's that sometimes shit happens. And even if none of that were true, Tula needed something to focus on.

Tula stilled then. The way a wolf does when it gets a first scent of prey. "She's not dead. I would know it if she were dead."

I struggled with how to respond. I didn't love Constance the way Tula did. I barely knew Constance, which wasn't a bad thing. I might have been incapacitated by grief or worry if I had spent a lot of time around her. Even as things were, I was having a hard time dealing with Constance's abduction. One of the ways I cope with horrible things is by making dumb jokes, and dealing with a kidnapped infant isn't exactly prime comedy material. I felt like a wind sock stretched taut in a storm, barely hanging on and being shaped and pulled as something big and ancient and elemental moved through me. I don't know if it was duty or guilt or my geas or some kind of wolf instinct or what. The hardest thing I ever had to deal with was the death of a woman I loved, Alison Garcia. Maybe Constance's abduction was reminding me that it's impossible to keep anyone safe, that life isn't safe, and it was taking me back to some dark places.

But I had to stay out of that frame of mind where I felt like it was my duty not to relax, or enjoy anything, or love anyone or anything, to always act as if things were going to be okay and never really believe it. Monsters, human or otherwise, do the things they do to send people to that place. To make them feel helpless or afraid or full of pain and hate and anger. Monsters do that because that dark place is where they live, and doing horrible things is how they communicate.

"I believe you. Now try to believe me." I took Tula's hand and willed her to hear me. "You didn't do anything wrong. You are not powerless. You are not alone. And love is never pointless."

I was in Dawn's makeshift lab, examining the file that Bob had reluctantly handed over and left with me. The magic had finally died down enough for wireless connections to work again, and Dawn was sitting on a stool in an unconscious imitation of Rodin's *Thinker*, huddled over her computer keyboard while she did some kind of research. Her hair was green now, and at some point, Dawn had stripped down to a T-shirt that revealed a variety of tattoos coiling over her arms, most of them Celtic. Yeah, Dawn definitely hadn't liked growing up in a Catholic order.

"What?" she said when she caught me staring at her hair. She touched it self-consciously. "You don't like it?"

"It doesn't smell like fresh dye," I said.

She laughed. "Oh. It's something I invented. It's a dye made out of chameleon scales. I can make it change color."

"Can anybody use it?" I asked. "Or do you have to have mojo?"

Dawn seemed amused. "Why? Do you want some?"

"Sure." I said. "It'd be useful."

"You have to be able to experience the chameleon," she said, whatever that meant.

"Oh," I said. "Darn."

We went back to our respective studies, interrupted by occasional random comments from one or the other of us. Dawn had some pretty impressive powers of concentration. She didn't move for a solid hour, then out of nowhere, with no inflection, just said a single word over and over. "Shit. Shit. Shit. Shit."

I looked up from my medieval smartphone—I mean, my thick folder—but Dawn didn't look at me or elaborate. "That's not how you talk shit," I said. "In case you're wondering."

Dawn laughed slightly but still didn't look up or comment. I'd overheard the conversation that she'd had with Simon on the phone. Simon had told Dawn that if she didn't pull her act together, he was going to send her away and ask for another merlin, had in fact told her that he had someone named Gloria Waterhouse on standby, and despite her misgivings, Dawn didn't want that. I kind of had a feeling that Simon had chosen this Gloria because she was some kind of rival that Dawn hated. And Dawn was obviously upset about Nathan's death, but she was also...well...upset about Nathan's death. She wanted to do something about it.

I hadn't asked what Nathan had meant to her. Dawn was still

dumping out rage and fear and frustration smells at odd intervals, but that could have been because Nathan was her mentor or her lover or her friend or her surrogate father, and I wasn't sure that it mattered which. Merlins aren't trained in a combat capacity, and people can be traumatized by having someone die next to them even when the person isn't someone they know or care about.

A little while later, I exclaimed, "Simon Templar!"

Dawn blinked. "What?"

"I just realized, there was a character called the Saint whose name was Simon Templar," I said a little lamely. "Whoever named Simon had a sense of humor."

"Simon didn't know his real father," Dawn murmured.

"Did he grow up in one of our orphanages too?"

"Not exactly," Dawn said. "The Order has a special center for kids who grow up in the normal world being Templar bastards and not knowing it. Since the Pax doesn't keep them from experiencing the supernatural, they grow up seeing and hearing things that nobody else around them can, and they don't know why."

I processed that. The Templars are pretty fanatical about keeping track of bloodlines, but knights are physically fit, generally high-testosterone, and mostly male specimens under a lot of stress. It wasn't surprising that sometimes knight seed wound up sprouting in unexpected places. "I can see where that would mess with someone's head."

"These kids grow up half convinced they're insane," Dawn said. "Nobody believes or understands them. It's like typical adolescence on crack. And then this man comes along and makes sense out of their world for them. He accepts them. He teaches them a way to take control of their lives and introduces them to other people just like them for the first time."

There was something strange in her voice. "That would be

kind of like growing up psychic," I ventured. "Are you talking about Simon and Emil, or you and Nathan?"

She flashed me a complex look. "Maybe that's why I get it. But I've met a couple people from Simon and Austin's training center, and they all try to outknight the knights. Maybe it's because they didn't grow up knowing where they belonged like most Templars do."

I actually knew a little about that myself. "Is that why Simon is being so hard on you?"

Dawn shrugged. "That's some of it. Simon's in his mid-forties and trying to fight being put in an administrative position too."

"I would have figured him for mid-thirties myself," I commented.

"He's in crazy shape," Dawn said. "Simon's been Emil's number one go-to for special assignments for a long time. He's refused to marry or have kids, and the only reason he's gotten away with it is that he's so good at what he does. I don't think Simon ever planned on living past his mid-forties."

"I could help him with that," I said.

Dawn laughed, and I went back to my file. Not too long after that, I picked up an essay Austin had written as a squire on why he believed he would be a good knight. The page still had faint traces of the oil that Austin's fingers had left behind when he was a kid, and I smelled something strange. I held the stationery up to my nose to get a deeper whiff.

"What is it?" Dawn asked, still not looking up from her own endeavors.

"This paper smells like Austin," I said. "But it doesn't."

"How can it smell like Austin but not?" Simon's voice was coming through a cell phone that Bob was holding up. We were out on the porch, where reception was better. "And why are you calling him an it?"

I had Ben on a speaker phone myself, and I held up the essay, even though half my audience couldn't see it. "The scent on this paper isn't the smell Austin has been leaving behind in the house. It's more like a brother or a father's smell."

"Are you going to tell us that Austin has an evil twin?" Bob inquired skeptically.

"Bear with me for a second," I said. "I smelled this kind of thing once before, in Boston, in 1965. It was when I killed that skinwalker I told you about."

"Another skinwalker?" Simon managed to pack a lot of different emotions in that word.

"Yeah," I said. "I think a skinwalker killed Austin Denham. It peeled his hide off, ate a part of him, cut sigils on its own flesh with a knife that had been dipped in Austin's blood, and then made a magic suit out of Austin's skin. When it put on the suit, it looked and moved and sounded exactly like Austin."

"But magic doesn't work on knights," Sig objected. "How could a spell..."

"Any kind of magic that depends on getting inside our minds doesn't work on us," I amended. "But nothing would keep a cunning man from using our hide once we were dead."

"Wait a minute. Magic doesn't work on knights," Sig repeated slowly. She wasn't asking a question this time. "And it wasn't Austin."

"Sig?" I asked.

"So, magic should work on it. Dawn should be able to read his things." Sig turned to Dawn. "Did you try?"

We all watched Dawn as something...well...dawned on her. She ran through the front door, and we followed her into the house and up toward Austin's room.

"Dawn?" Bob called after her, but we stayed downstairs so that we wouldn't lose cell phone reception. "Is everything all right? Do you want me to do something?"

"Just give me a second!" Dawn called down. "Sig's right. The skinwalker doesn't have a geas that protects him against every kind of mind magic!"

We listened to her pulling things out of Austin's closet for a moment, then Ben's voice came through my phone. "Are you talking about a *yee naaldlooshi?*"

"I don't know if this was one of the Navajo skinwalkers or not," I admitted. In the United States, the term *skinwalker* has spun out of Native American tradition, but the practice is alluded to in Gallic, Norse, and Celtic mythologies too. Maybe others. "The one I saw in 1965 wasn't."

Dawn appeared at the top of the stairs, wearing some of Austin's clothes, specifically grey sweatpants, a navy blue sweatshirt, and some socks, all of which were way too large for her. She had a highlighter in her right hand, and she stopped next to the roll of tape that I had left hanging on the wall beside Constance's doorway. "Show me where Austin anchored that tape on the rail again. Exactly."

I told Ben I'd call him back later.

"Dawn, what are you up to?" Bob asked.

"I'm such an idiot!" Dawn exclaimed. "It's like we were talking about in the car. I knew Austin wouldn't leave any psychic impressions behind, so he didn't. I blocked myself!"

Then Dawn shushed us. She attached the roll of tape to the bannister in the exact same spot that Not-Austin had, then pulled the roll so that a strip of tape was exposed. Dawn evened her breathing out, drawing in slow, deep breaths. Her eyes glazed over. In some indefinable way, she began to seem less like Dawn and more like a human-shaped part of the house sticking out of the floor. Then Dawn suddenly began drawing runes of a kind I'd never seen on the roll of tape, pulling the tape tight.

When she was done, the lights began flickering and our phones went dead.

Dawn didn't seem triumphant about the magic she'd activated. She left the tape hanging from the rail and recoiled against the far wall, pulling her borrowed clothes off as fast as she could. When she was done, she was huddling in her bra and panties against the stairwell wall. There was an expression of intense disgust on her face, and she was rubbing her hands over her arms as if she wanted to scrub her skin off. It was a particularly disturbing picture with the strobe-light effect, and I went ahead and tore the strip of tape in half, careful not to irreparably damage any of the sigils.

It didn't take long for the lights to stabilize. It took Dawn a little longer. "This was one sick man," she gasped. "It feels like my soul's covered in grease."

"Did you get inside his mind?" Bob asked urgently.

"No, just inside his shadow," Dawn said.

I'm usually pretty interested in those kinds of distinctions, but not then. "Can you use those runes to take us wherever that assbag took Constance?" I asked impatiently.

"What runes?" Dawn asked dazedly.

Wow. I showed her what she had drawn.

"I don't think so," she said regretfully. "It was tuned to that specific door, and we broke it. We'll never be able to fit those two door halves together perfectly again."

Sig knows more about runes than I do. She can do some of that kind of magic herself, though in a limited capacity. So, when she looked at me over Dawn's head, I felt my scalp tighten. "Maybe we won't have to," Sig said.

7

LET'S NOT GET A HEAD OF OURSELVES

We were back in Dawn's makeshift basement lab, examining the two halves of Constance's bedroom door while we waited for our cell phones to come back online. Dawn was back in her own clothes but still hadn't fully recovered from her brief psychic contact with the skinwalker. She was staring at the door halves with an unfocused expression while she mechanically ate chocolate-covered espresso beans. Occasionally, her body would convulse as if she'd just stuck her hand in something disgusting.

"We don't have to try to put the door halves together," Sig said. Like me, she was sipping a cup of some Mexican coffee I didn't recognize. It was pretty strong. "We need a doorframe made out of balete wood lining the doorway, and a door made out of balete wood to fit in the frame, right?"

"That's how it was set up on the second floor," I said. "It's probably the door making contact with the frame again that completes the spell."

"So, this is what we do," Sig said. "We take the bigger door half and size it down into a two-and-a-half-foot door. Then we take strips from the door frame upstairs and size them down into a two-and-a-half-foot door frame."

"Elias knows something about carpentry," Bob said thoughtfully, and when Sig and I looked at him blankly, he explained: "One of the guards outside. I might have to run out and get him a plane saw, though."

"Hold on there, Sparky." I removed my pocketknife and unfolded the blade. "None of us are going anywhere until we do a simple skinwalker test."

No one eyed my pocketknife with anything resembling enthusiasm.

"What test?" Dawn asked suspiciously.

"This test." I made a slash on the back of my right hand. Blood began to well up in a thin line.

"The skinwalkers' magic flesh suits work as some kind of magic armor. I've seen it personally."

Sig held out her hand for the knife. "Works for me."

Bob didn't waste time arguing. He knew I wasn't going to let it go, and he tried to surreptitiously remove the M9 holstered at his side. He was presumably going to start shooting all of us, but I wasn't the only one being watchful. Sig grabbed Bob's pistol before it cleared his side and punched him in the face with her free hand, hard...and the punch didn't draw blood.

Yeah. Bob was a skinwalker.

If that seemed to come out of nowhere, how do you think I felt? Dawn wasn't the only one who wasn't operating on all cylinders. I had just offered the knife because I thought I should, acting on general principle. I hadn't really expected this. If I had, I would have handled the whole situation a lot more cautiously.

Sig punched the skinwalker again, harder, hard enough to

put her fist through a wall. The punch still didn't faze Bob—or the thing that was pretending to be Bob—but Not-Bob couldn't move his gun either. He might have been virtually invulnerable, but Sig was still four or five times stronger than he was.

Not-Bob's left hand came out with a small resin bag that seemed to appear out of thin air. Sig blocked the skinwalker's left hand at the wrist, but it still managed to release a small cloud of some kind of white, mealy powder into her face. Sig choked and released the thing, stumbling back, her face going slack.

The skinwalker tried to shoot Sig as soon as she let go of its gun, but I charged in at full speed and halted its gun hand halfway, causing a bullet to slam into the west wall. The skinwalker kept pulling the trigger, but I whirled inside its grasp, and even though I couldn't budge his arm, I got my hands on the M9's butt. The bullets rebounded, and one ricochet actually sliced past the outside of my left calf, while another wound up in Dawn's ass. She yelped and stopped in the middle of some incantation she'd started, then cursed angrily. I couldn't pry the gun out of the skinwalker's hand, but my fingers found the magazine release, and when the clip fell out, I kicked it across the room.

We could hear people yelling and wolves yipping and the sound of bodies thundering down the basement stairs.

The thing that looked like Bob tried to lean in and tear out my carotid artery with its teeth, but when it bent forward, I went with the motion and flipped the thing into a cabinet. The cabinet's door shattered, but none of the skinwalker's bones did. It stayed on the floor to save time and began making some kind of passes with its freed hands, whispering something in a language that I didn't recognize.

There was a small bowl full of salt on a table—I have no idea why. I grabbed it and tossed the contents into the skinwalker's face. His skin may have been invulnerable, but he still had to breathe. Whatever the spell was, the skinwalker choked on a mouthful of half-inhaled salt and didn't finish it. Two knights slammed the door open at the same time that Dawn hobbled up with a metal canister that looked like a small fire extinguisher and pressed it close to the skinwalker's face. It wasn't foam that came out when she pressed the nozzle up to Not-Bob's face though. It was a stream of compressed liquid nitrogen.

The thing about cold is, it's not a form of energy that can be conducted. Cold drains energy.

The part of the skinwalker's suit covering its face hardened and whitened. The thing's tongue shriveled and its eyes withered while the liquid nitrogen traveled through its open mouth and froze any screams dead. The skinwalker tried to rise up, but when it did, its head fell off its shoulder and shattered.

"Oh," Dawn said in a small voice.

The knights ordered us all to freeze, and I was too concerned about Sig to even make a smartass joke about that. "I'm checking on her," I told them, but I held my hands up while I walked.

"Don't touch me," Sig warned. She was blinking and shaking like someone having a bad trip, but she was lucid enough. "This bone dust I'm covered with is some kind of death magic."

I moved forward anyhow, crouching down a few feet away from Sig. "What do you need?"

"Just a damp cloth. This bone powder sends people's souls to the spirit world." Sig smiled briefly at my expression, though her forehead was coated with beads of sweat. "It's okay. I'm used to it."

Okay. File that one away in the come-back-to-later category. I didn't trust any of the cloths in a merlin's lab, and I'd recently set my handkerchief on fire, so I peeled my shirt off inside out and soaked it with a bottle of water.

"There you go, taking your clothes off in public again," Sig joked, but she said it kind of weakly.

I made an attempt at a smile and handed the shirt over. If Sig had died, it would have been because I messed up. Which is why I picked my pocketknife off of the floor and went back over to Dawn. She was sitting on the floor with her back against the wall, staring blankly at the headless torso and the shattered remains of a face, trying to explain things to the knight who was watching her. At least the cold had frozen the blood in the skinwalker's veins at the point of separation. I gently removed the canister of compressed liquid nitrogen from her unresisting hands and took out my pocketknife. "Give me your hand."

"I'm bleeding from a bullet wound in my butt!" Dawn said with what was probably justifiable asperity. "Doesn't that count?"

"I know, but I'm freaked out, and you're a cunning woman," I said. "You could have done some sleight of hand with some dye or something. Do you want to do this, or do you want me to stick a finger in the bullet hole?"

The knight cleared his throat. "I could examine—"

"Shut up, Shane." Dawn snapped. "Two pains in the ass is enough." She offered me her hand.

Wait. Two pains in the ass? Well, I probably deserved that. I didn't really believe Dawn was a skinwalker, and this time I was right.

∾8∾

THE FINE ART OF FLYING BLIND

I was really tired, and everything that proceeded afterward had a kind of strange nightmarish quality: rushed, dreamlike, fragmented, and dark. It was a massive headache, isolating every knight and wolf in the vicinity of Constance's house, cornering them, giving them a slight cut, and enlisting their help in testing the others. But eventually, we—that is, the five survivors of the Dogtown pack ambush—reassembled in a small family room built around an entertainment center with a widescreen TV and a music system. The shelves were full of DVDs and CDs and books that seemed almost quaint in the cold new digital age.

Ben had brought more werewolves back with him, and Simon put on an Amy Winehouse CD that was probably tradecraft against beings with enhanced hearing more than an attempt at coziness. I liked the music anyhow, in an abstract this-would-be-good-if-I-wasn't-full-of-tension way. There was something about her voice that took me back to the female singers I had grown up listening to. The room was twelve by twelve, and everyone except Dawn was sitting on a wraparound brown leather couch that took up two walls. Dawn's bullet wound had only torn off a small piece of the...edge? Tip? Border? What do you call the outer fringe of a butt cheek? Flank, maybe? Anyhow, she was sitting on a doughnut pillow on the floor at an odd angle. Dawn had also fixed enough of some kind of detox Yogi tea for everyone, and I drank it without protest. It was hot.

"There's no way the skinwalker you killed was the same one pretending to be Austin Denham," Simon said glumly. He was wearing a black suit coat over a dark-green turtleneck shirt and slim-cut black slacks. His dark shoes somehow looked fashionable and serviceable at the same time. "Even if the skinwalker took Constance to this dalaketnon world and came back to ours, there was no opportunity to isolate Bob and take his place. The man we thought was Bob spent half the time since Constance's disappearance on a plane and the other half here surrounded by security cameras and guards. He must have been another skinwalker all along."

I took a sip of tea without really noticing the flavor. "So, at least two skinwalkers are working together."

"At least three," Ben corrected. He seemed a little better now that he had the beginnings of a direction, but he still wasn't projecting his usual air of laid-back stoicism. "You don't think it's a coincidence that you killed a skinwalker doing the same kind of thing here in Massachusetts back in the '60s, do you?"

"So, we're talking about the possibility of some kind of colony or cult of skinwalkers," I said. "Or a far-reaching conspiracy. Or both."

It was a lot to wrap my head around.

"If this is an organized group, what do they want?" Sig asked quietly. She hadn't wanted to risk getting that bone dust on anyone, and she was still damp from a shower, wearing spare jeans and a thick white sweater over a T-shirt that she'd gotten from her backpack.

"They want to eat away at the Knights Templar from the inside and take them over," Simon said flatly.

"Is that something Dawn picked up from Austin's psychic impressions?" Sig asked. Dawn's hands were wrapped around her own mug of tea, and she shook her head emphatically. She didn't seem to like being reminded of that experience.

"You just have to look for patterns," Simon said. "We have magic doors made out of a parasite tree from a parasite world. We have skinwalkers who take over other people's forms and wear them. We have a werewolf pack from the Round Table that was supposed to make it look like the whole werewolf alliance was a larger conspiracy. The attacks all reflect a way of thinking. Whoever is calling the shots likes to make their enemies weak by hollowing them from the inside out, making them turn on themselves."

I stared at Simon, kind of wishing I'd put that together. I was impressed and a little competitive and a whole lot of tired. But what I said was, "That's a good insight."

But Simon was watching Dawn. "Do you think skinwalkers are the real enemy, Dawn?"

She shivered. Dawn had psychically read some of Bob's possessions, and she hadn't liked that experience any more than she had enjoyed wearing Austin's clothes. "I still can't believe the thing I read hid all of that hate so well. It feels like it was Bob who shot me."

People are funny. Some people respond well to outward shows of compassion, and some people enjoy sympathy so much that they take it as an excuse to keep feeling sorry for themselves, and some dislike having their vulnerability pointed out so much that they refuse to ask for any kind of help or admit any kind of weakness, and some only snap out of funks when they have to rise to a challenge. I'd been watching Dawn for a while, so I took a shot. "Are you still going on about that bullet wound? I thought you'd put it behind you."

Dawn shifted on her doughnut cushion and glared at me. "Is that a joke? Why don't you kiss this butt?"

"Well, his last name is Charming," Sig observed. "That might magically make your butt better."

I looked at Sig. "That is wrong on so many levels."

She stuck her tongue out at me.

Simon clearly wasn't a fan of using immature humor to emotionally decompress. "I repeat: Do you think the skinwalkers are the real enemy, Dawn?"

Dawn thought about what she wanted to say hard, and when she spoke, it was with a certain distaste. "I don't understand how they're working together. When I read those things, I get a sense of really dark self-loathing. These things are gross! They don't pretend to be other people just because it's a good strategy. By the time they're finished doing whatever it is they do to become skinwalkers, they *need* to get out of their own skins. They probably wrap that up in a power trip and don't admit it to themselves, but it's true. Being around other things just like them would be like standing next to mirrors, and these things don't like mirrors."

"That's why I still can't believe they're working together too," Simon agreed. "Skinwalkers would know what they each had to do to become skinwalkers emotionally before they could become skinwalkers physically. Hard to build a foundation of trust on that."

"It's not the sort of thing you usually see on a Roommate-Wanted ad," I agreed. I made an air frame with my hands. "Wanted: murderous sociopath with no moral boundaries, deep-rooted hostility, and trust issues."

Sig snorted. "Been there. Done that."

There was an awkward silence. I wasn't sure if the others knew the details about Sig's relationship with a man named Stanislav Dvornik or not, so I changed the subject. "It sort of sounds like some powerful outside party would have to be forcing skinwalkers to work together."

"Whoever is behind this, it may be that the Order working with werewolves is what forced these skinwalkers to expose themselves." Simon rubbed some focus back into his bleary eyes. "The last thing skinwalker spies would want is a bunch of werewolves with supersensitive noses running around."

"Then we should spread this knowledge around as soon as possible." I yawned. "Right now, everybody who knows about this is right here. That makes us vulnerable."

"John's right," Sig agreed, and unfortunately I didn't record it. "When John figured out that Austin was a skinwalker, and Dawn figured out how to activate the dimensional portal, Bob tried to slip away."

Dawn shuddered. "We have to stop calling that thing Bob."

Sig got a little impatient. "I don't care what you call it. The point is, that skinwalker wanted to warn somebody we were on to them and might be coming soon. But it didn't."

Even exhausted, I saw where she was going. "That means we've got a very short window where this enemy that's been spying on us doesn't know what we know and isn't expecting us."

Simon added, "It also means none of us can be alone for a second from this point on."

I didn't have any problem following his logic. It wasn't just to keep anyone from sending word out, although Simon was probably worried about that; it was to keep people from being snuck up on and replaced by skinwalkers after they'd already been tested. In a horror movie, this would have been the part where people started splitting up and wandering off one by one.

Sig took my hand. "If we're doing a buddy system, I call John." When I looked at her, she added, "I'm still mad. But we're sleeping in the same bed anyway."

"And I have to figure out how I'm going to test the Grand-master," Simon said. "Then we have to figure out the best way to test every knight in the Order discreetly."

"That's your job," Ben said unsympathetically. He was eating homemade peanut butter crackers, smearing thick gobs of the stuff on saltines and eating them mechanically. I think he'd forgotten to eat earlier. "Getting Constance back is ours."

9

SPEAKING OF EVERYTHING HAVING A STRANGE NIGHTMARISH QUALITY...

I was lying on the ground. It felt as if I was pinned there, and then the world started spinning and I was looking down at myself. My katana had pierced my stomach and anchored into the grassy field I was lying on. My chest was peeled open and the flaps were spread out like two bloody baby angel wings that somebody had put on backward. Then I was back inside my body, and I could feel blood pooling out of my stomach and sinking into the earth beneath me, turning the ground into warm, wet quicksand. It was oddly pleasant until I saw Sig's face above me. Her eyes were remote and beautiful, her face solemn.

"I love you," I said, but all she said back was my name, and she said it like a question. She kept repeating my name, and that was odd because her lips weren't moving but the earth was, and then—

~10~

LOCKER ROOM TALK

John, wake up. Are you all right?"

I groaned. My eyes felt glued together and my chest still felt hollow. I rubbed it. "Not really."

Sig sounded really concerned. "You were making a weird sound."

I opened my eyes and found myself staring at a ceiling light. My head was pressed against the back of the couch. Sig and I were alone in the room where we had talked about going after Constance. "I'm having a little trouble shaking this chest injury. I'm not sure why."

Sig laughed softly, and I felt a rush of warmth and relief. "Because that's sane?"

I moved my head so that I could see Sig standing before me in a knight's armor. It wasn't metal but a full black bodysuit of some kind of spider-silk and Kevlar weave. Fire-retardant, bullet-proof, and more light and flexible than straight Kevlar, the suit would stand up to small mortar fire, though the impact of such a thing would leave the knight inside pulped. Some kind of jet-black space-age plastic strips were built into the suit too, providing additional impact protection and support around vital organs and joints or areas where a sharp edge might penetrate when a bullet couldn't.

More importantly, Sig was holding a big mug of coffee. I made an effort to rally. "Give me just a moment." My whole body was still stuck in a sitting position on the wraparound couch. "I'm discovering a whole new range of sex fantasies."

Sig smiled faintly and gestured at herself. "It's not like we're going to blend in with the locals, anyhow."

"How long have I been out?" I asked.

"Not as long as I'd like," Sig said. "But probably longer than I should have let you. I can give you five more minutes to drink that coffee, but the magic portal will be ready in another couple hours. If you're going with us, you have to start getting ready."

"I'm going," I said. I didn't feel great, but at least my head wasn't full of silt. My chest still had those phantom aches though, and I rubbed it some more. "Did I miss anything important?"

"Dawn's been researching these dalaketnon things," she said. "Simon already knows most of it anyhow, and I told her you probably would too."

"Mmmn," I grunted. "Not really. I know they're supposed to be tall and pale and beautiful. Kind of like elves, but they're not immortal."

"That's it?" Sig asked skeptically.

I puffed out a heavy breath. "I think they're all supposed to live in big mansions or palaces on another world. But maybe that's because the only ones who can cross worlds are the rich, powerful ones. I know they like to kidnap humans and turn them into slaves by feeding them some kind of black rice that steals their willpower. And they can make duplicates of themselves. I have no idea how many or how fast. And they can also move things with their minds."

"That's pretty much what Dawn said too, except she told us that their hair turns white when they use their powers," Sig said.

I'd heard that too, but it sounded like something that had started up on an online game or Japanese anime because it looked cool. But if Dawn said it was a fact, it probably was. "I take it that Simon agreed to let the Round Table handle the rescue?"

"Mostly. Simon and Dawn are going to be with us, and other knights will be coming behind to back the advance party up. Make sure we have a fallback position."

Seven was too big for a scouting party but not too bad for a search-and-retrieval team. I yawned.

"Dawn wants to be there to keep us from doing something that could mess up the space-time continuum," Sig explained. "Something about the universe being sucked inside out through a small hole like a bedsheet down a vacuum-cleaner nozzle."

"That doesn't sound good," I agreed.

"And she's the only one who might get us back home if we get stranded over there."

I yawned again.

Sig was concerned. "Are you really going to be able to do this?"

"I'm not a hundred percent," I admitted. "But if I thought I was more likely to get somebody killed than help, I'd step aside."

Sig snorted skeptically.

I took a sip of the coffee and winced.

"Is it that bad?" Sig's voice was a little sharp, and I realized that she must have made the coffee herself. Sig has the worst kitchen instincts I've ever encountered. I think it's all tied up with the fact that her mother never taught her how to prepare anything, and her overly critical father expected her to take care of him domestically when Sig's mother died. I've seen Sig enter vampire hives and werewolf dens without losing her cool, but the simplest kitchen task involves all sorts of defensive anger and resentment and tension.

"Strong coffee is what I need right now." I reached out and put my free hand on her hip. "It's perfect."

She smiled a you're-full-of-it-but-I-appreciate-the-effort kind of smile and squeezed my hand before sitting down on the couch next to me. "The other thing you missed was that Dawn's upset about this black rice that makes humans slaves. She doesn't like that we might get attacked by people who aren't in control of themselves."

"I'm not too crazy about the idea either." I took another sip of the coffee. It didn't get better with time. "If it helps, I think if there are any human guards, they won't be zombies drugged out of their skulls. How could they be? They'll be the same kind of men who worked on slave plantations or became policemen in the Nazi ghettos."

In a movie, we could have flooded the portal with sleep gas or something, but sleeping gas is a myth. There's no such thing as a gas that knocks people out instantly and painlessly and doesn't do any lasting damage. The closest thing to that sort of gas that I've ever heard of is the gas that the Russians used in the Moscow Theater Crisis in 2002. It knocked out the terrorists instantly, but it also killed one out of seven hostages, and a lot of the survivors had serious neurological damage and side effects. And that's just the stuff the Russians couldn't cover up. This is the same society where it's illegal for people who live near Chernobyl to own radiation detectors. We couldn't use anything like that kind of gas when we didn't know where Constance was located or how soon we might be bringing her back through the area.

Sig's mind was somewhere else. "It's always going to be like this, isn't it?"

"Well, I don't think there's always going to be a cabal of cunning folk killing knights so that they can make magic suits out of their skins," I replied. "Or that we'll be tracking stolen werewolf babies through dimensional portals that lead to some other world."

The fact that I could piece that many weird words together that fast was a good sign.

Sig punched me in the shoulder lightly. That was another good sign. "I mean the people we care about always being in danger."

I felt a spasm of uneasiness. Sig and I had both lost a lot because of the lives we led and the world we lived them in. But people were depending on me staying focused, so I made another effort to spackle myself back together. "This really isn't the time to get too emotional or talk about big pictures, Sig."

Not that Sig seemed inclined to do that too much herself. She hadn't mentioned the fact that I'd said I loved her, for instance, and I didn't know if that was for her sake or mine. I wasn't going to bring it up again while there was so much going on either. "It's okay." She kissed my cheek. "It's not like either of us can retire. Your geas wouldn't let you. And me...well, dead souls that haven't moved on can be pretty insistent."

I couldn't leave it at that in spite of myself. "I also have some pretty basic instincts to take care of my mate. If that means finding a quiet place where my geas won't get triggered as much, I can do that. I've done it before."

She put her head on my shoulder. "Me too. But there are ghosts everywhere, John."

"So, you tried to find a peaceful place before?" I asked.

"A few times," Sig said quietly. "Drinking was a place like that for a little while."

I turned slightly and kissed the top of her forehead. "You watch my ass, and I'll watch yours. That's the deal."

Her face was hidden, but I could hear the smile in her voice. It was a small and slightly crooked smile, and I could have traced it with a finger without looking. "Is that why I catch you staring at my ass so much?"

"I take my responsibilities very seriously," I said.

"Hmmn," she said. "I haven't forgotten that you're going to pay for keeping secrets from me."

"You really hold a grudge, don't you?" I asked.

"I really do. You should know that about me." Sig stood up and held out her hand. "Come on."

We went down to a small arsenal in the basement. I wasn't surprised to see Dawn already in knight armor too, but it was a little odd seeing werewolves like Ben, Tula, and Virgil in black Templar field suits of their own. "Excuse me," I said. "Is this where they're casting the next Tim Burton film?"

Virgil gave me a wry look. "How's it going, John?"

"I've been better, Virgil," I said. "But it's good to see you here." And it was too. Virgil is a widely built black man, bald-headed and broad-shouldered. He's about three inches shorter than me and a hundred pounds heavier. He's solid in more ways than just physically, though. Virgil defines calm under pressure, which for a werewolf is no small thing.

"Are you up for this?" Ben asked point-blank. There wasn't any aggression or accusation in his voice, which was good.

The closer we got to actually doing something, the more Ben seemed to be like himself again.

"I'm up for it." I stripped down to my boxers and began getting dressed in a suit of armor that had been set aside for me. "I'll need to rest again at some point, but that nap helped clear my head."

"I can give you something that will have you on full alert for about eight hours," Dawn offered. "But the crash is fierce."

"I'm good," I said. "What about you?"

"Define good," she said tartly.

"It's an adjective describing whatever or whoever can help us find Constance," I answered.

Dawn released a deep breath. "Then I'm good."

We'd see. "How about your...umm...injury?"

"It was just a slice," Dawn said, a little awkwardly. "I whipped up a local anesthetic that doesn't make me groggy."

"Maybe you should market it," I couldn't help suggesting. "You could call it Assprin."

Dawn got a little pissed, but she laughed too, and either was better than being too tense. "I could call it *Shut the Fuck Up*."

"Probably not the best marketing strategy," I observed. "Where's Simon?"

"He's busy delegating," Ben said. "He's been prepping us, though. Did Sig tell you he's going to lead us?"

"She told me he was coming along." I remembered what Dawn had said about Simon resisting being gradually forced into an administrative pasture.

"Simon's trained for this kind of op, and the knights who are gonna back us up trust him," Ben explained. "I would have preferred you, but we don't have a lot of time and you really needed some sleep."

I just nodded. I would have preferred me too, but trying to start a power struggle now would just cause confusion, so I turned my attention to Tula. "What about you, Tula? Can you handle this?"

She held up her right hand. It was steady.

"Okay." Asking Tula too many pointed questions to try to reassure myself would only tear her down, so I asked her some questions about the submachine guns we'd be using instead. Just to give her a chance to remind herself and us how expert she was at that kind of thing. I continued examining my gear while I listened to her talk, though. We had different scenarios to prep for and only a few hours to do so.

Making a small-scale version of the magic door presented some challenges. The culture that had created the first magic door had been doing that kind of thing to raid our world for centuries, and doing it with impunity. With that kind of mind-set and history, the door's creators probably didn't believe that we would be able to come after them, not really. But by the same token, the door's creators were in some kind of communication with a skinwalker who was very familiar with the Knights Templar and what the Order was capable of. So, they might have taken some basic precautions; for example, there might be some sentries waiting on the other side of the magic door if it worked. Or there might be booby traps.

So, we filled the bottom half of the doorway with cinder blocks and bound those together with quick-drying concrete, and set our smaller door on top of them so that it was two and a half feet off the ground. That way, we wouldn't step on any mines or trigger any trip lines on the other side. We made another change too: instead of opening horizontally, the door dropped down towards us like the flap of a mailbox. That way, nobody could block it, and our viewpoint of the sides of the room wouldn't be impeded as the door opened.

Someone had pulled out an office table from upstairs and set it in front of the flap. Tula was kneeling behind the table, facing the flap with a suppressed MP5 because she was our best shot. Her face was a cold mask even if she smelled like stress. I was standing on one side of the table, aiming my MP5 at a right angle. Simon was on the other side, aiming his MP5 at a left angle. It was risky and not textbook for very good reasons, but as long as none of us swept, swiveled, or fired at anything outside our designated field, we should be able to cover three different directions simultaneously. If there was nothing in our designated area, we would hold our fire no matter what else was going on.

Our weapons were set for single shot, but we could switch them to rapid fire, and if we did, we'd see how long the silencers held up. I'd read that high-quality suppressors made especially for the military can function through thousands of rounds, but I'd never used one before.

As the physically strongest, Sig was standing behind Tula so that she could shove Tula through the opening like a torpedo or pull her back in. Dawn was standing behind Simon with a strip of tape that had almost all of the sigils necessary to activate the portal. The rest of our raiding party was spread out along the hallway. The knight strike team that would attempt to secure the doorway while we wolves went hunting was lined up in the stairwell, along with a series of assault packs and drop bags that contained ammo, medical supplies, camping gear, and rations just in case we wound up in some cabin or cave in the middle of nowhere. Ideally, we'd have all been carrying those on our backs, but the size of the access point and the need for a fast entry made that impractical.

Simon looked at Tula. "Let's go."

∾11∾

TRY TO SEE IT FROM
THE OTHER SIDE

Somewhere, on another world, four guards were in a moderate-sized chamber that was lit by mounted torches and made of stone. The room didn't have any windows or a fireplace, but that world was warmer than the one the guards had grown up on, or at least warmer than Massachusetts in late winter/early spring. That's probably at least partly why the guards looked like mean cabana boys, dressed in loincloths, sandals, and leather harnesses that sheathed short steel swords behind their backs.

And they were guarding an empty doorframe that led to nothing but a closet.

One of the guards—let's call him Gary—was facing the empty doorway with a spear that was more like a pike. There were wedges on the floor placed to halt any doors that materialized and tried to swing open, and poison caltrops too, but Gary was supposed to have the spear pointed at the doorframe in case somebody got sneaky and made a door that swung inwards. To hell with that, though. Gary had been there for hours, and it was a damned heavy weapon, so Gary had the metal point of the spear resting on the floor while he leaned on the wooden haft. If the masters of that place wanted Gary to do a good job, they could give him one of the assault rifles or shotguns they occasionally picked up on earth during their slave runs. Fat chance of that happening, though. The dalaketnons couldn't drug Gary with that black rice that turned humans into cattle—not if they wanted Gary to be even halfway alert or effective—but that meant that the bastards couldn't entirely trust Gary, either. They gave him rewards for turning on his fellow humans, then acted like that made him unreliable. Assholes. He had about as much chance of getting his hands on a firearm as he did of finding a magic lamp.

Another guard—his name could have been Harry—was standing next to the empty doorframe on the right side with an axe. Harry was more like a strike-breaker or a bouncer than a member of an elite military unit, but Harry could swing an axe and break a door as soon as it materialized. And if he didn't, there was another guard with an axe who might have been called Larry on the other side of the door. Or at least, Larry was supposed to be there. Larry had set his axe down so he could go take a leak in the bronze pot in the corner.

The last guard—probably not named Barry, because that would have been way too big a coincidence, but whatever—was standing next to a gong with a war hammer. Barry was burly, but he had the tip of his weapon resting on the floor too. As far as Barry was concerned, somebody ought to just rip out the wood from the doorframe or fill the whole space in with stones if they were that worried, but that was the point, wasn't it? Nobody was really *that* worried about a door appearing and some SWAT team coming through. No, they were just making Barry waste his time standing there. Who cared about him?

God forbid anybody have to build another doorframe or find a different doorway.

Then a wooden square appeared two feet off the floor, floating in the middle of the doorway. It dropped down into another world, and the bottom fell out of Barry's.

Gary died almost immediately. He had the closest thing to a front-row seat, and he saw long, brownish-blond hair and a rifle barrel, and then he didn't see anything else.

Harry hesitated. His axe was braced to swing horizontally, not vertically, and the flap was falling away from him. He had to shift his stance. It was only for a moment, but something was wrong with the way time was flowing. Harry probably didn't know that the tachyon rate between worlds was different and that time flowed at least two-thirds slower on his adoptive dimension. But he knew that the people on the other side of that world seemed to be darting like insects. And then Harry took two bullets in the center of his chest and staggered back, trying to suck air in through his ruptured lung. The next bullet put a stop to that.

Barry managed to lift his hammer off the floor, but as soon as he turned to swing it, a bullet went through his temple.

Larry took the time to tuck little Larry back in its loincloth and then paid for it by getting shot in the back of his head.

They died quickly, but they didn't die quietly. The sound of all those exclamations and falling bodies carried.

Two rooms down a stone hallway, four more guards were in a crude barracks. The four of them were the next shift, sleeping while their compatriots were dying in the portal room. The sound that woke at least one of them up had been loud, but because it had woken them up, they were also disoriented.

The most alert guard or natural leader, let's call him Jake, didn't waste a lot of time debating. He slapped the other guards awake, and shrugged on his sandals, and reached for a sword. If there was any conversation, it probably went like this:

JAKE THE ALERT: Arise, arise, you laggards! The fox is at the henhouse and the chicks begin to peep!

SECOND GUARD: In which event, 'twere best to let us sleep. To any wolf come here, we are but sheep!

THIRD GUARD: True! Better a brief nap than eternal rest. If some fearsome foe arise, less than our best is best.

JAKE THE ALERT: For shame!

FOURTH GUARD: How shame? Those I protect I love not. Those I oppress I hate not. Come, come, the hour is late. 'Tis you who dream, who call shame at our gate!

JAKE THE ALERT: Fie! Did any man e'er choose his fate?

Well, okay, maybe not. Actually, if there was any conversation, it probably went like this:

JAKE THE ALERT: Fuck! Wake up!

SECOND GUARD: What the hell was that?

JAKE THE ALERT: It's our ass if we don't check it out. Wake up.

THIRD GUARD: Shhh. Listen!

JAKE THE ALERT: Fuck that! Anonymous guard two, you follow me and keep your signal horn at your lips. Anonymous guard three, you cover us with your crossbow. Anonymous guard four, fucking wake the fuck up, you fucking fuck!

FOURTH GUARD: Ow! Fuck!

The prudent move would have been to just start screaming, but the masters of that place were cruel, and their security measures were extreme. None of the guards wanted to draw attention to themselves unless it was undeniably necessary. That's something that a lot of would-be leaders who think of themselves as hard-ass disciplinarians don't really get: being too harsh is just as bad as being too lenient. It kills initiative, loyalty, and quick response time. Nobody wants to step up and claim responsibility for anything when death is the door prize for everything.

Jake, or whatever his name really was, exited the barracks and moved down the stone hallway toward the portal room.

~12~

OFF GUARDS

Tula scooched up to a sitting position on the table and gingerly eased feet-first through the portal. "Be careful," she hissed. "There are iron spikes on the floor, and they're covered in something." Her words and movements were stretched out, but that didn't surprise me. It had been bizarre, watching those guards falling while their blood sprayed in slow motion.

Somewhere, in some other room not too far away, I heard more mutters, movements, and thumps.

Simon handed Tula her MP5, and I gave him mine and made my own way through the crawlway. Time shifted, and Tula began moving at normal speed again. I took my MP5 back and made my way to the room's main door, stepping carefully. There were at least three separate and distinct movements...no...four...and fresh human scents coming from a ginormous crack under the wooden door. I smelled the skinwalker and Constance and something else I'd never smelled before too. The skinwalker and the alien scent were almost a day old. Constance's smell was fresh. I peeped under the crack and saw another door about ten feet across from us, and there was some kind of soft firelight coming from under it. Someone tried to step quietly in that room, and it caused the shadows to shift. I angled my neck and saw that a segmented stone wall was three feet to my right. Our room was at the end of a hall.

Screw symbolism. The dead end was a good thing. It meant we only had two directions to cover. Speaking of which, there were men in that hall creeping slowly, trying to approach quietly, but whichever genius was leading them hadn't considered how the torch he was carrying would cause the light to shift. I could see that the first shadow was carrying a sword, not a gun.

I signed the basic information to Simon while Ben made his way through the portal, and I could see Simon processing the logistics: Constance was nearby. We were at the end of a hall. Four guards in the hallway. At least one person in the room across from us. Probably armed like the men we had just killed. Approaching in a rough line. Speaking a language we didn't know.

There was no way we were going to be able to kill them all instantly and silently, no way to deceive them when we didn't speak the local language, and going out blazing with MP5s on full auto wasn't an option, not if Constance might be close by. It was a messed-up situation, but it was the one we had.

I gently regained my feet and held my MP5 at ready position. Simon nodded, moved to the door, and put one hand on the handle. Tula didn't sign, so he subvocalized, the words barely leaving his mouth. "John, take the hall. Tula, take the room across from us. I'll back up whichever one of you needs it."

Simon eased the door open slowly, casually, as if he had every right to do so. A voice called out, but as soon as the door slanted enough, I stepped through. The first guard was three feet away and I shot him in the face, then stepped past him and shot the second guard in the chest twice just as he was putting a wooden horn to his mouth. He had been ready to exhale powerfully, and the air came out of him in a loud grunt. I would have shot the third guard too, but the fourth guard shot him in the back of the head with a crossbow bolt. Was that on purpose or a happy accident? I kept walking forward with my MP5 trained on the fourth guard just in case, but the guard hissed, "Take me with you!"

Should I kill him, knock him out, or listen to him? I covered him while behind me, Tula shouldered a door open. There was a yell, muffled single-round bursts from her MP5, and bodies falling. Then, most significantly, a baby cried.

I didn't know it at the time, but Tula knocked one guard who was next to the door backward, hard, and when he went sprawling, she saw another guard holding Constance awkwardly with a knife to her little throat. It was why Constance was located so close to the portal. The master of that place wanted to use Constance as a hostage to immediately contain any ugly situations in the unlikely event that any pursuers did show up. But Tula didn't hesitate. The guard holding Constance was just starting to say something like "Stop" in English when Tula shot him through his forehead. Then Tula let Constance fall down with her captor's toppling body while she shot the other guard on the floor. That was cold. That whole bouncing-baby thing? Trust me, it's just a figure of speech. But Constance didn't break anything, and fortunately, screaming your head off is just a figure of speech too.

I had my own problems. At the other end of the hallway, in the direction I was facing, another voice yelled something through the closed door. I took in a long, dimly lit corridor about an eighth of a mile in length. The hallway was really some kind of a cave passage. Stone walls and floors had been built inside and over the cavern to make some kind of dungeon complex, but the ceiling was the original natural rock formation. What was I supposed to say? The men I'd killed had made a lot of noise going down.

The guard with the empty crossbow ignored the submachine gun I was aiming at him and yelled something over his shoulder. I don't know what. It was in that language I'd never heard. I made a snap judgment and let him. It wasn't like he could say anything that would make the situation drastically worse, and he might just make it better. His voice sounded nervous, but the tone was obviously meant to be reassuring.

While the guard was talking, I noticed two things. One was that the door at the end of the hall didn't have any crack under it. The other was that the door had been carved out of a solid piece of wood. Every other door on the hall had a huge crack and was made of boards held together by steel bands. That's when I had a very, very bad thought. In fact, it was so bad that if I had been in a children's story, that's what the name of the chapter would have been: JOHN AND THE VERY, VERY BAD THOUGHT.

The voice through the door yelled something else, and the guard—my guard now—yelled something back with a laugh that didn't sound all that convincing. I didn't care. Constance was still screaming, and I could hear Tula's voice saying something low and soothing. If the guard I was covering could buy us any time, any time at all, every second was precious.

"Tula, get Constance out of here now." I muttered the words so low that only a werewolf could hear them. Then I began pulling my guard with me back to the portal room. "Ben, tell the people who can't hear me to bug out."

The voice at the end of the hall said something else, louder and more belligerently, and my guard called out something in response, his voice strained. Even not speaking the language, I could tell he was full of shit.

The door at the end of the hall opened, but only partially, and an arm covered in some kind of scale armor emerged through it. The hand was holding something that looked like a cross between a steaming iron and a rubber stamp. Later, I figured out that the flat metal plate had shapes carved into its surface that were either heavily inked or sharp enough to cut into wood—designed to imprint runes into the door with one thump. But all I knew then was that the hand smashed the plate into the door.

The hand did this because the door at the end of the hallway was made out of balete wood. And it had just become magical.

A man dressed up in enough plate mail to armor a tank came through the door then. He slammed it shut and opened it again while I was still firing on him.

∾13∾

THE WORLD'S WORST KNOCK-KNOCK JOKE

Something like this must have happened. The dalaketnon built a boat large enough to have a cabin in it. Next, it built a magical doorframe leading to that cabin. Then it punched a hole in the bottom of that boat and sank it. Probably not into an ocean—he or she just wanted to flood the dungeon level, not have water burst through the stone walls and flood the whole region. The dalaketnon probably sank the boat to the bottom of a lake.

And the magic door that the man in armor had opened was keyed to the door or doorway in that boat. The connection was made, and the lake came crashing in with God only knows how many tons of weight behind it.

It had to be something like that.

~14~

IN WHICH A LOT OF PEOPLE WET THEMSELVES

All of my impressions of leaving the dalaketnon world are jumbled. I'm sure there was yelling, but I couldn't hear any of it. Maybe the lake had been invited in, but it was a pretty rude guest anyhow, knocking things over and making a hell of a lot of noise. I saw Simon duck back into the portal room and Tula dash across the hallway holding a screaming bundle, her MP5 forgotten. I rushed forward and didn't look back until I reached the door and realized that the guard who'd helped us was six feet behind me, the column of water closing in on him in a liquid avalanche.

Fuck it. I threw the MP5 aside and reached back and grabbed the guard by his baldric. That sounds mildly obscene, but the baldric in question was a leather contraption that strapped across his chest so that he had a back sheath. I swiveled, pulling the guard violently into the room and throwing him into the wall beside me while the same motion helped me shoulder the door shut. Water roared like a thousand lions while it rushed past an instant later, then crashed into the stone wall at the end of the hallway.

I don't know if it's fortunate or unfortunate that the man-made stone wall at the end of the hall held. Maybe it would have taken some pressure off if the water had burst through it and gone rushing down whatever subterranean passages this dungeon had been built over. Or maybe it would have brought the cavern down on top of our heads. The rebounding water seemed to create some kind of resistance as it surged back and pressed against the rushing water behind it, and the door to our room held for maybe three more seconds. That was barely time enough for me to pick up the guard by his back sheath and half carry and half lead as I rushed him across the room.

Simon was just being pulled into the portal—with the speed distortion accelerating the motions on the other side, he looked like a trout being yanked on the end of a fishing line. He must have stayed while Tula passed Constance through. I guided the guard forward in a kind of bent-over shuffle, mostly dragging him, and threw him through the portal with a sideways hip pivot. Unfortunately, that didn't leave me in a good position to dive when the door behind me popped off its hinges like a champagne cork and several tons of water came barging in.

Someone had kicked the office table on the other side over so that Sig could pull others through the portal more efficiently. I bent forward and tucked into a ball as I dove through the square opening at an angle. Some water from an advancing wave still came through the opening, and somebody scraped the hell out of my shin while they slammed the flap upward and shut. Somehow, I wound up taking Sig's feet out from under her, and she fell on people who were still lying on the floor where they had been yanked through, knocking Dawn over in the process, and I found myself in a tangle of thrashing and yelling bodies on the floor while the water that made it through sprayed over us. We probably looked like some kind of walrus orgy.

When people were done crawling out from under and over each other, I wound up sitting with my back against the wall next to Sig. I looked over and grinned at her. The corners of my mouth stretched so wide, it probably looked like the smile was trying to take wing and fly off my face. I couldn't help it. Constance was still screaming her head off, and it was the most beautiful sound I'd ever heard. My heart was pounding and my nerves were frayed, but at the same time, the sense of grim dread that had sunk into my bone marrow ever since I found out Constance was missing was beginning to evaporate through the pores of my skin. The combination made me feel a little lightheaded. I looked at Sig and said, "I love the way you smell and feel and taste, and when we make love it feels like we're really making love. I really want to be with you, and I want to really be with you. Your presence in my life is a gift, and I swear to God I'm going to try to become someone who deserves it."

Well, okay, that's a total lie. What I really did was look over and say, "Hey there. Did you get drenched by a flood, or are you just happy to see me?" I blame the stress.

Sig rolled her eyes, but she was smiling too. "Give me a moment. I'm reevaluating."

"Wow," Dawn said flatly. She was to my left, lying sprawled on her side on the floor and not giving any indication that she planned to move anytime soon.

"What?" I asked.

Dawn raised her head enough to look at Sig pointedly, then looked at me and shook her head. "You must be doing something right in bed."

Sig smiled wryly. "He's got a lot of enthusiasm, anyway."

I reached down and squeezed her hand. "Who wouldn't?"

Simon wasn't amused. "So, who's this man you risked your life for?" Simon was standing in the middle of the hall, looking down at the guard I'd dragged with me. Except for the puddle on the floor, there was no sign that Simon had scrambled for his life and gotten soaked with the rest of us. He reminded me a little bit of a cat that refuses to acknowledge any momentary lapses in dignity.

I answered before the guard could say anything. "I wouldn't have had a life to risk if it weren't for this guy. He saved all of our asses back there."

The guard flashed me a grateful look over his shoulder, and Simon allowed a brief cynical smile to flit across his face while the subject of his scrutiny wasn't looking. The guard was thinking that in me he had at least one ally in this strange new old world. Simon was thinking that I'd saved the guard for his intel value—that now we had someone who could tell us about the dalaketnon and why it had helped the skinwalker kidnap Constance. Simon thought that I was encouraging the guard to think of me as an ally so that he would confide in me when it came time to get information out of him.

They were both right.

Ben didn't waste any time. The wolves were taking Constance somewhere safe, and they weren't telling any knights where that was until the knights got their Order in order. Even Simon could see the sense in that. Virgil went outside to get the cars warming up before he even took his field armor off, and Ben had other werewolves standing around the vehicles to make sure that no one tried to put tracking devices on them. Tula was staying glued to Constance, but she let me hold the baby even though she wrinkled her nose when she did so. I hadn't showered in four...or maybe five...days, and between camping over the weekend, stewing in an insulated field suit, and getting soaked in lake water, I smelled a bit funky even after toweling off and changing into a flannel shirt and jeans from my backpack. My other clothes were in a washer.

"Do you want me to go with you?" I asked Ben. Part of me wanted to go with my packmates—I trusted them in a way that I would never trust a knight again. And part of me needed to stay behind and help the Templars clean house. "I've got a lot of experience hiding."

Ben smiled at that. Or maybe he was smiling at Constance. I had her cradled in one arm, bobbing her up and down gently with a slight sway to the motion. She was staring at me placidly with that Baby Buddha stare that makes you think infants know something adults have forgotten, though the effect was slightly ruined by the small grunts she made while her mouth worked on a pacifier. I reached out awkwardly with my other hand and smoothed the thin wisps of hair on her head.

"Do you have any idea how old I am?" Ben asked.

"You said that your rez was attacked by a werewolf a hundred years ago," I said. "And it looks like you were in your forties when it did."

"I forgot I told you that." Ben looked at me a little sourly, but then he squeezed my shoulder. "I'm leaving Virgil with you. I want you to hunt the people who will be hunting Constance. Keep them too busy to focus on us."

"Yeah," I said. "I can do that."

"I know it," he said. "I trust you with this."

I nodded at Constance. "And I trust you with her."

"It's good," Ben said. "Having people you can trust."

"It feels like we're about to break into a musical dance number," I observed. "Should I put the kid down?"

Ben laughed. "I just don't want you to forget you have family when you're hanging out with the crazy people again, John."

"They're my people too," I admitted. "You both are." Constance chose that moment to stop grunting. Her eyes took on a slightly unfocused look. "I think she's pissing herself," I told Ben.

Ben laughed again. The back-and-forth of extreme emotions had him a little off-balance too. Normally, he would have just smiled wryly. "I know how she feels."

God, I was tired. Constance was safe, and the physical and emotional toll of the last few days came calling like a four-hundred-pound loan shark. I had to focus to make sentences with more than one word, then words with more than one syllable. But when Simon handed me a cup of coffee and asked me to explain how things were to the guard I'd dragged back with us, I led the man to the kitchen downstairs without arguing. He was a tall, rangy guy with curly blond hair and slightly outdated slang from the west coast. His skin hadn't been tan in a long time though.

When we got to the kitchen, I opened the refrigerator and stepped aside so that he could look at its contents. "Do you see anything you want?"

He stared at the fridge as if I had just opened the Ark of the Covenant. I don't think he'd really had time to accept that everything happening was really happening until that moment. "Lemonade," he gasped, and I couldn't tell if he was making a request or pronouncing a blessing. He collapsed against a counter and barely managed to prop his ass against the edge before he began to cry into his hands. Big, fat tears soaked his cheeks and his chest while he heaved and gasped.

I poured some lemonade—or at least that bullshit concen-

trated sugar that grocery stores call lemonade, but whatever—
into a tall glass and waited until he cried himself out, then led
him to the dining room table in the next room. "Come on."

He grabbed the glass with both hands. The hands were
shaking so hard that he spilled some of the drink onto his shirt,
and I put a palm on top of the glass and gently forced it back
on to the table. When I went back into the kitchen and got
a paper towel and a straw, it was as much to give him some
time as anything else. He sipped the lemonade slowly at first,
then greedily, and I went back and fetched the whole bottle
and topped his drink off again before sitting down across from
him. Eventually, a little color began coming back into his
damp cheeks. "That's awesome," he sighed. "Do you got anything stronger?"

"Probably," I said. "But give that a minute. What's your
name?"

"Dan," he said cautiously. "Dan Lacado."

I reached my hand across the table. He shook it warily. "I'm
John. Thank you for saving my life, Dan."

"Uhhhm," he said. "You're welcome?"

"So, when did you get kidnapped, Dan?" I asked. "And from
where?"

"1983." He said the date as if he were trying to tattoo it on
the air between us. "I was night-surfing on Redondo Beach.
That's in California."

"How old were you?" I asked, thinking about how time had
seemed to flow differently on that world.

"I was twenty, man," he sighed. "I guess it's been about ten
years, right? Their calendar doesn't work the same as ours."

If he thought it was 1993, he didn't know the half of it.
But I would let someone with a clear head, tact, and seda-
tives on hand break that to him. "Here's the thing," I said.

"We represent a group dedicated to keeping the supernatural a secret. Sometimes, that means killing supernatural beings who can't stay in line. Sometimes, that means taking care of humans who have seen too much and can't keep their mouths shut, one way or the other."

He opened his mouth. "I..."

I waited, but he trailed off. The expression on my face probably told him that there was nothing he was going to say that would be sufficient by itself.

"Do you want the good news or the bad news first, Dan?" I asked.

He laughed shakily. "I don't need any more bad news, man."

"Okay," I acknowledged. "Here's the good news. We owe you. Also, you're a valuable resource. We don't know much about the world you just came from, and we want to. You play your cards right, you'll never have to work a nine-to-five job. We'll set you up somewhere nice with a stipend, and all you'll have to do is teach people about the world you just came from."

"I could just hang on a beach?" he said wistfully.

"Yeah," I said. "We like remote beaches. The bad news is, your old life on this world is over, and we're going to make sure we can trust you before we ever let you out of our sight. We're particularly going to be asking you a lot of questions about the guy who brought that baby to the castle."

"I don't know anything about that dude!" Dan protested. "Mistress Malea must have met him on your...on this world. He just dropped off the baby and paid her and bailed."

It made sense that the skinwalker wouldn't hang around on a world where the time rate was different, not if he had concerns on ours.

"Mistress Malea is the person who abducted you?" I clarified.

"Naw, that was her mom." Dan said. "But she's dead. Mistress Malea runs the castle now."

"And she's a dalaketnon?" I was basically there to give him a heads-up, not go into an eight-hour question-and-answer session, but curiosity got the better of me.

"Yeah."

"Paid her how?" I asked.

"They're in the middle of making some kind of trade," Dan said. "The dude belongs to some group that wants Mistress Malea to join them. They want her to teach them how to make magic doors, and they're gonna teach her how to make something that will give her an edge over the other amos."

The word sounded familiar, but I couldn't remember if it was Filipino or Japanese or what. "Aw-mohs? Doesn't that mean chief or noble or something like that?"

"Dude, how would I know?" Dan said with some justification. "Amos rule that place."

"What kind of magic did the man who brought Constance want to trade with her?"

Dan grunted. "You think she told us? I wouldn't know any of this if I wasn't guarding the door in the dungeon when he came through. All I know is, he gave her some kind of parcel, and they talked like they were letting each other sample the goods."

"What did the parcel look like?" I pressed.

"It wasn't big." Dan stretched his thumb and index finger apart to indicate size. "Like those boxes they used to put earrings in."

"They still do, Dan," I said gently. "Here."

Dan swallowed. "Yeah."

"Yeah," I said.

Dan gulped. "It's . . . it's still hitting me, you know?"

"I know," I said. "And the hits are going to keep on coming for a while. Do you know what rope-a-doping is?"

Dan scrunched his face up. "Never heard of it."

"It's a boxing technique Muhammad Ali used," I said. "A lot of the impact of a punch comes from you resisting it. When Ali was up against a heavy hitter, he would just lie up against the ropes and let the punch send him backward into them, then use the ropes to spring back."

Dan wasn't much for metaphors. "All right."

"Don't try to avoid or fight the feelings," I advised. "They're just feelings. Let them go through you if you can. Rope-a-dope it."

Dan just nodded tiredly. It was an easy thing to say. Hard to do.

I picked up the conversation and dusted it off. "There must have been something pretty important in the tiny little box that guy gave your mistress."

"You have no clue, man," Dan sighed. "That door magic is, like, religious shit. Whatever was in that box must have been beastie. But I don't know what it was."

"You might know more than you think," I said finally. "But I'm too tired to question you myself. Just cooperate with these guys, Dan. Seriously. They won't hurt you if they don't have to, but you don't want to mess around with them."

"Or what?" he asked dully.

"First, you're going to get plastic surgery no matter what," I said. "That's nonnegotiable. As to the rest, well . . . my group runs a couple of insane asylums. Assuming they don't just kill you, they'll produce records that show you've been a John Doe in a padded room for years. They'll also make you take LSD and put lots of needle holes in your arms. If you go to some reporter or cop with your crazy story, the LSD will show up in certain kinds of tests for a long time. They'll also take lots of DNA samples from you. Enough to frame you for any number of insane crimes connected to cult activity. Anybody who starts investigating your story will find evidence that ties you to other people who have gone missing over the years. We know a lot of those."

"Dude..." Dan protested.

"They'll also send people to test you occasionally," I said. "People claiming to be reporters who know about us. E-mails from bloggers who have been writing about this kind of stuff for years. People claiming to be detectives hired by your family to find you. If you talk to any of them, we'll kill you. But Simon can tell you a lot more about that side of things than I can. I'm here to tell you the real reason you don't ever want to try to go public with this."

"Dude," Dan protested faintly. He looked like he was about to start crying again.

"It really can't wait, Dan," I said. "The worst of it is, we won't have to silence you. Maybe somewhere in the back of your head, in a place you're not even fully aware of yet, you're thinking that if you play along, one day you'll wind up in some press conference or FBI office where you can get your story out. Maybe you think you'll be protected by bodyguards, or we won't be able to do anything because your story is out there and killing you would just confirm it. But the last thing you want to do is draw attention to yourself, Dan. There is a big, dark world out there full of things worse than this Mistress Malea— things that don't want humans to know they exist."

"Like what?" he asked uncertainly.

"I'm talking about beings who can kill you in your dreams and make it look like a heart attack," I informed him. "Things that can possess you and make you recant in the middle of an interview and confess to unspeakable things. Creatures who can change shape and take your place, or the place of someone you're in love with. Monsters who can hypnotize the people around you and make them believe or say anything about you that they want. Monsters like Mistress Malea who can cut you right out of time and space. There's not an FBI office or press conference in the world that can protect you from them."

Dan started getting angry. It was a healthy reaction. "I'm not gonna say anything!"

"I'm telling you this for your own good, Dan." I leaned forward. "It's not just about these monsters' abilities. It's about their nature. There are things out there that will paralyze you and eat you one bite at time over the next ten years. There are things that will play with your soul as if it were a chew toy. Look into my eyes, Dan. Think about what you've been through and really look, and tell me I'm lying."

Dan glanced at me while I thought about some of the things I've seen, and then he looked away quickly.

I settled back in my chair. "I owe you, Dan. I will do what I can, but I can't save you from yourself. You have to believe me when I say that we won't have to silence you or discredit you. If you draw attention to yourself, all we'll have to do is step back and get out of the way."

I didn't waste much time before asking Sig to join me in a shower.

She regarded me levelly, without enthusiasm or hostility. "Don't you think we should talk before we get naked?"

I was too tired and emotionally drained to try to figure out all of the nuances and subtleties behind that question. "I'm tired and I stink."

She smiled faintly at that. "You probably shouldn't lead with those as your selling points."

I sighed. "We can talk in the shower. If you're willing to get in there with me."

She seemed to read more into that than I'd intended. "All right."

We faced each other nude under the hot water with our lips next to each other's ears, our soaped hands sliding over each other's backs and bottoms. Movies always have two people standing romantically under a steamy cascade that manages to gently engulf both of them, but I think there must be somebody with a shower head on a hose just off camera, standing over the actors on a step ladder. Maybe that's what a key grip does. Sig and I had to do an awkward little shower dance and rotate around each other to share the water. It was either that or stand there, blinking and spitting while water splattered into our faces, one side cooked and one side underdone.

We were speaking low, our bodies pressed tightly together. I shouldn't have been feeling randy, but people react to stress in different ways, and the truth is, survival makes me horny. I kissed Sig directly below her left ear, then nibbled down her neck.

I couldn't see her mouth, but I could hear a reluctant smile in her voice when she asked, "Do you really think we're being bugged?"

"What?" I was honestly puzzled. "There's too much magic still in the air. And even if there wasn't, who cares? We don't know anything that everybody else on this property doesn't know."

"I thought that's why you wanted to get in the shower," she said. "So we could talk privately."

"I don't need an excuse to want to get in the shower with

you," I said. "Besides, I promised you a good scrubdown, remember?"

"That's right," she said. "Your word is so important to you."

Uh-oh. I rubbed a cake of soap in my palms. "I guess you're still pissed at me?"

"Yes. No. Yes. We haven't had time to talk about it yet." She adjusted her jaw slightly and sank her teeth into my right earlobe, biting down hard.

I laughed and gasped. "Just take the damn ear if you want it. I'll grow another one."

Sig released my earlobe and pushed me back slightly with her palms on my chest. "You kept secrets from me. Big secrets."

I put the cake of soap on a shelf built into the shower wall, then took Sig's hands by the wrists, lather oozing between my slick fingers. I awkwardly tilted down and kissed her wrists. Her palms squeezed my pectorals. I couldn't tell if it was a warning or a very firm caress. Those same fingers had cracked my chest plate not too long ago, and I winced at a brief flashback. "I didn't lie to you, Sig. Ben and Emil Lamplighter and I agreed to keep Constance's existence a secret. So, I didn't talk about it."

Sig took her palms off of my chest and put her hands around my back again. "Everybody needs their private spaces, John. But you don't get to do the brooding-loner-with-a-dark-past thing if you want to be with me. How do I know you aren't still keeping secrets?"

I guess when your former lover tries to break up by killing you, it creates some issues that don't just go away. I ran my soapy palms down the slick surface of Sig's back, over the upper swell of her rear end, squeezing her just to feel the warmed skin slide under the pressure of my fingers. "Maybe I screwed up," I admitted. "This issue seems kind of complicated to me. But if you're worried about me having secrets, just ask me."

Sig gasped slightly and dug her nails into my shoulders. Fortunately, she keeps her nails short. I pulled her in still closer. That part of me that has a mind of its own kept prodding her insistently, and judging from the places where her own rushing blood was causing her to swell up, Sig wasn't completely unaffected by our proximity either.

"Are you keeping any more secrets?" she asked.

"Yes," I said.

Sig arched her back so that she could look into my eyes, and it made her slide over me. "You'd better explain that."

"I don't kill every supernatural creature I meet," I groaned. "Some people have helped me too."

"Like Sarah White," Sig said.

"Yeah," I affirmed. "It would be pretty shitty of me to repay them by going around broadcasting their existence to the world. Don't you have stuff like that?"

Sig kissed me lightly. "Constance wasn't a little thing. And this stuff about how your geas really works isn't either. These things affect me."

It was a hard point to argue, given the circumstances. "I don't have any more big secrets." I returned her kiss a bit more intently, and my body moved to adjust against hers in a way that opened up some new possibilities.

"Okay." She pushed me back and tilted her head so that her long blond hair was completely under the shower jets. She pulled a shampoo bottle off the high ledge built into the shower and poured some shampoo into her palm and closed her eyes as she began to rub it into her hair.

I took a step forward and she opened her eyes. "Nuh-uh."

"What?" I said stupidly.

Her smile was pure evil. "I'm getting back at you, remember?" She moved her hands behind her head so that her torso was fully on display.

"Are you kidding?"

She closed her eyes and went back to shampooing, moving her hands behind her head slowly. "What do you think you'll remember more the next time you think about keeping secrets from me? If I have sex with you now, or if I don't?"

"Sig, come on," I protested.

"I'm really not ready yet," Sig replied calmly. "I'm still processing what I'm feeling. I'll let you know when I want to use you sexually."

I held out my hands. "You're really going to leave me like this?"

"You have hands." She plunged her head back into the shower jet.

"I was raised Catholic," I protested. "I only do that alone and with feelings of intense shame, the way God intended."

She laughed but didn't say anything.

"Sig," I called out gently. "We promised we wouldn't go to bed mad, remember?"

She smiled at me sweetly, and somehow, that made the expression even more fiendish. "I'm not mad."

The worst part of it was, I had to wait for her to finish because we had agreed not to let each other out of our sight. I tried to get back at her by adopting some seductive poses of my own to torment her with, but that just made her laugh hysterically, which sort of defeated the purpose. But I showed her. I was so tired that as soon as we found the folding cots set up in the office on the second floor, I passed out anyway.

PART THE SECOND

In One Fear and Out the Other

～15～

IS IT TWO DOOR, THREE DOOR, MORE DOOR, OR MORDOR?

It was after the field trip to Dalakit that I really got to see Emil's number-one fixer at work. Knights and lay sergeants that Simon could trust began showing up at the house in groups of two to twelve. The first group brought along some of the community tents used at town festivals and church revivals and set up a training camp in the woods outside Constance's house.

Next, a portable CDC lab disguised as a moving truck arrived at the house, complete with a team of scientists. Within eight hours, they had studied samples of the water that we had brought back with us from that other world and concluded that it came from an underground lake in Canada.

This was good news. If the water had been from Dalakit, we would have had to destroy the magic door we'd refashioned; there was no way we could risk a flood of water that might contain alien organisms making its way to a local stream or creek. But as soon as Simon got the all clear, he had knights breaking holes in the walls and floors of the house, then digging a trench in the yard. The idea was to make as straight a channel for water as possible so that we could continue to use the stairwell once the floodgate opened.

And then Simon opened our magic door. Water shot out through that hatch in a solid column and just kept going. And going. And going. Sig and I took one shift on guard duty, watching the magic doorway from the attic above the second floor, staring through an open access panel. After three hours watching a solid stream of water pouring through the hatchway, I said, "It's starting to feel like Canada is pissing on us."

"This is good," Sig contradicted. "That hallway they flooded would have drained a long time ago. This means they haven't closed or destroyed the magic door that's letting water in from that lake."

"Maybe they can't," I observed.

I'm not a metaphysicist, but bear with me for a moment. Take the front door of a house in Massachusetts. On one side, there's the front yard. Call that side A. On the other side, there's the living room of the house. Call that side B. Now suppose magic makes it so that the front door of the house opens up into a diner in Arizona instead. Call that side C. If the front yard of the house now opens into that diner in Arizona—if side A opens into side C—what happened to Side B? Where's the living room of the house?

More to the point, what if someone was in the living room when the door changed? Say someone is looking at side B of the door from the living room, which should open into a front yard. It can't do that anymore, can it? Because the other side of the front yard is now a diner in Arizona. So, what's on the other side of the living room now? Can that person in the living room even open the door? What would happen if they did? An antimatter explosion as two doors—side B and side C—were forced to occupy the same space? Would all time and space and matter between Arizona and Virginia be sucked through that doorway and get turned inside out like a jacket whose sleeves were too small? Was a side D somehow created?

This kind of stuff usually makes my ass twitch, but it mattered because those guards beyond the hallway in that Dalakit castle had turned a door into a magical water pressure release valve. Then they had sent another guard through to open that door from the other side—from our side of the hallway. This suggested that they couldn't open the door from their side. Why not? Whatever the answer was, it might explain why they couldn't close the magic door once they opened it either.

As an experiment, Simon and Dawn and Sig and Virgil and I knocked a hole in the wall from the room next to Constance's bedroom. The bedroom that was theoretically behind the magic hatch that was pouring out water from Canada now. We looked through the hole in the wall and saw...Constance's bedroom. The crib. The bookcases. The changing stand. We even saw the back of the cinderblocks we'd put in the bottom of the door. Freakiest of all, we saw the back of the hatch we'd made. The hatch was closed. Except that was impossible because the hatch was open on the other side of the room, jetting water out.

What the hell? Was Constance's bedroom frozen in some kind of time stasis field, caught in the moment before the hatch opened? Could that be why there had been some kind of time distortion on the other side when we'd first gone through the magic door? Some kind of bleed-through effect?

It was a bad idea, but Simon stuck a yardstick through the hole in the wall. We watched the yardstick's progress for about two seconds, and then about a foot into the room, the yardstick disappeared. The tip was just gone. Simon pulled the yardstick back, or tried to. All he pulled back was the first two feet; the tip of the yardstick had been so cleanly sheared off that there wasn't a jagged edge to be seen, and we couldn't spot the sheared-off tip of the yardstick on the floor of Constance's bedroom either.

We backed away from the hole in the wall very carefully. As near as I can figure it, when dalaketnons make a magic door, they basically tie time and space into a slipknot. The part between the two ends of the rope gets crimped up and cut off, and the rest of the world just slides around that area.

But all I really needed to understand was this: When Constance was first kidnapped, Tula had run upstairs and kicked the bedroom door down. As soon as Tula broke the door, the magical connection was severed. If we could go through the magical hatch we'd restored, travel back down the dungeon hallway, and destroy the second magical door, the dimensional link those guards had made to Canada would be disrupted. We would have access to the castle and the dalaketnon beyond the hallway again.

Dan was looking tired, but he also looked calmer and cleaner, and I didn't see any overt signs of long-term harsh treatment or malnutrition. To be honest, Dan looked better than most Americans his age after my own world's brutal and sadistic regimen of financial debt, time-consuming jobs that mostly involve sitting or standing around, processed foods, and evenings spent holding down a sofa while staring at some kind of electronic screen. The only real signs that Dan had been through an ordeal were his too-wide eyes.

Dan was also still drinking lemonade like...well, like he'd just spent decades in a place that didn't have lemonade. Me, Sig, Virgil, Dawn, Simon, and two knights named Angel Solis and Steven Hunter respectively were all seated around Dan in the living room.

"So, how many duplicates of herself does this Mistress Malea have wandering around?" Dawn sounded a little cross. I don't think she was an early-morning person. Or maybe she just wasn't a have-your-beloved-mentor-die-before-your-eyes-and-then-experience-the-world-through-the-emotions-of-a-psychopath-and-get-shot-in-the-ass-and-freeze-the-face-off-some-sleazeoid-playing-*Invasion-of-the-Body-Snatchers*-and-go-to-another-world-and-almost-get-drowned kind of a person. Come to think of it, that's probably a pretty select group. In any case, Dawn looked tired and smelled like stress and cigarette smoke. Her hair was now blue. Maybe it worked like a mood ring.

"I don't know, man," Dan said nervously. "The bogies all dress the same, and they kind of shuffle themselves around like three-card monte, you know? They like to keep us guessing. There's at least four, but there could be six or seven."

"Bogies?" I asked. "As in enemy aircraft?"

Dan shook his head. "No, dude. Like bogus."

"Can this thing just whip up a...bogey...of itself anytime it wants to?" I asked. "Does it just split off into clones like microbes?"

"No, man. Mistress Malea always locks herself in her bedroom for hours when she makes a bogey. She screams a lot too. Like she's giving birth or something."

We kept questioning Dan in that vein, and in fairly short order, we determined that (A) Dan said "man" a lot. We also determined that (B) the dalaketnon world—or at least one continent of it—was loosely ruled by these nobles called amos. Amos were distinguished by their ability to move things with their minds and create duplicates of themselves. (C) The palace and/or feudal lands that Dan had been abducted and transported to were ruled by the female dalaketnon Dan called Mistress Malea. (D) Mistress Malea and her bogies shared some kind of telepathic link. (E) If the bogies had a hive mind, the original Mistress Malea was some kind of queen bee, and the bogies always took pains to protect her. (F) There were modern weapons from our world in the castle, but Mistress Malea and her bogies were the only ones allowed to use them.

It was a lot to take in.

Virgil was focused on practicalities. "Are there any more of these things in the palace? Is there a Mr. Malea? Little baby Maleas?"

Dan's mouth made a strange twist. "No, man. Mistress Malea and her mom used to fight about that a lot. Mistress Malea's dad died in a duel with some other amo, and Mistress Malea's mom thought the mistress needed to stop messing with Makisig and start looking for a husband. The old lady nagged Mistress Malea so much that Mistress Malea finally got sick of it and killed her."

We waited for him to expand on that little nugget, and when he didn't, I cleared my throat. "Who's Makisig?"

"Oh," Dan said, remembering that we didn't know. "He's another guard like I was. His real name is Mike. They liked to give us names from their language that sort of sounded like the ones we were used to when we got there. Like they called me Danilo."

"So, this Makisig is another human?" Dawn probed.

Dan shook his head sorrowfully. "I don't know if I'd say that, man. Makisig is one sick dude. I mean, like twisted. I don't know if Mistress Malea messed Makisig up, or if he messed her up, or if they were just two warped people who fit together, you know?"

"So, when they came together, it was like the Charles Manson version of Romeo and Juliet?" I asked.

Dan smiled a bit ruefully, but Sig jumped in before he could respond. "Tell us more about this Mistress Malea killing her own mother."

"The old lady always made Mistress Malea eat dinner with her back when she ran the place," Dan said. "See, they're, like, big on being proper over there. Not proper like we think of it. Those dudes don't see anything wrong with kidnapping us and making us slaves and stuff. But proper the way they see it. And over there, it isn't, like, proper for a woman to have power, so Mistress Malea's mom was always nagging at her to marry some amo's son. It wasn't proper to like a human either. They could have sex with us, but treating us like equals is sick to them. Then the old lady put Makisig in a torture cell and told Mistress Malea that if she didn't start going along with the plan, her pet human was going to die bad. The old lady keeled over during dinner right after that, and all of her bogies dropped at the same time. We always figured she was poisoned."

Sig and I exchanged a glance at that information. So, when you killed the original dalaketnon, you killed all of the duplicates? Simon noticed the silent exchange and coughed to get my attention, subvocalizing so that only Virgil and I could hear. "We want to get some information about the skinwalkers from this Mistress Malea. Not kill her right off."

Dan continued. "Next thing you know, Makisig is captain of the guard, and he's living in Mistress Malea's chambers. She even lets him carry a gun and grow a beard. Things were never good over there, but that's when they got bad. Like I said, those two feed off of each other in a sick way, man."

"How bad?" I asked quietly. I wasn't being sadistic or voyeuristic. Anything that would help me predict the dalaketnon's actions would be useful, and I wanted to know if the human captives in the castle were likely to rise up and revolt.

Dan didn't answer, and Simon filled in. He had either sat in or read Dan's interrogation. "The dalaketnon and this Makisig are basically running their own little S&M palace, but it's not based on mutual agreement or setting boundaries. There are no safe words."

"It's not just sex, man. They practice shooting fruit out of people's mouths with handguns," Dan added. "And Makisig isn't that great a shot. They make people kneel down on all fours beside them and use their backs as ash trays when they smoke. Stuff like that."

"So, there's no way to tell Mistress Malea apart from her duplicates?" Sig verified.

"No, it's easy, man." Dan laughed bitterly. "Once her mother was gone, Mistress Malea started packing on the pounds."

"And her doubles didn't gain weight when she did?" I asked.

Dan shook his head. "Naw, man. They all still look like Mistress Malea did when her mom was alive."

That was helpful.

"Let's go back to how bad things were getting. Is that why you shot your partner in the back?" Virgil's tone was neutral, but it was hard to ignore the element of judgment in the question. A werewolf's pack loyalty runs pretty deep.

"The dude was an asshole," Dan mumbled. "Seriously."

"Do you think any other guards would revolt like you did?" I asked.

"I don't know, man." It was starting to become a refrain. "Most of them are the kind of dudes who get off on having a little bit more power than people who got none, you know? And Makisig just eggs them on. He's, like, the kind of guy who gets off on bullying other people into bullying other people. I don't think most of them'd want to have to deal with some of the shit they've done if anybody else took charge over there.

That's why I had to take my chance. I wasn't getting with the program, man."

Dawn intervened. "We seem to be focusing an awful lot of our energy on this Mistress Malea, but she's not really the one who kidnapped Constance. The skinwalker who did just used the dalaketnon's castle like a hotel. We don't even know if this Mistress Malea really knows anything useful."

"She's the best lead we have." Simon didn't look too happy about that either. "We know the skinwalker represented a group that wants to recruit her. They have to have told her something."

"We know they paid her off with some kind of rare magical item too," I added, thinking of Dan's description of a box barely large enough to hold a pair of earrings. "If it's as unique and precious as all that, finding out what that gift was ought to tell us something about where they come from."

That was true, but the deeper truth was, I would have gone back to that world whether it was tactically advantageous or not, whether the knights supported me or not. This wasn't a fairy tale and I wasn't a fairy godmother, but this Mistress Malea had helped kidnap the wrong damned goddaughter.

∾16∾

FUCK SOUP

When I was a kid, my favorite movie was *Duck Soup*. Groucho Marx plays the leader of a small Eastern European nation, and in the climactic scene, he's holed up in a command center while telegrams about the chaos erupting all around him keep coming in. The days I spent studying the maps we had made with Dan and training with the knights Simon had assembled were a bit like that.

Simon was gone. Apparently, fires were breaking out all over the place, and Simon left Angel Solis in charge of leading the second foray into Dalakit. Angel was a lean and seasoned Latino whose English and body language both held no trace of a Hispanic accent—probably a product of one of the Templar orphanages like me, or a third-generation American at the very least, or maybe even a graduate of that special training center Dawn had told me about, the one that had produced Simon and was starting to sound like an Assassins R Us. Angel didn't talk more than he had to, but when he did speak, he was clear and to the point, only voicing reservations and criticisms when they accomplished something.

What? Like Simon was really going to put me in charge. But Virgil and I were Simon's liaisons to Ben, and as such we got updates. The Grandmaster had tried to contain the flow of information and quietly investigate a number of Templar higher-ups to see if they were skinwalkers before proceeding on a wider scale, but that option disappeared quickly. Maybe someone talked, or maybe the skinwalkers knew something was up when they didn't hear from Bob. Either way, things went nuclear when a skinwalker led an assault team of knights to kidnap Silas Carlson, the English head of the Warhound chapter.

The skinwalker who led the abduction attempt had used a combination of truth mixed with lies to convince the knights in question that Emil Lamplighter and several key higher-ups were skinwalkers, that the Templars had been compromised, and that they were on a holy mission to save the Order. The attempt had failed, barely, and only because trying to take the leader of the most aggressive and paranoid chapter of knights alive, in his own territory, had proved problematic at best. Silas had killed the attackers moving through his house, but he had also lost his wife and two trusted bodyguards and was now trying to pursue all leads and vengeance by himself. If the goal of the raid was to keep the Warhounds from readily cooperating with Emil, it might not have mattered to our enemy if Silas survived or not.

Our enemy had also conducted a simultaneous raid on the Templar Loremaster, but that had done much less damage. The Loremaster had a number of arcane defenses derived from centuries of capturing magical artifacts that no one else knew about. Apparently, most of the attackers had wound up trapped in a magic painting. Still, the attempt itself was raising alarms.

"Did we capture any of the skinwalkers?" I asked.

"No," Angel said. "The one who led the attack on the Warhounds had his whole body covered in flames when he ran away, and he didn't seem to mind. They found the skin suit he was wearing in a nearby sewer."

A few hours later, Angel gave me another tight-lipped update. "One of the Grandmaster's houses just blew up."

"I take it Emil wasn't in 'it?" I was pretty sure Angel would have mentioned that first.

"He was supposed to be." Angel barely seemed to know I was there. "That's why he wasn't."

I understood him perfectly. Emil Lamplighter is one twisty son of a bitch.

Virgil came back from a chat with Ben with his own summary. "Things are getting out of control. This rumor that the Grandmaster is a skinwalker is spreading everywhere. Some people think the security measures he's taking are really an excuse to capture and replace people. The Crusaders are saying the real reason the knights made an alliance with us werewolves is because the Grandmaster is assembling an army of monsters to wipe the knights out."

"Whoa," I said. "Have the Crusaders tried to capture or question any werewolves?"

"He's still trying to drum up support from the other chapters," Virgil said. "The Grandmaster has been reminding the other chapter leaders that you held the Sword of Truth in front of half a dozen of them and that this head of the Crusaders refused to. Ben's been using the time to get werewolves in the Midwest to gather in large numbers or make themselves scarce for awhile."

What a fustercluck.

Soon after that, Dawn told me, white-faced, "Maxime Allen was assassinated."

"Who's Maxime Allen?" I asked.

The knight who had been shadowing Dawn as part of our skinwalker protocol, Steven Hunter, looked at me as if I'd just walked out of a UFO, but Dawn just said, "The head of my chapter."

"The Swords of Solomon?" I had never actually asked. But assuming that Dawn came from the chapter that was the most adamant about using magic to fight magic seemed logical.

She just nodded.

"Isn't he located in France?" I asked.

Dawn frowned. "Does that matter?"

"No," I admitted. "I'm just trying to wrap my head around all this. Now I know why Ben wouldn't tell me where he's taking Constance."

"This has got us all paranoid," Dawn said ruefully. "I can't even talk to my niece on the phone without Steven listening in."

"Just don't start talking about twerking or clickbait," I said. "Steven'll tackle you if he thinks it's code."

"Maybe even if I don't," Steven said. He was silent most of the time, an average-sized and leanly muscled man with skin the color of mahogany and hair shaved way down on his skull to the point of being whiskers. He had a coiled-spring kind of alertness about him and didn't like to be called Steve for some reason, but when he did speak, he had a quiet sense of humor.

Dawn laughed. "My niece is six. She's not quite at that level yet."

It made me glad that my task seemed, if not simple, relatively straightforward by comparison. Finally, though, there was a crack between the top of the magic hatch and the water as the levels finally began to lower, and by early evening, the water finally trickled off. We were...well, I won't say we were ready. I'm not sure anyone is ever ready to deal with a series of dimensional loops and crimps between them and another world where they plan to hunt a telekinetic sociopath who can create doubles of herself. Honestly, I would have preferred a few more years to prepare. But we waded knee-deep into that hot mess anyhow.

~17~

MAMA MIAHHHHHHGGHHH!

We were halfway down the submerged hallway on the other side of the portal when Sig made contact with a ghost.

There were four of us in the advance party, with me in the lead and Sig backing me up. The water had finally leveled off, two and half feet deep on the other side of the magic portal, so I went in with basically the same gear as the first raid, only my field armor was the Templar's amphibious version, a bit more skintight, completely watertight, and much more efficient at keeping body temperature contained. It was pitch-dark and cold, but at least my enhanced senses weren't picking up any signs of life that weren't at the basic bacteria stage.

Suddenly, my skin prickled and the hair on my neck began to stiffen. My heart pounded harder; I had to focus and ride out the adrenaline spike while someone depressed a flush handle in my skull. I knew the sensation: ghost. Active ghost. They're far more likely to manifest when Sig is around. I whispered, "Is it hostile?"

"Very," she whispered back. "But I don't think she'll bother us. It's the mother."

Which mo…oh. That wasn't a euphemism. Sig meant the dalaketnon parent that this Mistress Malea had supposedly killed. I didn't find the realization all that comforting.

"Go on," Sig said. "I've got this."

I didn't like it, but it was Sig's area of expertise, so I continued forward and gave the other two knights in our detail, Steven Hunter and a dour hunk of gristle named Slater, a few terse commands in Latin.

It wasn't until we rippled to the end of the hall that I activated the penlight mounted on the barrel of my MP5. The door that had been opened on us like the world's biggest can of whoop-ass was intact, perhaps because it was thicker than any normal door and mounted on five sturdy hinges rather than the usual three. It was pressed against the wall and open to cold, impenetrable darkness. I gestured, and Steven Hunter moved forward with a portable explosive about the size of an ashtray.

When a button on the side of the bomb was pressed, metal joints with sharp prongs could be unfolded like spider legs from an indentation in the bottom of the explosive device. When the button was pressed a second time, the joints snapped back, bear trap–style. The rig was designed to wrap around small protrusions or dig its metal claws into doors or plaster walls. Built into the top of the bomb was a metal dial that resembled the old-fashioned wind-up timers that people used to set on their ovens before everything went digital. You had to rotate the dial to three specific notches first, like a combination lock, but once you did, you could deactivate the bomb or set it to go off anywhere from five minutes to six hours later, and unlike modern bombs, it would work in magic-rich environments.

Steven placed the bomb over the surface of the wooden door and was about to trigger the switch that would secure it when Sig said, "Wait."

I echoed the command.

Steven and Slater and I stood there awkwardly. Sig didn't move or say anything else. I waited for perhaps a full minute before speaking, more for the knights' benefit than mine. "Can you tell us why we're waiting, Sig?"

"Not yet," she said tersely, still just standing there. "But it's important."

I leaned against the wall to indicate to the knights that I wasn't seriously worried. "All right."

In a way, it would have been better if the hallway had been filled with ghostly lights or unearthly shrieks gradually gaining in intensity. Our bodies were pumped full of adrenaline, and even with a knight's training, it is no easy thing to wait silently in cold, waist-deep water for the better part of ten minutes while someone dramatically does nothing. Then the temperature dropped about five degrees and the lights mounted on our MP5s dimmed. Steven pulled a glow stick out from somewhere—his ass, if the pained grunt he made was any indication—and Slater cursed and swiveled his weapon around.

Revealed in the chemical light was a tall, pale, slender woman with long silver hair who had materialized behind Sig. The dalaketnon was wearing a green silk gown, but the cloth didn't seem to be affected by the water she was standing in. The freakiest thing about her was her eyes. The shadows that hid them seemed darker than the inefficient lighting could account for.

Sig turned around to face me, her arms held out from her sides, and when she did so, the ghost stepped forward, passed through the back of Sig's body, and... didn't emerge. Sig didn't seem to care. Her body language when she began wading toward me was still hers, but it was... I don't know... flavored differently. There was a cold arrogance there, and a purpose to her stride that didn't permit any hesitation. She drew a knife from a sheath at her left hip. "We've got a new source of intel."

"I'm pretty sure this isn't what people mean when they talk about having someone on the inside," I pointed out quietly. I would have said a lot more, but not in front of knights.

"I'm still at the steering wheel," she said calmly. Too calmly for me. "I've just taken on a backseat driver. Hold your light on the door."

I held the chem stick on her instead. Her gaze was so focused on the door that it didn't seem capable of focusing on anything else. "What's your favorite movie, Sig?"

Somewhere in there, she seemed distantly amused. "*Run Lola Run.*"

"Good," I acknowledged. "Now, what's your *real* favorite movie?"

That made her pause and look at me with an irritated mouth twitch. "It is NOT *Toy Story 3.*"

I had to consciously refrain from releasing a deep, relieved breath. "There's nothing to be ashamed of. It's a fine film. What's my favorite?"

"*Monty Python and the Holy Grail,*" she said. "I'm here, John. I don't like this bitch, and she doesn't like me, but we've reached an agreement."

"You couldn't just pinky swear?" I demanded.

"No," Sig said shortly. "And trust me, we need her." She walked up to the door. Steven Hunter got out of Sig's way as if she might be radioactive, but he focused his flickering target light on the door so that he could see what she was doing. The runes that had turned the door into a magic portal were still visible, grooved into the wood, and Sig took her knife and began to carve into them, changing their design.

"Ummmm...Sig?" I said.

"If we blow the door, we'll find ourselves a couple of hundred feet below the castle, in a narrow cave tunnel loaded with dynamite," Sig explained.

"And the alterations you're...she's...making...in the design will change that?" I ventured.

"She says it would be better if we could come out on the top floor." Sig stepped back and examined her work critically. "But the symbols are too different. This will have our door appearing in a storeroom in the cellar."

"Don't open it yet," I said. And perhaps it's a measure of how freaked-out I was that I added, "Either of you."

Again, Sig regarded me with that oddly distracted amusement. "I really am in control. I've just got a little Jiminy Bitchit chirping in my ear. Go ahead and tell your team what's going on."

"They already know," I assured her. Down the hallway, through the flap into our world, I could hear Virgil explaining the situation to Angel. Our enhanced hearing was the best we could do to compensate for a lack of working headsets or radios. Oddly, with the time rate difference, it sounded like Virgil had sucked on a helium balloon.

In a moment, I heard Virgil's voice. "Dan knows the storeroom she's talking about. Go for it if you trust her."

Of course I trusted her. It was Sig's polterguest I wasn't too sure of. "Are you sure your passenger isn't leading us into some trap to save her daughter, Sig?"

Sig gave a short, strange laugh. "It's not a mother's love keeping her here, John. Believe me."

"Okay," I said, and Sig shot me a grateful look that told me what she was doing was more difficult than she was letting on. "So, does your...guest...know how many doubles there really are?"

"In this world?" Sig paused while she searched someone else's memory. "Five. I mean, four. There are five of Malea in all. The original is in the top floor of the castle. There's a secret passage in the library that will get us there faster."

I've never actually had a secret passage built myself, so I have no idea why they always seem to be in libraries. But what I asked was, "The mother can sense her?"

"Like a burning rash," Sig confirmed tightly. "I can take you straight to Malea no matter where she goes."

"That's good," I said, not at all sure that it was.

Four more knights came forward, pulling small inflated rubber rafts with supplies in them: extra magazines, heavy weapons, spools of barbed wire, portable mines, med kits, and so on. The hall we were in had just been elevated from entry point to extended fallback position.

"Turn off your lights," I reminded the others. "I don't want them going off and then coming all the way back on while we're trying to hide in the dark."

Then I opened the door a crack. The air in our hallway was pulled roaring past me, and I jammed my body into the opening to keep the door from being yanked shut again. That impulse was a huge mistake. I found myself being sucked through the door as the differences in air pressure continued to negotiate, with my side losing. A strong wind yanked me violently off of my feet, and then I was falling through an empty canyon, thousands of feet above the earth.

~18~

DOUBLES, DOUBLES, TOILS AND TROUBLES

No, just kidding about that whole falling-through-a-canyon thing. Sorry. That just seemed more interesting than the actual process of opening a door half submerged in water. It took Sig and me both to force the door open, and the water resistance got even worse when we cracked the portal open and the water we were wading in began rushing past us into a storeroom. There were large shelves threading around the walls, and I could just make out stacks of priceless treasure looted from our world: batteries and bars of chocolate and cartons of cigarettes and packages of toilet paper and bottles of bourbon on the first two rows near the storeroom's opposing entrance. Then that far door facing us was gone. The storeroom's other door ripped off of its hinges and came hurtling at Sig and me. Don't get me wrong; the door was still intact—it was more as if it had been picked up by a giant hand and thrown forward than blown up—and its corner caught against the door Sig and I had half-way opened and started to push it closed again. I ducked and squeezed past both doors right before our portal was forced shut again and saw a large, open cellar where a tall, pale woman in a flowing green robe was pushing an outthrust palm at me.

Hesitation isn't really my policy in such circumstances. I thumbed the MP5 to full auto and began firing, running and splashing as I did so. There was an awkward moment where I bounced off the door that was still hovering in the air instead of shouldering it aside, but I recovered quickly enough and kept firing.

Halted bullets floated in front of the dalaketnon like a swarm of bees, and even in lantern light I could see a thin stream of blood pouring from her left nostril over that pale chin. Apparently, it is no easy thing, stopping a bullet in midair with your mind. Catching a continuous stream of them is even harder. The dalaketnon—or more accurately, her double—was standing frozen some twenty feet away as I charged through the now-open entrance to the cellar, still firing. Her slender Eurasian features were framed by long brown hair so light that it was almost blond, and it was getting lighter by the second. She would have been beautiful if her face hadn't been contorted in a rictus of pained concentration.

I kept firing right up until the moment I charged through the floating bullets and slammed an elbow into the bridge of her nose, snapping her neck backward with a sharp crack. Ammunition dropped into the water washing around our shins while I stumbled over her. Six human guards with medieval weaponry had been giving her a lot of room, and now they came at me from all sides. Two crossbow bolts nearly got me, one hissing in front of my face and another thudding painfully into the polymer guard over my kidney.

A guard came forward swinging an axe two-handed, and I had to shift my grip on my MP5 so that I could use its barrel to catch the haft of his axe. The impact was jarring, and I cursed. If this asshole caused my weapon to jam at some point...

well, okay, I might kill him anyhow, but it still pissed me off. I expressed this sentiment by trying to put my knee through his ribcage while his hands were full of overextended axe. At least three of his ribs shattered, and he stumbled into a second guard who was running forward with a spear cocked over his shoulder. It slowed them down enough for me to shoot around the first guard and catch the spear carrier in the shoulder. They both went down, and my MP5 still worked, so it was all good.

Another guard came from the side with a war hammer swinging. A sliding drop under the swing of the hammer, and I swiveled to my side and brought my leg behind the attacking guard's knees while water sprayed all around us. He collapsed next to me awkwardly. If we hadn't been clothed and cursing, it would have looked like we were getting ready for the 69 position. Or, I don't know, maybe that's how some people get started. I don't mean to judge. In any case, I managed to untangle my leg enough to coil it, and then I slammed my foot into the haft of his hammer, smashing it under his chin while I held on to his knees to keep him anchored. He was done.

Dropping down also had the added bonus of giving the rest of my team a clear field of fire, even if I hadn't planned it that way. Sig and Steven had cleared the door by then, and several enfilading rounds tore into the walls over the heads of the guards who were still standing, and they all dropped their weapons and fell to the ground, either holding up their hands or trying to hide behind them. Only the guard with a spear tried to get up out of the water, holding his weapon in his other hand—his fight-or-flight response must have been in overdrive—but Sig calmly walked forward and plucked the spear out of his hand and head-butted him with a sickening smack of bone against bone. He dropped again, and this time, he didn't get up.

Now that I had time to take a look, I saw that we were in a large room lined with sacks of grain and wooden barrels that smelled like wine from a fruit I didn't recognize. Roughly thirty feet separated the ceiling from the floor, and instead of a stairwell, open wooden stairs with handrails like you'd see leading up to a dock wound their way to a large wooden door twenty feet above us. There were other doors in the room too, but I couldn't hear any movement and all of them showed darkness beneath their cracks. Well, securing the areas I left behind was what the lay sergeants were for. The dalaketnon had seen Sig and me and only us through the eyes of its double, and every moment I kept her focused on dealing with us would buy the knights more time, so I told the others to trail Sig and me from a distance, and began moving up the stairs.

Here's an odd SAT question. You are on the first floor of a castle with three floors, and you have been told that a dalaketnon has made four doubles of herself. You kill one double in a cellar. Now, you have also been told that the original dalaketnon always keeps one double at her side at all times and that she is on the top floor. If there are two doubles left between you and the original, and you are moving toward the dalaketnon at point B from point A at say, five miles an hour, and the castle is a fifth of a mile long and filled with humans who might be hostile guards or drugged slaves or innocent victims, how long will it take you to realize you're screwed?

The large, deserted kitchen area was designed in a way that was familiar and subtly foreign at the same time. It was a hodgepodge of cultural influences. The cast iron stoves were distinctly European, but the stone counters and cupboards that had open shelves without any doors or drawers were not.

Glasses and clay cups were narrow in the middle and looked like they were wearing a tight girdle. The stone floors were covered with smooth mosaic triangle tiles, and instead of paintings, pictures carved out of some kind of sandstone hung on the walls. I had other things on my mind than anthropology, but I kind of had an impression of a magpie culture, which made sense if the Dalakit way of life was based on scavenging off other worlds.

There were no doors in the castle proper once past the kitchen wing, which probably used them to contain heat. I suppose if I lived on a feuding world where other people could use doors as dimensional portals, I wouldn't want to be surrounded by them either. Rooms were connected by round, open arches, their spherical ceilings high and their tables low. There were no chairs, only mats and cushions lit by hanging paper lanterns. Tables were roughly a foot off the ground, large bronze circular tops placed over eight wooden supports that unfolded from the center like tentacles.

I moved through several halls and chambers in the general direction of the library, occasionally eliciting shrieks as terrified servants caught glimpses of me and ran away. I was glad they were running but wished they would shut up about it. There was no wind, and the dalaketnon—or at least her doubles—all smelled the same so that their scent trails overlapped.

Slater was trailing me and Sig now, Steven guarding our back to make sure no one came up behind us. Dawn and Virgil had come up with the second group, which was now securing the kitchen, and Dawn's voice began booming through the house, somehow magically amplified: "ATTENTION, ALL HUMANS! LIE DOWN AND YOU WILL NOT BE HARMED! WE ARE HERE TO FREE YOU! HELP US IF YOU CAN! STAY OUT OF OUR WAY IF YOU CAN'T!

ANYONE CARRYING A WEAPON WILL BE KILLED!"
Dawn began yelling it again in Spanish.

My MP5 was back on the single-shot setting, and when a guard with a crossbow popped in the doorway of a large sitting room, I put him down with a single shot. He was just the preliminary, though—a shadow darted across the archway, too small and too fast to be a human. I pivoted and put one leg behind Sig's knees, sweeping her sideways into a dive that had us land on the edge of a sitting table. Our weight caused the heavy bronze top to slide off of its supports, and the top got seesawed, leaning against its old foundation and slanting up between Sig and me and the archway as we lay on the floor.

That was actually more than I'd hoped for. I'd thought the shadow might be some kind of explosive or combustible, and I had some vague idea that Sig and I would wind up next to the tabletop on the floor and I'd be able to lift the edge up with my hands to give us some cover. But we were still behind the heavy bronze shield when an AK-47 held by nothing but willpower floated across the entrance to the room some two and half feet above the ground. The assault rifle looked like nothing so much as a weird and hostile puppet in a goofy kids' show, bobbing on invisible strings as it swiveled and sprayed rounds over the room.

Welts formed in the bottom of the thick tabletop as bullets hammered into it, some of the protrusions punching against my back, but the metal held. Slater sank into a fetal position, the bracers built into his forearms and knees helping shield his head and torso while bullets thudded into his field suit. Steven Hunter was guarding the archway we'd entered, and he managed to swivel around its stone edge as bullets spattered off of the wall behind him.

The AK-47 clicked dry, and Sig shoved me off of her. This seemed a little rude, but I'm pretty sure that somewhere in the *Miss Manners' Guide to Etiquette While Under Fire*, there's a section on how a lot of the normal social conventions get suspended when an AK-47 is involved. Besides, the sound of many humanoid feet was coming from the same hallway where the assault rifle had appeared, and I was scrambling myself. It wasn't guards who came running into the room, though. It was more than two dozen women all dressed identically in plain short white dresses. They had some kind of green scarves tied around their head and faces so that only their eyes showed, and they all bore some kind of weapon in their hands—mostly knives but a few pokers and hand axes, and one had a big-ass crocheting needle. Their eyes were blank, almost unseeing.

Black-rice slaves.

If this Mistress Malea had been planning on us being reluctant to fire on women, she didn't understand knights very well. Slater had lain down in a firing stance—I'm not sure he could stand up—and he began firing into the mob's shins and knees. The first rank went down like wheat in front of a combine, but what was really creepy was that they didn't scream; in fact, after a few seconds, they began to crawl forward on their arms. Slater thought that all of the attackers were just drugged human servants, and to be fair, I didn't realize that a disguised double was hiding somewhere in the middle of all those human shields either. Not until Slater went flying backward and hit a wall with an impact that didn't bode well for his future chiropractor bills.

The hidden double tried to telekinetically pluck Sig's MP5 out of her hands and turn it on us next, but Sig is stubborn and supernaturally strong, and her wrists didn't break when she hung on to her weapon. Instead, her body was lifted and dragged behind the MP5 as if the weapon were a trapeze bar.

The submachine gun was firing the whole time, some of its shots hitting the double's servants, but when the fire began to come my way, Sig managed to kick one of her feet off the ground and tilt the barrel of the weapon up so that the bullets went over me. It brought me enough time to hurl my flash-bang grenade underhanded into the middle of the group while the dalaketnon was concentrating on Sig.

The grenade went off with a bright retina-searing light and a deafening force that sent several bodies crashing to the ground. Sig dropped to her feet as her weapon was released, but she'd been blinded as well. Oops. I began to move through the bodies on the floor, trying to figure out which one was the double, when several of the writhing women were picked up and flung towards me by a force blast that I couldn't escape. The same widespread mental wave that had scooped the servants up picked me off of my feet and threw me into the wall some ten feet behind. The only good side was that dispersing the force blast that widely apparently depleted a lot of its power. I dropped to the floor, but I wasn't seriously hurt except for a throbbing in the back of my head. I was conscious and watching when another blast picked up more bodies and sent them and Sig cartwheeling across the room.

I fumbled for my Glock with a hand that felt so large and unresponsive that I might as well have been slapping the weapon with a bowling ball, but Steven Hunter swiveled around the archway he'd been hiding behind and put a bullet through the double's head. She was easy to spot. Everyone in front of her had been tossed away. I won't describe the effect of that bullet, but I will say that there was no need for a double tap. No pun intended.

Two bogies down. Still assuming one was with Mistress Malea, that left one unaccounted for.

∽19∾

THE GAME IS AFOOT. ALSO AHEAD. AND AFEMUR. AND I THINK THAT'S ASPLEEN...

A hallway, a dining room, some screaming people, a firefight involving homemade Molotov cocktails thrown at us from a balcony, and then we were in the library even if flames were still licking over Steven's right arm. The fire-retardant properties of our armor were so effective that he didn't seem to notice.

I stepped aside and Sig took the lead. Dakota Ashworth, a young knight who had stepped up to take Slater's place when we briefly made contact with a backup group, started to protest, but I cut him off at the knee-jerk protests. "Guard the hall and be quiet."

I gave Sig a look that asked if she was still in there and knew what she was doing, and she gave me a look that said yes and to get off her ass and let her concentrate.

So I did.

It turned out that the secret passage wasn't behind a bookcase; it was accessible via a trapdoor beneath a shaggy rug whose hide had come from an animal I'd never smelled before, but even once Sig pulled the rug back, the panel was hard to spot. She opened it by pushing on three triangular floor tiles in sequence, and the trapdoor dropped to reveal a ladder leading to an extremely narrow passageway. We ignored the ladder and jumped down.

I actually had to tilt and walk slightly sideways not to rasp my field suit against the stone walls. The passage was dark and cold and full of sharp angles, but when it began sloping upward, it became dimly lit by small square patches in the walls. They were spy holes. I looked through them as we went by and saw a number of private bedrooms, many of them containing humans who were trying to barricade themselves but were hampered by their minimal furniture and possessions. They were piling futons and rugs in front of the strands of hanging beads that passed for doors. One room I passed held a naked man screaming through a gag and thrashing around on a water bed, his ankles and wrists chained to iron rings embedded in the walls. I didn't blame him for being apprehensive. The sound of gunfire and yells was loud in the background.

The passage ended in a door that seemed to be nothing but a depression in the stone wall with a metal handle and an outline. Sig braced her back against the wall and put one hand on the lever, positioning her submachine gun so that the stock was securely braced by her biceps. Then she turned to me and whispered, "Are we ready?"

"Do you think it's too late to pretend to be Jehovah's Witnesses?" I asked.

The question was punctuated by a distant explosion.

"Never mind," I said.

Sig threw open the door, firing a single shot into the back of the head of a double who had been waiting for someone to come from the opposite direction. The double had been sitting behind four ranks of kneeling humans, each row holding six people. All twenty-four of the servants were crouched behind the kind of transparent polycarbonate shields that riot cops use, armed with short, curved stabbing swords that looked a little like truncated cavalry sabers. The humans weren't dressed like guards, though—males and females both were topless and barefoot, wearing nothing but black... kilts? Miniskirts? The important thing was that they weren't wearing scarves wrapped around their faces, and their stillness and orderly placement made it easy to verify that none of them were doubles.

That didn't stop them from turning around and looking at us with expressions that fell somewhere between dazed and crazed. More rice zombies. Sig began yelling words in a language she shouldn't have known, in a voice I didn't recognize. Apparently, the rice slaves recognized it though, and in the absence of a recognizable authority, it was enough. Their expressions went from slack and aggressive to just slack. As a group, they began listlessly dropping their blades and shields, and Sig continued to harangue them in that language I almost recognized until they stumbled out of the room. Thank God. Putting those drones down would have been like clubbing baby seals.

We were left in a large, eight-sided chamber that was mostly empty except for the cushion the double had been sitting on. Now that I had a moment to really look, I could see that there were eight doors around us, each built into a different section of wall.

"The real Mistress Malea doesn't know that we know she's gained weight," I commented, looking at the dead double's body. This bogey was dressed more elaborately than the other doubles had been, in a red silk robe that had elaborate yellow swirling designs over it. Her hair was done up in two tight lay-ered buns, and her face was completely covered in white face paint, like a mime or a Chinese opera singer. "She wanted us to think that this double was her, making a last stand."

"It's more than that." Sig pointed at the door directly behind the double. "If she couldn't kill us, this double was going to run through that door while her guards delayed us and hope we followed her."

"What's behind it?" I asked.

"Death," Sig said. "Eventually."

"All doors lead to death eventually," I replied a little impatiently.

Sig conceded the point with a tight smile. "The Faerie Realm."

As far as I know, nobody has heard from the Fae—at least the full-blooded ones—since they created the Pax Arcana and went home almost a thousand years ago. That does suggest that wherever the Fae went, they have a strict no-trespassing policy. Would we have followed the double right through a magic door if things had fallen out differently? Yes. Or at least some of us would have.

I would have.

Steven was getting edgy. "So, where did this Mistress Malea really go?"

Sig pointed her index finger up at the ceiling. "Up there."

"I'm going to assume you don't mean heaven," I said evenly.

"Not hardly. My guest can't sense her daughter on other worlds, but that's how she knows we just missed her on this one." Sig jumped up and grabbed at the ceiling. It was the first time I really registered that the ceilings on the upper floor were made of wood instead of stone. Her fingers found some kind of indentation or purchase in the surface that I couldn't see, and she pulled a secret panel down. A wooden ladder unfolded and dropped to the floor. "This goes to their bolt-hole."

I peered up the ladder. It didn't lead to an open attic. The new opening in the ceiling had some kind of weird sloped wooden cover over it.

"That's the lid to a chest made from a balete tree," Sig told me.

I squinted at her. "Why a chest lid? Why not just a trapdoor?"

Sig seemed to be having a hard time articulating. "I think the dalaketnons got tired of having to make doors out of balete trees and replacing other doors on our world every time they wanted to establish a new portal. So, they made a portable chest."

I climbed up the ladder for a closer look. A set of horizontal hinges joined the lid to the ceiling opening so that it would swing up like a submarine hatch. When I looked back down, I was a little nonplused. "Are you saying that if we open the chest lid over the top of this ladder, we'll wind up crawling out of a wooden chest that could be anywhere on our world?"

The look Sig flashed me was almost grateful. She was scrunching her brow as if she had a headache. "Yes."

So, that's what we did. Oh, there were other details. I smelled for explosives. Sig's "guest" had to reactivate the magic because Mistress Malea had used that tape trick to activate the portal, use it, and turn off the mojo again before dropping the lid back down. There was stuff piled on the lid from the opposite side, though none of it was deadly. Stuff like that.

But that's what we did.

If anyone had seen me climb up through the storage chest, it probably would have looked like some kind of bad sight gag, but nobody saw me. I found myself in a concrete room with a metal panel door that looked and smelled like one of my world's storage silos. Trust me on that—I've been in a lot of storage silos.

Between the dim light coming through from my side and the fading moonlight shining around the edges of the silo door, I could see a variety of items—small firearms, textbooks, gun cartridges, MREs, rolls of toilet paper, dental floss, propane, helium tanks—don't ask me why the dalaketnon needed those—and so on. It was obvious that some items had been hurriedly shifted and some boxes rifled through, and the smell of auto exhaust was strong in the air. Somewhere—and not too far away either—I could hear a running car engine. Just one.

In retrospect, I think the dalaketnon had reasoned that even if someone did come after her—and that must have still seemed pretty unlikely despite how far we'd come—the different time rate between worlds would give her time to transport her wooden chest to a storage silo. She was intent on escaping to someplace safe, and she didn't want to take the chest with her because we had demonstrated an ability to use her magic portals against her, but she didn't want to leave a valuable item like the chest unguarded either. She also didn't want to destroy the chest, because it was possible her double would come through it later and mentally contact her and tell her that everything was all right.

Whatever. All I really cared about was that the dalaketnon had just been there and wasn't there any longer. She might not be in the wind, but it was definitely getting drafty. Still hanging on to my Glock, I climbed up the top of the ladder and worked my way out of the chest. Then I pulled Sig up and through with one hand until she could get a foot on the floor. "Can you get the door?" I asked her. Storage silos are sturdy, and Valkyries are physically stronger than werewolves.

"Always the gentleman," she muttered, but she was already moving. I stood next to the entrance with my Glock ready while Sig bent her legs, straightened her back, and put both hands on the handle of the sliding door. Then she pulled until something metal snapped. The door slid up and open on its rails with a sound like a passing train and thudded loudly into concrete.

Steven was still guarding the ladder on that other world until more knights came along, so Sig and I stepped outside. We were in the middle of a long row of storage silos in some cold, remote place. It was night now, even though it had still been daylight when we'd last been in our world, and I could see red lights from the tail end of a dark grey car as it disappeared around a corner. It was more than a dozen storage silos away. Apparently, the occupants of the car had heard the ruckus we'd made too, because the driver gunned the engine as soon as it straightened past the turn.

"Give me a boost," I said, and Sig made a pair of stirrups with her hands. I stepped onto them with one foot and touched her shoulder, and Sig hurled me straight up into the air and onto the roof of the opposite storage silo. From that vantage point, I could see that we were in one grade-A large storage facility. Each silo was part of a row some twenty-four silos long, six pale rows in all forming five dark spaces between them. It felt like I was standing on a giant keyboard, though I don't want to even think about what kind of music it would play. "Follow as fast as you can," I called, and I was off.

There were a lot of buildings and streetlights nearby. We must have been located on the outskirts of a city, but I couldn't tell which city as I darted across a silo roof and took a running jump over to the next row. Two more to go. I'm faster and jump farther than a normal human, but I couldn't overtake the grey car in a straight race; thankfully, the large lot was square and covered in speed bumps and hemmed in on all sides by a chain link security fence with barbed wire running over it—the driver had to slow down to turn around the last corner, and I hopped over to the last row of silos as the car was regaining speed and rushing toward the entrance.

A security guard—yeah, we were definitely near a large city—was stepping out of a booth to see what the hell was going on. He was a weedy-looking kid in his early twenties with scrubby-looking shoulder-length brown hair, his hand instinctively going for a cell phone rather than a gun. Suddenly, he flew backward for no discernible reason and smashed against the side of the concrete booth he had just stepped out of. When he slipped to the pavement, there were several dark smears on the pale yellow concrete wall.

So, yeah, the dalaketnon was in the car. I celebrated this discovery by slinging the MP5 off of my shoulder and firing down into the hood of the automobile until my clip ran dry. I didn't fire through the windshield or the roof, though. I was still willing to try to take Mistress Malea alive.

The engine died, and the driver instinctively hit the brakes, the car skidding past me and half spinning to a halt. I threw down my MP5 and ran alongside the roof, drawing even with the car and leaping off of the silo at roughly the same time that the double in the back seat managed to unbuckle herself and throw the back door open. I hurtled through the air like a spear of vengeance, passing over the roof of the car in one great bound that ended in a downward side kick, smashing past the double and snapping her neck. I landed in a smooth crouch and pulled the Glock from my side, ready to settle accounts or my name wasn't John Carter of Mars.

Oh, wait, my name wasn't John Carter of Mars. Maybe that's

why my massive running leap actually ended with me hurtling through the air like a flailing chicken who has just realized that it can't fly. I really did manage to land on the edge of the car roof and kick the double in the face and snap her neck, but the car roof buckled more than I thought it would when my left knee stopped bending. My ankle then turned in a way I'd thought it wouldn't, and my torso decided that it liked falling through the air so much that it might as well keep going. My foot slipped, my back scraped over the roof, my legs got tangled up with the door that the double had opened, and somewhere in there, I smashed the back of my head against the edge of the car and then the ground.

It was the second time I'd hurt the back of my head, and I guess the third time's not always the charm. I was turned into a frog for a little bit. A groggy frog. Before I could finish lurching to my feet, I was lifted up off of the concrete by some vast unseen pressure. I had maybe one second to stare at a plump woman who sort of looked like the doubles though she was bundled up pretty heavily, standing outside the dead car in a light blue winter jacket made of some kind of heavy felt, red mufflers on her ears and a green scarf over her throat. Then giant invisible fingers pinched my head and abruptly twisted it to the side. The top of my spine snapped.

I was dropped limply to the ground, and given my lack of options, I decided to stay there. I tried to be paralyzed heroically, but it didn't seem to make much of a difference. My head had landed on its side and Mistress Malea was still in my line of sight. So was the man who got out of the car. He fit the description of Makisig that Dan had given us, a guy who might have been good-looking if he hadn't started getting gaunt. He had cavernous muddy brown eyes and scraggly facial growth.

Dressed in several layers that ended in a puffy black coat, he was cursing in my language.

Makisig circled around the car and pulled a .38 out of his blue parka. I have no doubt that he was going to start emptying it into me, but then someone started shooting at him from the roof. Tufts of fabric fluffed into the air where bullets slammed into his back, but Makisig didn't even wince. He didn't even stumble with the impact. But it wasn't until I saw the hair on the back of his head rustle without even a sign of blood or discomfort on his part that I realized the truth.

Makisig was a skinwalker. For a moment, all the things Dan had said about Makisig being a serious sicko who had maybe twisted Mistress Malea around over time flew through my head. Had the skinwalker somehow taken the real Makisig's place to influence Malea? Had the skinwalker studied the dalaketnons' hunting patterns and preferred type of slaves and put itself in a position to be abducted? I didn't have time to think about it, because Sig dropped down from the roof of the storage silo, only I don't think she was Sig anymore. Sig wouldn't have tossed her MP5 away.

The dalaketnon screamed again, only this time she was putting more than her lungs into it; Sig's body recoiled in the face of some psychic gale, her hair flying backward. Sig's body stayed rooted, though, and then she was leaning forward and screaming back. Little bits of debris between them—twigs, flakes of concrete, bits of napkin, a penny, and then the skinwalker itself—floated up into the air and lurched violently back and forth, first in the direction of Malea, then Sig, and the whole time, the two women were yelling at each other. The skinwalker's defenses seemed useless; either psychic energy was something the skinwalker's magic suit couldn't channel, or he was being grabbed by the bones beneath his layers of skin. Gradually, some balance of power shifted. Sig began to move forward, one step at a time, and Mistress Malea was the one whose body began to bend backward. Her feet slid over the pavement in the last few seconds and then her body was lifted off the ground. Mistress Malea and the skinwalker both floated there, heads tilted up, arms flung out and mouths opened wide, but instead of screams, it was everything else that came out of them. Everything. Their eyes popped out, and then blood began spraying out of their eye sockets and ears and nose and mouth, and then other fluids and bits of bone, and then liquefied things that used to be tissue.

So much for taking the dalaketnon alive.

And yuck.

Two sets of wet skin flopped to the ground. A few seconds later, Sig collapsed some twelve feet away from me, face hitting the concrete in way that made me wince with what facial muscles I still controlled. Sig's hair was silver. Not grey. Not white. A pure, startling silver. I lay there and stared at Sig and marinated in my own helplessness, waiting to heal enough to move or for Steven to arrive because there was absolutely nothing else I could do.

∽20∾

SO, WE WEREN'T DEAD.
WE WERE JUST IN CANADA

It wasn't the first time I'd been paralyzed, and it wasn't the worst time I'd been paralyzed, but let me just say right now that spinal injuries aren't something that get easier with practice. I was lying on a crude pallet of clothes taken from some of the many suitcases in Mistress Malea's car. It took maybe four minutes for the cold from the concrete floor in the storage silo to seep through them, and two more minutes for my teeth to start chattering.

Dawn was watching me because Sig knows a thaumaturgic ritual for burning away blood and bodily fluids, and was helping with the cleanup outside. That kind of magic takes a bit out of Sig, and she'd already had a bit taken out of her—more like a bite taken out of her, actually. Sig had woken up disoriented, shaken, and tight-lipped, and she left as soon as Dawn arrived. I think Sig needed some time alone in her own head again.

Steven Hunter was busy going back and forth between our world and the dalaketnon's. He'd gotten Dakota and a lay sergeant to help him move all of the bodies, including mine. They'd basically bundled all of the corpses into the car, put the wreck in neutral, and pushed it back to the storage silo, where it was currently parked next to me. We weren't sure how long we had before the security guard's shift was over, and we were making haste. Two lay sergeants had already dropped the corpses through the storage chest and into the dalaketnon's world—including the body of the security guard—and now they were methodically transferring the contents of the silo down that dimensional rabbit hole. Another lay sergeant who was about Makisig's size had taken some clothes from his suitcase, then started walking with a cell phone in his hand. When he was far enough from the ambient magic, he went to work with his smartphone, then came back and told us that we were on the outskirts of Vancouver, Canada, and that Simon was sending some knights with blowtorches and toolboxes through the dimensional doorways. He didn't want to contact any of the local Canadian knights under the circumstances, and the plan was to send the dalaketnon's car through the chest in pieces.

"Yuh...yuh...yuh...you're gon...nuh...nuh...na...have tuh...tuh...to...guh...guh...get me some puh...puh... pillows and...bluh...blankets and food," I tuh...tuh... tuh...told Dawn. "If...I...shuh...shuh...shake too much...I muh...muh...might juh...jar my spine and sluh...slow down...thuh...thuh...the healing."

"And that's the only reason you want to get warm," Dawn said dryly. "Efficiency."

"That's...whuh...whuh...why...I *nuh...nuh...need* tuh... tuh...to," I said. "I *whuh...whuh...want* you tuh...tuh...help muh...me warm me up becuh...cuh...cuh...cause I'm freezing muh...muh...my ass off." If I just lay there cold, dehydrated, hungry, and constantly shaking, it would probably take me three days to heal. Given warmth, stillness, and food, I would be walking again in an hour or two.

"I can't believe I was getting tired of my lab," Dawn said, a little raggedly. But she found a set of blankets and a couple of pillows without pillow cases. When she brought them over, she laid the blankets down and got down on her knees, one of the pillows held between her hands. For a moment, it looked like she was planning to smother me, and Dawn paused. "Boy, does this give me ideas."

"Hey," I protested.

Dawn smiled evilly. "Let's talk about those jokes you've been making about my butt."

"I was muh…muh…making jokes about a buh…buh… bullet wound," I said. "Come on."

Dawn suddenly froze. A growling sound was coming from behind her.

"Step away from him." Virgil finished climbing up through the storage chest with pack instincts on full throttle. With Mistress Malea gone, the castle on that other world had fallen quickly, and there was no question where Virgil's real loyalties lie. He took in the sight of me lying motionless on the crude mattress of clothes with Dawn leaning over me with a pillow, and almost attacked her right then and there.

"I love the smell of testosterone in the morning," Dawn said in a dry tone that meant the opposite, and she ignored Virgil and finished fluffing the pillow. When she was done, she put it under my head. By that time Virgil was standing next to her, something protective and hostile in his steady stare and his body language that said outsiders weren't welcome. I'm not even sure Virgil realized that he was doing it.

"Virg…juh…gil, it's ah…ah…all right," I assured him. "I asked her tuh…tuh…to fetch thuh…thuh…those."

"There's something else I can do too." Dawn took a red plastic cigarette lighter out of her armor and flicked it until a flame appeared. Then she put her right palm on the floor. The flame from the lighter died down to a small blue aura, barely perceptible, and then disappeared some twenty seconds later. When Dawn was done, the floor beneath me was warmer.

"Thuh...thuh...thanks," I said.

She shook her head and put her right hand on my cheek. Her fingers were warm despite having been in contact with cold concrete. Then heat began to flow through my body. When Dawn removed her hand, I was warm, and she was the one who was shivering, her teeth chattering and her lips blue. "Yuh...yuh...yuh... you...cuh...cuh...can't tell...anee...nee...nee...nyone...I... did that," she stammered.

Manipulating fire and transferring heat isn't defensive or scrying magic. Having figured out what her geas really would and wouldn't allow, Dawn had been experimenting with magic in ways the knights wouldn't approve of.

"I won't," I sighed, and then added, "Except maybe Sig," because Sig and I still hadn't worked out that whole secrets thing yet. "Of course, Virgil here is the real chatty Cathy."

Virgil had relaxed a little by this point. "One part of your whole damn body's working, and it had to be your mouth."

"Speaking of which, can you dig me up some food?" I asked. "My body's been doing a lot of healing lately."

Virgil grumbled something about me not being his claw leader anymore, but he found a box of MREs—meals ready to eat—that hadn't been chucked down the magic portal yet. When Dawn was done tucking two blankets around my shoulders, he began feeding me crackers, smoked almonds, and some kind of beef strips.

"Gah," I said when I tasted the latter. "What kind of meat is this?"

Virgil looked at the back ingredients. "Says here it's Asian style."

"Remind me never to eat any Asians." Werewolf humor. You wouldn't understand.

Virgil smiled and shoved another hunk of the stuff into my mouth.

Vancouver is one of my favorite places in the world when it isn't raining, and I like it okay even when it is, but when Sig and I opted to stay in Canada awhile, it wasn't because I wanted to sightsee. I tried to explain this to Simon over that week's burner phone, but he wasn't really listening and I didn't really care. I was already driving Sig away in the car that had belonged to the dead storage-facility guard. I was worried about Sig; her hair was still pure silver, and she looked as weak and trembly as I felt.

That hadn't stopped me from taking advantage of the confusion and the time differential between worlds while Angel Solis was busy consolidating the knights' control of the dalaketnon castle. No one had said that I wasn't still in charge of the advance team, so I'd had a lay sergeant swap the license plates from Mistress Malea's car with the ones on the dead security guard's, and also had a list of the numbers taken from Mistress Malea's cell phone delivered to me. I'd known better than to ask for the phone itself—Mistress Malea and the skin-walker's possessions were being treated like religious artifacts.

As soon as I got the info I wanted, I scrounged through the pile of clothes I'd been lying on and found an outfit that fit Sig, then found another that almost fit me. Once changed, we took a suitcase full of Canadian ten-dollar bills that Mistress Malea had been running away with, packed our field armor and weapons in another suitcase, and slipped away in the dead security guard's car. I used the excuse that I needed to ditch the vehicle and talk to Simon on the phone wherever he was on our world, and I really did need some distance from the magic portal to do both of those things.

"We need to find out what the Valkyrie learned while she had that ghost in her head," Simon's voice crackled, and I'm not sure it was the cell phone connection. "Especially since she killed our best lead."

"I'll question her," I told him tersely. "But she needs some downtime. You're not going to put her in an interrogation room, or drug her, or start asking her if she killed Mistress Malea because she's secretly working with the skinwalkers and wanted to silence them or whatever paranoid bullshit you come up with. Sig wasn't Sig when she killed those assholes. Just the way they died should tell you that much."

"You're supposed to be our werewolf liaison," Simon tried. "Not some bleeding heart with a hard-on. Man up. Both of your tribes are in danger here."

"Virgil can be Ben's man on the scene for a while," I said, knowing Virgil would love that. "I think this Mistress Malea had a residence on our world somewhere around here. You should check it out. I'll put the battery back in this cell phone in twelve hours."

Things got a little nasty after that, and then I heard a voice in Simon's background say, "Let him go." It was Emil Lamplighter. The Templar Grandmaster.

"But—" Simon started.

"Have you forgotten that one of us killed a woman John loved once?" Emil asked. "You're never going to win unless you capture John and use force, and our relationship with the werewolves is too shaky right now."

Simon didn't translate that very accurately. Instead, he told me, "People like you and me can't afford romantic notions, Charming. It makes us vulnerable and erratic."

"Just do what I said, Simon," Emil's voice snapped from the background. "In fact, tell everyone John's doing this on my orders. Right now, John's an asset. Push this, and he'll be an ass sore."

"Tell Emil I love him too," I told Simon. Then I turned off the phone and gave it to Sig.

"That sounded like it went over well," Sig said from the passenger's side, still a bit too listlessly for my tastes. But she took the battery out of the cell phone without me having to ask.

"Let's hope so," I said tersely. Emil's reference to Alison had upset me a little. "Emil knew I could hear him in the background. I wouldn't put it past him to have said all that just to get me to relax my guard while he sends a retrieval team after us."

"Trying to think through all that who-said-what-and-why-and-what-does-it-really mean stuff when you and Emil start playing your weird chess game just makes me tired," Sig grumped. Yeah, *that* was what was making her tired. The fact that a ghost had possessed her and used her to telekinetically squish two people like ticks had nothing to do with it. But Sig wasn't ready to talk about that yet.

Bill Murray used to do a bit where he played a hokey night-club singer, alternately crooning and belting out snatches of old songs with cheesy faux passion, and I began mock–power ballading a few lines of that old Bob Seger song "Night Moves," trusting Sig to catch the obvious homonym, "Knight Moves," given the context of our conversation.

"Oh God," she said, and began looking for a radio station.

I can't sing, by the way, not that this always stops me. I like music, and I spent a lot of years alone with the sound of my own voice. It's become a bit of a running joke between Sig and me. Sometimes with Sig actually running. I ran out of lyrics, but that didn't stop me. I took the story to strange places Bob Seger never intended, both thematically and on the note scale. Pretty soon the teenaged protagonist found himself in the land down under, and then there was a Swedish guy named Gunter, and then the gravelly voiced narrator I was imitating met a girl and shunned her, and that was a huge blunder, and it rent his heart asunder. I admit, when the narrator went back and wonned her, I probably should have been ashamed of myself.

Sig turned up the radio's volume, and I turned up mine, and finally she laughed and begged me to stop, undoing her seat belt and cracking the car door open, acting like she was going to jump out.

It was an improvement.

We passed a Tim Hortons, some kind of Canadian franchise restaurant that was all brown and white and looked like a prefabricated attempt to cross a Burger King and a ski lodge. I asked Sig if she was hungry. She had a moment of self-evaluation, and then a surprised look came over her face. "I'm starving."

"Telekinesis probably burns calories." I regretted the comment when Sig's face closed down again. We wound up in a corner booth with something called aged cheddar biscuits that tasted a lot better than they sounded, and five boxes of doughnuts. The place had people in it, but that early in the morning, they were all out of it, and the only person in a position to see us was facing the other direction. Neither Sig nor I talked much, and I put a foot up under the booth and rested it next to her leg, sipping a dark roast blend coffee that was pretty good as far as franchise coffee goes.

"Didn't they get curious when you ordered five boxes of these?" Sig asked as she stuffed an apple fritter doughnut into her mouth.

"Canadians don't get curious when American tourists buy lots of food," I said. "If the guy thought about it all, he probably figured I wanted to take the doughnuts home, or to my church group or academic conference or whatever."

Sig eyed my clothes doubtfully. "How did he know you were American?"

"I made sure I talked loud," I said.

Sig began alternating among apple fritter doughnuts, blueberry doughnuts, maple glazed doughnuts, and strawberry doughnuts. I guess she was saving the chocolate ones for an emergency. Usually she manages to eat daintily even while stuffing food down, a trick I've never been able to figure out, but that morning, she was barely pausing between mouthfuls. She did stop long enough to shake her long and newly silver hair around her face, though. "So, what do you think of my new look?"

Even with supernatural women, you have to be careful when they ask you to comment on their appearance. "It's beautiful," I ventured. "Kind of attracts attention, though."

Sig nodded. "I've been thinking about that. Maybe I should stop letting police departments keep it quiet when they consult me as a psychic. I could just go all-out public as a medium and tell everyone my hair changed color when I contacted a ghost. Hide in plain sight."

I just kept listening.

"We wouldn't have to spend so much time hunting down paranormal incidents," Sig went on. "People would come to us."

"A lot of nutcases would too," I replied. "And reporters. Bloggers. Reality show producers."

"But I'd have a legitimate source of income," Sig said. "And an excuse for being around weird events all of the time. Instead of trying to prove that there's something weird about me, people would be trying to prove I was a fake."

She had reeled all of that off pretty rapidly. "You didn't just think of all that because your hair changed color," I said.

"I've been considering it ever since we met Holly Blake," she admitted. Holly Blake is the pen name for a nymph who writes a successful series of paranormal romances. Or maybe they're autobiographies. Holly Blake had tried to get Sig and me in a threesome pretty aggressively when we'd met her in New York. "I could probably stay in the spotlight for ten or twenty years before I'd have to disappear or fake my death or something. People are looking a lot younger for a lot longer these days."

I reached over and took a blueberry doughnut. I thought it was a terrible idea. The public psychic thing, I mean, not the doughnut. It's a lot harder to disappear once you've become famous these days. Those YouTube videos and blogs don't go away like newspaper photos and articles used to, and unlike Holly Blake, Sig doesn't blow out a stream of illusions and charms every time she sneezes.

"So, what do you think?" she probed.

I thought that Dawn's magic hair dye was a better solution. She'd said that merlins could make the dye change color by somehow tapping into the spirit of the dead chameleon it had been made from, and that sounded right up Sig's alley. But what I said was, "I think it's a mistake to talk about the future when you're trying to avoid the present."

Sig gave me a stormy look that boded no good. I didn't cringe.

"Like I said," she reminded me, "I've been thinking about this for a while."

"I believe you," I granted. "I just don't want to talk about it right now, because we'll get in a fight, and we won't be fighting about what we're really fighting about."

Sig clasped her hands together into one big fist and stared at me over it, her fingers white with the pressure she was exerting on them. "And what should we be fighting about?"

"I'm not saying we *should* be fighting," I said evenly. "But I think we're both freaked out by the fact that you were possessed by mommy dearest for a little while back there."

"I have rules about what kind of spirits I let in." Sig's voice shook slightly. "The only reason I broke them was because I was trying to keep you and your stupid knights alive."

"I'm going to die sometime, Sig," I said quietly. "I can live with that."

"That's because losing Alison fucked you up!" Sig said angrily. "Sometimes, I think you're more scared of outliving me than you are of dying."

How did the discussion become about what was wrong with me? That's the problem with arguing with Sig. We start at point A and then go straight to step thirteen and wind up in phase orange and then, you know, we're in the linen aisle looking for windshield wipers. I was struggling with how to respond to that last statement when Sig continued. "Do you think I don't know why you jumped out of a moving car and tried to put yourself between me and a werewolf pack? Or why you left me behind and threw yourself off that roof without even stopping to think about it?"

"I'm pretty sure we'd all be dead if I hadn't thrown myself out of that car," I protested.

"And I'm pretty sure we'd all be dead if I hadn't channeled Dalisay!" Sig countered.

That was the mom's name? Whatever. "The problem is," I said, "I only risked my life. You risked something a lot more important."

"The problem is," Sig corrected, "you just said you *only*

risked your life, and you really think that way. Trust me on this; dying is nothing to take lightly."

"Sig," I said gently. "You only see the dead people who are so messed-up, they can't move on. You're like a ghost plumber, pulling out stuff that's been stuck in the pipe for a long time. Of course it's not pretty."

"I just don't want to have to see your ghost someday, John." Sig sounded exhausted.

"Well, I'm going straight to heaven," I told her. "So you don't have to worry about it."

She smiled wanly in spite of herself. "Does heaven have a service entrance I haven't heard about?"

"I'm walking through the front gate ass-backwards," I said. "It's all part of the plan."

"I'm serious, John."

I nudged Sig's leg with my foot. "And I'm not as reckless as you think. When we got ambushed in the SUV, I jumped out to divide their focus. I'm not saying it wasn't crazy, but having us all lumped together in one big easy target was crazier."

"And the silo roof?" Sig asked skeptically.

"There were two people in that car who could stop bullets with their mind, and I was supposed to bring one of them in alive," I explained. "What was I supposed to do? The back door of the car was opening. I couldn't see into the car, so I couldn't just pump bullets into it and hope Mistress Malea lived. I could have just faded back out of sight and waited for you, but then what? That would have given them time to get out of the car, and our only advantage was that they needed to see to use their telekinesis effectively. Our guns would have been useless, and we couldn't get in close, and we didn't have any cover to work with."

"Oh. Now it all makes sense." Call me paranoid, but I thought I detected an element of insincerity.

"I wanted to take whoever was coming out of the back door by surprise," I elaborated. "Then I was going to fire through the front edge of the car roof at an angle. It seemed to me that Malea or her double might have a hard time focusing with bullets in their knees. But I messed up the kick landing."

"Because it was a crazy stunt to pull," Sig said.

"Well, yeah," I admitted. "But I figured at the very worst, I would take one of them out and distract the others so that you could surprise them. That would be better than having two telekinetics up and on guard. And that's how it worked out. Sort of."

"The very worst would have been if she'd ripped your head off instead of breaking your neck," Sig said grimly. "You should have said 'Screw the mission' and killed them. Or you could have let them run away and trailed them from a distance with your sense of smell until we could take them by surprise."

"That's easy to say, but they wouldn't have run away on foot," I argued. "The security guard's car was right there. And what makes you think they would have run away in the first place? What would have kept Malea from levitating upward and taking us on? Or tossing that car up over the roof at us with her mind and turning it into shrapnel? I still don't know how powerful their telekinesis can get, but I do know that when you give your enemy the initiative, you give them options you can't predict or control."

"Most people aren't as creative as you are when it comes to mayhem, John," Sig said. "Malea wasn't a warrior. She was a spoiled sociopath."

"A spoiled sociopath who had information about people who are a threat to Constance," I countered. "And I didn't want to risk having to fight Malea another day either. She had a really nasty habit of putting innocent people between her and harm's way."

Sig leaned back in her booth and sighed. "God, you're a butthead."

"I'm not saying all of this because I have to be right, Sig," I said. Maybe that was even true. "It's just I'd rather be wrong sometimes than start second-guessing myself and hesitating in the middle of every fight. That really will get me killed."

Sig's appetite seemed less all-consuming, and she took a maple glazed doughnut and dunked it in her coffee. I've never been able to do that. I like coffee too much to have little bits of pastry floating around in it. "I've seen you almost die twice in the last week, John, and for some reason, I didn't like it. So, back the fuck off, okay?"

"Okay," I said, then confessed. "I'm a bit shaky too."

"You think I don't know that?" Sig said. "When you told Simon that I was the one who needed some downtime, you were doing that male thing."

"Yeah, I was," I admitted.

She shrugged. "It's okay. You and Simon have some competitive thing going on. Probably because he's Emil's favorite."

"I don't want to be Emil's errand boy," I protested.

Sig didn't exactly disagree, but she didn't agree either. "As big a shit as Emil is, he's still some kind of a father figure to you."

"I'm older than Emil is, Sig," I pointed out.

She wasn't impressed. "And you're still a Templar orphan who never felt totally accepted. He isn't just a human. He's the face of the whole organization for you."

"Let's not take the Freudian stuff too far, okay?" I requested.

Sig's mouth quirked an agreement. She finally got around to the chocolate doughnuts while I went to get a refill on my coffee. Maybe she'd just been waiting until she was eating slowly enough to taste them.

"So, what about you?" I asked when I got back. "If you had

to do it all over, would you let that Dalisay byatch back into your head again?"

The sudden reversal caught Sig off guard. She had turned the conversation around so successfully that she'd forgotten how it started. "I don't know," Sig sighed. "She didn't exactly take me over. I let her use me."

"What?" I said stupidly.

"I fired at that damn skinwalker and the bullets just bounced off!" Sig said miserably. "It was about to blow your brains out, and the daughter was about to go psycho psychic on me, and there was nothing I could do about it! And Dalisay's spirit was urging me to let her handle them..."

"Huh," I said.

"Yeah," Sig said. "Huh."

I tried one of the chocolate-covered doughnuts but didn't really taste it. "I'm still not okay with you risking your soul for me. Or your psyche. Whatever."

Sig nodded, but her words weren't an agreement. "I can't stop communicating with the dead, John. It's what I am."

"I know that," I said.

"There are different levels," Sig admitted. "I haven't let any spirits share my body since Alison."

Why did she keep bringing up Alison?

It was as if I'd said it out loud. "You tense up every time I say Alison's name," Sig observed. "But you and I wouldn't be together if I hadn't channeled her. You acted like a real jerk the first time we met. The only reason I came back was because I saw you through her eyes. I'm not sure you'd have fallen for me so hard so fast either. I think you sensed her inside me."

Oh. That's why she kept bringing up Alison. "How long have you been carrying that around?" I asked.

"What?" she said suspiciously.

"This idea that I only care about you because I've got you confused with Alison," I clarified.

Sig shrugged unhappily. She's an odd combination of fierceness, confidence, bravery, and low self-esteem. Well, I guess I am too, actually. Maybe everybody is.

"Everybody has issues, Sig," I said.

She laughed starkly. "Everybody doesn't have issues like us."

"Maybe they do," I said. "We could be having a variation of this conversation if I was a fireman and you were maybe spending too much time on the Internet. Human nature is human nature."

"If we're human at all," Sig mumbled.

I squeezed her hand. "Listen to me. You're brave. You're smart. You're sexy. You care about people, but you're not a doormat. I don't care how we got started. I just want to keep going."

She looked at me solemnly, and for once, I couldn't tell or smell what she was feeling. There were powerful currents moving inside her, mysterious and deep. Finally, she said, "So let's go."

~21~

RITE OF THE VALKYRIES

There's a fine line between finding a place to stay that won't ask too many questions if you want to pay in cash and finding a place that isn't full of cheap locks, drug addicts, and bedbugs. It's a line that I've walked a lot, though—hell, sometimes I've run it while looking over my shoulder, emitting high-pitched screams—so it didn't take too long to find a bed-and-breakfast called the Maud Montgomery. It was a reasonably nice-looking white building, old but going for historic more than run-down. The establishment was in the middle of Vancouver, not out in the country like a lot of B&B's, but it had a walled-in court-yard out back and a small yard where a couple of cedar trees had been planted. It also had a FOR SALE sign out front.

A series of posted arrows led us around the front of the building, down a street, and to a large lower parking lot behind the place. The lot was shared by several other houses that had been converted into small businesses. We found the owners, an elderly retired couple, in a basement office that shared space with a dining room and a kitchen. It was the husband, a big man with small glasses and hunched shoulders and retreating grey hair who took our money without offering his hand or his name. The wife was cooking crepes and omelettes and bacon for a family that was talking French around a table.

"We don't make pancakes," the husband told us firmly as he gave us our keys. I have no idea why that was so important to him. He didn't make conversation, either. We weren't allowed to use the stairs—at a guess, they led through the couple's private quarters—so Sig and I took our bags back up the street and around the house. The front door opened to a large living room with a huge fireplace and old but comfortable couches and armchairs. There were pictures of a stern-looking woman all over the place.

"Who was Lucy Maud Montgomery?" I asked, reading a plaque.

"She wrote *Anne of Green Gables*," Sig said. "I loved that book when I was a kid."

"I guess one of the owners did too," I commented. "Wasn't that book set in the country or something?"

"Prince Edward Island." Sig didn't want to start a book club. "Come on."

We went up a set of rickety stairs. The house had two upper levels, and I could smell that only three of the eight rooms were occupied. One of the rooms had towels stuffed under the crack beneath the door; well-to-do people cheating on their second or third or fourth spouse have started doing that because private investigators can loop cameras on the end of fiber-optic cables through small crevices these days. I guess the unfaithful spouses learned at least one thing in divorce court.

As soon as Sig and I got into our room, we started tearing each other's clothes off.

"Wait," I said while Sig was throwing my belt across the room. My shirt was on top of an end table and she was stepping out of her pants while my foot held them pressed against the floor.

"What?" She gasped.

"I'm withholding sex to get back at you for that shower," I explained.

"The hell," she said. It wasn't a question so much as a warning.

"Hold on," I said.

She stared at me.

"Okay, I'm finished." I grabbed her and pulled her over onto the bed.

I don't know if it was good sex or not. There was no foreplay, no teasing, no tantric breathing, no establishing a mood. We made a lot of noise, hands gripping so tight they hurt a bit, bodies slick with sweat, each of us trying to merge with the other's skin. When it was over, and it was over for both of us a lot sooner than normal, we were tangled together and motionless, as if we'd just been washed up on the bed by a violent storm, and in a way, I guess we had.

"I need to talk to someone," Sig said a few sessions of more intimate lovemaking and a five-hour nap later.

We were still in bed, drained and nestled around each other, and I found a good place for the hand that was draped over her and kissed her softly on her neck. She tasted salty with sweat. "What, you mean like a therapist? Molly?"

Sig nestled her bottom into me, craning her neck back to kiss my cheek for a moment. "Another Valkyrie."

Huh. Sig had once mentioned an older Valkyrie who had helped show her the ropes, but we'd never really talked about it in detail. It was one of those Stanislav Dvornik topics we skirted around. Her previous lover had introduced Sig to the woman while helping Sig get clean and sober, and it was all tangled up in the codependence that had turned into guilt and obligation and desperation and resentment when Sig and Stanislav's relationship went on far longer than it should have.

"Okay," I said simply. "Where does this Valkyrie live?"

"I didn't say she was living," Sig said gently.

Oh.

I drove to Vancouver International Airport in a brown business suit I'd gotten from a consignment shop, and parked the security guard's car in long-term parking. I used the sun visor to avoid getting my face on any cameras. The lots were pretty crowded, and I parked at the fringes and waited for the right moment. I used to have to get creative in order to sit around in a public place for hours at a time without drawing any attention or suspicion, but now all I have to do is get out a burner phone and pretend to be texting. It took about an hour and fifteen minutes for someone who looked like a lone businessman to show up, hurriedly parking and leaving a vehicle that had all the makings of a company car. It took longer to get out and disable the wireless module beneath the vehicle, but only because there was still foot traffic around, and my elbows didn't have much bending room under the car.

Company cars are a bigger pain in the ass to steal than normal cars—they're a lot more likely to have elaborate electronic monitoring systems and a lot less likely to have spare keys magnetically attached to the undercarriage. Leased and rental cars also have special license plates that cops can spot, which meant I would have to find some junker plates to swap out. But company cars also have some advantages. They tend to get serviced regularly, and I'd rather steal a well-insured vehicle from a corporate entity than from Joe Shmo who got laid off two months ago, or Jane Shmuckatelli whose mom has cancer. Getting into the vehicle was actually a lot easier than getting under it. You can make an improvised slim jim—I'm talking about the tool that cops use to unlock cars, not the meat snack—with two items you can find in any store that sells office equipment. Pardon me if I don't go into detail.

The ignition cap wasn't a cap; it was recessed and surrounded by slight ridges that would make it hard to pry off with my knife, so I had to go down and do a little damage to some plastic paneling to hotwire the car, but in the end, I drove out of the long-term parking lot in my new temporary vehicle, leaving the car I'd gotten at the storage silo behind.

There was a pretty good chance that I wasn't going to be able to make any phone calls near Sig for a while, so I stopped by one of my favorite places in Vancouver, Quilchena Park, and wandered around until I found a bench with a nice view and a lot of wide-open green space so that no receivers were likely to pick up my conversation by accident or design. It was in the "Dog Off Leash" area, but I chose to ignore any obvious metaphors.

Simon was happy to hear me check in. "Did your Valkyrie remember anything useful?" he asked without preamble.

"It's not like Sig actually became this Lady Dalisay," I said. I was going to keep saying it until I completely believed it too. "A man claiming to represent a powerful organization approached Malea's mother while she was on our world two years ago. She and Malea were staying at a luxury suite in Los Angeles at the time, and this Dalisay told the guy to take a flying fuck at a rolling doughnut."

"Does this organization have a name?"

"Not yet," I said. "Anyhow, Dalisay didn't suspect the guy was a skinwalker at the time, but Sig figures he somehow managed to make contact with Malea and seduce Dalisay's daughter way back then. Maybe he had charms in more ways than one. You know, like a little magic involved too, not just wine and dances and smoldering glances."

"I understood what you meant," Simon said irritably.

"Anyhow, he might have killed whoever originally looked like this Makisig and made arrangements for Malea to abduct him," I continued. "A lot of things would make more sense if the skinwalker had been working on Malea for years." And they would too. Things like how the skinwalkers had maintained contact with Malea's world, why she was willing to kill her mother, why she was willing to sell her people's sacred magic, and so on.

"That's all you got from the Valkyrie?" Simon griped. "Theories?"

A few years earlier, I would have just told Simon to fuck off. I had gone through a lot of long-delayed personal growth though, so now I took a few seconds to think about it and said, "Her name is Sig. Fuck off."

Simon responded by one-upping me. "We know how the skinwalker's organization bribed Malea to use her teleportation magic for them."

I bit. "How?"

"They have a drug that causes the user to have a high fever, sweats, aches, and delirium dreams for several days," he said. "But the dreams also include brief glimpses of the future."

"Holy shit," I said.

"Probably," Simon agreed. "We think someone has synthesized one of the drugs that ancient priests used to take to have visions of the future."

"But you're saying this drug gives people precognition without years of training and discipline," I clarified. "Not spiritual insights or vague prophecies cloaked in metaphor. They actually see the future."

Simon sighed. "We're still testing the blotting paper Malea had in her purse. But basically, yes."

"Like the Oracle of Delphi," I pressed. In ancient Greece, the temple at Delphi had operated a kind of prophecy drive-through in exchange for donations or political influence.

"And others," Simon said.

"You said blotting paper is the medium," I reminded him. "So, it's a kind of acid? You put it on your tongue instead of shooting it or snorting it or swallowing it?"

"I'm not ruling those ways out," Simon said. "But the blotting paper is what makes us think the drug is being synthesized for mass production. Blotting paper is easy to carry and conceal and ship in large quantities. The paper was produced by professional equipment too."

Mass production?

"Dan said Malea was trying to hold on to power in a society where a bunch of male nobles disapproved of unmarried female nobles," I recalled. "I can see where a drug that let her see the future would be pretty useful. Maybe she wasn't just Makisig's pawn. Maybe she and the skinwalker both thought they were using the other."

"That's fine, but Malea was just supposed to be a stepping-stone to the people we're really after," Simon reminded me. "Which is why we needed her alive. All I know is what we found out from the human servant Malea tested a sample of the drug on. The man lived, but he's still feverish and half delirious."

I had to search my memory, but it paid off. "Gordon Porter told me something when I saw him in New York not too long ago. He said the knights were looking into homeless people in

Boston who were having seizures and spouting prophecies right before they died."

"Very good," Simon said. Like I'd earned a gold star. "We think someone was testing this drug on vagrants in Boston while they were trying to synthesize it. Working out the kinks."

"It started out killing its users? That's one hell of a kink," I observed.

"You would think so," Simon agreed. "But now I know why we never found the people responsible. Every time we had a lead, it dried up or died or disappeared. That would be a lot easier to pull off if you had a drug that let people see the future."

"It's more likely skinwalkers on the inside were tipping them off," I argued. "Knights don't show up on psychic radar." This is part of the trade-off of being bound to a magical geas. Clairvoyants can't read us. Precognitives can't predict us. Telepaths can't dominate us.

"True," he said. "But what if you had a calendar and a cellar full of test subjects who were raving about the future in delirium states, and April sixteenth kept coming up blank? And you knew that knights were after you and can't be predicted?"

I saw what he was getting at. "I'd pack my bags and go find a rabbit hole by April fifteenth. You're right. Hold on."

Some kind of little froufrou dog—I think it was a bichon frise—had run up and started yapping at me from forty feet away. I know it smelled werewolf, but I don't know what it thought it was going to do about it. The dog's owner came ambling up, a soft, pleasant-looking man in his thirties and a heavy sweater, with hair down to his chin and a rounded face. He scooped the dog up in the curve of his arm and called out a mild apology, then said, "Perhaps she smells your dog. Is it close by?"

He was being territorial. I considered telling him that my Alaskan husky liked to free-range so that it could hunt fancy lapdogs, but he wasn't being huffy or confrontational, or at least not directly so, like a lot of people in a lot of big American cities would have been. "She died last month," I lied. "She used to love to come here. I know it's silly, but..." I trailed off.

"Ah," he said awkwardly, then mumbled a few condolences and wandered off to leave me to my grief.

"I still don't understand how a skinwalker could pretend to be a dalaketnon servant for years," Simon said when the sound of the dog was no longer in the immediate background. "Suffering and discipline and working toward a long-term goal for a group just isn't in their makeup."

"Somebody else really has to be pulling their strings," I agreed. "Somebody who scares these skinwalkers, or has something they want very badly."

"The mysterious organization that doesn't have a name," Simon said darkly.

"Not yet," I amended. "You said these prophecy-farting vagrants started showing up in Boston. That skinwalker I killed back in the '60s was in Boston."

"Don't make too much of that. Massachusetts has always been a trouble spot," Simon cautioned.

"So you think it's a coincidence?"

"Hell, no," he said in a rare lapse of dignity.

"I should go there," I said. What I really meant was that I was going to go there, but I was giving Simon a chance to agree with me. I would do what I could to help the Templars, but I had sworn to protect Constance, and I had told Ben that I would put pressure on the people who wanted to use her like a playing piece. That was more important than playing Simon Says.

"You will," Simon half agreed and half told me. "But you should stop by a lake house outside Vancouver first. Malea owned it."

"And you haven't already sent knights there?" I asked skeptically.

"Of course I did," he said. "But the only thing they found was a dead double of Malea."

"What about the other numbers in Malea's cell phone?" I asked.

There was a long silence while Simon wrestled with his inclination to not tell me anything I didn't need to know. "We've verified that doubles of Malea have dropped dead in Los Angeles, London, Paris, and New York. Probably Tokyo and Hong Kong too, but we haven't found the bodies there yet."

Sig had said that making too many doubles was dangerous for a dalaketnon, that it divided their focus and could have weird repercussions, maybe even drive them insane. If Malea had been spreading her psyche out like butter on too many crackers, that might explain some of her actions too. But Malea was dead, her doubles were dead, and I didn't want to go back to talking about all of the things that Sig might know with Simon.

"What about Boston?" I asked. "Did the cell phone have any numbers there?"

Another silence. "We have a number with a Boston area code in the phone's contact list. It doesn't seem to exist anymore, and we're having a hard time proving that it ever did. Just check out the lake house."

"No," I said.

The line went quiet.

"I know you have whole teams of knights looking into whatever identity Malea was using to buy cars and lease lake houses, Simon," I said. "And you have other people trying to identify the DNA of the skinwalker who was calling himself Makisig. That house has been gone over, gone under, and gone around. I'd be about as useful as a blowtorch on a blimp."

"You have your senses," Simon pointed out.

"So does Virgil," I said. "And he's a damn good detective. It's not like I'm going to examine the carpet and tell you that someone wearing high heels with a limp they got from a ballet injury is hiding in a secret safe room somewhere in the house."

"You found some things nobody else did at Constance's house," Simon argued.

"We didn't know anything, and your chief investigator was working for the enemy," I responded. "We already know how the double died."

"What about your girlfriend's ability to talk to the dead?" Simon asked. "She's what this is really about, right? You still think I want to put her in an interrogation room."

"We don't even know if doubles have souls, and even if they do, very few souls leave ghosts behind, and if this one did, I don't want Sig trying to talk to the ghost of a psychotic bitch that she killed personally," I said. "Especially not one who can toss things around with her mind. And I *know* you have something planned for Sig. I don't know what, but something."

And he did too. I didn't know how much of that stuff Emil had said about the alliance with my pack being shaky and Simon needing to give me rope was true, but Simon would do something. Maybe just find a way to have a private conversation with Sig. Maybe find some way to threaten me and use that as leverage over her. Maybe find a way to get a drug into Sig's system or magically enchant her. Maybe try to seduce her. Simon had some kind of plan or strategy—hell, I would—and if he had been upfront with me about what that plan was, we would be having a different conversation.

Simon didn't deny anything. "We can't have two people in charge, Charming. You need to work for me or I need to work for you, and there's no way that I'm going to work for you."

"Don't think of me as a soldier," I said. "Think of yourself as a CIA handler, and I'm a double agent out in the field."

To his credit, he was still listening to me. "What are you talking about?"

"I want to go check with some of the contacts I've made over the years," I said. "People who would never talk to a knight. You've already got knights doing the stuff that knights can do. Drop the pissing contest and let me do the things that only I can do."

Simon's voice was taut. "You mean talking to the naga and the witch."

"I mean talking to whoever I mean," I said flatly. "I don't tell you about them. I don't tell them about you. That's the only way this is going to work."

Simon's voice got even tighter. "You want to go off the reservation."

"Don't use that expression around Ben," I told him. "And having me go after this group outside the normal channels a knight might use makes sense for all kinds of reasons."

Simon was torn between the need to assert his authority and the appeal of having a secret weapon that no one else knew about. "Promise me," he said at last.

"What?" I said.

"Give me your oath that you will check in with me and tell me when you find something useful," Simon repeated. "Or I'll come after you personally."

Simon had been making some judgments about me too.

"You have my word," I said. "If I don't check in, it's because I can't."

Simon still wasn't happy. "Someday, you're going to have to decide if you're still a knight or not."

He was probably right about that. My no longer not being a not-knight didn't even make sense grammatically.

The power was off for an entire block when I went back to the Maud Montgomery to check on Sig, a fact that seemed to have the male owner befuddled. He was feeding logs into a fire in the fireplace area and assured me that someone was looking into it.

"That's all right," I told him airily. "Have you seen my fiancée? She said something about going out."

His face turned red for some reason. I don't know if it was because he'd had an encounter with Sig or if someone had complained because she and I were making a little too much noise that morning. "I'm sure I haven't," he said a bit stiffly.

"Ah," I said. "Well, I hope you get the power thing sorted out."

"I wouldn't mind, but it's so unseasonably cold," he complained.

I stood there and savored the sentence for a moment. I'd never actually heard anyone say "unseasonably cold" out loud before. You have to take your small pleasures where you find them. "It's all good," I said as I went up the stairs. "The cold just makes the fire feel better."

He grunted.

The air got colder the higher I climbed, and I'm pretty sure thermodynamics aren't supposed to work that way in an enclosed space, but then, it wasn't thermodynamics at work. A pale grey brightness was coming through the lone window at the top of the stairs, and small slivers of light gleamed under the doors as if auditioning for an Emily Dickinson poem.

There were no sounds coming out of our room, no wind, no fresh smells, but there was…something. Something that went straight through my skin and made my muscles and gums tighten, pressing against my…my what? My soul? My chi? It didn't feel evil, but it didn't feel natural either.

Sig obviously wasn't done talking to her spirit guide yet.

I sat down at the top of the stairs and waited. I spent way too many years terrified of a dark demon wolf taking over my soul to be nonchalant. Unbidden, part of Saint Patrick's "Breastplate Prayer" came to me, and I chanted it silently to myself, as if I were back in a room with Father Eric glowering, and at me in particular. He always stayed close to make sure I was actually saying the words while the class learned guards and wards.

I bind unto myself today
The power of God to hold and lead,
His eye to watch, His might to stay,
His ear to hearken to my need.
The wisdom of my God to teach,
His hand to guide, his shield to ward,
The word of God to give me speech,
His heavenly host to be my guard.
Against the demon snares of sin,
The vice that gives temptation force,
The natural lusts that war within,
The hostile men that mar my course,
Or few, or many, far or nigh,
In every place and in all hours,
Against their fierce hostility,
I bind to me these holy powers.
Against all Satan's spells and wiles,

Against false words of heresy,
Against the knowledge that defiles,
Against the heart's idolatry,
Against the wizard's evil craft,
Against the death wound and the burning,
The choking wave and the poisoned shaft,
Protect me, Christ, till Thy returning.

The prayer both comforted me and made me feel like I was a nine-year-old boy terrified for my soul, and if you don't understand how a prayer can do both, all I can say is that you were obviously never raised Catholic. Somehow, I doubted that Father Eric would be all that surprised to find out that I was a werewolf now, sitting on a landing while my inhuman premarital lover communed with the dead.

I almost charged into the room to confront my fears, but I made myself wait like Sig had asked, not sure if I was being passive or wise. Often, the reckless things we do to make ourselves feel better when we're anxious have a nasty habit of masquerading as bravery, but they're really selfishness and desperation, and they don't take their masks off until you've already messed up and hurt somebody you care about. Surprise.

I rubbed my own breastplate absent-mindedly even though my chest shouldn't have been hurting anymore, not logically. Not literally. It felt like my heart could stop again at any moment, which is odd, because I have no idea what that feels like. I had been unconscious at the time. I obviously had some fresh PTSD to work through, but I couldn't afford to take an extended vacation. Someone had kidnapped Constance, and I was sworn to protect her. Everything that didn't fall between those two facts would just have to go play in traffic for a while.

I consciously slowed my breathing and focused on a spot

on the wall, focused on it so intently that it felt like the spot was getting bigger, actually moving toward me as its smaller details came into focus. When it felt like I was on the verge of squeezing through that spot, I widened my focus again, slowly expanding it around the spot in all directions until it included the floor and the ceiling, and then my awareness moved to the world behind me, the hall at my back, the owner still puttering and grunting downstairs. I put my right palm on my leg and focused on what I could feel with my fingers. Me. Here. Now.

I had felt Alison move through me after she died, because of Sig. That hadn't been evil. That had been a blessing. And if there was a God, I really believed that he, she, we, they, or it wasn't some sadistic referee calling technical fouls and violations. I just had to do my best and admit it and deal with it and try to do better when I screwed up. That's all any of us can do, and then we die, and then it's out of our hands.

Sig opened the door. She was dressed to leave, and she came over and sat by me at the top of the stairs and took my left hand in her right. "Hey."

I squeezed her hand back. "Did whatever you just did help?"

"Herja always helps. She thinks you're right, by the way. About drawing firmer boundaries."

"Mmmn" was the only comment I felt safe making.

"She also thinks men are a distraction that Valkyries can't afford," Sig said. "She says it always ends badly."

"That's what the ancient Greeks thought life was," I said. "A distraction that ends badly."

"If that's the kind of stuff you think about, I'm not going to leave you alone on steps anymore," Sig informed me.

"Yeah, well, the ancient Greeks weren't a real cheerful bunch," I said. "Neither were the ancient Norse, for that matter. How about we try to figure this out for ourselves?"

"That would be nice," she said.

Succeeding would be nice. The trying was probably going to be a pain in the ass. But it wasn't the right time to say that, so I filled her in on my conversation with Simon instead.

"How are we getting to Boston if we're staying away from the knights for a while?" Sig asked.

I actually had some money and fake identification hidden away in two places in Canada, but I hadn't made those kinds of provisions for Sig. I would have to start thinking about that kind of thing now. "I can get you there," I said.

And I did.

PART THE THIRD

*Your Mission, Should You
Live to Regret It*

~22~

PROXY LADY

The Scarborough Lodge was a small, posh hotel in Beacon Hill, Boston, one of those new buildings that try to look old and dignified while keeping everything unmarred, mass-produced, shiny, and symmetrical. Sig and I were sitting in the lounge area past the customer service lobby, in front of a fireplace that wasn't putting out any real heat. Scattered around us were men trying to maintain that precarious balance between dressing professionally and appearing young that characterizes the technological industry. They were all casting covert glances at Sig while they played with themselves. Well, okay, played with their electronic devices. It's not exactly the same thing, but it's close.

"You're thinking something sarcastic," Sig ventured.

"As often as not," I agreed.

"Your eyes have that glint," she elaborated. "And I'm bored."

"It's not really sarcastic," I explained. "I was just thinking about new buildings that try to look old. We have all of this advanced technology now, and nobody makes anything half as impressive or long-lasting as buildings that were built over a thousand years ago. It's a little sad that we might not ever have another medieval cathedral or ancient pyramid."

"You could look at it as encouraging," Sig argued. "Most of those places were built with generations of serfs or outright slaves."

"True enough," I conceded. "And I guess things like space stations and submarines and the Internet are pretty spectacular in their own way."

The men around us—and with only two exceptions, they were all men—were there to attend the Laissez Faire, a week-long symposium on the ongoing advances, applications, and legal ramifications of certain fields of virtual reality. Sig and I were waiting for her friend Parth, who was conducting a seminar in one of the small conference rooms that the hotel was using to host the event.

Like a lot of nagas, Parth has dealt with the boredom, apathy, and cynicism that often accompany being centuries old by devoting himself to the constant discovery of new things. Maybe he also bungee-jumps and studies craniosacral therapy and skateboards and swims with dolphins and that sort of thing, but most of Parth's attention seems to be devoted to exploring unsolved mysteries, which is often the same thing as a search for forbidden knowledge. This is one of the reasons Parth has evolved into a hacker of some skill while most beings with long life-spans tend to stay several generations behind the technological curve, myself included.

At some point, Parth's Internet explorations evolved into the creation of a software company, which evolved into a corporate entity that produces apps, online video games, website designs, and search engines. Parth still has his old hacker connections, but now he also has lots of legit cyber slaves sifting through the nets of raw data that his services pull in every day, and maybe some of his helpers are in the know, or maybe they all just think they're doing market research or looking for new ideas for fantasy games or PR gimmicks. I just don't know. Either way, Parth knows a lot, and what he doesn't know, he can usually find out fast. Sig calls Parth up on her smartphone whenever she needs to know something right away, and it's like she's talking to a magic mirror.

That's partly why I've never fully warmed to Parth. Fair or not, I have a hard time trusting anyone who makes himself that indispensable that quickly. It's the kind of thing I do when I'm pretending to be someone else so that I can find something out.

Which is why I observed, in a mild voice that didn't fool Sig for a second, "We rely on Parth an awful lot."

"Well, I suppose we could stand in the middle of South Station, yelling, *HELLO! HELLO! DOES ANYONE HERE HAVE A DRUG THAT LETS PEOPLE SEE THE FUTURE?*" Sig reflected thoughtfully. "It might alert the people we're after, though."

I smiled but stayed on track. "Does it strike you at all odd that Parth just happens to be in Boston, which just happens to be starting to look like the center of all the chaos that's swirling around the knights right now?"

"No," Sig said simply. "We already know he's a nosy bastard who's always poking into things. That's why he's useful."

She had a point. And I didn't really think Parth was the mysterious enemy we were trying to identify. I just wasn't ruling anything out.

As it turned out, though, Parth wasn't actually in Boston, anyway. When Sig and I entered the small conference room, it was Parth's...umm...I'm not sure what to call her. I mean, her name is Kimi, but I don't know if she's Parth's lover, protégée, partner, servant, or worshiper. She's an Indian woman in her mid-twenties, but all I know for sure about Kimi is that she comes from money, is some kind of business major from Virginia Tech, and seems to serve Parth with unswerving devotion.

Today, Kimi was wearing the sort of retro Miami Vice–style attire that Parth favors, a loose-fitting cream-colored suit over a light blue shirt that didn't have buttons. Her normally long hair was cut short and cinched tight in a samurai knot, and she was wearing some kind of monocle. The left eyepiece was a lens surrounded by a circle of thick, high-tech-looking plastic with the radius of a mini-pancake. Goggles were lying on the conference table in front of the empty seats. When Kimi spoke, she sounded like Parth, which was a little disorienting until I realized that the voice was coming from a pendant suspended from a necklace around her throat. "Hello, Sig. John."

"Kimi, swallow three times fast if you're still in there and need help," I said.

It was only because of my enhanced hearing that I heard Parth's voice come through much more quietly from some kind of device planted in Kimi's left ear. *Don't respond to him.*

"Don't listen to John," Sig said as she stepped forward to give Kimi a half-hug, which Kimi didn't avoid or return. Sig had once knocked Kimi out during a particularly tense exchange, and though they have made up, Kimi tends to move carefully around Sig. "You know how he is about interconnectivity. I don't think he actually knows what a hashtag is."

"I really don't," I agreed. "It sounds gruesome."

"What's that underneath your suit, Kimi?" Sig asked while Kimi stepped back.

"They're sensors." The slightly annoyed expression on Kimi's face actually matched the tone of Parth's voice. "Put on the VR goggles and you'll see why."

Since it was the probably the fastest way to get past all the nonsense, I did as instructed. When I slipped the goggles over my eyes, the room around me didn't look any different. I stared at my hand, half expecting to see a virtual version of it, or at least have it lit up in infrared, but when it appeared the same, I looked over at Kimi. Parth was sitting in her place. He was so lifelike that it took several seconds and some concentration to spot the telltale signs that he was a virtual-reality construct superimposed over a real background. Part of that was the way Parth was holding himself motionless. When he moved, his image blurred around the edges at certain transition points, and the juxtaposition was easier to spot.

"Kimi has agreed to act as my proxy," Parth said with a hint of smugness.

"Is that why you said you were the one meeting us here?" I asked. "To make a point?

"I am the one meeting you here," Parth said.

I thought about that. "I take it you can see through her monocle?"

"Yes," Parth said.

So, the real Parth could be hundreds or thousands of miles away, sitting somewhere with the same types of sensors coming out his wazoo. I don't know that any of the technology Parth was demonstrating was new, unless the feat he was pulling off was being done more cheaply or at a higher level of resolution than previous innovations. Still, it was a cute gimmick for a conference.

"Is the real you wearing any pants?" I asked.

"Shush, John," Sig cautioned. "You're about to get Parth started on what constitutes reality."

That was actually one of the most effective threats I've ever received. I shut up.

"Sig, is your hair pale, or is something wrong with the visual resolution?" I couldn't tell which possibility concerned Parth more.

"I had a bad ghost experience and my hair really turned white," Sig said. "I kind of like it."

"It suits you." Parth said it pleasantly, but I wondered what he meant by that.

"Speaking of different hair, why has Kimi cut her hair and dressed to look more like you?" Sig asked. "And why won't she talk to me?" Maybe Sig's own recent experience acting as someone else's proxy was making her sensitive.

"Part of the reason that I look as realistic as I do is that your brains are filling in gaps to resolve the differences between my virtual body and the background," Parth explained. "The human mind constantly struggles to impose order on the universe so that it will make sense, and because of that, it sees what it expects to see. We're testing to see if having a proxy remain silent and dress the same as its subject cuts down on the amount of cognitive dissonance."

Even I could see some of the useful applications of the technology Parth was messing with. Brilliant surgeons. Bomb-disposal experts. Businessmen making physical transactions. Military leaders. All of them could monitor and direct subordinates to act on their behalf far more effectively with the kind of gear Parth was using than through a cell phone or a laptop screen.

"Is it working?" I asked.

"Let's just say that I wouldn't invest in hotel or airline stock if I were you," Parth said smoothly. "In another ten years, middle-management business trips will be an unnecessary expense." Then I heard his voice whisper in the ear of a Kimi I couldn't see. *Check your watch.* The image of Parth in front of me checked its watch. "But maybe we should focus on why you're here."

Sig just came out with it. "We're trying to track down a drug that gives visions of the future."

"You are?" Parth asked. "Or John is? Or the Round Table? Or the Knights Templar?"

"Sig's helping me," I said. "And I'm helping them."

"That's what we do, Parth," Sig reminded him. "We help each other."

"I will tell you this much," Parth said. "A few months ago, a dead woman approached me and told me that she had a drug like the one that you are describing. She said a group she represented wanted to set up a system of exchange."

I didn't bother pointing out that Parth had never mentioned any of this at the time. "Why do you say she was a dead woman?"

"Because," Parth said, "I had her fingerprints analyzed, and the person they belonged to had died in a fire months previously."

"That would do it," I agreed, but what I was really thinking was that a skinwalker had skinned a victim so it could use her image and then burned her actual body to disguise the fact.

"What did she want from you?" Sig asked.

"Whoever she represented wanted me to give them access to my channels of information," Parth said. "Contacts. Passwords. Accounts. And in exchange, they would give me a small but regular supply of their drug."

The deal Parth was describing sounded similar to the one that had been offered to Malea. Then something occurred to me as I worked it through. "You sneaky bastard," I said. "That's when you became interested in the chen."

Smile appreciatively, an electronic voice whispered in the background, and Parth, or the pixels that looked like him, smiled. "Yes, it was."

Chen are ageless beings that live on the bottom of the ocean and look like giant clams. Some people say they're shapechanged dragons. Some say they're sleeping gods. All I know for sure is that chen release bubbles whose shimmery surfaces reflect visions. I'd had such a vision in the tea house of Akihiko Watanabe, and after Akihiko was dead, Parth had laid claim to the chen for services rendered.

"Wait." Sig was reorienting. "Are you saying these people somehow harvested this drug from a chen?"

"I doubt it," I said automatically. "The visions the chen give aren't necessarily the future. Sometimes they're visions of the past or someplace else in the present."

"You would know," Parth agreed. "Besides, the chen's visions enter the brainstem through the visual cortex. The drug we're talking about travels through the bloodstream."

"Yeah, that too," I said. "And the visions a chen gives aren't fatal, and people were still dying when this drug was being tested a few months ago."

"The drug is dangerous for *human* people," Parth emphasized. "I tried a sample and was just fine."

Yeah, well, nagas can pretty much survive anything this side of a direct nuclear strike. Still, that was an interesting nugget. "You wanted the chen because you got obsessed the way nagas do, but this time it was with the idea of seeing the future," I accused. "And that gave these people leverage over you. So, you used us to try to get you your own kind of future fix."

"You have a very real gift for making the miraculous sound shabby, John," Parth observed. "Sometimes, it's amusing. Sometimes, it's a bit tiresome."

"Walking around in a state of awe all the time would be bad

for my pants," I explained. "Anyhow, the chen wasn't exactly what you were looking for, was it? The chen only shows what it wants to show when it wants to show it."

Sig was tired of recapping. "Why did you say you'd only tell us *this much,* Parth?"

"Because I am willing to work with you and John," Parth said. "But I can't work with knights."

Sig absorbed that silently. I didn't. "Politics?"

"Business," Parth corrected, as if the two were different these days. "Our interests don't coincide right now. I want to find out more about this drug, and the knights will want to locate it and destroy it, or keep it and not share its secrets with anyone."

We didn't deny it. Instead, Sig said, "What if I tell you that the people behind this drug are truly evil? That any information you give us might save our lives? Or that we might save other lives?"

An electronic voice whispered, *Spread your palms out.*

Parth spread his palms out. "Any information you give me might save *my* life, Sig. I'm your friend. I am not your employee or your...what is that unfortunate expression? Bitch? I will not be taken advantage of."

"Taken advantage of?" Sig repeated incredulously.

"You want me to tell you everything, but you don't want to tell me anything," Parth pointed out. "That is not a relationship between equals."

It occurred to me that Parth might have another reason for acting through a proxy. Maybe he didn't trust me any more than I trusted him. If that was the case, whatever was going on between him and Kimi didn't quite seem like a relationship between equals either.

Enough bullshit. "I'll trade you one piece of significant information for another," I offered.

I really didn't want Parth to get his hands on the drug, but I would rather risk that than delay.

"That is acceptable," Parth acceded. "If you go first."

"The dead person who visited you?" I said. "That was a skinwalker."

Parth considered this. *Nod,* that electronic voice hummed in the background, and he did. Or Kimi did. Whatever. "The drug you're looking for is being called *Glimpse.*"

I decided that was a trade of equal value and continued. "The people who tried to deal with you also tried to make a deal with a dalaketnon," I said. "They wanted access to the dalaketnon's door magic."

Somewhere, the real Parth made a grunting sound through Kimi's pendant. I thought I knew what he was thinking. More rivals. "Did you kill the dalaketnon?"

"This is an exchange, remember?" I reminded him. "It's your turn."

Wave your hand dismissively, the digital voice whispered, but the Parth I was looking at got it wrong. Virtual Parth made a *get away from me, peasants* gesture instead of a *that doesn't matter* one. "You killed it. Of course you did."

I kind of resented that.

"We're still waiting," Sig said. She smelled a little pissed and a little sad at the way things were going.

"The chen gave me a vision," Parth said reluctantly. "I saw the dead woman...the skinwalker, if you are right...with a bunch of young men dressed like members of a street gang."

"Which gang?" I demanded. "What were their colors? What was their ethnicity? Did they have any significant tattoos?"

"The information I gave you was of the same level of usefulness as the information you gave me," Parth asserted, and I couldn't really disagree. I wasn't telling Parth anything about

Constance or the Templars, but did I want to tell him that the skinwalker was working with other skinwalkers? That fact seemed minor and harmless, but it was confusing, and figuring out the bit that doesn't make any sense is often the key to figuring out everything else. Besides, if Parth was my rival, pursuing a lone skinwalker might lead him down some false trails.

"There's more than one skinwalker working together," Sig said, and I kept my expression neutral while I cursed silently. She wasn't being stupid. Angry or not, Sig cared about Parth and didn't want him running into more trouble than he was expecting.

"Ah." Parth exhaled softly. He seemed to find that information worthwhile. "The gang members were Caucasian, and they all wore red baseball caps."

"I've heard enough if you have," I told Sig, and she agreed. We made reasonably polite if somewhat stiff farewells after that. No one said any thank-yous. Instead, Parth asked, "Would you mind filling out a form and answering a few questions about your experience with my proxy?"

He was serious.

∾23∾

EXCUSE ME, WAITER? THERE'S
A GUY IN MY SOUP…

Intermittent licks of far-off lightning lit up the bay as Sig and I strode along the shore of Boston Harbor. We were weaponless but far from defenseless, wearing black hoodies beneath our winter canvas jackets and waterproof waders over our shoes. The beam of the Graves, the tallest lighthouse around for miles and miles, swooped through the dark at regular intervals as we drew closer to the wharf.

A high and light voice tinkled out of the fog like distant wind chimes. "Is that you, Liam? It's been a long time."

"Hey, Babe." I indicated Sig. "This is Britte." While I was talking, I unshouldered the waterproof knapsack I was carrying—most definitely not sealskin—and held it out to the air.

"Babe?" Sig asked.

"My name is Babette," a voice said without inflection, and then its owner materialized out of the fog like the unearthly being she was, all five foot four and one hundred and sixty pounds of her. Babette looked like she was still sixteen though she had to be at least twice that, wearing an olive tank top and blue shorts despite the cold. Her curly black hair didn't seem to be lank or lifeless despite the damp either. "Liam likes to tempt fate."

"I never noticed." Sig's voice was dry. It was about the only thing around that was.

"I was starting to wonder if you were going to show up," I told her.

"Pietr told me to ignore any new werewolves." Babette kept her eyes on me while she spoke, but I couldn't tell if she was really looking at me or not. She had a kind of far-off stare that seemed to see everything and nothing. "Some of them are working with knights now. But I know you."

Babette took the knapsack out of my hands and opened it, sifting through some dark chocolate bars, a box of cigarette cartons, and a bottle of whiskey.

At some point, either Babette had committed suicide by drowning herself or someone else had drowned her. Whichever it was, for some reason the ocean had spit Babette back. There are theories about whether rusalka are living or dead or undead, about why rusalka are always female, and why the suicidal ones seem to be lonely and looking for love and the murdered ones seem to be homicidal and looking for vengeance, but these are like the theories people come up with to explain gravity and time. Sometimes, the universe just does what the universe wants to do, and screw you if you can't take a joke. I would like to think that Babette's return is a second chance rather than a blessing or a curse—that all existence is what we choose to make of it. But let's be honest: I have an obvious motive for not wanting to believe that monsters are predestined to walk a dark road by their very nature.

Apparently, my bribe was sufficient. Babette shouldered the knapsack without comment and looked at Sig. Somehow, her neutral expression and passive tone contained an inexplicable and chilly menace. "Does *Britte* know the rules?"

Sig wasn't offended, but she wasn't impressed either. "First rule of Tide Club: do not talk about Tide Club. Second rule of Tide Club: do not talk about Tide Club."

That could have been a little awkward since only God knew how long it had been since Babette had seen an electronic screen of any kind, but the rusalka was used to letting cultural contemporary references slide off and around her. She just kept staring.

"She knows," I assured Babette. "Does Nikki still come around?"

Babette's mouth was straight and unmoving. If her face had been a heart monitor, she would have been flatlining. "You act like it's been a hundred years instead of one or two."

It had actually been closer to thirty, but it seemed rude to point that out. If Babette's awareness of passing time was a little shaky, that was probably a good thing. So I waited.

"Of course Nikki still comes around." The rusalka turned and walked beneath the large network of piers. "And around and around and around." The solid, tangible knapsack I'd brought was slung over Babette's shoulder, but the water washing over her ankles didn't foam or splash when it made contact with her skin, not upon arrival and not when it went back into the sea.

Sig and I followed, and I had to force myself not to hurry. I had a feeling that if the fog closed entirely around Babette, I would never see her again, but that was just me trying to maintain some illusion of control. The rusalka didn't want to lose me, and if she decided otherwise, there wasn't a whole hell of a lot that I could do about it.

We splashed beneath a boardwalk, my cheeks beginning to sting in the bitter damp, and then Babette stopped, and the sand beneath her feet oozed and shifted into a sinkhole. I'd seen this before, but it was still the damnedest thing. Instead of rushing in to fill the hole, water oozed out of it as if a giant invisible fist was pressing down onto a wound. Then the hole caved in and a set of descending wooden stairs was revealed. Babette disappeared into the dark tunnel.

"What kind of a bar is this Buried Treasure?" Sig said doubtfully.

I wanted to say a sandbar, but I resisted the impulse. "Come on. The clam chowder is really good."

We went down the stairs, and after a brief interval of darkness and a sharp right turn, we found ourselves on a wooden walkway. Kerosene lamps hung from the planks over our heads, and I could see that the wooden rails on either side of us were surrounded by solid walls of packed damp sand instead of open air. Unlike Babette's bare feet, our boots were splashing in the inch of water that covered the walkway. Be it lake, river, sea, or ocean, rusalkas have to stay in physical contact with whatever large body of water they drowned in. According to some tales, rusalka wander the shorelines, never aging, until they've lived out the life-span that they would have lived out naturally, and then they just disappear. Other stories claim that rusalka don't go away until they have found love or been avenged. I don't know if either is true, or both, or neither. Rusalka only become knight business when isolation drives them over the edge and they start drowning people, either out of rage or in a calculated attempt to create other rusalkas for company.

Sig reached out and almost touched the sand walls surrounding us, then pulled her hand back, afraid that the walls would burst apart like a popped bubble. "I had no idea rusalkas were this powerful."

"They're not," I said. "This place is run by the Tomovs, a bunch of half-breed vodyanoi."

Water trolls.

I heard chanting before we got to the bar proper, not some sorcerous ritual—or at least I don't think so—but English words spoken in the cadences of freestyle rap with a slightly Gaelic lilt. The scent of more than half a dozen species intermingled with a musk of brine and mild decay and cigarette smoke. A lot of the supernatural creatures that can pass for human picked up smoking between the 1800s and 2000s, and most of them don't have to worry about cancer.

There was no door to the Buried Treasure. The walkway just opened up into a large square room whose walls were hardened sand and whose floor and ceiling were planks propped up by the same kind of round wooden columns that hold up docks. Wreaths of cigarette smoke curled lazily in the lamplight, creating a slight haze. The room was still submerged in an inch of water, and there were tables and booths that looked like they'd been made out of packing crates, but the bar was sturdy-looking and the glasses were clean and there were enough customers to half fill the place.

The source of the rapping was a medium-sized blue-skinned man standing next to the bar. The sleeves of a flannel workman's shirt emerged from beneath the red tee he was wearing over cargo pants, and the strands of seaweed coming out of his skull were braided. His swaying was both rhythmical and slightly inebriated, and it brought him stumbling into my path. I might have thought that it was an accident if Babette hadn't somehow managed to disappear after leading me toward him. The blue man continued chanting, his solid-black eyes looking directly at me, his breath a salty puff of alcohol and burnt ozone. *"I don't care what you be knowin',"* he proclaimed. *"Don't care where you be goin' / don't care where you come from / you march to your own drum!"*

The blue man stopped expectantly, and the bar went quiet for a moment, not that it had been that loud to begin with. The Buried Treasure wasn't that kind of place. The blue man didn't have a six-gun strapped to his side, but there was a distinct tension in the air. I picked the verse up, though my cadences lacked his flair. " *'Cause the people who will lead you / are only gonna feed you / enough to survive / but you'll never be alive."* The intense focus melted off of his face as he considered that, but the offering must have been good enough, because he picked his rap up, dusted it off, and made his way back to a more open space, still chanting.

That could have been bad—storm kelpies take their poetry challenges seriously—but the hard truth is, anyone who can't handle impromptu rhyme and riddle contests has no business being in my world.

In the absence of the rusalka, there was no hostess. Pietr nodded at me from where he was sullenly towering over the bar like a big craggy rock that some pranksters had put an apron and bifocals on. He yanked his big greying head towards the common area, so Sig and I threaded our way through the tables. As we made our way past a bunch of boisterous *fir darrig*—rat boys—one of them furtively darted a hand out to either pinch Sig's ass or pick her pocket, but I grabbed his hand in midair and bent his fingers back painfully. He basically looked like a hairy hipster—his nose and jaw were a little elongated, but the beard would help him pass for a norm—but when the rat boy snarled, he exposed some seriously prominent buck teeth. His neighbor tried to stand up, but I stepped on the hairless tail that was emerging beneath his shirt and over the back of his pants, and he was pulled back down into his seat. Another rat boy tried to rise, but Sig turned and casually put a palm on his shoulder. Or maybe it wasn't so casual if the creak of bone and the way his face paled were any indication.

"Pietr!" I called out as I forced my rat boy's hand down and pressed his palm flat on the table. "Buy this table a round on me." The rat boys stilled, their noses all instinctively tilting upward in a way that was almost comical while they smelled what was coming off of me and didn't pick up any particular fear or overt aggression. I winked at them, patted the top of the rat boy's hand as I released it, and then Sig and I kept walking. Several of the rat boys cursed, but none of them got up to follow.

We passed another table where a normal young human male was staring rapturously at the undine who had brought him there. The undine was dark-haired, dark-eyed, pale-skinned, curvy, smooth, and beautiful. The human was pale-skinned as well, but there the similarities ended. The man's jacket had come out of an army surplus store, presumably for ironic or economic reasons, and he had a shy, gentle quality. Curly-haired, skinny, and clearly besotted, he was the closest thing the Buried Treasure had to a Happy Meal.

Sig and I had been partners long enough to know to find a table instead of a booth, sitting across from each other so that she could watch over my shoulder and I could watch over hers. Booths would have offered more protection, but we both like our freedom of movement. "Is your friend here?" Sig asked.

I looked over the rest of the place without making any pretense about it. There was a hag drinking by herself. I couldn't identify her exact species by scent, but the old crone had powerful-looking shoulders and long arms and very sharp nails. A heavily bearded male with olive skin and sandy blond hair was sitting with a selkie. The hair on the underside of his jaw almost covered a patch of skin that had been burned in a way I'd seen before. Sometimes, hybrids will scar their gills just enough to make them look like damaged skin but still be functional. They call such patches *watermarks*. I knew the woman was a selkie because she'd draped her seal skin over the back of her chair like a coat.

The only thing that really concerned me was the male naga talking to a gorgon. Gorgons can see the future. Was it really a coincidence that another naga was talking to a precognitive? Was the naga an ally of Parth's or a rival? Or had this naga been approached by our enemy just like Parth had and reacted in a similar fashion, pursuing alternative means of seeing the future? I would have used my hearing to eavesdrop, but the two were speaking in a Mediterranean-sounding language that I didn't know. Greek, I think.

"Not yet," I told Sig, and then Denis Tomov came over and took our orders. There was no menu. The daily offerings were scrawled on a piece of slate for those whose noses weren't sharp enough to smell them. Denis was Pietr's son and looked like a tall yet squat old man. The tips of large ears stuck out from Denis's tousled hair, and he had an unfortunate propensity for skin infections—his fingers were thick with warts and slightly webbed. Denis made a grunting sound with a question mark at the end of it, and parallel slits in his neck puckered. He did the table-serving because he was the social one in the family.

If Denis remembered me, he gave no sign of caring. Sig and I both ordered clam chowder, and after Denis departed, Sig picked up where she'd left off. "So, you think this Nikki will show up tonight?" Sig was too smart to bad-mouth a place where the regulars were highly irregular and many of them had extra-sensitive hearing—but I could tell that she wasn't thrilled at the idea of spending several days hanging around.

"If not tonight, soon," I said offhandedly. "Nikki's a creature of habit."

Sig's brow furrowed. "You said it's been a few decades. I thought nixies were supposed to be impulsive and always changing."

"Sure," I said. "Just like werewolves are always hot-tempered and territorial."

Sig's look spoke worlds. Hell, it contained alternate universes.

"Come on, us supernaturals might be closer to our primal instincts than most norms," I defended. "But you know we're not all the same."

"That's true," Sig granted. "And this Nikki goes against nixie stereotypes?"

"Well, maybe not on the surface," I admitted. "But I think so much of Nikki's life is in a constant state of flux that she clings to whatever rituals and habits she can."

Sig gave me another look that wasn't hard to read. I rarely establish regular routines, varying times and routes and destinations out of instinct. I still go through burner phones like some people go through cigarettes, use cash whenever possible, and rarely form attachments to any material possessions that don't have sharp edges. But that said, I have a lot of habits for channeling stress that have assumed the importance of religious ceremonies. My reading, coffee, meditation, hot baths, hikes, katas—if I neglect them for too long, I start to get cranky and tense. But Sig let it go.

Denis brought us the appetizer, a fish stew served in a large polished oyster shell. The stew smelled delicious. It was a thick and slightly yellowish brown soup with onions, garlic, parsley, tomatoes, mussels, clam strips, and thick wedges of potato floating around in it. Sig had half raised the spoon to her mouth when I said, "Hold it."

Sig slowly lowered her spoon. I picked up the whole oyster shell in front of me and held it under my nose. Yeah. I knew that smell. Human flesh. Was it a test or a gesture of disrespect? Or had the place just gotten that rough around the edges in the last few decades? I put the bowl back down and gestured to bring Denis back over.

The vodyanoi positioned himself so that I was entirely in his shadow. There was a reason the Tomovs didn't have a bouncer. "What?"

"Some of this meat is human." I said. "And no offense, but I still kind of think of myself that way."

Denis's features gave no hint of what he was thinking. I had leaned back in my chair by this point, tapping the oyster shell with the edge of my finger. These motions put my hand near the bowl in case I wanted to hurl it in Denis's face and also put my foot close to his knee in case I wanted to kick out and propel myself backwards.

Unexpectedly, an ice fissure of a smile cracked across Denis's craggy face. "It must be that marine biologist who kept coming around the docks. I guess Mom finally had enough of him."

"I guess so," I agreed as if that made perfect sense, and I suppose it did from a purely rational perspective. Get rid of a pest and add to the soup stock. Win win. "Could we just have some scallops and fried potatoes while we wait for the chowder?"

Denis grunted something that might have been agreement and took the oyster-shell bowls back into the kitchen. A moment later, a guttural voice began cursing in some Slavic language, and Denis snapped something back in the same tongue before two splashes punctuated the discussion. I assume that was the stew returning from whence it came. God, I hope that was the stew returning from whence it came.

Sig had an odd expression. "Who's talking to him?"

"The cook, Lenke," I said. "Pietr's wife."

Sig made a humming sound. "I thought there were only male vodyanoi."

"No, there are females," I said. "But the vodyanoi like to keep them out of sight. I don't know why." And I really didn't. It's a mistake to judge supernaturals by human standards.

There was another guttural rattle, and Sig smiled faintly. "She just called us weeping hemorrhoids."

"Well, we did send her food back," I reminded her. "All artists want to be appreciated."

"If you didn't have such a good sense of smell, I would be a cannibal right now," Sig said mildly. "I'm tempted to express some displeasure of my own."

"I guess I could ask Denis if they have any of those little comment cards." Which was my way of saying that I was pissed too but there was no percentage in starting a fucking fight with a bunch of fucking vodyanoi on their home fucking turf, because even if we won, the sea that their fucking magic was holding back would come crashing through the fucking walls, and between a burst fucking dam in New York and a flooded fucking hallway on another world, I'd had quite enough of being two steps in front of massive columns of rushing fucking water, thank you very fucking much. Especially since werewolves aren't immune to drowning.

"Do that," Sig said, which was her way of letting me know she'd follow my lead since I knew the territory, but she wasn't happy about it. Then she reached across the table and twined her index finger around mine. My girlfriend was agreeing not to remove anyone's vital organs with a salad fork for my sake. It was a sweet moment. Too bad cell phones didn't work in places like that. We could have taken a selfie.

In any case, the scallops and fried potatoes were excellent, and the clam chowder was better. Sig and I were still working on second bowls of the latter when a leanly muscled, brown-haired male in a tan all-weather coat and a young female in a green slicker followed the rusalka in. The female was human. The male was not. Babette stepped aside and the man focused on me with shrewd, alert blue eyes. His face was hard but not necessarily unkind, the lips looking like they were on the verge of a slight smile, the nose straight as a blade. His hair was just short enough that it wouldn't be easy to grab in a fight. I didn't recognize his features, but his smell was familiar. I mean, her smell. I think. The nix wasn't particularly happy to see me, but it didn't evidence any displeasure either. We weren't enemies.

"That's Nikki," I murmured to Sig.

"How close were you and this nix again?" Sig asked in a low voice of her own.

"We got along," I said. "Why are you asking like that?"

"The coloring is different, but he looks a little like you," Sig commented.

The man approached our table, careful to keep his hands visible. "Liam, is that you? I figured you'd be dead by now."

"I get that a lot," I said, and made a slight face as if I was struggling to remember him. "Nick, isn't it?"

A grin flashed across his face. "Nikki is fine, if you want. Adriana knows the truth. And anyone else who cared would just assume you were ending it with a Y instead of an I anyhow." The last time I'd seen this particular nix, it had been a beautiful woman. While a human's body is two-thirds water, a nix's is more like nine-tenths, and their bodies move fluidly in more ways than one.

"I call him Nicholas," the woman offered.

"And she's the only one who does," the nix added firmly.

"This is Britte." I tilted my head at Sig. "My partner."

"So, it's okay if I refer to you as a male and call you Nick, then?" Sig offered her hand and the nix took it. "Nicky makes me think of a little boy."

Nick pulled up a chair for his date. She was short, with even shorter brown hair and big eyes, round and curvy. Her smile was shy and delighted, and when she took her slicker off, she was wearing a black T-shirt and a lot of tattoos. "Hmmmn,"

Nick said thoughtfully. "A little boy. Maybe I should try that. I don't think I've ever really spent a lot of time being a child. Especially when I was one."

"Watch out," I warned Sig. "A few drinks and he'll start crying and saying *Rosebud* over and over."

Nick laughed. "Watch out yourself. Most people under thirty don't watch *Citizen Kane* anymore. You don't want to give yourself away."

"I've seen it," Adriana scolded Nick archly, but she was at least half putting it on. "And you'd better not become a little boy either. I'm not into that."

"So...ummm...Nick here can look like anyone he wants to?" Sig asked Adriana carefully.

Adriana was very animated. She smelled scared but also excited, riding the feeling like a surfer on a very big wave. "He sure can. I've been working my way through the whole Celtics lineup this month."

I could see Sig processing that, and I felt a pang of alarm and jealousy. I'm not proud of it; I'm just not denying it.

Nick coughed. "Adriana, this is Liam. He's a werewolf I met a few times back in the eighties. Or was it the nineties?"

"It blurs for me too," I admitted.

"An honest-to-god werewolf?" Adriana's eyes were shining, and maybe it explained some of why Nick was with her. Some long-lived supernaturals like to hook up with mortals to re-experience the world vicariously through unjaded eyes. "I've been hoping to meet one of you."

"You should be hoping the opposite," I said dryly. "Whatever you're thinking, I guarantee it's not like that."

Adriana looked slightly hurt, and Sig patted the back of her hand. "It's okay. He's actually saying that because he's protective."

"And old-fashioned," Nick proclaimed loftily. "Another thing that people like us have to watch out for."

"Liam refuses to get involved with social media too," Sig told Nick.

Nick's face grew serious. "That's actually a good thing. It's gotten way too easy for corporations and governments to track people. That's starting to be a real problem for people like us."

Maybe it wasn't odd that the conversation had gone this route. You meet a sports fanatic, you wind up talking about sports. You meet a nix, you talk about the ins and outs of constantly changing identities. But I wanted to move things along even if I didn't want to be too obvious about it. "That's actually why I was hoping to meet you here, Nick."

Nick wasn't surprised, but his face only showed polite interest. "Why is that?"

"It's time for me to build a new cover identity," I lied. "I'm either going to have to retire the name Liam or start dyeing my hair grey and using a cane. But doing that kind of thing right takes money."

"And that's a problem?" Nick asked blandly.

"It's been a lot harder to find my kind of work with all of these stories about werewolves teaming up with knights," I said. "I was hoping you could help me find something around here."

Nick stroked his chin. "I know about a car wash that's really a drop-off and pickup point for meth. It's a pretty smooth operation. Any car can come and go at any time."

"You do that sort of thing?" Adriana asked, looking first at Nick, then at me with a different sort of speculation. She was in her mid- to late twenties and seemed very young to me, and it made my heart ache. What the hell was Nick doing, bringing an innocent like this to a place like this?

"That's how Liam and I met," Nick told her, and then his face grew somber. He mouthed the name "Chris."

Adriana's face cleared, and she looked sad for a moment. So, Nick really had told her everything. Not just the supernatural stuff. Heroin had been pretty big in certain parts of Boston the last time I'd passed through—it probably still was, even if meth was getting all the headlines currently—and I had been pretending to be an addict and hanging out in a flophouse so that I could find just the right kind of dealer to rob. I was looking for a middleman in the drug pipeline, someone not too bright with a lot of money lying around in cash—a low-level unconnected guy who couldn't go to the police and wasn't likely to report a missing ten thousand or so to his suppliers because even if they believed him, they might kill him on general principle.

Nick—actually Nikki back then—had just lost a lover named Chris to the drug. The dealer I was zeroing in on had cut the shit he was dealing too many times, and this Chris had overdosed, trying to find the right balance. Nikki had been tracking down everyone involved and killing them. I had stopped Nikki from beating information out of one of Chris's former acquaintances by plunging a hypodermic needle full of heroin into her—a nix's system absorbs drugs quickly and processes them very quickly, so you have a very short window where you can inject them with something disorienting and soluble and attack them while they're having trouble holding themselves together.

We'd had a long conversation when Nikki woke up, a ranting, sobbing marathon session. Nikki promised not to kill me if I would give her the name of the dealer we were both looking for. Then she offered to let me keep any money we found on the dealer's premises—but I refused. I'm not sure why. I was perfectly willing to rob the dealer and wasn't inclined to interfere if Nikki did track the dealer down and kill him. But I wasn't willing to hand over the dealer's name so that someone else could kill him while I stole his money. I had no idea why then, and I'm still not sure now, which made it very hard to explain that particular moral boundary to Nikki, but she seemed to have worked more than one kind of poison out of her system when all the screaming and threatening were over. I'm not sure it really mattered what we said. Just the fact that we were talking was enough.

It was Nikki who later introduced me to the Buried Treasure. Now it was a new beginning and Nikki was Nick, and I was saying: "I'd prefer to stay away from the human criminal world as much as possible for a while. I might have gotten in a little situation."

Nick smiled, more to show that he understood than because he was amused. "So, your kind of work . . . I never did figure out what that was exactly, Liam."

"That's because there is no *exactly*," I said. "I find things. I deliver things. I protect people or property. I collect debts."

"So, you two are professional improvisers," Nick suggested as Denis brought him a red wine in a tall beer glass without being asked. The kelpie was rapping about war and children in the background, and it was kind of interesting, but I maintained my focus.

"That's a very polite way of putting it," Sig said. "Thank you."

Nick's answering grin had a bit of a roguish quality. "How did you wind up with such a striking partner, Liam?" Something about the way he said *striking* suggested that six-foot-tall women who looked like a slightly more buxom and long-haired versions of Ronda Rousey weren't really his thing.

I shrugged. "I got lucky."

Adriana made a noise of sentimental approval, then looked at Sig quizzically. "Umm...if you don't mind me asking, what are you?"

"I don't mind," Sig said gently. "But I'm not going to answer."

Nick cleared his throat and looked at Adriana a little uncomfortably. "It's considered rude to ask questions like that unless you're offering something in return."

"Well...I'm a music teacher?" Adriana said uncertainly.

I gave her a faint smile. "The thing is, a lot of the people in this room can hear us and smell what we are and what we've been doing and even what we're feeling. There's sort of an unspoken understanding that privacy is extra important in our world because it's so hard to come by."

Adriana was a little taken aback. "Oh."

Nick seemed a bit uncomfortable too. "Britte doesn't know anyone else here, Adriana."

She turned her answer into another question. "Well...I don't either?"

"As long as nobody else knows what Britte is, they have to think twice about messing with her because they don't know what she's capable of," I elaborated. "Your situation is a little different. Everybody knows what you are. Most of us don't think you're a threat, and you're a guest of Nick's, and he's a regular. Britte and I aren't."

"Oh," Adriana said again in an even smaller voice.

"It's okay," Nick assured her. "But it's best to let people like us offer information voluntarily, or formally offer an exchange."

"But you introduced Liam as a werewolf," Adriana said. She wasn't arguing. She was refusing to be intimidated and trying to learn. I respected that.

"Everyone who can smell me knows what I am anyway," I explained. "Werewolves and vampires aren't really the most powerful supernatural creatures around; we're just the most numerous. It's because we don't have to have kids to reproduce. Britte is more exotic."

"She certainly is." Nick looked at Sig thoughtfully, and Adriana smacked him on his arm. He laughed, then grew serious. "You know, Liam, it's too bad you didn't show up a few days ago. The Redcaps were asking around about werewolf packs. I think they were looking for someone who might be willing to work with them."

If I weren't so careful about monitoring my breathing, my pulse would have quickened. "Redcaps?"

Nick took a pull off of his red wine as if it were ale. "A new gang in Boston. But you know, it's probably better that you weren't around, now that I think about it. They're nasty pieces of work."

"Is this like a gang that wears red baseball caps, or are you talking about actual Redcaps?" I asked.

Nick's mouth kinked. "A bit of both. The leaders came over straight from the old country."

This was bad. Very, very bad. Back in the day—by which I mean at least eight or nine centuries ago—Redcaps were the uncouth thugs of the unseen world. They were one of several species that acted as leg-breakers and bully boys for the Fae, and Redcaps looked the part: squat and muscular sociopaths with sharp talons and needle teeth. What made the Redcaps truly dangerous, though, was their speed. Unlike most Fae, Redcaps don't study magic, can't charm for squat, and as far as their ability to shapechange goes, Redcaps are limited to appearing like old men or teenagers. Redcaps are blurs in motion when they've got their elf on though. It is axiomatic that no being on two legs has ever successfully outrun one.

The Redcaps in the old tales had a reputation for crudity as well as cruelty, and they weren't welcome at High Fae functions. Supposedly, Redcaps belch and fart when they feel like it, relieve themselves wherever they feel like it, and have sex with whatever they feel like however they feel like it, which is why some of their half-breed castoffs are still around today. And a Redcap's lust for violence is a thing of legend among legends.

What I find interesting, though, is that the Redcaps' supposed nature seems more like a case of nurture. The Fae have a caste system that makes medieval feudalism look socially liberal and progressive, and it is clear that the High Fae found having an entire species specifically designed to do their dirty work extremely convenient. Redcaps always sport red headwear because they have no choice. They are under an enchantment that compels them to wear hats that are dyed with the blood of their victims and lined with skin from those same victims' scalps. According to lore, if the red color of a Redcap's hat ever completely fades, the Redcap dies.

Redcaps are also born under a compulsion to wear heavy footgear weighted down with metal. Supposedly, it's the only thing that keeps their speed manageable, because the High Fae don't like their servants being too powerful. It all sounds like a spell meant to ensure that the Redcaps never give peace a chance and never get too dangerous at the same time. It would be entirely Faelike to sneer at the Redcaps for their limitations while taking great pains to make sure that the Redcaps could never rise above them. That tends to be the way with all oppressors, come to think of it.

And I knew firsthand how good the Fae were at making enchantments that would ensure an entire class or species would serve them loyally over centuries.

"Redcaps are muscle," I said. "Who are they working for?"

"You'd have to ask them. Not that I'd recommend it." Nick did a slight double take as something occurred to him, and he scanned the bar more carefully. "Actually, there are usually a few of them hanging around here."

At those words, my sphincter dilated. Sometimes, I know things, and my conscious mind goes into overdrive trying to trace the connections back so that I can figure out how I know what I know. Simon had said something about trying to track down people who had access to a drug that let them see the future. He had said that even though knights don't show up on a psychic's radar, if psychics couldn't see the future at a certain time or place, they would know knights were going to be there. A kind of precognition by omission.

I was a knight in this bar, looking for the people who had threatened Constance. The people who had threatened Constance had a drug that let people see the future. Parth had said that a gang wearing red baseball caps were involved. Nick said the Redcaps usually came here. Now the Redcaps weren't here. Put all that together and...

The Redcaps weren't here because someone had shaken their Magic 8 Ball about this evening and the answer had come up REPLY HAZY. TRY AGAIN, and they had figured out that a knight was going to be here looking for them.

Right now. Right here. Me.

I cast around for possible weapons while Sig asked Nick why the Redcaps were looking for werewolves. I already knew why. They had been looking for some werewolves who would ambush Ben if given a chance, and eventually, the Redcaps had found the Dogtown bunch that had attacked us.

I saw some kerosene lamps that would spread flaming fuel around. Some reasonably sharp dinner knives. Thick table legs whose joinings were pretty heavy. Pietr didn't let patrons bring in blades or guns, but like Nick had said, I'm an improviser. Pietr. Wait a minute. I calmed down slightly. It would be really stupid to attack the Buried Treasure just to get at a knight. The place was full of some seriously badass supernatural predators, many of them members of species that held grudges for centuries. Why risk pissing them off and making enemies? It would be much smarter to stake out the shoreline and attack me later if they wanted to attack at all. Even in the worst-case scenario, Sig and I probably had some time to prepare.

I was still thinking that when the gorgon at the next table began talking excitedly, and it's never a good thing when a gorgon begins talking excitedly, even if it's in a language you don't understand. Especially if it's in a language you don't understand. I looked over my shoulder as the precognitive rose up from the table and began to rush out while the naga hurriedly threw too much money down on the table. The gorgon's hair was distended, writhing about her skull the way a gorgon's hair does when they use their psychic abilities.

I don't know how much Sig had figured out for herself, but she stood up and stared after the gorgon as the precognitive departed. "Something's up. Nick, you'd better get Adriana out of here."

The gorgon didn't make it to the exit. Her spine stiffened and greenish-tan scales began to emerge and cover her skin. Everyone in the room was staring at her now.

"What's this about, you dead-eyed bitch!?!?" Pietr called out. A large fire axe that Pietr had pulled out from under the bar was in his fist.

As if in answer, a hand came out of the wall of hardened sand behind him.

∾24∾

DEAD MEN BEHAVING BADLY

What was really odd about the creature that came through was that its arrival didn't disturb any of the hardened sand that the wall was made of. The dead man was all fish-nibbled flesh and exposed bone, and it had to be solid because it grabbed Pietr's shoulder and turned him sideways, but the monster hadn't burrowed or clawed through the wall. Its molecules had either merged through the hardened sand or else its mind had psychically moved and rearranged the sand out of its path and back into its wake as it passed. That's how I knew we were dealing with a draugr.

There's a couple of things that make draugar (plural form) different from the kind of zombies that are basically shotgun fodder in apocalypse movies. For one thing, all draugar somehow wound up dead and dumped in a large body of water. Oceans, seas, rivers, lakes, and swamps are where the bodies went in, and that's where the draugar come out, even if they're not bound to the water like rusalka are. Mankind basically uses the ocean like it's a giant toilet; maybe rusalka and draugar are the ocean's way of reminding us that it doesn't have a flush handle.

Another difference is that draugar aren't slow and shuffling; in fact, draugar are like humans on PCP because their bodies are basically lifeless puppets being animated by an evil spirit. It's not decayed or shredded muscles making draugar move; it's an animating will that was strong enough to give the afterlife a big middle finger. This is also why you can forget about that putting-a-bullet-in-their-brain-to-put-them-down stuff; draugar aren't actually seeing with those dead eyes, their hearts aren't actually pumping blood through those dead limbs, and they have no need for a nervous system. Decapitation might halt a draugr, but it might not; you just have to keep dismembering the thing until it stops. Almost all ghosts are bound to something, and draugar are bound to the physical remains they used to live in. Eventually, the shock and trauma of having those bodies torn apart will wind up performing an impromptu exorcism on the spirits that are pouring so much energy into holding the draugar together.

But the main difference between a draugr and a Hollywood zombie is that a draugr can move through water and earth like those elements are a thick fog. I don't know how or why; it's some kind of psychic skill those evil spirits evolved in order to move their old bodies through the tons of silt and sand and water pressure keeping them down. Draugar can even move through stone, though that takes them a long time. Not wood or metal or plastic or anything like that, though.

And the sandstone walls that the Tomovs' water magic was maintaining were doable.

The draugr was holding a rusted lug wrench with a sloped end for prying off hubcaps, and it plunged the crude metal weapon through Pietr Tomov's ribcage. The lug wrench must have found something vital; a runny sea-green fluid began pouring out of Pietr's mouth and he dropped. So did his axe. I would regret Pietr's passing later, if there was a later. I wanted that axe.

I was already rushing across the room toward the draugr when other walking corpses began to emerge through the walls all around us. One, two, three, fuck, five, shit, bloody hell, eight... I stopped counting. Draugar only attack in numbers when a very powerful necromancer has cast a very powerful summoning spell, and then draugar get out of control quickly. It's sort of the magical equivalent of releasing piranha into a crowded swimming pool.

The draugr was still pulling the lug wrench out of Pietr when I put my palms on the bar and vaulted over it, my feet smashing into the draugr's side. The draugr didn't weigh anywhere near as much as a fully fleshed human body, and it was flung off of its feet and against the wall. My feet landed on the ground at the same time that the draugr did, and I picked up Pietr's axe. Unfortunately, two more draugar came through the same wall while their fellow was picking itself up, and I straightened and threw myself backward, shoulder-rolling over the bar again to put the wooden barrier between me and the new arrivals before I was overwhelmed.

I didn't land smoothly, but I did manage to stay stumbling on my feet. It gave me room to swing the axe when I stepped back up. One of the draugar had climbed onto the bar, and I took its head off with a full-body whirl, twisting away with the momentum just in case the draugr's left hand kept coming. It did. I spun again and knocked the draugr's body off of the bar and most of its left arm off of its body.

I didn't have time to finish the damned thing off, though. Another draugr took a running jump onto the bar and tried to dive on me, and I caught it in the middle of the torso with the tip of my axe while it was still above me. I guided its leap and lifted the draugr over my head as if I were pitchforking a load of hay, tossing my unwelcome burden toward the naga. The naga had changed into his combat form—a scaly man's torso atop a gigantic snake body that was two feet thick at his navel and tapered into a tail that was roughly twelve feet long. He looked formidable as hell but was content to wait in the center of the crude protective circle being formed by bar patrons around him.

Screw that. Welcome to the circus, clown.

I had bought myself maybe three seconds, and I used them to check on Adriana. Sig could take care of herself. In fact, Sig had positioned herself on the other side of a protective wedge in front of Adriana while Nick took point. Sig had just used a disjointed table leg with a heavy hunk of wood still attached to its end to splatter a draugr's skull like a grapefruit and knock it onto its back, but her blunt weapon wasn't going to do her much good when it came to dismembering.

"Hey, Britte!" I yelled. Sig looked up and I straight-armed the axe through the air between us. Sig dropped the table leg and caught the axe with one hand. I turned back around. Wait, what was I going to do now? The draugr with the lug wrench was back on its feet and scrambling onto the bar.

I stepped forward and pulled a chair over as I passed, so that the chair's back and seat both touched the ground and its legs were slightly tilted up and toward the bar like a pike wall. Then I did a kind of crude, converted uchi makikomi throw—turning in and under the draugr's descending arm so that the lug wrench passed over me. I guided and pulled the arm that thudded across my upper chest with my left hand while my own right arm snaked under the draugr's shoulder. It was basically behind me now, and the draugr tried to crouch and bite my throat, but I dipped and let the draugr's bending motion and my own descending weight take it over me, using my right arm to guide its body down off the bar and onto the chair legs. Two of the chair legs burst through its rotted back and out its front, and when I released the draugr and stepped back, I kicked the tip of one of those chair legs viciously, tearing both the chair and the draugr apart.

Ugggh. No more clam chowder tonight.

We really could have used Molly right then. She could have sent the unholy things running for whatever passed for their mommy. But we didn't have Molly, and a draugr without a head or a left arm was on the ground, crawling towards me. I lifted the corner of a table up and pulled the edge over the creature, then threw all of my weight down on the table so that its lead leg went through the draugr's shoulder blades. The dead man's fist flailed upward at me and I grabbed the wrist, put my foot against the draugr's shoulder, then twisted its arm over my upper thigh. I kept turning my whole body, still pulling after the bones of that decomposing arm began snapping and its ligaments began tearing. The draugr's spirit left its body at the same time that its remaining arm did, and I threw the limb across the bar and took another precious second to glance around.

Dammit, where had that lug wrench gone?

At least the bar wasn't full of scared teenagers who had just read an occult book for kicks while partying in a graveyard. Sig was using the axe to good effect, disconnected limbs flying around her like shrapnel. The storm kelpie was smashing through a body that it had managed to freeze solid. So, that was why the air had gotten so cold so fast. I hadn't had time to wonder about that. The hag was using her steel-hard claws and gaunt muscles to literally tear a corpse from limb to limb, and the snake tail of the naga's lower body had completely encircled the draugr I'd tossed at him, tightening and rupturing and popping the corpse apart. Nick's right arm had somehow grown sharp ridges, and I saw him deliver what looked like a stereotypical karate chop. The side of Nick's hand didn't cut through a tree, though; his forearm sliced through a draugr's neck and down into its chest. And Adriana? She had rolled up the sleeve of her black T-shirt and was baring a shoulder at two draugar, and both of them had stopped in their tracks. I couldn't see what kind of holy symbol it was, but Adriana must have believed in it. More importantly, Adriana was keeping her wits about her under pressure. It's a rare quality.

Denis Tomov, for example, didn't have it. Denis was paralyzed by shock; the vodyanoi just kept staring at the bar where his father had fallen, and I moved to intercept several draugar that were coming out of the wall some twenty feet behind him. I needn't have bothered. Fluid was pouring out of the draugar. Not off of them. Out of them. A deep, scummy, dark, viscous fluid full of little squirmy parasites. I guess they were the ocean's version of maggots. The fluid was leaving a slick pool on the floor, and the draugar seemed to be slowing down, their limbs making cracking-branch sounds. Then I saw a female vodyanoi for the first time.

Lenke Tomov came bellowing out of the kitchen with a large cleaver in each hand, and she tore into those dead bastards like a buzz saw. Now I think I know why vodyanoi keep their females hidden. Lenke would never be able to pass for human. She was a size and a half bigger than her husband and her son, eight and a half feet tall and very wide, with a snub nose and ears that stuck out of her head like a bat's. Based on the water manipulation I was seeing, it was also actually Lenke's magic that was holding the Buried Treasure together. The sand walls hadn't shown any signs of weakening when Pietr died—I think the female vodyanoi must be homemakers in more ways than one.

It wasn't all going our way, though. One of the rat boys had tried to grab a hanging kerosene lamp and use it as a weapon, and now half the rat boys were down while fire spread on the tables and floor around them. A draugr's hand punched through the wood planks in the floor and grabbed the undine's date, the human. He had sensibly hidden beneath a table, and he was pulled screaming down into the sand beneath. When the human's screams stopped, the undine's began. Undines are water elementals, and in order to stay on our plane for a long time, they have to anchor themselves to a human presence, usually a lover. That human love and devotion somehow become a tether to our dimension, and when her human died, the undine fell apart, literally. She wailed and collapsed into a puddle.

Worse still, draugar just kept coming through the walls, and another dropped onto the selkie from the ceiling. The draugr got its arms and teeth around the selkie's neck after she was knocked to the ground. Her companion, the sandy-blond whatever-the-hell-kind-of-hybrid-he-was, tried to pull the draugr off of her, but it was too late.

A draugr stopped as if surprised, and if anything could surprise a draugr, I guess it would be a slender fist punching out of its chest from the inside. Then the stiff tips of another hand ripped out of the side of the draugr's neck, and then both of the small emerging feminine hands grabbed the draugr by its shoulders and ripped its body vertically in half as if the damn thing came with a zipper. Babette, the rusalka, was left standing where the draugr had been, like a freshly peeled banana. I have no idea how she did that.

Another draugr who'd lost a hand came at me from behind, swinging a thick rusty chain, but I ducked under it. The draugr tried to grab me with its other hand, forgetting that it didn't have it any longer, and I slid around the flailing stump and grabbed the end of the chain that was now swinging behind the draugr's neck. Then I grabbed slack chain with my other hand and turned so that the draugr and I were back to back, the chain tight against its neck. I bent and pulled the draugr sharply off of its feet and broke its decayed spine on the anvil of my shoulder blades.

When I dropped the draugr, its legs were still staggering around while its upper torso flopped behind it. Thank God we weren't in a limbo contest.

Babette was taking care of the remaining two draugar, not even giving them a chance to regain their feet. I'd had no idea rusalka were so physically formidable. It made me glad I'd never hunted one. Other draugar kept emerging from the walls, though, more rapidly if anything. Despite our best efforts, the draugars' numbers were getting larger, our numbers were getting smaller, and the hits just kept on coming. How many angry spirits who died from violence or suicide could have bodies lying in Boston Harbor, anyway? Oh. Yeah. Shit.

I took another precious second to cast around for some kind of game changer or inspiration while I picked a fallen baling hook off the floor—any idea at all would do—and I saw the giant serpent tail that was the naga's lower half sweep a draugr aside so that the gorgon he'd been with could run through the kitchen area. The gorgon who could see the future. The gorgon who had showed no interest in anything but her own survival. That was good enough for me.

"WE'VE GOT A WAY OUT!" I screamed. Even if it wasn't true, at least we could pull our ranks in tighter. "BRITTE, NICK, ADRIANA, WHOEVER, COME ON! FALL BACK!"

The crude circle formation began to cave in as Sig came to me immediately, and Adriana followed her closely while Nick watched their backs. Not everyone did as well. The hag—she must have been one of those incredibly tough-skinned water hags who haunt ponds and sandstone caves like Jenny Green-teeth or Black Annis from legend—was deep in a killing frenzy. Her body was buried beneath draugar, but one of her arms reached out from the squirming pile with a draugr impaled on her hand and flung it violently to the side, only to have the damned thing regain its feet and charge again. Two of the rat boys broke free, but a third was pulled down as he turned, and his comrades never looked back. The selkie's companion, whatever he was, was laying about with a fishing gaff that was too large to use effectively, and he didn't seem to care. I saw a draugr run up and intentionally impale itself on the steel edge at the end of the pole, pulling its dead body over the pole stomach-first in order to get closer to its prey, and the blond humanoid bared some seriously pointed teeth and waited for it to arrive.

And Babette? Ever see those old Bugs Bunny cartoons with the Tasmanian Devil? She was a blur of destruction. Literally. A draugr knocked her into the water covering the floor, breaking a plank beneath her and sending a jagged tip upward, and then somehow Babette was behind the draugr and on top of it, driving its skull through the fragment of wood that her own body had just dislodged. It was as if she'd splashed up behind him.

"GET YOUR MOM!" I slapped Denis Tomov on the shoulder and ran for the kitchen, spearing an oncoming vodyanoi through its forearm with the baling hook and whirling it around, not even trying to destroy it, just tearing it off its feet and sending it tumbling over a table and out of my way. When I reached the doorway to the kitchen, I saw that a large icebox had been shoved aside and a section of the sandstone wall behind it torn away, revealing what looked like a large obsolete culvert drain. Sand and debris that had clogged the opening were piled around, and the naga's snake tail was disappearing into it. Those buttmunches were leaving us behind to slow down any pursuers.

"Go!" I yelled as Sig came running up with the axe still in her hands, but she had other ideas.

"You can track them!" she yelled, positioning herself to guard the doorway as Nick came up. "Get Nick and Adriana out of here."

It was weird how Sig and I had both taken responsibility for those two instinctively. My own reasons weren't complicated. I knew what it was like to live with the guilt of having a human lover get killed because you'd involved her in your world. Nikki...Nick...wasn't a friend, exactly, but he was something, and what little I'd seen of Adriana, I'd liked.

And Sig was right. Even in the dark, echoing cold, I would be able to follow the gorgon's scent trail, and Sig was pretty good with an axe, even if she was better with a staff or spear, and we didn't have time to argue about it, so I shut up and ran into the kitchen and grabbed one of the three kerosene lamps while Adriana and Nick followed me. Then two rat boys came rushing in so far up Nick's ass that they almost knocked him over. In the background, Denis's mother was bellowing her son's name and a bunch of other words I didn't recognize.

Rat boys are the ultimate sewer guides. I gave the one who was the most composed, which wasn't very, the kerosene lamp. "Follow the gorgon's scent." That seemed simple enough, and he was gone before I finished the sentence. "Nick, take Adriana and follow them."

He was about to protest, but then a draugr's ravaged face came snarling out of the sandstone, and Adriana screamed. The draugr's midriff slammed against the wood counter set against the wall. I grabbed the draugr's hair and slammed its face down into the counter. There was a wooden knife holder with six large blades in it, and I grabbed a knife that was a foot long and very thick and slammed it through the draugr's partially decomposed neck and into the counter beneath. It flailed about with its hands, but I pinned one arm and then the other, slamming two more big knives through its wrists and down into the counter.

When I looked up, Nick and Adriana were gone. So was one of the kerosene lamps.

Denis's mother came barreling through the door, dragging her son behind her as if Denis were a very large stuffed doll, and she took in the culvert and made for it at once. It was a little larger after she was through it. Another draugr broke through the planks of the floor, and I pulled a large cabinet full of bowls and pans down on top of it, pinning its arm against the wood surface while its lower body was still in the sand. Sig yelled at someone else to come on.

There was some kind of device that was basically a heavy cleaver the size of a machete hinged to a cutting board by a bolt hole through its tip. It looked like an industrial paper cutter to me, but maybe Lenke Tomov had adapted it to meat slicing because she had to work without electricity a lot. Either way, I grabbed the long handle of the blade and rammed it side to side violently several times. I had to pause in my efforts because a draugr broke through the ceiling, but I took a running leap, grabbed it by the collar of the filthy longshoreman jacket it was wearing, and pulled the zombie headfirst down through the hole. Its backbone shattered on the edge of the counter, and I broke its arms like kindling. Maybe the renewed adrenaline helped, because I when I got back to the slicer, I tore its blade free.

Sig finally gave up on whoever she was waiting for and

backed into the kitchen—maybe I should say hacked into the kitchen. I ran and got behind the huge icebox that had been pulled out, and as soon as Sig danced to the side, I tilted the freezer over and sent it slamming down over the pursuing draugar, ramming it through the doorway that was actually too small. Sandstone crumbled but then held, and the icebox wound up wedged at a forty-five-degree angle, emerging counters sealing off the crawlspaces beneath its slanted side.

"John, go!" Sig yelled. She was already grabbing the huge oven and dragging it sideways, propping it against the bottom of the freezer to keep it from sliding, so I took the last kerosene lamp and went down the culvert, hoping my light would give her something to follow.

❧25❧

SEE JOHN RUN

Dammit, John, hurry up!" The metal head on Sig's axe had finally flown off the handle—oh...that's where that expression comes from—and Sig was using the wood haft to shove draugar back down as they tried to climb up through an open access panel. I think we were in some of those underground air tunnels from the old-fashioned heating systems that used to run beneath every house in areas several blocks long, but I'm not really sure. I'm not even sure how we got there. I'd only had the flickering light from a jostling kerosene lamp to see by while hungry nightmare sounds from behind drove me after the gorgon's scent. We had scrambled through drainage pipes which led to some kind of pumping station which led to a grate which led to a duct which led to an access panel which led to these cramped tunnels. It was hard not to blank out and just start running mindlessly, but we were still managing. The narrow opening had seemed like another good choke point for Sig to defend while I tried something.

There was no way we were going to lead a horde of undead into Boston proper, where they could run wild, so Sig and I had been fighting a battle of attrition, trying to string the draugar out and destroying them one or two at a time from defensible positions, hoping to whittle their numbers down to something manageable. A lamentable result was that the stopping and starting had let a horde bunch up and gather behind us. I kicked the hilt of my machete where it was lying on the ground and sent the weapon hissing over the tunnel's galvanized steel surface toward Sig. "Take this and shut up. I need to pray."

"Nice"— Sig paused and grunted as she kicked out and literally tore a draugr's head off, sending the face rolling down the tunnel with rotten teeth still gnashing. It gave her time to grab the machete, though —"spiritual attitude."

We had found some ripped-out chicken wire back in the duct—I'm not sure what it had originally been meant to filter or keep out—maybe bats—and I was using it to tie two metal pipes together into a crude cross. Again, I have no interest in being a sales representative for any kind of ism or ity, and I'm nowhere near as effective as someone like Molly Newman, who probably could have made a symbol that would have blasted the draugar apart, but I can make undead turn away. I sincerely believe a higher power exists, and I sincerely believe that things like draugar aren't part of its plan, and I sincerely believe that said higher power is willing to use me to do something about it. Fortunately, there aren't any holy books that actually say you can't drop f-bombs or use slang terms for excrement— I checked. That's stuff humans just made up to give other humans a hard time.

"Hello, God?" I said. "It's me. Margaret. No, just kidding."

"John!" Sig bellowed.

"Dear God, source of my soul," I said hastily. "Please accept this cross as an offering of a symbol of hope. I would like to live, and I would honestly like to figure out how to do a better job of it. Please help. Amen." The cross I'd made was suspended from chicken wire that was wrapped around the tip of a screw that was sticking out of the ceiling, and I'd jammed a stick up the hollow shaft of the cross's vertical pipe and braced it against the floor to keep it from spinning. "Sig, move it!"

Sig cursed and scrambled in a low, crouched shuffle and threw herself beneath the left corner of the cross in a dive, and I grabbed her wrists and pulled her the rest of the way under and through. A draugr erupted through the panel as if the ground were vomiting it up, and other hands and skulls bubbled up after it, but the draugr stopped crawling when it got within seven feet of the cross that I had suspended above the ground. It stopped and then tried to crawl back.

"Come on." I grabbed the kerosene lamp again and we took off. The cross wouldn't hold the draugar for long. Either the building pressure of bodies would eventually force the first few forward, inching them along until they were pushed into the cross, tearing it down, or the draugar would smash through or pass through the walls of the tunnel itself to get around the icon. Whichever was fastest. Maybe the cross would burn the undead, or maybe it would send the spirits animating their bodies fleeing, but either way, if enough unnatural corpses were shoved over the cross they would eventually conceal it or defile it.

Even if only because that's what I believed.

When the heating tunnel came to a corner, there was a big rusted-out hole that had been enlarged by someone with greater-than-human strength. A loose scale hanging on a sharp fragment of twisted metal suggested that it had been the naga. The gorgon's scent trail led down the opening, so I followed suit and found myself in a concrete corridor that would have been comfortable if the metal heating access tunnel hadn't been

running halfway through it. We were probably in an improvised service corridor. Every major city with elaborate sewers
and subway systems has a vast network of abandoned tunnels
that don't show up on any map. Underground construction
workers—in my day, we called them sandhogs—worked on
power grids, heating ducts, and plumbing throughout their
lives, and they found it convenient to make shortcuts that met
a variety of demands, not to mention storage areas, personal
lockers, common rooms, kitchens, chapels, or just places to
have a drink or a smoke or a moment alone.

The heating duct disappeared into the ceiling, and we had
a little more room to move for maybe forty yards, and then we
found a security door with a lock bar that that been torn down.
It led to a little storage room that was mostly full of trash, and
there was another torn-down door and another service corridor on the other side. We wasted a little of the precious time
we'd gained looking around, but unfortunately, I didn't see
any chain guns, flamethrowers, antipersonnel mines, glowing
green lanterns, swords embedded in large stones, or hammers
that some Norse god had left lying around. I did manage to
craft another cross while Sig whipped up a torch out of a broken broom handle, a torn piece of canvas cloth, and some very
old motor oil that had turned into paste.

"Do we have a plan?" Sig asked while she lit the torch.

"Well," I said. "If we keep running, maybe we'll find
a big red button that says Press Here in Case of Zombie
Apocalypse."

"Oh, good," Sig said. "I was afraid you hadn't thought this
through either."

It's not like we had a lot of options. We could keep looking for some way to destroy the draugar en masse. We could
find a place to trap them in. We could find a place where one

of us could hold them off indefinitely while the other got far enough ahead for cell phones to work and call for help. Or we could die.

So, we kept running and looking.

I don't know how much distance we covered before we stepped over another torn-down access door and emerged into an old abandoned subway tunnel. The air was stale and the tunnel was cramped, probably more so than modern safety regulations would allow. There was just one set of rails, a low domed ceiling, and barely enough room on the little raised concrete platform on the side for a person to stand with their shoulder against the wall. Actually, I'm not sure *platform* is even the right word. It was more like a big curb raised four feet off the ground.

The old T trains must have rocketed through this place like torpedoes through a tube. Black rats scurried away wherever the light from my lamp fell. Behind us, we could hear the echoes of approaching grunts and screams and yells, hatred and hunger trying to express themselves through punctured lungs and ravaged vocal cords. It sounded like hell's own accordion.

"John, speed up." Sig's voice had acquired a new urgency. Not that it was more urgent—just different. An element of purpose and hope rang in her intonation.

"What are we looking for?" I grunted as we shuffled down the tunnel.

"Room," she said enigmatically, and the quality of sound in the tunnel changed when the first of the draugar stumbled into the tunnel somewhere behind us.

I don't know how far we ran while the draugar gained on us. They didn't have to slow down to keep from tripping on a railway slat, or worry about the light from a lamp being completely jostled out. We didn't have much longer before we would be overtaken when Sig stopped and gasped, "This is going to have to do. Can you buy me some time?"

Here? The tunnel was cramped for a subway train, but not for a lone person trying to keep from being surrounded by a horde of undead fuckwits who didn't experience little things like fear or pain or survival instincts. But it's not like I had any better ideas. "Okay," I said simply. "But let's move up a little."

Sig looked around. "Why?"

I pointed at a metal bar that ran beneath the ceiling of the tunnel. There were two clamps where something had hung from it—probably a destination sign or warning for the subway conductor's eyes only, but whatever it had held was gone now. "I want to hang the lantern on one of those clamps. Give me a hand."

We walked towards the crosspiece, and Sig obligingly knelt down and held a palm out. I stepped on her palm and she straightened up and lifted her arm up over her head. I rode her palm up as if I'd just stepped on to an escalator, grabbing the bar with my left hand to steady myself when I neared the ceiling. It only took a moment to hook the kerosene lantern's handle over one of the clamps, and then I jumped down to the ground.

"Now you can't take the lantern with you if you run." Sig had to speak up because the sounds of pursuit were getting louder. She sounded troubled.

"It's almost out anyhow," I said, not quite managing to sound casual.

Sig handed me the machete back. "Don't die."

"Then do your thing fast." I turned around to face the sounds of growling and scrambling limbs. I didn't want to see Sig disappear into the shadows. The kerosene lantern was giving me a fifteen-foot radius of light, and its glow turned red at the edges as it was swallowed by darkness. What I could see of the tunnel looked like a giant inflamed throat.

I set my machete aside, hurriedly yanking my jacket and shirt off over my head. I didn't want to get my hand too slippery to hold a weapon, so I bent down and ran the shirt over the rails and between the trestles, then smeared cold slippery mud and grease over my arms and chest. Freezing to death wasn't way up there on my list of worries at the moment; getting grabbed by bony fingers and pulled down into an angry sea of teeth was.

I didn't see any way to make a quick wall of crosses. If I braced a slat against my machete and improvised one, the draugar would just run around me on the sides and head for Sig.

It wasn't a long wait. As soon as the first silhouettes appeared at the edge of the light, I charged. Cut a leg out from one of them before shouldering it off its remaining foot, whirled and took a forearm off, evaded a bear hug, took off another forearm, and then a draugr ran onto my machete and tore the damn weapon out of my hands. Some flailing limb broke my nose with a loud crunch as a draugr fell scrambling, but I was too busy too care, kicking my leg free from another draugr who had almost tackled me by grabbing my legs. My knee lunge broke a neck, and I stumbled backward, weaponless, swallowing blood. At least the mud covering me helped me turn and slip out of several bony clutches. Long fingernails tore furrows between my shoulder blades and another lunge ripped the lower part of my left earlobe off as I gained speed.

My plan, such as it was, had been to use the open space to cripple a few of them and totally focus them on me before jumping up on to the more easily defendable narrow platform. But that plan had also depended on hanging on to the machete. Screw it. I ran and leaped on to the raised concrete platform, then jumped up at the wall and kicked off it, grabbing the metal rod that the kerosene lantern was hanging on. Fortunately, the lamp was on the other side of the tunnel.

A draugr grabbed at my ankle, and I swung myself up and managed to wrap my feet around the pipe so that I was hanging horizontally. My torn-up back had little lines of fire running down it. The draugar could actually leap a little higher than a normal human, but not quite as high as an NBA star. Several bony hands passed beneath me and then a draugr smacked against the platform. Shit. I began to inch down toward the center of the pipe to lure them away from the platform, and the gathering mob shuffled beneath me obediently. My earlobe and broken nose were still bleeding, and while I was looking down over my shoulder, I saw one of the draugar who were facing upward open its jaws and catch a couple big fat drops of my blood in its mouth. It looked like nothing in the world so much as a desperately thirsty man trying to catch raindrops. The draugar weren't really physically hungry for my flesh. They just desperately wanted life, any piece or scrap of it, wanted it with an animal frenzy, and the fact that it was denied them drove them insane with hatred and pain.

Not that I was feeling too sympathetic at the moment.

"YO, UGLIES!" I released my hands and hung upside down from my legs, waving my arms. Several draugar jumped and I straightened back up and grabbed the pole again as they passed beneath me. I couldn't physically prevent them from going after Sig in this position, but maybe I could continue to keep them focused on me. "The buffet's right here, bitches!"

I heard even more bodies running forward, and then one of the draugar who'd missed me the first time came running back and collided into one of the new arrivals jumping from the opposite direction. They both fell and other draugar stepped over them. That wasn't good. I didn't know if draugar were smart enough to form a pyramid or not, but if they started clambering over each other, it would have the same effect. "Hey, did you all shit yourselves when you died, or do you just smell that way?" I called to the gathering throng. There had to be over fifty of them crowding into the radius of the lamplight now, and still more growls were coming from the darkness. "What's the matter, catfish get your tongue? Graaghhhrhh! Uhnggh! Blarghkclach! Ghaaaaah!"

I managed to pull myself up so that I was lying on the pipe instead of hanging under it. That was good, though I had to be careful when I hooked my ankles on the pipe and adjusted to find a comfortable position for my testicles. It felt as if I'd been holding the world up. For an insane moment, the sound of the draugar below became background noise, and I had an impulse to take a nap. Then a leaping draugr managed to tear a strip off of the side of my knee, and I almost fell off of the pipe.

For one of the few times in my life, I seriously began to contemplate ways to kill myself quickly. If I dropped, could I change to a wolf before I was torn apart?

Then the sound of an approaching subway car filled the tunnel.

~26~

A TRAIN OF THOUGHT

The air was filled with a loud mechanical roar and the piercing shriek of lost souls. A light cast from some impossibly bright source turned my hands so bright that they were colorless, and then a subway train passed beneath me.

I closed my eyes and held on, but there was no wind pulling at me, and the bar I was holding on to wasn't shaking at all. That was impossible, not that I was inclined to let go of my perch and prove it. I could feel the pull of some indescribable suction that didn't seem to have a physical source, and I held on even tighter and shut my eyes while bright flashes sparked behind my eyelids. I had a definite sense of some loud, vast, and powerful force whipping past me just beyond a very thin barrier. The closest I can come to describing the sensation is that it was like burning up from a massive fever and sitting next to the open window of a car going ninety miles an hour.

Sig had summoned a ghost train.

When the light and the noise were gone, I still hung there. The kerosene lantern should have been hanging too low to have survived, but it was still burning, if faintly, and the protruding slopes and edges of what were easily half a hundred bodies were lying on the ground beneath me. The draugar had always been dead, but now they weren't moving, outlined in the lamp's fading glow. The odd thing was, their bodies weren't broken. The draugar hadn't been hurled aside or splattered. They had just... stopped.

"John?" It was Sig's voice. Somehow, I had gone temporarily deaf until she spoke up. I didn't want to move, didn't want to do anything but hang on to that metal pole like a scared cat, but I'd had about enough of paralysis recently, so I moved anyway, forcing myself to drop down to the ground. At least my nose wasn't bleeding anymore, though it was pretty clogged up. Sig was shuffling forward stiffly, only her silhouette visible at the edge of the lantern light. "I found that red button you were talking about," she said, and then she collapsed. If I weren't faster than a normal human, she would have hit face first on the railway.

I guess summoning a ghost train takes a lot out of you. My heart sped up, which at least warmed me a little as I checked Sig's vitals. That was when I discovered that Sig was covered with a thin layer of frost. She had a heartbeat, and a steady one too, if just a little slow. I ran back and found my hoodie and the machete in the dark, then wrapped the jacket around Sig and pulled her into my arms when I came back.

How the hell was I supposed to help her? I didn't even understand what she'd done.

The sound of the train had still been audible in the background all of this time, but now it ended with a high-pitched wail that made every nerve I had vibrate like a struck piano key. The sound of that piercing scream echoed in the subway long after a normal sound would have died out. It sounded human. Horribly human.

And yes, phantom locomotives are a real thing. Lincoln's

funeral train and the St. Louis ghost train are probably the most famous ones in the United States, but there are literally dozens of famous ones; every country has them and nobody knows what they are exactly. I'd never heard that a phantom train could run over zombies and deanimate them, but then, that's not something that comes up a lot in casual conversation.

I wiped the thin layer of frost off of Sig's face and hands, and I was kissing and rubbing her skin, trying to get some circulation back into it, when the kerosene lamp finally died. I could see a light from around the bend of the tunnel that Sig had traveled down, so I carefully placed her forehead on my shoulder and picked her body up in my arms, carrying her back toward the light. Despite my best efforts, the jostling woke Sig up again, and she came to, cursing. That was my princess.

"What happened?" Sig sounded out of it.

"You summoned a ghost train and saved our asses," I reminded her.

"Oh," Sig said vaguely. "Right."

"And then we had a long conversation where you agreed that I was completely justified in keeping a few secrets," I continued. "You forgave me once and for all. Oh, and you're going to go see Elvis Costello live with me this summer."

Sig wrapped her arms up around my neck. "So, I've been delusional?!?"

We rounded the gradual curve, and I could see that the light was coming from the torch Sig had made. She had set it upright and embedded it in a mound of debris that she'd found or slathered together. "So, how did you do that thing with the ghost train, anyway?"

"Ask me again," Sig said.

"Why?"

"Because I like it when you're the one who has to have

something about the supernatural world explained to him," she said.

"Oh, bite me," I grumbled. But when she didn't say anything else, I obliged. "So, how did you do that thing with the ghost train?"

"Ghost trains aren't really ghosts of trains. Most ghosts look like themselves when they appear, but there's no law that says they have to." Having to think that through had Sig sounding more alert. "That body you see is just how they picture themselves."

"Are you about to tell me that a lot of ghosts picture themselves as trains?" I asked.

"All it takes is one lonely drifting soul who died down here and doesn't want to be itself anymore, who thinks of trains as a place where people come together and go somewhere," Sig said. "And then another lingering spirit senses the train projection and wants to go somewhere and be a part of something too. And then another."

I thought about all the people who had probably died in Boston's subway tunnels over the past two centuries. Gas explosions. Tunnel floodings. Derailments. Suicides throwing themselves in front of trains. Homeless people dying in abandoned tunnels unnoticed. Murdered bodies dragged and abandoned there in the dark for the rats to feed on. Hell, how many elderly or sick people had died on trains while riding them around and around because they needed a cheap, safe roof over their head while they slept, or because they didn't feel quite so alone that way? Then I thought about that indescribable pull I'd felt. "You're saying ghost trains are some kind of communal ghost projection? That they become like a rolling stone, except instead of gathering moss, they gather lost souls?"

Sig nestled her head further into my shoulder. "I could sense a powerful one as soon as we stepped into this tunnel. I thought maybe if I could call it, it might pick up the spirits animating those corpses."

"Like a lint roller," I said.

"Uhmmmmmnnhmn." Sig nestled her head further into my shoulder. Then she lifted her head. "You're covered in mud."

"Well, you know, things got a little tense back there," I said. "I thought I'd treat myself to a spa day."

Sig snorted and put her head back against me anyway, and I gently lowered her to the ground and set her upper torso on my lap, her head against my chest. I didn't have anything warm or dry to lean back against, so I rested my chin on the top of her head. "Are you going to be all right?" I finally asked.

"I just need to stay in this world for a while," Sig half explained. "Part of summoning a ghost train is tapping into that part of yourself that always feels lost and alone."

"Oh," I said inadequately, and I pulled myself around her a little tighter. Eventually, I heard far-off voices—and with my hearing, "far-off" means "far-off." Which wouldn't have been a bad thing, necessarily, but I wasn't inclined to assume it was a good thing without a damned solid reason. I didn't quite know what to make of the fact that the voices were coming from the same direction that Sig and I and the draugar had come from, either.

"I hear something," I told Sig. "It might just be some homeless people or transit cops coming to see what all the noise was about. I'm going to go check it out."

Sig really was wiped. Not only did she not argue, she didn't notice that I was leaving the crude machete with her. "Don't be long."

"You bet," I agreed. "You and I have a date with a hot tub."

"That sounds good," she said, and I kissed her on the forehead again.

∿27∾

COLD-BLOODED KILLERS

I didn't make another torch. I climbed up on the not-quite-platform and moved through the dark quickly and low to the ground, keeping one hand brushing the wall. What airflow existed was at my back, but there was nothing I could do about that. When I could almost distinguish what the voices were saying, I climbed down off the platform and covered my body in mud again, damn it. Then I moved down the trestles until I encountered another thick patch of bodies scattered on the ground. How many draugar had there been? I stopped when I found a mound where several bodies had clumped together. Then I lay down flat on the ground and pulled several of the corpses over me. One former draugr in particular was large and fairly intact, and I arranged it so that its torso was lying over my lower half.

It was uncomfortable on all kinds of levels I don't want to go into. I was actually relieved when I saw floating spheres of bluish-white light bobbing around like fireflies as they approached from the depths of the subway tunnel. I hadn't factored in what staying still under those conditions would do to my circulation. There was a point of diminishing returns where staying hidden from infravision wasn't worth impairing my ability to fight.

On the other hand, the lights I saw weren't exactly good news either. I recognized them. They were will o' wisps, disembodied spirits who died lost in the wilderness and whose souls glow at nighttime as if still searching, though I don't think they remember what it is they're looking for.

Call me paranoid, but whoever had summoned the draugar was a necromancer, and now here somebody was, trailing the zombies and using will o' wisps like floating glow lamps. Coincidence? I could make the voices out now, and they came with thick Irish accents and some surprisingly heavy footsteps. Some of the voices were nasal but oddly deep at the same time. They said mostly inconsequential things but eventually got to something I found interesting.

"These shites aren't torn up either. Not fresh-like."

"You saw the train same as we did, ya gammy tool! That was no normal engine that sent everythin' arseways."

"I'm just sayin', whoever we're after got further than this, is all. And I'm not so sure it was a knight neither. It's only the two humans I've smelled, and one was that undine's lad and the other is a lass."

"At least now we don't hafta clean up after these banjaxed fookers."

"Hssst! Silence yourselves." A feminine voice, light but normal-sounding if all you listened to were the range and volume of it. But... have you ever hated someone at first sight? I hated this woman from first sound. It was the cold savagery and the certainty of being obeyed that made the voice anathema. "Someone's listening. And listening fiercely too."

I didn't move in the silence that followed.

"There's hot wolf blood mixed up with all the rotter stank," one of the males finally said reluctantly. "But I don't think the wolf's alive. Its tracks fade out right where I can see them."

I had stopped leaving discernible heat impressions when I'd smeared cold mud all over myself again. The Redcap—and it was one of the Redcaps that Nick had talked about—thought I'd died.

"How can you tell someone's listenin'?" another male demanded.

"I can taste the tension in the air," the female almost purred. "It's a hunter waitin' out there in the shadows, sure and it is."

"If there's anythin' there, it's too cold to be a wolf," one of the males argued. "Those fookers burn hot."

"I smell some cold-bloods," another one offered. "A gorgon and a naga. Or it could be that Denis and his Ma."

"Ah, don't act the maggot! Those water trolls are pussies," another male voice chimed in. "This thing's not squirting any fear, whatever it is. Or no more than the usual amount."

"Is that you, then, Mr. Naga, whoever you are?" the feminine voice called out. "We mean ye no harm. We just found a right mess at the Buried Treasure and followed along to see if we could help."

Pull the other one, lady. One of the males had said something about expecting a knight raid. And another had said the ghost train had sent everything arseways, meaning that having the draugar running around had been part of a plan that had been messed up. And yet another had casually said that they didn't have to clean up after the draugar *now,* as though there had never been any doubt that they would, as though they'd been planning on it.

When I didn't respond, the female said, "Well, I'd best be leavin' you lot to it. Here's a little summat to give you luck." I heard the slight sound of a cap being unscrewed and liquid gurgling from what sounded like a canteen. Could it be a liquid version of the mysterious future drug? Some kind of magical enhancer or focuser? "Not you, Billy. You come back with me."

I decided to speak up after all. They already knew I was out there anyhow, and I wanted to know more about the female. "Hey, now, lady, are you really coming to the party late and leaving early? That's a little rude, don't you think?"

One of the males cursed, and the female asked what I'd said. So, the female had normal hearing. On the other hand, the female had somehow picked up on my presence before any of the males despite their senses and my geas. After the male repeated what I'd said, the female laughed, and the raw spite in that laugh chilled me in a place that my low body temperature hadn't. "No poor soul has called me a *lady* in over a thousand years, you foolish man. And the last one who did regretted it."

"Sounds like we both need to work on our social skills, then," I said mildly. One of the males—Billy, I guess—relayed my message, and he kept doing so for the rest of our conversation. I didn't need the slight scrape of gravel and slap of mud to tell me that the woman's other enforcers were creeping forward quietly under the cover of our conversation. My right shoulder was uncomfortable to the point where my whole arm was going to go completely asleep if I didn't shift it, so I went ahead and adjusted my weight, making sure I could peek down the tunnel while I was at it. I saw two heat impressions, hotter than a human's would be. Most Fae are slightly colder than humans, but Redcaps have an extremely high metabolism rate.

"Didja hear that?" a male voice whispered.

"Shut yer bake!" his partner hissed back.

Their boss, farther off, didn't hear any of that exchange. "Speaking of manners, I don't believe you've told me your name."

"Fair trade?" I offered. "My true name for yours?"

Billy repeated the offer and she laughed that laugh again. "I think not. You're one of those werewolf knights I saw bust up the Crucible in New York, aren't you? Who cares what you call yourself?"

Come to think of it, I'd seen a few Redcaps in the crowd at the Crucible that last night, shooting dice with a bocor.

"Then you can just call me Trouble," I said. "Pleased to meet you."

"You have it wrong there," the woman said. "If you're trouble, we've met before. And I expect it's soon enough we'll be seeing each other again. I know all about you knights and your big secret plan."

Big plan? It was distinctly possible that Simon and Emil were keeping something from me, but it sounded more like she was on a fishing expedition of her own, trying to trick me into revealing something. Her voice was so far away that even I could barely hear it now, and the light of the will o' wisps was gone. Damn it.

"Phir milen-gay," I called out, which was Hindi and roughly meant, "See you later." I wanted to see if I could get them to think I was the naga again, just to sow some confusion.

Billy almost got the words right, and they made the woman he repeated them to pause. "That's fair fancy talk for a knight in a stealth suit."

All I knew about the naga was that he'd been at the Buried Treasure with a gorgon, so I used what little information I had. "You're off base with this knight nonsense." I laughed. "I came here for the gorgon."

This time, the pause was longer. I had the distinct impression that she was unsettled. When she spoke again, her words were even fainter, and all she said was, "Then whoever you are, you've made a terrible, terrible mistake." She went on to add something in Gaelic that I didn't get.

One of the two approaching males began firing some kind of automatic weapon along the surface of the tunnel floor. Automatic fire raked around me, and some of it thudded into the bodies I was hiding under, but none of it touched me.

The other Redcap advanced behind the line of fire, fast. Hoping that I was still too cold to give off a clear heat impression, I used my legs to prop up the corpse on top of me like a scarecrow while I yelled.

The Redcap's heat impression became a blur. It darted forward and something stabbed into the corpse I was propping up, repeatedly, the blows so fast they sounded like someone hitting a wet speed bag. My own movements were a little slower than normal, but that was okay. I had the element of surprise when I reached under the corpse's arm. My fingers were too cold to grip as strongly as I would have liked, but when my hand slid over the Redcap's wrist, I encountered a thick metal stud-covered chain bracelet—probably bling. I managed to wrap my three middle fingers under and around the band tightly. Startled, he tried to yank free, and I pulled him off of his feet when he rocked back. The Redcap fell on top of the fat corpse, and I rolled both of them over, pinning the Redcap beneath the dead body and breaking his wrist in the same motion.

The trapped Redcap tried to free some kind of submachine gun that was really too big for this kind of close-up work. I only had to move a few inches to pin the gun barrel that he brought up between my elbow and ribcage. When the Redcap squeezed the trigger, he wound up firing several rounds into the gut of the partner who was about to stab me in the back. Like I said, Redcaps move fast.

The bullets didn't seriously harm the Redcap behind

me—it's complicated, but the short version is that the Fae made a kind of magical nonaggression pact with our earth a long time ago, and naturally occurring elements like lead won't harm them. This is why the Fae are constantly portrayed as tree-hugging environmentalists living in harmony with nature, and also why the pure-blooded ones left around the same time that mankind started developing alloys and chemical compounds that confused the Fae's wards.

The bullets had the same effect on the Redcap—who was only a half-blood Fae, really—that they would have had on someone clad head to toe in padded Kevlar. He was startled and had the wind knocked out of him. I managed to kick back with my foot and catch him right in the middle of his face, and that was all she wrote. The Fae never made a magical nonaggression pact with mortal flesh. That would have meant they had to respect human bodies, and what fun would that be?

The Redcap beneath me used my shifting weight to free his submachine gun, and this time, he managed to fire several bullets through my arm and along my rib cage. That was enough of that. I used my weight to shift the corpse between us to my left, pinning the Redcap's gun hand down and exposing his face. I came over the corpse's right shoulder and punched the Fae again and again and again, both of us screaming, me using the side of my numb hand and the heel of my palm until the bones of his face collapsed and his body stopped moving.

Once we'd both quieted down, a voice from very far down the tunnel called out, "Tom? Dylan?"

I didn't answer, and a moment later, there was a loud rumble. I closed my eyes. For a second, I honestly thought that the female had some kind of magic spell that caused earthquakes. But the sound of falling rock died, and I didn't.

~28~

YOU'D BETTER SHREK YOURSELF BEFORE YOU WRECK YOURSELF

John?" Sig's voice came through the darkness.

"Hey, honey," I was going over the Redcaps' bodies, looking to see if they had anything useful on them. "Sorry. I got held up at work."

It turned out that the Recaps had come prepared for a running battle. Both had the kinds of belts that usually go over wetsuits, the pouches full of chem sticks, flares, spare magazines for their submachine guns, zip ties, Swiss army knives, a couple of thousand dollars in cash, and some chocolate-flavored protein bars loaded with nuts. I guess the latter made sense. Anybody who moved as fast as the Redcaps did had to burn up a lot of calories. The jackets they were wearing were heavily insulated too, and they had gloves in their pockets.

There was a flare of light as Sig lit another torch that she'd managed to cobble together. From the look and smell of her, she'd torn off the lower half of her shirt, soaked it in some kind of flammable axle grease, and tightly wrapped the fabric several times around a broken railway trestle. "What was that explosion all about?"

"I expect it was a woman I just met covering her escape," I said. "A real Miss Nasty Pants. Want to go check it out with me?"

"Not really," Sig said, a sentiment I heartily agreed with. "But we're not separating again."

I agreed with that sentiment too.

When Sig saw how badly I was shivering, she insisted that we wait until she started a fire, and I didn't argue. I had a pretty good idea what that collapsing rock had been about, and it diluted my sense of urgency. I held the torch while Sig continued to break wooden trestles off the railway by the light of one of the flares, and the heat gradually brought my aching hands back to full, stinging life.

Neither one of us talked much. Sig asked me a few questions while she worked, and I only had a few answers to give her. When I braced one of the Redcaps' feet on a subway rail, Sig asked what I was doing. "Trust me," I said, and broke the Redcap's ankle with a sharp downward kick. Then I did the same with his friend. Neither one woke up.

After Sig and I were warm and clothed and armed again, we began walking down the tunnel, each of us dragging a Redcap behind us. With their heads bouncing up and down on the railway slats, there wasn't much chance of the Redcaps waking up, and the zip ties we'd bound them with would slow them down if they did.

About a hundred yards down the tunnel, we found two canteens that the Redcaps had left behind so that they wouldn't slosh around when they tried to sneak up on me. I held them directly up to my nose and smelled them carefully just in case the woman had left them as a trap, but the contents were just water. It was the best and earliest Christmas present I'd ever gotten. I never got to thank the Redcaps, though. About three minutes later, Sig halted in midstride and announced, "Are you sure these guys are Fae? They're dead."

I didn't doubt Sig or question how she'd figured that out.

Instead, I bent down and tried to smell near their lips through my still-healing nose. "Dammit."

"What?" Sig asked.

"The woman I told you about gave them something to drink before she sent them after me," I said. "She said it was for luck, but it must have been some kind of poison that works on half-breed Fae. If they'd succeeded, they'd have been back in time for the antidote and none the wiser. But since they didn't..."

"We don't have any prisoners now," Sig finished.

"Yeah." I took one of the Redcaps' thumbs in my hands.

Sig made a face, but she wasn't freaked out. "They're not faking."

"I know. They've lived among humans, though, and knights keep their own database of fingerprints." I won't go into detail about how you remove a thumb when you don't have any blades that work on Fae flesh. There was nothing else to do after that, so we kept walking. I was really, really tired of walking. But eventually, Sig and I found pretty much what we'd expected to find. The explosion we'd heard had collapsed the tunnel. Whoever the woman was, she believed in covering her tracks.

"How did she do this?" Sig wondered. "Magic?"

"Sure," I said. "An ancient dark ritual using plastic explosives."

"Let me see your profile," Sig commanded.

I obligingly turned my face when Sig held up a chem stick so that she could look at it closer. "What is it?"

"Your nose didn't quite set right. Hold still." Sig reached out and grabbed my nose sharply between two fingers and broke it again with a sharp crack, maintaining a firm pressure while she positioned it. "You'll thank me later."

"I'll thank you now," I assured her while I contorted my jaw muscles, and then I proved it. "Thanks."

"Hmmn," Sig grunted thoughtfully. "Didn't you say something about a hot tub?"

"I did," I agreed. "I think I'm up to jogging now. Are you?" She was.

We never did catch up to the naga or the gorgon, and the rat boys who had escaped from the Buried Treasure split off from the main group and went their own way soon after Sig and I picked up their trail again. Eventually, the sound of distant but active subway trains began to make itself heard, and the drafts of fresh air got stronger. Denis Tomov and Nick and Adriana had gone on back to the surface world, but Denis left his mother behind and below-ground while he went to go make some kind of arrangements for the next few days and see if their restaurant could be salvaged.

The reason I know that is because Lenke Tomov was waiting for us when we finally made our way to the big hole that subway sounds were coming through. My nose was still numb and clogged, and Lenke was cold-blooded and unnaturally still, but the light from Sig's chem stick glinted off of Lenke's eyes in the dark. When I stopped, Sig stopped, and Lenke unfolded herself from the shadows and walked into the periphery of our light. All eight and a half feet and four hundred plus pounds of her. The vodyanoi was still holding two cleavers in fists the size of baby cantaloupes, and her pointy ears were lying flat in a way that would have signified trouble if she were a horse. Her eyes were bloodshot and crazy and glaring at Sig.

"You summoned ghost train," Lenke accused in a voice that sounded like a grindstone. The Eastern European tendency to omit articles is a real thing among people who don't speak English frequently, by the way, especially when they're upset. Hollywood has abused this to the point of parody, and some people think it makes the speaker sound less intelligent, but it's actually a much more efficient way of communicating. The truth is, English is at least fifty percent word flab.

"I did summon it," Sig admitted. "That train saved our lives."

"What necromancer shit have you gotten my family in?" Lenke half growled and half sobbed. It wasn't an illogical assumption.

"I..." Sig started, but she didn't get a chance to finish, because Lenke charged, howling. Then Lenke collapsed, howling. Largely because I had just fired several automatic rounds into her kneecap.

"That's enough, Lenke!" I snapped. I had, by God, had too much. After a moment's thought, my mind caught up with my mouth though, and I added lamely, "But I'm truly sorry for your loss."

"I could have handled that without shooting her," Sig tried, but it was a pretty lackluster reprimand. Sig was exhausted too.

"I know," I sighed. "But the bullets will do less damage. Look."

It was true. Lenke was already up on one knee, experimentally putting weight on her leg and glaring at us in a way that made me very, very glad that we weren't in a sewer with water all about. Her voice was ragged because the heart behind it was in shreds. "I'll kill you both."

"Britte here didn't have anything to do with the attack on your place tonight," I said coldly. Forget sympathy; Lenke was dangerous. "But I talked to the cunning woman who did."

That got her attention. "What cunning woman?"

"I don't know, but she had an Irish accent and she was following the draugar she'd summoned," I explained. "I think she meant to summon them back to some nearby place as soon as they were done and blow them all to hell. She was packing some serious explosives."

"Who is this slut?" Lenke demanded.

"I don't know," I said truthfully enough. "But she had a bunch of Redcaps with her. That's what you're smelling all over me."

Lenke growled again, but hatred and anger weren't the predominant emotions coming through on the pheromones she was releasing now. It was fear. Lenke was probably realizing the same thing that Nick had verbalized, that no Redcaps had shown up at the Buried Treasure that night. Supernatural or not, dangerous or not, vodyanoi aren't natural predators. Lenke was a restaurant owner and a chef, not a vigilante. "What she want?"

"I don't know. She seemed interested in that gorgon, though," I said. "First she accused me of being a knight. Then she got really pissed off and upset because she thought I had something to do with the gorgon. Do you know anything about that gorgon or the naga she was with?"

"No," Lenke hissed, glaring at Sig again. "They are strangers too."

"Well, that's all I know," I said. "If you want me to find out more, you'll have to pay me."

That went over like a belly flop in a kiddie pool. Or put another way, it made a big impact, followed by a stunned silence while everyone struggled to believe what I'd just done, trying to figure out if they should laugh or if I should be ashamed of myself.

"What?!?" Lenke choked.

"John," Sig protested mildly.

I shrugged at Sig. "Lenke is obviously scared, but she also wants revenge. I've already killed two of these knobgoblins, and I've never met a Fae yet who didn't hold a grudge. If I stay in Boston, they'll come after me anyway."

Despite the raw emotions she was struggling with, Lenke's leathery face settled into a certain impassive cunning. "So, why I pay if you fight anyhow?"

"Because I don't have to stay in Boston," I lied. "What's me sticking around and becoming a pain in the Redcaps' asses worth to you?"

Look, I didn't really care about the money. I wasn't indifferent to it—setting up fake identities and maintaining storage silos and

PO boxes and bank accounts and credit cards in other names all takes money, and anybody who thought I'd given up those practices just because I'd reached what might be a temporary détente with the Knights Templar didn't know me very well—but Lenke had lost a husband because people were trying to get to me, and I wasn't looking for an opportunity to profit from that either. It was strategy guiding me, not greed. I was going to be hanging around Boston, asking questions of people who didn't like knights or any werewolves who worked with knights. Operating on Lenke's behalf would give me camouflage and credibility.

"I could maybe pay ten thousand," Lenke said reluctantly.

"We're talking about a gang of Redcaps and a powerful necromancer and maybe a gorgon and a naga," I reminded her. I didn't have the energy to get really theatrical, but I did make to move around the vodyanoi. "Look, this was a bad idea. I'm sorry for your loss, but it wasn't Britte's fault. We're out of here."

"Why I pay more?" Lenke demanded suspiciously. I don't think she gave a shit about the money. She just didn't want Sig and me to leave her alone in the dark. Denis had better come get his mom soon. "Maybe you just take money and leave."

"I could make sure he doesn't cheat you, Mama Lenke." I lost several cool points when Nick emerged from the hole in the wall. In fact, I barely kept from shooting him. It takes a lot to sneak up on me, but my sense of smell was impaired, and not only was Nick cold-blooded, quiet, and naked, but he had turned his skin and the irises of his eyes jet-black so that he could move in the shadows better.

And since when did Nick call her Mama Lenke?

"You believe wolf?" Lenke demanded.

"Yes," Nick said simply.

"Nick, get out of here," I said irritably. "You should be with Adriana, you idiot. Take her someplace safe and stay with her."

"See?" Nick asked Lenke, though I'm not sure why. Then he turned to me. "I had Adriana make arrangements in case anything like this ever happened. Even I won't know where she's going or how she's getting there for a couple of days."

"Go try real hard to find out," I suggested.

"No. I owe somebody for tonight," he said. "I owe you and Britte too."

"You don't owe me anything," I contradicted uneasily.

Nick shook his head. "You saved Adriana's life."

Thirty years, and the nix was still a hopeless romantic. But then, if I've learned one thing hanging around beings who live for centuries, it's that people really don't change all that much or all that often.

"Then *you* pay wolf and his bitch," Lenke snapped at Nick. "You owe them so much."

"Bitch?" Sig asked mildly. She was still a little out of it.

"I think she means because you're hanging out with a wolf," I said helpfully.

"Oh, good," Sig said. "I think."

"We want a million dollars, Mama Lenke," Nick told the vodyanoi. "Each." I guess Nick had a pretty good idea of how much money the vodyanoi really had, or he was an extreme bargainer. Lenke and Nick lapsed into a flurry of some kind of Russian-flavored conversation that left me speechless. Sig seemed able to follow along with most of it, though she frowned occasionally.

The long and short of it is that eventually Sig and I got back to a working subway line alive, and a water troll agreed to pay us a million dollars that Nick and Sig and I could split three ways if we killed the bitch responsible for her husband's death. I felt a little bad about that, but Lenke could apparently afford it. It was as close to a happy ending as the night was going to get.

ᕙ29ᕗ

OUT OF HOT WATER AND
INTO A HOT TUB

Nick, Sig, and I had a subway car all to ourselves. There had been a few other people in it, but then they saw my muddy and bodily fluid–stained pants, got a whiff of what I smelled like underneath the jacket I'd stolen, and took a good look at my face. My smile definitely seemed out of place. Sorry, Smokey Robinson. They got out, off, and away at the first opportunity. "What do you know about these Redcaps?" I asked Nick.

Nick seemed distracted and a little sad, probably wondering if he should stay in Adriana's life. "Not much. I heard they wiped out a vampire hive in their territory. Turned those mothersuckers into blood smears too. They never got over the line at the Buried Treasure, but they weren't a lot of fun to hang around either, you know what I mean? They were driving away customers, but Mama Lenke wasn't going to say anything."

I hesitated a moment myself. "Have you ever heard of a drug called Glimpse?"

Nick gave me a quizzical look. "No. Why?"

"I haven't told you everything, Nick," I admitted.

Sig put her hand on my knee. I don't know if it was a warn-ing or support, but I didn't try to ease into it. "I'm one of the werewolves who work with knights now. The draugar might have attacked tonight to get to me."

Nick didn't tense up. I don't think I've ever seen a nix tense up; their bodies are too fluid. But he stayed quiet, and his eyes had a lot going on behind them.

"That's not a hundred percent," I added hastily. "There's a naga looking into them too, and the naga and the gorgon who were there tonight might have been working with him or for him. The necromancer running the Redcaps really did seem upset about the gorgon for some reason. I wasn't lying about that."

"You work with the knights," Nick repeated. "You're one of those Round Table wolves."

"Yeah," I said. "I could use your help, but I understand if you don't want to hang around."

"You want me to help you con Mama Lenke," Nick accused.

"I aim to do that. She put a bounty out on whoever killed her husband," I said. "And I'm really not convinced the Buried Treasure got attacked just to get at me. That's crazy overkill."

"Besides, your *mama* tried to feed me human being tonight," Sig said flatly. "If you don't have a good sense of smell, there's a chance you've had more than a couple of extra ingredients in your food recently too."

Nick shook his head as if there was a fly rattling around in it. "That doesn't matter," he said without conviction. "I'm not a human."

"It's not like you just play one on TV either, Nick," I argued. "You're at least half human, and you love them. You're in love with one now. Lenke would have fed Adriana human tonight too. Are you saying that doesn't matter?"

Something occurred to Nick then. "This woman called you John. You're him, aren't you? John Charming? You're the werewolf and the Valkyrie who killed a djinn in New York. Were you working with the knights when I showed you where the Buried Treasure was way back then? Are you some kind of informant?"

"No," I said, but I don't think he believed me.

Nick stood up abruptly. "Whatever I do, I'm not doing it with you. And if you do kill the person you're after, I'm taking a third of the money just for keeping my mouth shut."

"That's fair," I acknowledged. "But you ought to look for that gorgon too. I'm going to be busy going after this gang, and the gorgon was important to the necromancer for some reason."

My opinion didn't seem to matter much. "Don't ever ask me about finding you work again," Nick said tersely. "This makes us even."

"Why did you owe John?" Sig asked softly.

Nick looked at her for a long moment, then shook his head and walked off to find his own damn subway seat.

"You've got my number," I called.

"You got that right," he shot back over his shoulder.

"Sorry about using your name," Sig said shamefacedly. "I can't believe I made a rookie mistake like that."

I didn't say that it wasn't a big deal. It kind of was. But Sig wasn't used to working my way any more than I was used to working hers, and we had bigger things to worry about, so I just shrugged. She would make more mistakes, and that was probably a good thing, because I certainly would. And I was pretty sure Sig wouldn't make that particular mistake again.

"Still, laying it all out for Nick like that was kind of risky," Sig continued. "And having a shapechanger of our own would have been really useful with all of these skinwalkers running around."

Huh. Sig was usually the one arguing for direct and honest communication. But there is a part of Sig that is always on the lookout for useful talent to sign up for causes and quests. I think it's a Valkyrie thing.

"The truth would have come out sooner or later," I said with complete conviction. "Nick would have been a time bomb as much as an ally. This way, he still might be a hole card for us."

Sig frowned slightly. "What do you mean?"

"Nixies are curious," I said. "It's one of their defining traits. Nick is going to be working this from his own angle now, and our trails might cross again."

"He might snarl us up too. That doesn't bother you?" Sig asked.

"Of course it does," I admitted. "But in a way, it's like taking out an insurance policy. If we get in trouble, having Nick in the shadows is more likely to help us than hurt us."

"I can never really figure out if you're being clever or insane when you say things like that," Sig confessed.

"It can be a thin line," I granted. "But I'm not wrong."

"How can you be so sure?" Sig asked.

"Nick is a romantic," I explained. "And we're the good guys."

Sig made a face. "Are you sure about that?"

"As long as we're talking comparatively?" I put my hand over hers. "Yes."

Sig made to snuggle in closer to me, but when she put her palm on my upper thigh, she frowned at what was still coated there. Then she wrinkled her nose as she realized what kind of smells she'd gotten used to over the last few hours. Examining her dirty palm, Sig said ruefully, "My knight in shining armor."

I leaned my head back on my seat and closed my eyes. The thin layer of plastic was cold and slightly sticky against the skin of my neck, and the metal seat beneath it was vibrating unpleasantly. "Why would anybody want a knight in shining armor? The guy would have to be a complete tool. Light would glint off of him and give his position away for miles."

"You're being too literal. Maybe the point is that he's got nothing to hide," Sig said. "He just puts it all out there."

"I'm sure all those damsels in distress really appreciate that," I scoffed. "Oh, here I am, being held hostage. I hope some sword-swinging moron with no grasp of strategy comes storming in here to save me with a hi-ho and a happy hard-on."

Sig made a *pffffft* sound. "You're overthinking this."

That didn't stop me. "And anybody whose armor is in parade shape obviously isn't doing his job, anyway," I complained. "It's like saying *a lumberjack with baby-smooth hands*."

Sig managed to nestle in against my jacket, shoulder to shoulder, without getting her pants or hair any more messed-up than they already were. "It's about the dream of the total package, John. A knight in shining armor means somebody who wouldn't have any doubts or play any games. He would look great, and his outside would match what was going on inside."

I looked down at myself. Even aside from my pants, my jacket was too short at the wrists and covered in spatters of dried blood. "Uh-oh."

Sig squeezed my arm.

I turned my head and kissed her on her cheek. "Did I mention that I like your new hair color?"

She closed her eyes and smiled.

"They don't call themselves Redcaps on the streets," Simon told me over the phone. "People call them 'the Pollys.' Polly like the parrot, not Paulie like the goombah."

"I'm guessing they're not Polish Irish?" I hazarded.

Simon's voice remained neutral. "They're definitely Irish

Irish. I've heard people say they're called Pollys because there are five brothers that everybody is particularly afraid of, and they hardly ever talk except to parrot what their older sister says. Too bad you didn't get a look at her."

"I'm pretty sure there's only three brothers now," I said. "And I don't think they're really related to the woman. But she's definitely the brains of the gang."

"I've also heard people say POL stands for piranhas on legs," Simon replied. "The five brothers are supposed to be very fast, and they like knives better than guns."

Working with knights again did have its advantages. Now that I wasn't hiding from Simon per se, I wasn't quite as particular about finding a place to hole up. Instead of dragging myself into a homeless shelter or breaking into a basement while I healed, I was at the Hyatt Boston Harbor, and I even paid for the presidential suite so that Sig and I could have that tub I'd promised.

So, while Simon's people were out doing all the groundwork, I was lounging in bubbling hot water and boiling the cold out of my bones. I decided that I could get used to this. Sig was sitting next to me so that she could listen to Simon on speaker. She was buoyant in very interesting ways, her feet intertwined with mine while the bubbles moved about and hid just enough of her to keep me staring. I did like her new hair but still thought it made her too visible.

"I figured you'd already know about the Redcaps," I said. "Does that mean you know how to find them?"

"Yes and no. The Pollys' hideout is an abandoned factory that used to make stamps for the US Postal Service," Simon said. "Unfortunately, it's in the middle of a neighborhood. We can't just go in guns blazing."

"How come this place doesn't still make stamps?" I asked

idly. "I thought places that made any kind of US currency were protected from overseas poaching."

"The demand has gone down." Simon said this as if it was something he'd always known, as if it was something I should have known. I'd never really thought about it, but it made sense. Between the advent of e-mail and texting, UPS, the decline in literacy, and the American public's nonchalance about handing out checking account information to companies who like to bill electronically, the US Postal Service has been taking a lot of hits. Internet shopping parcels and credit card offers are probably the only thing keeping them in business. "The factory tried to convert to making bumper stickers and customized stamps for a time," Simon went on blithely. "But that stuff is either handled by the Chinese or small private businesses now."

"Huh," I said. "I just thought of something."

"Uh-oh," Sig muttered drowsily. I ignored her.

"You told me that our enemy was putting this Glimpse drug on professional-grade blotter paper," I reminded Simon. "A facility that used to make stamps..."

"That occurred to me too," Simon said when I trailed off. "If this bunch really is gearing up to mass-produce, this factory might be important enough that they won't want to destroy it or leave it." Simon's voice took on a distinctly predatory anticipation. "Maybe they won't want to abandon the place even if they do get some kind of prophetic warning."

"You're using the word *maybe* an awful lot," I commented.

"Maybe." Was that actually a joke? "But Boston isn't like New York or Detroit. Less than one percent of the buildings here are abandoned." Simon really had been doing his research, or, more likely, someone like Dawn was doing it for him.

"I'm not following you." I tacked a yawn on to this admission.

"This place was in the process of being turned into a series of condos when the developer dropped dead," Simon elaborated. "And nobody has tried to do anything with it since."

I absorbed that information a little less efficiently than I normally would have, but I still worked my way around to the point eventually. Simon was implying that someone didn't want the factory owned by anybody else but didn't want to buy it and leave an official paper trail either. He was probably right too. Strange things probably kept happening to people who got interested in the place.

"Here's the thing," I said slowly. God, that hot water felt good. "Calling out all of those draugar just to wipe out me and Sig doesn't make any sense. It was like trying to kill a flea with a sledgehammer."

"Knights create a blind spot on psychic radar," Simon reminded me. "All this necromancer would have known was that some of her people had been hanging out at the Buried Treasure, and suddenly she couldn't see the future at that place at that time. She wouldn't have had any sense of scale."

"So you're saying she probably thought it was an entire knight raid going down there," I said thoughtfully. "Dozens of us."

"As far as she knew, that was the only way for knights to get in to that place. Speaking of which, you should have told me about this Buried Treasure." Simon's voice became a lash again. "We might have caught her. And if you had died, we wouldn't have learned anything."

I understood what he was saying, and he was right. But geas be damned, I wasn't going to repay people who had sheltered me from the knights during bad times by turning them over to Simon, no matter what. "How about we focus on the fact that letting me do things my way has gotten you better leads than any other approach so far?"

Simon couldn't really dispute my point, and he couldn't really agree with it, so he said, "That's true. It's also true that you poking around without giving us any clue about what you were up to led to a summoning that had hundreds and hundreds of sea zombies crawling out of Boston Harbor. We're still cleaning those subway tunnels out, and we've rounded up a dozen stray draugar. We even had to trot out that old bath salts excuse for a zombie that got out in traffic."

"Rounded up?" I said suspiciously. "Not destroyed?"

"I'm having Dawn examine them," Simon said reluctantly. "I want to see if she can figure out a way to enchant the draugar to return to the person who summoned them."

Now, that was interesting. "You mean like homing pigeons?"

"Like guided missiles," Simon countered.

That was a lot to take in, so I put it on hold for later. "Look, I wasn't bragging, Simon," I said. "I'm trying to convince you to keep giving me rope. I'll either hang myself with it, or I'll use it to strangle whoever's after Constance."

"I'm not sure which would make me happier," he muttered.

"Well, figure it out," I snapped. "Sig and I can't keep staying away from you if we're going to work together."

He couldn't really deny that, either. "If I see your girlfriend, I'm going to ask her some questions. That's just the way it is. You'd do the same."

I didn't disagree.

"But I won't try to spirit her away to some dungeon or drug her or whatever you're afraid of," Simon finished. "You have my word. I know you've got PTSD because of what happened with that nurse you lived with. You need to get over it."

Like it was that simple. What I was afraid of was that Simon was going to do some fucked-up thing to trick Sig or get emotional leverage on her so that he could feel like he was

274

in control. And if he did that, it was going to backfire. Most knights didn't understand how formidable Sig really was, and if they did, they wouldn't respect her for it. They would fear her. And knights don't respond to fear like normal people.

Sig put her mouth next to my ear, whispering. "I can take care of myself. Hurry up and finish." Then she nibbled on my earlobe.

"There's one more thing we should talk about," I said reluctantly, not sure which one of them I was talking to.

"What?" Simon said suspiciously.

"Even if you're right and she thought a bunch of knights were coming, unleashing a horde of draugar was still a desperation move," I said. "Do you know why the necromancer is desperate? Because I sure as hell don't. Where's the pressure coming from?"

"Us. Our secret enemy isn't so secret anymore," Simon said. "Would you want to be the person who pissed us off?"

In fact, I was a person who'd pissed the Knights Templar off, but whatever. I wasn't going to waste time talking about that. "The necromancer said she knew something about the knights' big plan," I said. "But I had the impression that she was fishing for information. Do you know what big plan she's talking about?"

"No," Simon said instantly, but then he gnawed on his answer for a bit. "The problem is, we're talking about someone with access to knowledge of the future. She might have gotten a glimpse of a big plan that we haven't actually made yet."

Sig groaned and sank her head underwater.

"Yeah, that sucks," I said. Of course, Simon could be lying and keeping some big plan from me, but there was no point belaboring that, either. "Hey, maybe that's why she overreacted. Think what it would be like to be used to seeing the future, and suddenly you couldn't see past a certain point any longer. What if we're going to kill her four days from now or something and just don't know it yet?"

"That would be enough to make anyone feel like they're under a deadline," Simon agreed slowly. "I like that idea."

"And I like that sending those draugar might be the mistake that causes the future she's afraid of to happen," I said. That actually got me thinking. Getting people who see the future into self-fulfilling prophecy mode might be the only way to stop them. But how did you encourage that sort of thing?

"Maybe this factory is the place where whatever's she's afraid of is going to go down," Simon said reflectively.

"It's definitely the place where something is going to go down." My voice was starting to slur slightly around the edges. "I don't like that. I don't like doing what an enemy expects."

"From what I can tell, you don't like doing what anyone expects of you," Simon sniped.

I definitely didn't want to get into that again, so I switched subjects. "There's something you aren't telling me."

"I'm not telling you so many things, it would make your head explode if you tried to take it all in too fast." Well, that was reassuring. "You're going to have to give me a context."

"You keep talking like we're laying all of our money down on this one particular number," I said. "This abandoned factory. What about our other leads? Did you find out anything about the dalaketnon's other numbers? Why aren't you capturing some of these Pollys and questioning them?"

Simon didn't like admitting what he said next: "The dalaketnon had doubles maintaining a long-term presence on our world, but they dropped dead. The Boston number went nowhere. And as to the Pollys, two days ago, we could have walked down a specific street and run into a Polly by closing our eyes and spinning in circles. But now that we know they're mixed up with this future drug, it's the same old story. They've disappeared. I've got knights and cops out looking for them, but they keep reporting in that they've just missed them, or that someone killed their informants before they even knew that they wanted to ask them a question."

"Ah. Future-drug problems," I said. "That's about all the metaphysical stuff I can handle tonight." We exchanged a few more unpleasantries, and then I set the phone on the edge of the tub.

"Why can't it ever be like *Mission Impossible* with us?" Sig wondered.

I closed my eyes contentedly. "What do you mean?"

"It would be nice to know exactly who our enemy is and what our objective is, and then plan everything out," Sig explained. "Ever since I started hanging around you, it's more like *Oh, look, something messed-up is going on. Let's poke it and see what happens. Wow, it's even bigger and more messed-up than it looked like. Let's poke it again. Oh my God, where did those giant fire-breathing woodchucks come from?*"

"Hey, that whole Akihiko Watanabe thing was your idea." I slipped and slid against her a little more firmly, though I really wasn't up for much more than a good cuddle. "Was it a lot different when you were working with Dvornik?"

Sig thought about that, then put her arms around my neck and gave me a slippery, sweaty kiss.

"You okay?" I asked.

"It *was* different," she murmured. "I prefer this."

It turned out I was up for more than a good cuddle after all.

∽30∾

BULLSHITTIN' ON THE DOCK OF THE BAY

I met Emil Lamplighter on a pier at noon. We were leaning against a rail, both of us drinking coffee from large Styrofoam cups while the sun overlooked the ocean. From the way it was beaming and glowing, the sun was also overlooking the fact that I'd just given Emil a small plastic lunch pouch with two messy Redcap thumbs in it. Noon and dawn are pretty much the best times to meet someone if you want to eliminate the chances of being tailed by about fifty percent of the unseen world, and the ocean is one of the most effective background-noise generators around, naturally or supernaturally. I didn't know if the area behind us was crawling with Templar snipers and strike teams or if Emil had slipped away and come here without telling anyone. Given the circumstances, I couldn't say which would have been safer, and the Grandmaster wasn't the kind to show his hand.

"Don't you have worse things to do?" I asked.

The Grandmaster was in his late fifties or early sixties, lean and weathered. His white hair was shaved close to his skull, his skin looked like it had been scraped out of leather, and his eyes were flint. He should have looked tired, but he didn't. "You could say that. The situation between the Crusaders and the Round Table is spiraling."

It wasn't surprising that the open resurgence of the Crusaders' anti-werewolf manifesto was beginning to have concrete repercussions. "Has something happened?"

"There hasn't been a Waco-style situation yet," Emil said. "But when Ben Lafontaine went underground, it made the Crusaders even more paranoid. So, they started looking, and not very politely, and Ben had the rest of the Round Table begin making itself scarce."

"That can't go on forever," I responded. "The Crusaders know a lot more about the werewolves since we've been working together. Like names and addresses."

"True." Emil blew lightly on his coffee before taking a sip. "But the werewolves have learned a lot about the Crusaders too. And let's not overlook the fact that the Crusaders' leader is an idiot."

"I've been wondering about that," I admitted. "How did a guy like Cassibury manage to become the head of his chapter?"

"Because I let him." Emil said this like I should have known it. I guess I should have. "And maybe that was a mistake, but I made that decision before I ever dreamed that our Order would be working directly with supernatural beings. The Crusaders have always been a problem. At least with Thomas leading them, they were a problem that was easy to predict and manipulate."

I'd actually seen a little of that for myself back when I was helping werewolves organize against the Templars. I'd gotten a distinct sense that the Crusaders' leader was better at ideological rhetoric and bullying than he was at strategy or foresight.

His lack of self-doubt made him attractive to people who were desperately trying to eliminate any anxiety or uncertainty from their own life, but it also made him override and micromanage the tactical decisions of his entire chapter, which hampered the efficiency and reaction time and flexibility of his agents in the field.

"Still..." I began, then faltered.

Emil picked up the slack. "Ben Lafontaine is a much better strategist than Thomas. And I have agents inside the Crusaders who are more loyal to me and the Order than to Thomas Cassibury. I've been sending the Round Table inside information."

Well, yeah, that would make it easier for werewolves to not be where the Crusaders looked, or to have more numbers and firepower when the Crusaders showed up, which would be a socially awkward situation, to say the least. Still, that would just make the Crusaders try harder, which would force the Round Table to go to greater lengths, which would make the Crusaders try harder. It was the kind of self-perpetuating cycle that usually ended in a collapse or an explosion.

"Why am I here, Emil?" I asked. "More to the point, why are you here?"

"Do you know you're one of the only people who talk to me this way?" Emil reflected. "It's refreshing, when I'm not fighting the impulse to have you assassinated."

"You scare me," I admitted. "It pisses me off."

"We're here because the way I'm playing Thomas has made me realize something," Emil confessed. "Like him, I am also looking for an enemy who is somehow managing to never quite be where I search."

The implication was obvious. "You think spies inside the Templars are still feeding this enemy inside information?"

"I do," Emil said. "And it's not just because of skinwalkers.

I won't say setting up the protocols has been easy, but there are definite steps to expose skinwalkers and root them out. But they've been busy implanting programs in our computer systems, bugging homes and meeting areas, bribing and blackmailing lay servants who aren't bound by a geas, emotionally manipulating and twisting knights who are until they're confused about what their duty actually is... It's a nightmare."

"You need to figure out what this enemy wants," I said.

Emil gave me a very eloquent look. But all he said was, "It would be easier to figure out what the enemy doesn't want. I think they want everything."

"But they must have priorities," I argued.

Emil sighed. "Our Order implemented the first church-sanctioned banking system back in the Middle Ages, John. We had spy networks and investments and holdings and political influence long before we went underground—that's one of the reasons we had to go underground. And we've been cultivating that power base for the better part of a millennium. We own a major corporation outright and have members on the boards and employees of almost every other. Knights are one of the least parts of what we do. We have geas-bound in every political branch, military service, intelligence-gathering agency, and law enforcement division. We have advertising firms who specialize in spinning incidents. We have bloggers flooding the Internet with so much insane and poorly written nonsense about the supernatural that finding anything real is almost impossible. We have real estate agents flagging properties that don't sell or sell repeatedly, insurance company employees investigating strange death and accident claims, hospital workers reporting strange accidents..."

"I know all this," I said.

"Have you considered that this might not just be about

neutralizing us?" Emil asked. "Do you know what a group that got control of our resources and wasn't bound by a geas could do with that kind of power base?"

"Rrrruuuulle the world," I said softly.

Emil didn't smile.

"I hadn't taken it that far," I admitted. "What I have been thinking about is how hard it would be to take over the Templars by inserting doubles into key positions. It wouldn't be like the movies, where just looking like someone is enough to pull that kind of scam off."

"It wouldn't be," Emil agreed.

The logistics were insane. This enemy would have to slowly insert skinwalkers up the ranks, having the low-level ones observing and gathering information until they could convincingly take over more visible knights higher up the food chain. It's not like most knights ever get more than a tiny peek of the whole operation. And skinwalkers are rare. The enemy couldn't have had thousands of them on hand, so in order to move up, the skinwalkers probably had to fake the deaths of the knights they'd been impersonating first. They would have also had to eliminate the people who could expose the targets they really wanted, or Templars in charge of verifying identities. It really would take a long, long time, and they couldn't have gotten too far.

"At least you're still you," I said. "I can smell it."

"Yes, you can," Emil smiled. "Whatever our enemy is up to, they must have had a bad moment when we introduced werewolves into the equation."

"Oops," I said.

"Then look at the kind of magical power our enemy has been trying to accumulate," Emil went on. "They're trying to synthesize and develop a drug that lets people see the future.

They're looking for ways to transport large numbers of goods or agents across physical distances instantly. That's time and space, John. They're looking for ways to control time and space, and those are just the two specific endeavors we know about."

"Okay, mission accomplished. You've officially freaked me out," I said. "What do you want from me, Emil?"

The bastard still didn't answer directly. "I want you to understand how close we are to falling apart when we need to be pulling together. The Crusaders are busy moving all of their Templar noncombatants out of the Midwest or transferring them to survivalist-type compounds. The good news is that it's buying us a little more time."

He didn't have to explain the bad news. If the Crusaders were getting their civilians out of the way, it was because they were getting ready for a war. "The Crusaders must be crazy. The Round Table still has the secret for creating werewolves." That was the only way Ben Lafontaine had managed to force an alliance between Templars and werewolves in the first place. We had killed the man who had identified the spell components of the original werewolf ritual, but not before he figured out how to turn them into a bioweapon for mass dispersal. I didn't think Ben would directly use that knowledge, but he wasn't above using it as leverage.

"Are you asking me if the Crusaders are capable of planning something big and stupid that would be a complete disaster?" Emil asked.

I sighed. "I guess not." It certainly sounded like the Crusaders were preparing for a Night of the Long Knives option.

Emil finally came out with it. "I need you to work with Simon. Quit distracting him with these power games and start helping him."

"He bothers me," I admitted.

"Of course he does," Emil said irritably. "You're fighting to have your own life separate from the Order. Simon's valuable because he's sacrificed any personal life he might have had for the Order's sake. You two are opposite sides of the same coin."

"You're grooming him to be Grandmaster someday, aren't you?" I guessed.

Emil gave me a strange look. "John, I'm grooming you both to be Grandmaster someday. And Ben Lafontaine is grooming you to take over the Round Table at the same time."

I sputtered.

Emil smiled that flinty smile of his then. "So, that's what it takes to make you speechless."

I opened my mouth. Closed it again.

"You're the one who started us down this path when you refused to just be polite and die," Emil said with a certain amused malice.

I had this sudden mental image of Darth Vader gesturing towards Luke Skywalker and saying, "JOIN ME, LUKE. IT IS YOUR DESTINY."

"Don't worry," Emil chuckled. "The Order has at least fifty years to a century of growing up to do before it's ready for that kind of transition. So do you." Emil chuckled again and shook the lunch pouch with two Redcap thumbs in it. "Let's focus on the problem at hand. So to speak."

He jawed around for ten mintues, dropped a bombshell like that out of nowhere, and then wanted to hurry up and get to the point? "You're just messing with me to keep me off-balance so I'll be more tractable, right?"

Emil blithely ignored me. "I'm fairly certain our enemy went after Constance because of Ben Lafontaine, not me. If Mister Lafontaine has one weakness, it's his tendency to adopt surrogate children and the lengths he'll go to protect them. As a result, the enemy has distracted the werewolves, and the werewolves have distracted the Crusaders, and the Crusaders are distracting me. Basically, the enemy is trying to turn you werewolves from a huge threat to an asset, and abducting Constance was part of that. I don't think they planned on you unmasking the skinwalkers, though."

"The fact that Constance is your grandniece has to play into it too." I don't know if I was asking a question or making a statement.

Emil didn't respond either way. "The only way to defuse this situation is to completely unmask our enemy, and right now, the enemy is still mostly underground. The Redcaps and this abandoned factory are just part of it. It's like glimpsing parts of a snake through a crack in the rocks. We still don't know how big the snake is or how poisonous or even what direction it's going in."

I went with the simile. "So, we need to dig carefully."

"But fast," Emil said, "before it disappears again. It's going to be hard to do both. That's why I have a task for you."

"I thought you might," I said dryly. "But all that buildup makes me think I'm really not going to like it."

"Oh, you'll hate this job," Emil assured me breezily. "That's why you're the right person for it."

Those were the worst kind.

∼31∼

SHAKE THAT MONEYMAKER

City Councilman Daniel Moran woke in total darkness. A thin wire was wrapped around his throat and binding it to the subway rail that his head was resting on, and his hands were zip-tied behind his back. The councilman was a big, soft man in his fifties, and I'm sure it was uncomfortable as hell. The sound of distant subway trains was in the background, but only because I'd recorded some. We were in a stretch of the abandoned sub-way tunnel I'd discovered the night before. I'd sprinkled bits of cheese all over him, and rats were crawling on his body.

"Huh?!" he said. It wasn't a particularly intelligent response, but I'm not sure there was one. He grunted and yelled then, probably because the wire was pressing into his neck. "WHUH?!? WHAT'S GOING ON?!? CHRISTINA?!?"

Christina was his twenty-four-year-old mistress. I had abducted the councilman from the parking basement of her apartment complex after his late lunch. He had never seen me coming, and the drug I'd used to knock him out had deleteri-ous effects on short-term memory. I won't say that I didn't keep the councilman in suspense, but I did provide some light. It came from his own cell phone, and it showed a picture of him and Christina that didn't leave much doubt as to the nature of their relationship.

I angled the phone so that he couldn't see me and I didn't have to look at the picture again. Morality aside, what a dumbass. The councilman was a professional politician who ran on a platform of family values, and most of his campaign money came from his wife's family. The phone also illuminated several of the rats, and they scampered off him while Moran screamed.

I spoke up, since I was wearing a ski mask. "Hi, Danny."

"What are you doing?!?" The councilman sounded outraged. "What is this? I'm not the president of the freaking United States!" It was an interesting reaction. Like he was personally offended by the situation's lack of proportion, not its morality.

"No, you're not," I agreed. "You're just a greedy asshole who took the wrong kind of money from the wrong kind of people."

That shut him up. It was probably taking Moran a moment to process how many bribes he was taking from how many people. That condominium loft his girlfriend was staying in was expensive, and so was her car, and I doubt he was paying for things like that with his wife's money.

I helped him out. "I'm talking about the abandoned factory. The one you've been helping keep abandoned."

Here's the skinny: Emil wanted to buy the building that the Redcaps were squatting in; more specifically, he wanted to purchase it using a Templar-owned production company as a front. There was a Templar named Brett Baker who hadn't made it through squire training but had gone on to be useful by becoming a director of low-budget action films. Apparently, Emil often sent Brett to locations where there either had been or was going to be a lot of unexplained gunfire and explosions and God knows what else. Once there, Brett would quickly assemble a specially selected film crew and movie set to explain the ruckus. It helped that this Brett had developed a long and colorful history of beginning projects without the proper licenses or permits, staging irresponsible publicity stunts, and failing to notify local authorities in a timely fashion. Brett Baker's films weren't exactly artistic successes, but from what I understand, they did sometimes make a small profit, and everyone knew that Brett loved blowing shit up.

More to the point, if we got into a huge fight with the Redcaps at the abandoned factory, Brett could claim that he was staging an action scene there as long as he owned the property and we got it done quickly. That part was simple enough. But Emil also wanted to purchase the building without providing the proper documentation to all of the people he was supposed to provide it to along the time frame he was supposed to provide it in. Emil wanted Dan Moran to stop blocking the purchase, then help us keep the transaction secret from the people Dan had been pulling strings for. As if that weren't complicated enough, Emil wanted to prove that everything had been done legally after the fact if things went sour. Emil wanted me to handle Dan because he wanted to keep as many extra people out of the loop as possible for as long as he could.

"Who are you?" the councilman asked. His voice was trembling, but he still wasn't admitting anything. Looking for information so that he could begin negotiating.

"You know those people who have been using that factory to make drugs?" Maybe he didn't know those people. Moran's wince seemed to have an element of worst fears being realized in it, and I was pretty sure the councilman had been getting paid in cash to not ask those kinds of questions. If the unexplained money in Moran's banking account had left an electronic trail, Emil's people would have found it. "I'm the reason those people don't want to sign any papers," I told him. "I represent the people they're hiding from."

I wasn't talking because I liked to hear myself talk. Emil was right; I didn't like this. The more I got the councilman in the proper frame of mind, the less physical damage I would have to inflict. I had just informed the councilman that he didn't want to go to the police because he was involved with something that might blow up his career at best, land him in jail or a coffin at worst. I had also just told him that if he was scared of the Redcaps, I represented people who they were scared of. And if the Redcaps were blackmailing him, I was offering Moran the hope that someone existed who might make his blackmailers go away permanently if he played his cards right. I had told him all of that, and he believed it because he thought he was a sharp guy and I was just dumb muscle who didn't know how much I was revealing. He needed to believe that. He was desperate, and playing angles was what he did.

"I don't know what you're talking about!" he tried, but it was pro forma, a feeble protest just to see what I'd say.

I turned off his cell phone. When I spoke, I sounded bored. "Don't waste my time, Danny. I have other people to see."

"What are you talking about?" Still trying to get information out of me instead of the other way around. Still not begging me to untie him, because he didn't want to draw attention to how little power he actually had. I almost admired the councilman for that. He was struggling to keep his wits in a scary situation; too bad he couldn't keep them in his pants. "What people?"

"That's the thing, Danny." I leaned forward in the dark, and when I whispered into his ear, I had a bit of a wolf snarl in my voice. He flinched. "You haven't told me yet."

On the tape, the sound of a subway train got louder.

~32~

AS A MATTER OF FACTORY

It was hard to get an estimate on how many bodies were in the factory, because the windows had been painted black and there was machinery running inside that made it hard for equipment that measured sound waves. Some of the spotters Simon sent out to discreetly canvass the area tried thermal imaging, but something had been done to raise the temperature in that place too, and that was assuming that everyone in the building had normal body heat and moved around all the time anyhow, which wasn't a safe assumption. If we were dealing with powerful cunning folk, there could be hundreds of corpses waiting to animate and burst through the ground on command, or some kind of elementals primed to materialize, and so on.

Simon considered using his influence to send a couple of cops to the factory to investigate it on some pretext or another—it's not like they would need a warrant for abandoned property. But anybody powerful enough to coerce skinwalkers and summon draugar was certainly powerful enough to entrance ordinary policemen and make them forget they'd seen anything. If Simon sent in any other kind of cops—say, Templars who had infiltrated the Boston PD and were immune to mind magic—it would be an open declaration of war instead of a probe.

Things weren't much better on the magical front. Some of the graffiti on the surrounding pavement was actually disguised sigils, defensive wards placed strategically so that they were just far enough away that technology could function in the factory, but spread out to form a barrier against scrying spells and bodiless spirits and wireless signals alike. There were probably warding stones buried under the ground at points too.

Knight observers spotted lots of people with red baseball caps moving on the roof or opening a window for some fresh air or occasionally going outside to take trash out to a large industrial storage bin in the back lot, but they all seemed to be human as far as anyone could tell. Whoever was there was hunkered down. Almost as if they were prepared for a siege. Jeepers.

Location was an issue too. The factory in question wasn't as isolated as we would have liked. It had a chain link fence with a thin layer of sheet metal draped over it and barbed wire on top, which was good, and a big decaying parking lot in front and railroad tracks running behind, which was even better, but there weren't any patches of trees around like there would have been in the South. The building's nearest neighbor was another factory that had been converted into a mall. Not a modern professional mega-mall, mind you; this place had probably been converted into a downtown shopping center back in the seventies when malls were just becoming a thing, and it was in the process of a long, slow death with very little dignity. Most of the converted storefronts were for sale, but there was a place that sold pet food, a carpet outlet, some kind of physical office for an online school, one place that became a dance studio three times a week, and another space full of rows of aluminum chairs that was apparently a church on Sundays.

The obvious solution was to start any action after dark, but there were problems with that approach too. It was the kind of area where the most foot traffic was going to occur after the sun went down, and that's when police would be more likely to swing by on their rounds as well. We had suppressors for our weapons, but there was no guarantee that the Redcaps did, and there would be less noise cover at night. Sparks and flashes and flames would be more visible too; they wouldn't be quite as visible at five thirty in the morning, but noise would be a lot more apparent then, and some early-morning traffic would already be on the road, anyway.

So, we decided to hit the factory in that sweet spot between the morning work rush and the lunch-break crowd. Brett Baker's "production company" had actually managed to quietly buy the abandoned factory, and he had crew members ready to cordon off nearby city streets, and assistants with loudspeakers and handouts to move through the neighborhood, assuring everyone that there was no cause for alarm. His FX crew was also preparing dry ice and fog machines for some really cool visuals that would obscure the view of the factory. The problem was that Brett couldn't warn the neighborhood days in advance. Still, it was the kind of stunt Brett Baker was infamous for, had even served jail time for. And if Simon was reluctant to send some the Order's geas-born cops into the factory, he wasn't at all reluctant to have them in the area to give Brett's enterprise every appearance of official approval. As an added benefit, they would be the first officers to respond if things went totally pear-shaped.

On the other side of the railroad, a knight had sabotaged a power junction so that a road crew was going to have to do some work with a jackhammer. It wasn't just a matter of providing noise cover—Dan Moran had pulled some strings, and the plans the road crew had been given for rerouting traffic with detour signs had maybe gotten a little more extensive than necessary.

And just to make sure that national media was busy, the Templars were arranging for a stolen sex tape of a pop star to be released on the Internet a few hours before we conducted any raid. From what I understand, the Order has collected several such tapes in case of emergency.

There was also an if-all-else-failed option. If worse came to worst, we were going to have some werewolves shapeshift in the middle of several strategic locations in broad daylight. This would cause the Pax Arcana to kick in on a massive scale; there would be a huge power outage, and traffic cameras and cell phones and security systems would stop working as magic poured into the atmosphere. As long as the werewolves weren't threatening anyone directly, the pedestrians and motorists would suddenly blank out and wander or drive off until they suddenly found themselves someplace nicer with better things to do.

You know all of those cases of missing time? It's not aliens.

That last contingency was the nuclear option, though—the whole point of the Knights Templar's continued existence was to keep the Pax Arcana from overextending like that.

I did my part to try to speed things along by helping scout out the area surrounding the factory, which is why I met Virgil the day before the raid. The factory was in a lower-income, predominantly white neighborhood, and Simon was concerned that a black man and a white man hanging out together there wouldn't blend in. I don't know if he was right or not. I can blend in among all kinds of settings—I can do homeless, hipster, drifter, soldier on leave, off-duty cop, white collar worker, blue collar worker, criminal, evangelist, news reporter, player, insurance investigator, federal agent, treasure hunter, paralegal, or corporate drone without blinking. But I'm used to scouting alone. So, I asked Sig for help.

"This is your chance," I told her, holding my arms out wide. "I'm going to let you dress me."

Sig clapped her hands and squealed excitedly. I really hoped she was being sarcastic. If that's what her excited squeal really sounded like, I was doing something very wrong in bed.

"Seriously," I said. "Simon says a white man walking with a black man in a low-income, mostly white Boston neighborhood will look like an undercover cop, or at least draw too much attention to be forgettable."

"What's the counterculture scene in the neighborhood like?" Sig asked seriously. "Is it just starting, or is it on the way to being kicked out by invading gentry?"

"Somewhere in the middle," I said.

"Okay," Sig said, and she held up a plastic object. "Let's start with this. This is a comb."

I made a cross with my fingers and staggered back against the bathroom door, yelling and averting my eyes.

Anyhow, after Sig and I visited a consignment store, I wound up looking like a graduate student trying to reflect culture and sophistication on a low income. I had just a little bit of a Scottish-gentry thing going on with a worn, bulky mackintosh coat, faded slim-cut jeans, an ascot, a Scottish tam, and a big pair of reading glasses at the lowest focus level. "Really?" I had asked. "You want me to disguise myself by wearing glasses?"

She had just laughed. "If you want to buy a blue bodysuit and a red cape to wear under your clothes, be my guest."

For his part, Virgil looked like he was going to go to a public reading of some really bad but very passionate poetry to support a friend. We met at a laundromat, both of us carrying bags with dirty clothes and maybe a few other things. There was a scary-looking guy with crazy eyes talking to himself outside the laundromat when we arrived. He looked and smelled like something that had been vomited out of a meth clinic, but that was only to discourage regular customers from coming in for a while. He was a knight, and the bulky clothing and filth concealed a body that was fit and formidable. Virgil and I smiled politely at his request for money, and I gave him eight dollars and went in to the place. It was a pretty grimy establishment, but all of the laundry machines were in use; it was supposed to provide noise cover and discourage any local hard cases who made it past the sentry.

"Looking sharp, Virgil," I commented while I pretended to walk around and examine the washers.

"You can just shut the hell up," Virgil snarled. "You're still on my list for leaving me alone with your buddies."

"You wouldn't hit a guy with glasses, would you?" I asked.

"I'd put my foot up his ass," Virgil assured me. I had sent Virgil a text after taking off, if only because I knew he had his own trust issues where knights were concerned, but he had a right to be pissed.

"I'm sorry I didn't warn you," I said. "I saw a chance to slip off the knights' radar, and I took it."

"Listen up, I expect being a black man and a police officer wasn't all that different from being a knight and a werewolf in some ways," Virgil said.

"Maybe," I said cautiously. "Where are you going with this?"

"I like Sig." Virgil said this with an edge of warning and reluctance. "But if you keep putting her over the pack, you're going to back yourself into a corner where you're going to have to choose between us."

"I've already lost somebody I cared about, Virgil." I didn't know what else to say.

He laughed ruefully. "Sometimes I forget. You've been a werewolf, but you haven't really been one of us."

"What do you mean?" I asked.

"We've all already lost somebody, John," he said, not unkindly.

"Wolves put their mates first," I said.

"They do," Virgil agreed. "*And* they put their pack first. It's not supposed to be a conflict. I don't know how you're going to make it so it's not a problem, but you need to figure that out or get the hell out."

"You make it sound like packs are perfect," I said. "I seem to remember a time when you and I found some werewolves being experimented on like lab animals."

Virgil glowered at me then. We had both seen some bad things when we realized what our first pack leader, Bernard Wright, was really all about. "I never said being part of a pack is perfect. It's simpler."

"The thing you don't get? Taking Sig away for a little while protected you as much as it did me and her." I kept rattling lids as I strolled around, creating a little more background noise. "It made you Simon's only liaison with Ben. He couldn't afford to mess with you too much."

Virgil crossed his arms over his thick torso. "Bullshit."

"Do I smell like I'm lying?" I asked.

Virgil actually inhaled deeply. He wasn't usually so dramatic. Being alone among knights must have been harder on him than I'd thought. Come to think of it, I'd never seen Virgil rattled, but I'd never seen him without other werewolves around, either. Maybe being part of a group was how he defused stress. "You're serious."

"Yeah," I said. "This is what it looks like."

"Who thinks like that?" Virgil wanted to know.

Being around Templars brings back all kinds of primal memories of feeling like a freak, and the aggression in Virgil's smell and the growl in his voice were really starting to push my buttons. But I made an effort. "I was learning how to survive the knights before you were even born, Virgil." I hadn't had to play those games for decades, but it was kind of like wrecking a bicycle.

"Yeah, well, while you're figuring your love life out, you need to figure out if you're a knight or a wolf, too." Virgil grumbled.

Him too? It was easy for Virgil and Simon to run their mouths. I was useful to the wolves because I had ties to the knights, and I was useful to the knights because I had ties to the wolves. Nobody wanted me to cut any of my ties, and everybody wanted my undivided loyalty. "And you need to relax," I told him. "We're supposed to be acting casual, and you look you have a red-hot poker up your rear end."

"You just need to remember why you're here," Virgil insisted.

"To do whatever I have to do to keep Constance safe," I said instantly. "Why are you here?"

Virgil worked his jaw. "To remind you that you have family if the knights start messing with your head." He said it like he was repeating someone else word for word.

I let him think about that. Then I said, "You're the one who'd better be careful, Virgil. The Templar Grandmaster thinks Ben is grooming me to take over the Round Table."

"Oh, *hell* no," Virgil said feelingly.

"That's right," I said. "You'd better start sucking up if you want to keep getting Christmas bonuses and casual Fridays."

"How about we both just shut up and do our job?" Virgil said irritably, and then he took his own advice. We took our laundry bags with us and walked out, crossing a street and moving through a large parking lot and on to an improvised bicycle path running behind a grocery store. The place I was currently living, Clayburg, didn't have bicycle paths in the lower income areas. Hell, most southwest Virginia towns don't even have sidewalks anywhere except on the main streets. The rare paved walkways tend to wind through parks or alongside rivers. But this big city path ran beside a neighborhood with drugstores and eateries and various parlors and warehouses that had been converted into apartments on one side, and a chain link fence separating us from the railroad on the other. A lot of the buildings had become brick billboards for local graffiti artists. Some of the graffiti would have stood up to any art gallery exhibit, and a lot of it seemed to involve gang tags or genitalia or very long tongues or scary-looking humanoids with occult characteristics and guns. All of it was colorful.

Virgil subtly relaxed. I don't know if he was letting his anger go, or if he had just spent a lot of time in places like this when he was in a missing children's unit, or if working with another wolf again was the real familiar territory. When we passed the area near the Redcaps' supposed hideout, I picked up on a tidbit of conversation from the direction of the factory roof despite the background noise.

"Look at that shit." The voice sounded like it had broken just recently. "Would you—"

There was a sharp slapping sound.

"Ow! Moth—"

"Sssst," a voice hissed, speaking so low that I could only pick up on the sharp consonants. "—t it!—what... told...K——up—k—uck—"

"What do you got to do all that for?" the first voice whined. "I—" And then the voice shut up with a pained grunt.

Just out of curiosity, I checked my cell phone. It wasn't working. My nose was getting a lot of elf stink, but none of it was fresh. Nobody followed us as far as I could tell, and if they did, a knight with a sniper scope would see them coming.

Virgil and I made a big, wide circle, but there weren't any young-looking guys in red baseball caps and steel-toed hiking boots patrolling the streets, which was weird in itself if this was Redcap territory. We eventually made our way back to the laundromat. Virgil gave the sentry eight dollars this time—it was the sign that everything was okay—and we went straight to the door in the back corner of the place.

Two knights were standing guard in a very narrow hallway, and six more were sitting around a folding table in a square room, cleaning weapons. Not playing cards. Not eating. Not talking. Just sitting there. Cleaning weapons. Staring at us wolves. There would be other knights setting up in similar locations around the area, and still others acquiring vans that they could use like Trojan horses to get inside the Redcaps' territory. Nobody greeted us, but one of the knights from the raid on the dalaketnon castle—Steven Hunter—nodded at me and indicated the door to his left. It wasn't necessary—I could hear Sig talking to Simon about whatever she'd sensed in the abandoned subway tunnel through the door—but I appreciated the courtesy.

Simon and Sig and Dawn were sitting in folded aluminum chairs, drinking Yogi tea from Styrofoam cups. Dawn's presence was a relief; if Simon had wanted a psychic around while he talked to Sig, it meant he was focusing on subtle interrogation. Simon was sitting behind a metal desk mostly covered by a laptop and a messy pile of city maps. Dawn was behind the laptop and seemed engrossed in it. Her hair was still blue. I waved at her and she waved back, though she didn't take her eyes off of the computer screen.

"Did you smell anything interesting?" Simon asked this blandly enough, but I could tell from the way he was looking alertly between Virgil and me that he was picking up on some of the unresolved tension.

"No," I said shortly, looking for a place to lean. The room was pretty bare-bones. It had an old-fashioned radiator that was making a lot of noise but not much else, and the walls badly needed a fresh layer of paint. "Nice place," I observed. "Did the Order buy it, or do we know the schedule of the guy who comes by to empty the machines?"

"We're in the process of buying a lot of properties in the area," Simon said neutrally. "This one will be useful." It probably would be too. Even after all of this was over—knock on skulls—a laundromat would be a great exchange or drop-off point, or a way to justify income for knights who didn't do anything for a living that they could declare on their income taxes.

"You're tense about something—" Sig began.

"That factory stinks," Virgil interrupted before she could go into the personal stuff that she was about to go into. "And I'm not talking about the way it smells."

"So, what are you talking about?" Simon asked.

Sig used their interaction to look a question at me. *What's going on with you and Virgil?*

I looked an answer at her while I closed the door and leaned against it. *I'll talk about it later.* And then I had to look another response at her. *Promise.*

"It's not what I saw. It's what I didn't see," Virgil was explaining. "There weren't any young kids."

"I noticed that too," Simon said cautiously. "What do you make of it?"

"I'm not making anything out of it," Virgil said. "But it's not right. Gangs draw kids like a hunk of bad meat draws flies. They got all kinds of uses for those boys."

That was true. The courts' reluctance to prosecute adolescents as adults made young kids a valuable resource. Gangs use juvies as lookouts. Human shields. Couriers. Salesmen. Someone to palm a gun off on if things get hot. And with the high mortality rate, they need to keep the recruiting pool stocked.

Sig frowned. "That's how human gangs work. This one's being run by some Fae."

"I didn't see any sign of that," I said. "I think Elve-us has left the building. I think these Pollys are just humans wearing red baseball hats, not actual Redcaps."

"Yeah. I think so too," Virgil grumbled. "They're using those gangbangers like scarecrows."

"No, they're not," Sig disagreed. "Scarecrows are designed to keep invaders out. These are being used to pull us in, and in large numbers too. Maybe that's why they sent the young kids away. One of the reasons gangs surround a place with young kids is to make it harder for cops to go in hot, right?"

"Explain," Simon said.

Sig obliged. "The Redcaps have to know we're coming no matter what. If the factory was empty, you would just send somebody like John in to scout the place out, and the Redcaps know it. They want us to have to invade in force without knowing what we're dealing with."

Simon gave a Sig a look I recognized. He was realizing that she was smart. Really smart. I wondered if people would underestimate Sig as much, now that she wasn't a blonde. I wondered if I should be worried about Simon learning to respect Sig. I wondered about Emil's comment about Simon and me being two sides of the same coin. And I wondered why I was wondering about so much crap when we were talking about how the factory was essentially a trap.

～33～

HOLY NO SENSE OF HUMOR, BATMAN!

The armored van was the same kind used to transport prisoners and bank deposits. Its windows were bulletproof and would stand up to anything this side of ammo that wasn't armor-piercing and explosive. The van's tires were thick, double-layered, and self-sealing, and if they did blow out, the round hubs they were wrapped around were tested to drive uninsulated for at least a hundred miles.

We were parked in the old loading bay of what used to be a grocery store and was now a church. The movie director, Brett Baker, had alerted people in the nearby dying mall about the shooting that was going to be going on—well, the film shooting, anyway—and the owner had gladly rented the space for the day. Both Sig and I were wearing knight field suits, though we weren't wearing helmets, and nobody had come by to ask us any questions.

"You know, we're about to do something stupid," I told Sig, who was in the driver's seat. "And this is still the safest I've felt in a while." I pounded on the thick door for emphasis.

She agreed in a kind of sideways fashion. "How much money does one of these vans cost, do you think? Choo would love one. Maybe if we got one as a group expense, he might come back a little faster."

"I'm not absolutely certain," I said. "But I'm pretty sure you need to get a special license to buy one, and you send up all kinds of warning flags when you do."

Sig made a face. Those federal regulators. They ruin it for everybody.

"How is Choo, anyway?" I asked. "Have you heard from him recently?"

My reluctance to have anything to do with social media often results in Sig being my social secretary, a fact which she sometimes enjoys and sometimes resents. "He wants us to meet his ex-wife."

"Really?" I didn't mean that to sound quite as surprised as that came out.

"I think he wants to tell her about our world," Sig said, then added, "I told him we were taking a vacation."

"Akh," I gritted while some compulsion to talk to Choo as soon as possible began to form and writhe around inside my skull like a saw-toothed snake. "If he's thinking of telling her everything, you should check her out before I do."

Sig looked at me curiously.

"To make sure she's cool," I explained. "And talk to Choo. My geas could be real inconvenient."

Sig changed the subject. "Maybe we really should take some serious time off when this is over. I hear they have a holographic ABBA show in Iceland now."

I stared at her. "That's the big draw?"

She laughed. "The coffee is really good there too. And so is the seafood and the saunas."

"That's intriguing," I admitted. "But what's wrong with the beach?"

"I hate it," Sig said simply. "It's hot. It's boring. It makes me want to drink. There's always sand up my crack. Plus, I have weird skin; I don't tan at all, even if lie in the sun for hours and hours and hours, and then I just go up like a bonfire."

I smiled.

"I'm not kidding," Sig said regretfully. "I have to seriously grease up, and I hate the way that feels. And then there are way too many swinging dicks around. I can feel eyes crawling over me like spiders the minute I take my T-shirt off."

"You just haven't been to the right kind of beach," I said.

"Are you thinking of the rocky kind that gets below zero degrees and has lots of black sand and walruses crawling on it?" Sig wondered. "Iceland has those."

"That does sound like heaven," I said. "But no. That's not the kind I was thinking of."

I reached over and gave Sig's shoulder a squeeze, and she absent-mindedly patted my knee. I would have rather had Virgil along, not because he pays more attention when he pats my knee, but because (A) people might be firing at us soon, and he regenerates, (B) it would have helped him and me work out the remains of our tension, and (C) I wouldn't care as much if he got killed. I mean, don't get me wrong; I would care. I would care a lot. I just wouldn't care as much. But Virgil was one of the werewolves who were going to help trigger the Pax Arcana if we needed them to do so. Rounding up werewolves was a lot harder since Ben had put our pack on lockdown.

Sig had been watching a side window the whole time, and she pointed at a mirror flash that kept repeating. "I guess that's..."

"Yeah." I got out and opened the sliding storage-bay door.

When I got back, I began to put my helmet on while Sig drove. Mirror signals are another one of the ways knights compensate for not being able to use technology reliably. This one meant that a train was coming and that Brett Baker had finished distributing announcements and had begun cordoning off streets and setting up roadblocks while his assistants yelled through megaphones.

"Whoever signaled me got the timing wrong," Sig fretted when we pulled up in front of the factory. "Should I wait?" There was supposed to be a cargo train coming up behind the factory. We'd wanted to arrive while the train's noise was at its loudest and its passing cargo cars would shield us from the view across the tracks. I could hear the train in the distance, but it was still, you know, in the distance.

I put my helmet on. "I vote we go now." Sig didn't wait for me to elaborate. She drove past the driveway, stopped, then reversed the van and stomped on the accelerator, gathering speed as she aimed us at the gate beside the factory. The chain binding the gate snapped, and the van barreled through. Yee-hah. As soon as we were clear, Sig angled the van so that no one inside the factory would have a direct shot at her window and stopped. Me, I jumped out of the passenger's side.

There was a duffel bag full of smoke grenades in the floorboard of the van—not the M18 kind—these were about the size of soft drink cans. Pulling the pin off one smoke grenade, I threw it over the roof of the van. The grenade was already belching red smoke before it landed. Several more smoke grenades followed. The trick to moving rapidly in a crazy tense situation is to find a balance between anticipating your next movement and not rushing the next move before you're completely finished with your last one. It would have been really embarrassing if I'd bounced a smoke grenade off the top of the van and had red smoke hissing around me and filling the interior of the van's cab, not to mention potentially fatal. But that didn't happen. I heard a few bullets smack off metal and concrete, almost experimentally, but then the train arrived and I didn't hear anything else.

Knights from various sniper positions began firing on the factory as soon as their noise cover arrived, mostly concentrating on the second story. Black duct tape was being pulled off premade holes in the blacked-out windows so that people could fire through them, but the knights were trying to discourage anyone from opening a window fully or going out on the roof. Even if our enemies did have something like rocket launchers in that factory, anything that could hurt the side of our van couldn't be fired without creating a hell of a backblast, and combustibles would require some arc room.

I climbed into the van, and Sig reversed again, backing into the smoke cloud and only stopping when smoke was at our window levels. She drove parallel to the factory and close to it so that when I got out again, the van was still between me and the people inside. My visibility was for shit, but my helmet kept me from choking.

Now I was carrying one of the time bombs that we'd been prepared to use on the dalaketnon world, and I crawled with it under the armored van. I didn't try to place the bomb directly on one of the storage bay doors. There's a time for precision; dragging an explosive through a smoke cloud while using a van like a turtle shell is not that time. I just left my special delivery on the ground and scooched back to the van, which began rolling forward as soon as I jumped back in.

When the bomb went off and leveled at least one large storage bay door, Sig pulled a lever that unlocked the back of the van. I couldn't see them, but figures in black field suits hurled themselves out of the van and into the red smoke. I don't know what kind of barricade had been set up behind those storage doors. I never saw that, either. The train sounds were fading now, and gunfire smacked against the van loudly, but I doubt the figures in field suits ever hesitated. When shot, they simply staggered or picked themselves up and continued on.

For her part, Sig took off. She wheeled the van out of the rough perimeter of the smoke cloud, turned, and plowed back through the gate that was still gently swinging.

If none of this quite makes sense, here's the missing puzzle piece: The invading knights we'd released weren't knights at all. They were some of the draugar that the knights had rounded up. Don't ask me how the knights had gotten them all dressed up in field suits. It must have been like trying to give baths to cats, times infinity. Thankfully, I had nothing to do with it.

The red smoke from those smoke grenades? It was laced with the smell of blood. I'd like to say that the knights had prepared those grenades especially for this occasion, but they hadn't. Apparently, they'd had use for this particular device before, and I suspect the smoke cloud somehow had real blood mixed in it. In any case, the draugar were hungry and enraged at being confined in armored suits that they couldn't tear off, and the scent of blood drew them out and onward.

We were on the street and driving away when the factory exploded. Gravel rained down on the roof of the van, and patches of dirt splattered against the windows. We had wanted to trigger the trap and see what see what kind of surprise was waiting for us, but this was definitely one of the worst-case scenarios.

I could see lots of black smoke and the twisted remains of fencing, and a telephone pole on the street behind us was on fire. Other vans and police cars driven by our knights or lay sergeants were appearing on the leading street that we had blocked off, and police officers and men in construction outfits who had gathered while the train was blocking them from the view of the factory began to advance on the scene. They were acting calm and unhurried, projecting an air of detached professional satisfaction, if anything. I still recalled my phone conversation with Simon. *"Every time we had a lead, it dried up or died or disappeared,"* he had said. *"That would be a lot easier to pull off if you had a drug that let people see the future."*

The Boston gang that this necromancer had assembled to help gather vagrants and produce and protect her drug had been our best lead, and she had just cut her losses in a big way. How the hell were we going to corner these people?

∿34∿

SCHOOLED

After dropping the armored van back at the dying mall, Sig and I wound up driving away in a stolen car that ought to be safe to use for another day or two. Then we got out and walked and then wandered onto a college campus—I honestly couldn't tell you which one. I think Boston must have more colleges than grocery stores, and we were just killing time. If the necromancer we were after hadn't left any living witnesses behind, she still might have left some of the other kind, and Sig was willing to check that out once it was safe to go back to the bomb site. Which meant more of Sig talking to the dead for my sake. Hurray. I was either going to have to resolve my feelings about her gift or stop expecting her to use it on my behalf.

Anyway, we made it hard for anyone who might be tailing us, friend or foe, physically or otherwise, and at one point that entailed wandering on to a no-driving campus, then finding a commons with a lot of foot traffic where tall women with exotic-looking hair didn't stand out quite as much. Then we wound up going through a series of front and side and back entrances, and somehow, that led to a college activity center where the student checking college IDs let us in for twenty dollars. The place had a bowling alley and a lot of Ping-Pong and pool and air hockey tables, and there was a common area with a big-screen TV. The snack bar served exactly the kind of food you'd expect.

Sig and I spent most of the afternoon eating carbohydrates covered with cheap cheese and watching television. The American Dream. I didn't learn much, although I do now know that I like Ellen DeGeneres, so that's something. We saw a local broadcast that showed Brett Baker on television in handcuffs once, but just once, and he waved at us cheerfully. I'd never actually seen Brett before. He was a round-shouldered, squat little troglodyte of a guy with a big beard and a friendly smile. I liked him instinctively. Two hours later, we saw reporters interviewing Brett's attorney. Nobody was questioning that the factory had been blown up as part of making a film, only whether it had been done so responsibly, and neither clip lasted more than ten seconds. There weren't even any sexy shots of the factory burning, just one image of smoking ruins with a lot of construction workers milling around. All of the reporters seemed more interested in whether or not a certain sex tape really did feature a well-known pop star.

Sig tried a conversation opener. "A lot of humans died today."

"Yep," I said.

"There ought to be more of a fuss about that," Sig maintained. "From somebody. They had families."

"Yep," I said.

"How are the Templars keeping them quiet?"

"I have no idea," I said. "Though a lot of them probably don't stay in touch with their families, and the ones who do, their families probably avoid the police."

"I guess those men wanted to live dangerous lives," she reflected. "But still."

"Yep," I said.

"You don't want to talk about this, do you?"

"Nope," I said.

She threw a French fry at me.

"It bothers me," I told her. "But I don't know what to do about it right now. And there's still a living person I need to worry about."

Sig wrinkled her nose. "Constance?" It wasn't that Sig didn't care. I think the connection between chasing down these people and keeping Constance safe had become a little abstract for her over the last week. It hadn't for me.

"Yes," I said. "Constance."

"You don't even know her, John," Sig sounded half exasperated and half fond.

"I will," I said. "Someday."

"Well, shouldn't we be going around asking questions and hitting people?" Sig asked.

"Not the right time." I nodded at the TV even though there wasn't any unusual activity on it. "I guess that was the point of blowing up the factory. Kill a lot of knights. Leave a lot of dead bodies behind instead of potential informants for us to take prisoner. Make such a big mess that we would be busy covering it up and hiding instead of actively looking for anybody."

"But it's not working out that way, is it?" Sig frowned. "Except for the part about all those gangster wannabes getting killed. I feel like shit. We should be doing something."

The truth was, the knights had been turning Boston upside down ever since they found out the Pollys had actual Redcaps mixed up with them, and the knights had a lot more people who knew the territory a lot better than we did, and they still weren't coming up with anything. Painting by the numbers wasn't working. I wanted to draw outside the lines and didn't know how yet. But I was pissed off and disturbed too, so all I said was, "I am doing something. I'm thinking."

"All right." Sig nodded abruptly. "I'm going to find some suckers to play some pool."

I blew her a kiss and watched her walk off a bit ruefully. Sig is an externalizer. She likes to talk or walk or dance or exercise or have sex or hit things when she's bothered. Molly wasn't around for her to talk to, and this sitting around was driving Sig crazy. I hadn't noticed, because I'm an internalizer and I was deep inside my own head. It's a trap I can fall into pretty easily when I'm processing bad things.

It was just...I felt so close to putting something together. The Redcaps were in Boston for a reason. They had to be if they wanted to avoid knights and were still sticking around. What was keeping them from just uprooting to New York or Chicago or Detroit? Figuring out that reason was key. Another thing that was bothering me was how big a gesture that factory explosion had been. As with the draugar, it was overkill. The Redcaps were connected to people or a person who had patiently been planting spies within the Templars for decades. Why were they acting so imprudently now? Where was the urgency coming from? And if the visions the Redcaps had access to couldn't predict knights, and they were avoiding us by omission, there had to be a way we could use that to herd them or mislead them. It was all whirling around in my head like safe tumblers, but I couldn't quite make anything click.

Sometime later—closer to two hours than one—Sig came back. She didn't sit down next to me. She leaned on her pool stick and faced me. "You know what the problem is? You're trying to play chess with someone who knows what moves you're *not* going to make in advance, and it's driving you crazy."

"It really is," I admitted.

"I might know how to level the playing field."

She had my fuller attention. "How?"

312

"We know these visions don't work on places and times where Templar types are present, right?" Sig didn't wait for me to respond. "So, how about the knights put their people everywhere?"

"I don't think Emil can spare enough knights for that," I said slowly. "Especially not with the way communication has broken down between the chapters."

Sig jumped on that. "Who said anything about knights? Use anyone with the geas. All those spouses and children and the people who usually provide secondary support."

Was that possible? Maybe the Order could have people posing as missionaries. Bums. Protestors. Kids on a treasure hunt. Surveyors. Motorists. Joggers. Cyclists. It would be a massive logistical undertaking to break that many geas-born into units and put them on a schedule, circulating up and down this city and creating a grid. But if it could be done, it could be a game-changer. "Sig, that's brilliant!"

"Who cares about that?" she said a little self-consciously. "Do you think it will work?"

"I think maybe it already has," I said slowly.

"What?"

"This would explain why somebody's been panicking and acting like their back is against the wall for no apparent reason!" I said with growing enthusiasm. "Let's say we manage to get all this organized and start using Templars to create a... what would you call it? A prediction barrier. Can you imagine what would it be like to be used to getting glimpses of the future, and suddenly you can't see past the next three days and you don't know why? It would drive you apeshit."

Sig groaned and glared at me as if it were my fault. "You're saying that these people have been reacting to the result of a plan that we didn't even have until twenty seconds ago?"

"Ummmh. Yes?"

"God, I hate this fortune-telling stuff!" Sig said feelingly.

"There is one big problem with your plan, though," I said.

"What?"

"I just wasted all that time sitting here brooding and thinking for nothing," I explained. "You were supposed to wait until I came up with something brilliant to amaze you with."

Sig reached down and ruffled my hair. "Don't worry about it, baby. You just sit there and look pretty."

I took her hand and kissed it and stood up. "Come on." We walked over to the area where bowling balls were racked up. There was a jukebox against the wall, or kind of a jukebox. It was shaped like a jukebox anyway, but it had a digital screen instead of a cardboard one under glass. There was a list of current popular songs displayed, but for a quarter, you could search some website for a song title and download...or is it upload...a song to play. For a dollar, you could pick five. What the hell was this thing? A Joogle box? I just went with it and found an old Etta James song, "Trust in Me."

"John?" Sig asked.

I led her out into a relatively clear floor space, basically a landing strip for people coming from the snack bar or going to the bathroom. "Let's dance."

Sig gave me a wry look but let me pull her in close, then settled her head against my shoulder while I smelled her. I put a flat palm on the small of her back and she draped a hand over the base my neck, and we moved so that we stayed together but pressed in closer at pulse beats. Etta James sang in the background, her voice a rich blend of hope, anger, longing, sadness, fondness, and desire, combining with the piano-driven instrumentals and somehow coming out sounding like love.

∽35∾

ICE FOLLIES

If you're going to look for spirits who died angry and unsatisfied before their time, the ruins of a bomb site where a lot of young would-be thugs were misled and killed isn't a bad prospect. Once the sun went down for the count, Sig and I made our way back to the abandoned factory to see if we could pick up something useful with our various senses while knights and forensic techs picked over the site using more conventional methods.

Well, more accurately, to see if Sig could pick something up. My senses were redundant; the werewolves who had been on call to trigger the Pax if necessary were sniffing around, Virgil in charge of them. Dawn was doing her psychic bit too, or at least I assume so. She was actually talking to some young knight who looked like a catalog model trying to look like a construction worker when I spotted her, but whatever. Steven Hunter drifted over to meet us, and Virgil nodded at me from a distance and sent two wolves named Gar and Tracy over to see if we needed any help. Or maybe just to guard us while so many knights were around, on general principle. It's not like the tension between knights and wolves had evaporated.

Gar was a big, pleasant-looking guy with curly brown hair and a lot of mass, some of it muscle. Tracy was a tiny and intense-looking woman, just a little over five feet, with long, lank, pale-brown hair. I only knew them peripherally.

I hadn't heard from Simon since getting ahold of him and telling him Sig's plan. He was probably tangled up in the hellish process of trying to set that plan in motion. He had snarled and called it "Operation Clusterfuck" and explained how impossible it was in such passionate detail that I knew he was going to do it. Later, it somehow got changed into "Operation Blindside."

The knights on site had compromised between providing some lighting and not illuminating everything like a stage for the surrounding city, so we had to pick our way through shadow. The ground was covered with rubble and debris, some of it sharp and some of it rounded, some of it made of things that had been fused together and some of it made of brick or board that collapsed beneath the slightest weight. Some of the rubble had a disturbing tendency to release puffs of smoke and dust when the ash beneath it shifted. Templars would have to lay down some board walkways when the wheelbarrows got into full swing, but they weren't at that stage yet. After Steven Hunter greeted us, he led us on a winding path through the site as if he was a tour guide for the apocalypse. We picked up some crowbars to use like walking sticks along the way.

Our destination was a fragment of the factory that had been left standing. It was bizarre; a small section of the building still had intact floors and ceilings but was missing a north wall, as if it were the end of a loaf of bread that had been sliced away.

"I can't believe the knights really managed to cover all of this up." Sig was waiting while two men in bright yellow vests and hard hats stepped out of the ruin, hauling a plastic bag between them that somehow drooped suspiciously. It was full of something heavy and wet.

"Local media is a lot easier to guide now that most of it is reported by freelance bloggers," I offered.

"I think the closest call was a woman who didn't believe that the leg that landed on her car was a prop." Tracy probed a section of flooring with her crowbar experimentally. "Virgil said the paramedics gave her something that wrecked her short-term memory."

"No, ma'am," Steven contradicted. The *ma'am* didn't sound all that respectful, but it wasn't hostile either. "The trickiest bit is some cops who got called out for not looking at all of Brett's papers and licenses close enough."

"That's only because Brett Baker's lawyers are countersuing the city for breach of contract or something." I'd actually seen that on the news. From what I understood, there was a document with an eight that looked like a three involved, and if I had to guess, I'd say that talented hackers were still busily updating certain files retroactively. A fire marshal would have to come by to inspect the site, but I suspected the inspection was going to keep getting delayed for one reason or another, even if knights had to set more things on fire to arrange it.

"Do you know where you want to go yet?" Steven asked Sig.

"The boiler room," Sig answered, then wrinkled her brow. "Or the furnace room? Some kind of concrete basement with lots of metal."

Of course that's where she wanted to go. One of the creepiest word combinations in the English language: the boiler room.

Gar had a similar reaction. Or maybe he just smelled something bad. With werewolves, that's always a possibility. "Why?"

"Because that's where the ones who took the longest to die were," Sig said bleakly.

"She's right," Steven admitted. "The door was open and channeled the bomb blast right down the stairs and toasted them. Then they lay there, choking on all the dust floating in the air."

"So, the bomb wasn't in the basement?" I don't know why that surprised me.

"No," Steven confirmed as he led us down.

Our flashlights were still working, but there were kerosene lamps all over the place, which was a good thing. The room was huge and cluttered at the same time, an unnatural gathering of cold, sharp angles and round, intertwined pipes and peeling grey metal organs. "This is what it would look like if Freddy Krueger ran a summer camp," I commented.

"Just nobody interfere, no matter what," Sig said levelly. "If ghosts were emotionally well adjusted, they wouldn't be ghosts."

By a kind of unspoken and mutual consent, we all began to spread out to give Sig some room to do whatever it was she did, exactly. I found myself in front of a wall that'd had a red smiley face drawn on it. Well, not really a smiley face. The flat line of a mouth had an upside-down triangle emerging from it so that it looked like it was sticking a tongue out at us. The design stood out, even faded and partially obscured by charred grease and ash. The icon was probably just a juvenile impulse some Polly had made to feel better about being in such a creepy place, but it bothered me, and I wasn't sure why. When I tried to turn my flashlight on to examine it more closely, the flashlight began blinking in a strobe-light effect and died. Sig was already getting started.

No one heard the high, piercing wail except for us werewolves. It echoed through a vent or vibrated along a pipe, even though the knights had been diligently checking underground conduits and connections. It was an eerie sound to begin with, but what really made my spine prickle was that I'd heard that shriek once before. I had it assumed it was the sound that a ghost train made when it left our world and went back to wherever it came from, but apparently not.

The room started to get cold. It always got a little colder when Sig did her thing, but now the temperature was really dropping fast. Turning around, I saw Sig standing rigidly with her head lowered so that I couldn't see her eyes, her hands palm-up at her sides. A wind from no place that I was familiar with was whipping Sig's hair around, and particles of ice began to form in the air and swirl in front of her as if caught in a dust devil. Or frost devil.

Sig had told us not to interfere, no matter what, so I stood there and tried to identify the sound I'd just heard and the thing that was taking form. Was it some variation of a funnel ghost? The whirling ice began to accumulate and condense, taking on a human outline that was roughly thirteen feet high. An albastor, maybe? No, they took shape out of hot steam and fog. This was something—different. The thing continued to solidify, forming two thick legs, a torso the size of a tree trunk, long jagged arms, and a head the size of a small boulder. "Ummm...Sig?" I said despite myself.

Sig's head shot up in sudden alarm. Her eyes opened just before a massive arm smashed her off her feet. I roared and drove my crowbar into the thing's back, where its spine would be if it had a nervous system. The tip of the crowbar emerged out of its side, and I pivoted and tore off a huge chunk of ice. The thing didn't even notice. It just moved one of those solid pillar-like legs in a huge, heavy step that took it closer to Sig, who was just lifting her head off the floor. Particles of ice were still whipping in and around the thing, and they began to gather and stick in the gaping hole I had just torn out of the creature's back, rebuilding it before my eyes.

Gar stepped between Sig and the thing, beginning to shift into a half-human/half-wolf hybrid. He never made the transformation. The creature—well, I won't say it breathed... I don't think it needed to breathe—it *emitted* a continuous stream of ice particles from an opening in its face that coated Gar, slowing his molecular rate and freezing his blinking eyes shut. Gar turned his blinded eyes away, stepped back, and kept going as the creature swung its arm like a giant croquet mallet and swept Gar aside.

"SIG! IT'S AFTER YOU! RUN!" I yelled.

"WHERE?!" The thing was between Sig and the stairway. She retreated anyway. The creature was slower than she was, and at least Sig was buying us a little time, but every step backward also brought her closer to being cornered or pinned against a wall.

Still behind the thing, I tried to break one of its legs off at the knee, and that *did* get its attention. The thing was a far cry from flexible and didn't turn easily; I would have dodged its backswing easily if the floor hadn't become coated with ice at some point in the last thirty seconds. My foot slipped, which is why the thing hit me and also why it didn't tear my head off. Instead of staying there and taking it, I went sliding across the floor, the entire left side of my body a new bruise in the making. Ow. Ow. Ow. Ow. Ow. Ow. Ow. Ow. Ow.

Steven Hunter got into the act, calmly firing his handgun into the thing's head and shattering off tennis ball–sized hunks of ice. Which would have been great if the thing'd had eyes or a flesh and blood brain. But it didn't. The monster threw a giant hand outward and upward as if brushing off a fly, the fist smashing into the ceiling between it and Steven. Steven had to jump back while chunks of concrete rained down. At least the thing didn't seem to be interested in methodically finishing the rest of us off one at a time so that it could concentrate on Sig; as soon as we stopped being distractions, it ignored us and went after her again. Like the only thing that was important was finishing her off before we finished it.

Virgil came snarling down into the basement, and he and Tracy tried to flank and the monstrosity, but they fell into the same trap I did. They both slipped on the floor when they tried to change direction and Tracy got torn off her feet by a backhand that flipped her through the air. Virgil jumped onto the monster's back, growling. He managed to lock his arms around the thing's neck and tried to rip its head off, but his legs slipped when he tried to wrap them around its torso for leverage, and then ice started to accumulate over Virgil's forearms and hands, encasing them and binding them to that massive neck. Virgil tore his hands free with a startled scream and fell back, leaving skin behind.

"WHAT IS THIS THING?!?" Dawn had picked up a kerosene lantern at the base of the stairs. She ran up and flung the lamp, but the metal bottom was heavier than the glass casing, and the base of the lamp bounced off the monster and fell to the concrete before bursting into flame.

I hadn't rejoined the fight because I was half dazed, lying on my side looking at the smiley icon on the wall. From that angle the mouth—the thin line with a tongue sticking out—looked like a capital D that was staring to sprout roots. Looked like... oh, shit. I knew what was going on. I scrambled and slid to my feet and managed to grab one of the dropped crowbars. Forgot trying to run and just threw myself sliding across the floor, as if I were trying to make it safe to home. I guess I was.

When I thumped into the wall, I pulled myself up to my

feet and began frantically chipping away at that spray-painted mouth with my crowbar. The first blow made a thin scrape in the concrete. A flat, straight line formed from the second shot. Anything to significantly alter the design. I heard yells, warnings, and the heavy crunching beat of those pile-driver legs making the floor shake. Ice coated the back of my head as the thing drew closer, no longer trying to ignore me.

It was the shadow cast by the light of the kerosene lamps and the rush of a large object moving through air that made me hurl myself to the side. The ice giant's fist went straight through the place my head had just been occupying, and hit the concrete. A large section of wall crumbled, altering that spray-painted line forever. The ice giant also broke off the end of its arm, but this time, the arm didn't grow back. Rolling into a crouch, I realized that the miniature ice storm swirling around the damned thing had finally stopped, particles of frost floating to the ground in a late snow.

The ice thing didn't have a face, but I swear to God it looked surprised. Then Sig rammed into it from behind, driving her crowbar where the hip socket would have been in a human being. She held on to the crowbar like she was clinging to a mountain piton for dear life, and when the ice golem tried to turn to reach her, she ripped its leg off. The thing fell to the ground, shattering more of its left arm, and then Sig and I were both on top of that icy body with our crowbars, smashing anything that looked like it wanted to hit us.

"What just happened?" Sig panted when we were done. She had a big streak of blood traveling between her nostrils and her throat, and a piece of her scalp was hanging loose on the side of her head.

I reached for the wound and Sig grabbed my wrist. Not hard. Just for emphasis. "What just happened?" she repeated.

"That was a *jötunn*," I said. "A frost giant."

"No, it wasn't," Sig said firmly. The blood soaking the lower half of her features made her expression seem particularly grim and foreboding in the lamplight.

"Well, the ghost of one." I pointed at what was left of the spray-painted mouth. "That was an Elder rune. The one associated with dark magic."

Sig frowned and squinted at the mouth. "Thurisaz?"

"Yeah," I said. "That one."

Sig moved a little unsteadily, but her focus was unwavering as she studied the wall. At some point during all of this, knights had come rushing down the stairs, and several of them had firearms locked and loaded, covering the room. I signaled Dawn. Her long winter coat went down to her ankles and spread out like a dress. The garment had a lot of pockets and pouches, and I nodded at it. "Do you have needle and thread?"

"Always," she said. "Do you want me to stitch her up?"

"I'll do it," I told her. "Her skin's tougher than it looks."

"This isn't just painted," Sig announced from where she was still studying the wall. "Someone scraped very small channels into the surface. It's spray-painted so thick that you can't tell. And this isn't just one rune, either. The runes combine to make sigils." Her fingers traced what was left of the spray-painted mouth. "Thurisaz is overlaying Isa, which means ice. One way to read this would be *ice regeneration*." Sig's eyes are sharper than mine, and apparently there were things hidden in the eyes of the icon too, runes or sigils denoted by slightly darker shades of paint. Come to think of it...I leaned forward and smelled the red paint more closely. I hadn't picked up on it because there was blood and burnt smell in the air everywhere anyhow, but there was a definite scent of blood mixed in with the paint.

"How do you know about Elder runes, John?" Sig asked

quietly while Dawn handed me some antibiotic cream and a pouch that had needles and thread neatly lined up. "That's a little esoteric even for you."

"You're a Valkyrie," I said. "I've been studying."

Sig looked like she wasn't sure if she was flattered or disturbed by this information. But yeah, I'd been studying up on Norse mythology because I wanted to know more about Valkyries and if they had any natural enemies. The *jötnar* were one of the most dangerous of the old Norse races, and they hated anybody or anything with Aesir blood.

We didn't have a conversation about that, though. Sig was swaying slightly. Hopefully, it was just the adrenaline wearing off. "Come here, champ," I said, and pulled her over to a place where a kerosene lamp on top of a white fire extinguisher box was providing a little better light. "Let's get you fixed up."

Sig refocused on me when I had her sit against the wall. "We're getting messed up even more than usual lately."

"We are," I agreed.

"The Templars still have leaks, John."

"Probably." I took out my new handkerchief and went over and scooped up some ice from chunks we'd just left all over the floor. When I got back, I told Sig to tilt her head.

"Why do you say we have leaks?" This from Steven, half asking and half protesting.

"Somebody knew we'd try to talk to the dead." Sig said it almost absently while she angled her head so that I could try to ice it down a little. Her skin may be tough, but it still has nerves beneath it. "No, knew *I* would try to talk to the dead. Somebody set a Valkyrie trap."

"Not somebody," I corrected darkly. "Some *thing*." This made three times we'd been attacked, but the last one had been one time too many. I finally knew what we were dealing with.

✤36✤

FROM BABD TO WORSE

Boston probably has as many country clubs as it does second-ary schools, at least in Greater Boston. Somehow, this simple fact resulted in Sig and Dawn and Steven Hunter and I meet-ing Simon on the golf course of a country club that was more exclusive than anybody knew. Virgil was out doing something for me. The club was walled in, had its own security team that amounted to a private army, and had all sorts of other perks. I'm sure the lawn sprinklers gave off holy water in warmer weather, and the PA system was live-broadcasting several Gregorian monks who were continually chanting live, though the volume was so low that only I could hear it. I suspect the conventional alarm systems wouldn't have been out of place at NORAD.

Simon invited us to play a few rounds even though we weren't dressed for that particular activity. It's not like any members were going to complain, and I suppose he was mak-ing some point about *sangfroid* and grace under pressure and all that. Or maybe he thought he and I could communicate more effectively if we got to smack the hell out of something while we talked.

"John thinks the necromancer is a banshee," Dawn told Simon bluntly.

Simon gave me such a glare that I pointed at Dawn and said, "She's the messenger. Shoot her."

"My hero," Dawn said dryly.

Simon sighed. "I'm guessing you don't just mean some weeping woman ghost manifestation like La Llorona."

"No," I said. "I don't." I understood Simon's reaction. Banshees are nothing like they've been represented in RPGs and video games and movies and monster-of-the-week shows and comic books and such, not that they're portrayed much more consistently in myth. Sometimes, banshees are just regarded as random minor spirits who have a piercing high scream that predicts death, not much different from a screeching barn owl, really. In modern-day Ireland, most people don't even regard banshees as particularly malevolent.

Older tales go to the opposite extreme and treat banshees as goddesses or elf queens. The war goddess Badb, for example, would single out people who were going to die in battle with a high piercing scream. The banshee Cliodna commanded a Faerie court. Some of the earliest banshee stories have them appearing as women washing bloody clothes until the water turns red, which is one of the symbols of the Morrigan. I really could go on. I'm not even bringing up the most infamous banshee, Aiobhill, because I have no idea how to do so briefly. I will say, though, that banshees sure as hell don't go around slinging their abnormally long breasts over their shoulder, or granting people wishes if they get between the banshee and water like some kind of leprechaun. Crap like that is one of the ways the Irish got a reputation for heavy drinking.

The truth is complicated. A long time ago, one of the Fae taught a cunning man, a druid with a name that sounded like some kind of blood clot, how to permanently anchor the ghosts of one of his ancestors into the body of one of his daughters. From the moment this spirit was unnaturally spot-welded into a new human body, it was mortal; the banshee ate, breathed, farted, slept, and slept around. But the banshee also retained gifts from that other realm—knowledge of the future, a kind of frenzied, hysterical strength, and a complete disregard for life. Most disturbingly, while the body of the banshee was part of the mortal realm, the scream produced somewhere between her human vocal cords and her unnatural soul was not. The banshee's wail became a sort of bridge between life and death, causing the barriers between the spirit world and ours to . . . thin.

It says something about human nature that the druid thought he could control his creation and make it work for him. In a way, the banshee essentially became a kind of ancient biowarfare. The druid used his new craft—soul smithing—for the five great Gaelic families, the O'Gradys, the O'Briens, the O'Connors (O'Conchobhairs), the O'Neils, and the Kavanaughs (Cahomhanachs). The banshees were supposed to function as bodyguards and battle leaders, and for a time, they did. Their wail was kind of like a smoke alarm, warning members of the five families that someone important was about to die, and their vicious strength came in handy at a time when battles were fought with swords. The problem was that as the banshees kept "dying" and being summoned back into new incarnations as not-quite-human weapons, they became increasingly unstable. The banshees' battle skills and knowledge of arcane arts grew, but so did their arrogance, misery, and contempt for the humans around them. It became common knowledge that wherever banshees appeared, death followed.

It wasn't Templars who shut the practice of banshee-making

down. The chaos and carnage became so bad that the five great families finally simply stopped by mutual accord. Banshees faded into myth, to the point where hundreds of years would pass before the next arcane fuckwit came along thinking that the forbidden arts held serious power that could be used without serious consequences.

"Give me your reasons, Charming," Simon directed crisply while he motioned for his caddy to give him a club. The club the caddy was carrying seemed unusually big. So did the caddy, for that matter. He looked like he could kill a rhino using nothing but his thumbs.

"I should have known something was up when I saw her in the subway tunnel wearing a T-shirt that said, KISS ME, I'M BEAN SIDHE..." I began.

"You told me you never got a look at her," Simon interrupted.

"Okay, fine." I started rattling off points. "This mysterious big sister who runs the Pollys is a she. She's a necromancer. She speaks Gaelic. She told me she's been around for at least hundreds of years, and I believe her. She seems obsessed with knowing the future, and that's one of the banshee's big parlor tricks."

Simon impatiently indicated that I was getting off track, so I dropped that point. "She's seriously into overkill when it comes to leaving dead bodies around, and banshees aren't exactly famous for their restraint in that area. And when she opened the way for that frost giant ghost to manifest, she screamed. She also screamed when she banished a ghost train. I'm making a guess, but I like those odds."

The caddy had finally selected Simon's club during this recitation. I don't know what kind. Golf isn't my thing, not that I have anything against it. It seems to me that people probably like golf for the same reason they like being in a batting cage, with the added bonus of getting to walk outdoors and looking cultured. So, I shut up while Simon swung. Despite what I'd told him, his swing looked smooth, and the ball seemed to go pretty far.

"That's at least worth looking into," Simon granted while he moved aside so that Dawn could line up her own shot. "It goes with what Dawn was saying about our enemy's mind-set too."

Dawn had been playing well, but she messed up then. Had Simon mentioned her just as she was about to take her swing on purpose? I kind of suspected so.

I thought back to what Dawn had said. "You mean the thing about parasites?"

"Exactly." Simon didn't say the word with any enthusiasm. "Remember when I made that list? Skinwalkers. Dalaketnons. Balete trees. Double agents. All things that weaken a host and take it over from the inside while pretending to be it on the outside. Banshees fit that pattern too."

Sig hit her ball very far and very straight. I don't think she had more than a basic grasp of the game herself, but Sig is good at games that involve hitting things at angles. She has hyper-acute vision, supernatural strength, and steady nerves. "Speaking of double agents," she said, "you know you still have a traitor pretty high up in the ranks, right?"

"We're looking into it." Simon sounded bored, which meant it was bothering him intensely. "But it's not necessarily true. We've routed out any skinwalkers who could be far up the ladder, and this banshee wouldn't be able to possess anyone with knight blood. And this necromancer guessed John was one of the wolves who were at the Crucible, right? And you two saw some Redcaps there as well."

"Right," Sig replied while I put my golf ball on the tee. I was good at that.

"And you were fighting at the Crucible too. You told everyone you were a Valkyrie and used the same name you used at this underwater bar. Britte, right?" Simon didn't wait for confirmation. "She's probably guessed who John is by now—he's getting a bit of reputation. And some monsters must have seen you and John together."

"Okay," Sig repeated a little more warily.

"Simon's right," Steven said. "This banshee might have put all that together and anticipated us the old-fashioned way. Just using her head, I mean."

Sig looked troubled. I think she preferred the idea of double agents. "I suppose. But if she's that smart, she might be smarter than us."

I frowned. "I'm pretty sure that's against the rules."

"If this plan to toss geas-born all over Boston like psychic radar chaff works, maybe we'll see how smart she really is," Simon said with a certain menacing satisfaction. "Assuming we don't just drive her away."

"Speaking of driving away, why don't you go ahead and take your shot, John?" Dawn taunted.

I almost pulled my Ruger Blackhawk out of its holster and shot the golf ball right there. But I was afraid the caddy might think it was an attack and pull a chain gun out of his golf bag, so I just hit the ball. I hit it farther than anyone, but I didn't hit it straight. I hope I'm not being too technical.

"We still have to figure out why Boston is so important to her," I said, carefully ignoring what I'd just done. "Could it have anything to do with the way she makes this future drug?"

"I doubt it." Simon grimaced. "It looks like a big part of making the drug nonlethal for humans is cutting it with anti-snake venom, and you can get that anywhere."

Anti-snake venom? My brain came lurching to a halt.

The gorgon.

∾37∾

BLOOD WILL OUT

Sig and I met the gorgon in the same conference room at the same hotel where we'd last talked to Parth. I mean Kimi. Karth? Pimi?

"You're the one who wanted this meeting," the gorgon greeted us, sneering. "So talk." She was a bronze-skinned woman with thick black hair bound tightly around her head. It sort of had to be, if she used her psychic gifts a lot. She was also wearing a formfitting, strapless white dress with a white layer of fabric draped over her left shoulder—not so much a toga as a hint or suggestion of one. The thick copper bracelets with some kind of runes on them looked a bit gaudy, but the emerald-chip earrings were subtle, which made me wonder if the bracelets had some utilitarian value. Maybe she blocked bullets with them. The big, thick sunglasses belonged on someone with a hangover, but at least they did a good job of hiding those stunning eyes.

"I made some wrong assumptions about you," I confessed. "I thought you were working for Parth. But you're not, are you? You came to Parth for help."

"I repeat," the gorgon said acidly, "what do you want?"

"We want you to confirm that the Redcaps are harvesting gorgons to make Glimpse," Sig interceded. "And maybe help us try to do something about that."

Gorgons can't see knights. They're technically blind, and they view the world around them with their psychic or third eye. But this one glared at me anyhow. "You're going to rescue my sister?"

Her sister? "I don't know. Can I see a picture of her?"

It was the gorgon's turn to be nonplused.

"If we're with the people who took her, it can't hurt," Sig pointed out gently. I was having a hard time being as tactful myself. I kept remembering how the gorgon had picked up on trouble and tried to abandon everyone in the Buried Treasure without warning them. "And if we're legit, it might help."

The gorgon tried hard, but she couldn't find any obvious flaws in that logic. She reluctantly picked up the smartphone that was lying on the table in front of her and pressed some keys without looking at them. I guess there wouldn't have been a point. In a moment, she showed us a picture.

I recognized the gorgon's sister. She had been running a fortune-telling booth at the Crucible back in New York. Maybe *that's* why there had been Redcaps there. "How did they capture her?"

"They?" The gorgon became incredulous. "*They* were knights too."

I guess *they* would have had to have been. Who else could have ambushed a precognitive? "Someone has tricked some knights into believing a false narrative, and now those knights are making mistakes," I said carefully. "I think your sister's abduction was one of them. That's why we want to capture the people responsible."

"And then what happens to my sister?" the gorgon demanded.

There was a pitcher of ice water on the table. I went ahead and poured myself a glass. "Our geas prohibits us from harming any supernatural creatures who aren't threatening the Pax Arcana," I said. "People keep forgetting that."

"And if you decide that gorgons are a threat because our blood can be used to make a dangerous drug, you won't blink at committing genocide, either!" the gorgon snapped. "No supply, no demand. Isn't that how you think?"

So, it *was* gorgon blood being used to make Glimpse.

"Let's just say that it's in all our best interests to keep this development a secret," I allowed. "That's another reason you should help us shut this thing down."

"You said that you would tell me why I can't see what happens past tomorrow," the gorgon replied sullenly. Yes, I had. It had been one of the only carrots I had to dangle in front of the gorgon. It had also been a sneaky way to confirm that the knights had in fact created a barrier for people who could see the future, even though we hadn't done the thing that would create that barrier yet. I was still having a hard time wrapping my head around that.

Sig told her.

The gorgon wasn't pleased, to put it mildly. "How in the nine bloody hells am I supposed to find my sister now?!"

Sig held up three fingers. "That's three reasons to help us."

"I wouldn't if I could!" The gorgon began making ripping motions, her body blurring and jumping oddly, and in a moment, we were staring at Kimi. She was dressed like the gorgon had been dressed; her hair was bound like the gorgon's had been bound, and sensor probes were visible on her temples and arms. She was wearing that weird-looking monocle rig too, even though the gorgon wouldn't be able to see through it. Probably to record the encounter.

I had a weird impulse to greet Kimi as if she had just gotten there. Instead, I said, "Well, I guess Parth knows how Glimpse is being made now."

"He's not the schemer you think he is," Kimi snapped in her own voice.

"And I'm not the paranoid lunatic you think I am," I replied. "I'm not going to try to kill everyone who knows this. I'm even willing to assume that Parth isn't going to start farming gorgons like alpacas." At least not until I had a reason to think otherwise, but there was no reason to go into that.

"How kind of you," Kimi said acidly. "Do you want points for not murdering people?"

Well...yeah. Sort of.

"It's good seeing you again, Kimi," Sig said, and I don't think I was imagining a double meaning lurking in that sentence. She took off her goggles, stood up, and gave Kimi a brief hug. "Whatever Parth's paying you, it isn't enough."

At least Kimi didn't give us a form to fill out this time. It's possible that the answers I'd written on the last one hadn't been particularly helpful.

"I don't think I'll ever get used to that," Sig said as we walked through the lobby. "It's creepy."

A little voice whispered to me. I don't know why it bothered; it was inside my head. But the voice rasped like crumpled newspaper skittering down a gutter anyhow. *How is what Sig does with ghosts any less creepy than what Kimi's doing? How is what the banshee's host does for the banshee any worse than Sig?*

Shut the fuck up, I mentally growled back. To myself, mind you. I mean, mind me. I mean...oh, to hell with it. I had to get away from the knights. Being around them again wasn't good for my headspace.

"Well, at least we know this Glimpse stuff has nothing to do with why the banshee is staying in Boston," Sig said when we got back to our car. The automobile was a little flashier than I usually preferred. A Redcap had left the car behind when he went into hiding. A couple of knights were driving Redcap cars around Boston, daring their former owners to come do something about it. Redcaps were supposed to be violent and territorial, after all, and even something as passive as reporting us to the police would require the owners to come to the station if we were caught.

"We know more than that," I disagreed.

"Like what?" Sig challenged.

"Well, for one thing, we also know that knights kidnapped the gorgon's sister." Is it okay if I say I smiled wolfishly? "And we know the Redcaps are using experts, facilities, and equipment for the transfusion and studying of blood."

"Well, yeah," Sig said grudgingly. Then: "Oh. Yeah."

~38~

PROBABLY NOT WHAT PEOPLE MEAN BY "POLICING YOURSELF"

Ironically, it was the knight-hating Virgil who arranged the meeting with a Templar lay servant. Jean Terry wasn't of the bloodline proper, but she was a Boston cop who had somehow become aware of the supernatural, and that was exactly what we were looking for. Sig and I had made more progress than anyone inside the knights, and as much as I'd like to think it was because we were just that much better than anyone else, I had a suspicion that it was the "inside the knights" part that was the sticking point. No matter what Simon said, as far as I could tell, Sig and I were the only ones not telling everyone what we were doing in advance and following strict chains of command. The fact that this was the only thing that seemed to be effective suggested that someone pretty far up those chains of command was compromised. Even if that was wrong, I was still inclined to stick with what was working.

In her forties, Jean was sturdily built and strong-boned, but she was starting to get soft and shapeless around the edges, both beneath her eyes and in them. There was an air of weariness about her that suggested she was just hoping to make it out of the Boston police force with enough of her soul left to enjoy it. Virgil had met her while they were both walking around after the factory explosion, trying to exude calm and authority, and they had recognized each other as fellow cops drafted into the Templars' service immediately. Strangely enough, Jean hadn't immediately assumed that Virgil was a werewolf.

The weather had taken another turn, this time for the warmer, and we met in Jean's backyard. She had a deck and a grill, and there were other signs that she had once had a family and no longer did. At least one kid out of high school and not living at home, if I had to guess. Whoever that tire swing hanging from a big elm had been for. Jean's mate was dead or just gone. I didn't ask.

Jean offered us a drink, and we accepted, though Sig asked for water. Jean was having a whiskey sour—no glass of red wine for her—taking tiny, slow sips and savoring them. I took the same just in case she was one of those drinkers who thought that was the polite thing to do. "I don't understand what you're asking me," Jean said.

"We'd like you to see if any genetics or medical labs have reported anything weird in the last two years." Virgil shifted uneasily in his metal deck chair. His spine had gotten twisted by that ice giant, and sometimes things pinch or kink without requiring regeneration. It didn't help that the chairs really weren't comfortable. Probably low maintenance, though.

"Weird like how?" Jean asked.

"Like missing equipment or scientists," I filled in. "Particularly labs having to do with all that bioengineering stuff. Or anything having to do with blood."

Jean took another small sip. "Why do you need me? You can get that kind of stuff easy any number of ways." Then she looked at me. "I mean, *you* can. You're not like me and Virgil and whatever she is. You're one of them."

She meant knights. Jean really knew how to hurt someone.

"We think the Order has a traitor," I said. "And maybe it's arrogant, but we think it's probably a lay servant. Like you. So, we're giving different lay servants small parts of a bigger task. That way, if you tell anyone, you can't really hurt us that much, and we'll know it was you."

"So, you're like an Internal Affairs officer?" Jean made an expression of distaste.

"Sure," I said.

"Well, then, why tell me all that?" Jean said. "That's no way to trap me if I'm a traitor."

"Jean, if you are betraying us, he'll find out anyway," Sig answered. "But I don't think you are."

Sig's attempt to make me the bad guy seemed to amuse Jean briefly. Very briefly. "What makes you think your group has sprung a leak?"

"Well, gosh, you're the detective," I said. "Maybe you can go to the massive bomb site where the factory we were going to raid just exploded and help us look for a clue."

Jean actually laughed a surprised little bark of a laugh. "You people never tell me anything. Are there freak-show terrorists out there now? I thought you just hunted..." Jean faltered and her voice dropped "...them." She shivered a little.

I don't know what *them* had gotten Jean involved with the knights, and I didn't ask. I wanted her to assume I'd seen her file. A little more conversation, a mild threat to let Jean sever her ties with us and be alone in the world with *them* if that's what she wanted, and another whiskey sour later, she agreed to get the information we wanted discreetly.

～39～

I'M GUESSING YOU HAVE A
STRICT NO-RETURN POLICY...

Later, Sig and I went to another college campus, this time a private-school library where the top floor was under construction. An anonymous private donor had given a lot of money to renovate the fourth floor and turn it into a collection dedicated to Proust. The elevators didn't go all the way to the floor, and a campus security officer who'd been waiting quietly in the corner of a stairwell landing told us that the top of the building was off-limits. He had an unlit cigarette in his mouth and a cell phone in his hands and looked for all the world like we'd just caught him about to take an unauthorized text and smoke break. What didn't quite jibe with that image was that most campus security guards don't look like they pick their teeth with a chainsaw, and their sidearms aren't made for moose hunting.

We gave him the special provisional school ID that was supposed to let him know that we had clearance, and he glared at us with a sullen and disdainful recognition that set me on edge a little. He squinted at the ID Sig had given him so long that I began making up sarcastic comments in my head just to pass the time. *Heat vision not working?* Or *Need help sounding out any of the big words?* But I stifled the impulse to say any of them out loud. Tension between the Templars and the Round Table was already bad enough, and I'm oddly inclined to behave in libraries. It probably goes back to childhood somehow.

He rewarded my restraint by calling out after us, "The periodicals are in the east wing, if you need to use some newspapers."

Use them. Not read them. Like a potty-trained dog. And the damnedest thing was, I'd just been firing off sarcastic comments in my mind, and for once I couldn't think of a snappy comeback to save my life, so I just said, "Piss off, assbreath."

He didn't look scared. "Bite me, freak."

"I would," I said. "But I don't want food poisoning."

Sig took my arm. "Come on, John."

Another guard on the other side of a heavy door let us through, and then we were in a library wing that had a tarp spread over the floor where a wall was being repainted and a lot of shelves were standing empty, but otherwise, the place didn't look like it was under construction at all. There were three people dressed like painters, but they weren't bothering to act like anything other than guards. We had to pass through a security checkpoint where a man who looked like the stairwell guard's big brother frisked us.

The section holding special historical documents was in a room behind a long marble library counter. A woman who was also dressed like a professional painter gave us a thick, rusty-brown folder full of documents and a flash drive, and we weren't allowed to leave the room with them. We found a table with comfortable chairs next to some computers that weren't Internet-accessible and made ourselves at home.

"So, the knights really don't send stuff like this wirelessly?" Sig asked.

"I'm not really current on all the ins and outs of their security standards," I reminded her. "But I doubt it's standard procedure to put this stuff on any computer that's Internet-accessible." This was me extrapolating a lot because the last time I'd officially been a knight, a computer that would fit in a smartphone now would have taken up three warehouses. But there's a reason that memorization is a huge part of a knight's training. The philosophy is to limit the amount of information that has to be written down as much as possible.

"Like keeping documentation in a public library is any safer?" she said. "Why not at least keep it in some corporate vault or something? How are they going to guarantee that the public doesn't read this?"

"Well, they did put it in a Proust collection," I pointed out reasonably.

She shot me a look with a little bit of hot sauce on it. Sig's a Francophile.

I laughed and made a time-out gesture. "Two things, okay? If the knights put everything they wanted to keep secret in one big bunker, they'd have to allow a lot of people in and out of the same facility with the Ark of the Covenant or whatever just to let them access the not-so-dangerous stuff like this."

"I guess that makes sense," Sig agreed grudgingly.

"And the knights deal with a lot of old manuscripts," I went on. "There's all kinds of stuff that goes with that: translating and restoring and transporting and collecting and scanning and preserving and binding and cross-referencing and blah blah blah. They probably have a lot of library facilities."

Sig got bored with the conversation. "I call the flash drive." She promptly plugged the drive into the computer so that she could do keyword searches while I went through the folder the old-fashioned way.

Most of the material we were reading was centered around Boston and banshees and wherever the twain did meet. There was a lot of it, but fortunately, it was all about one specific time period and one specific banshee. Apparently, a banshee had cropped up in Boston in the early 1900s, and she had made a serious attempt to unite the Irish mobs in a bid to organize crime. If only she'd known that Prohibition would soon come along and do it for her. It wasn't clear what the banshee intended to do with that power base when she was done, because the knights had destroyed her host body.

Sig and I drew each other's attention to little tidbits while we read.

"She called herself Aine," Sig said. "According to this, that translates to *radiance* in Gaelic. Do you think she was being ironic?"

"I don't know," I said. "Bad people don't think of themselves as bad. And it might be her real name." A little later, I added, "Aine was a Celtic goddess of fertility and beauty."

Sig gave me an eyebrow. "I still think that's weird. It's a weird name for a banshee to take, and it's weird if a banshee already named Aine was the basis for the myth about the goddess."

"I think most of the female Celtic goddesses had beauty and fertility somewhere in their job description," I said. "It's when you get down to the specifics that things talk to you. Like here—it says that the thing Aine was most famous for was biting off the ear of a king who raped her. The old Celts had a law that said blemished people couldn't rule, so this meant that he couldn't be king anymore. From that point on, part of Aine's godly province was proclaiming and removing rulers."

That made Sig thoughtful. "You think the banshee took the name because she wants to overthrow rulers?"

"Maybe," I said. "Or maybe she really was the basis for the legend. She said she was thousands of years old and didn't seem to like men much."

"With time comes wisdom," Sig muttered.

"Hey," I protested mildly.

She stuck her tongue out at me and grinned.

Later still, Sig told me, "It says here that before the knights killed her, this banshee tore a rift between this world and the spirit world." Sig looked queasy. "It says that ghosts and ecto-plasm were leaking everywhere."

Well, that certainly went with a tendency to commit over-kill. "How the hell did knights contain *that*?" I asked.

Sig kept reading: "It says here that they blew up a molasses factory."

I don't often go for big dramatic facial expressions like drop-ping my jaw or doing spit takes, but that one hit me hard. "Are you talking about the Great Molasses Flood in 1919?"

Sig laughed. "That's a real thing?"

"They were still talking about it when I was a kid," I said. "Molasses came pouring out of that factory waist-high. People and horses got stuck in that stuff and drowned. Cleaning it up was a nightmare too. Fermented molasses is flammable, just like alcohol."

Sig made a face. "You realize that's two factory explosions associated with banshees in this city, right? Maybe this really is the same banshee back in a different human host. Maybe she couldn't resist a little poetic justice."

"Maybe," I said thoughtfully. "This Aine tried to use an Irish gang to build a power base just like our banshee." And come to think of it, our banshee seemed pretty familiar with abandoned tunnels as well. That would be a lot easier if she was using them at the turn of the century when they were still active. But I didn't get a chance to say that out loud.

Sig stood up abruptly. "I need to pee and get something to eat. Let's hit that coffee shop by the lobby."

"All right." I turned and asked the librarian if we could just leave the documents on the table since there wasn't anyone else there and we were coming right back. She looked at me, and I smiled at her and began putting everything in the folders.

Sometimes you have to pick your battles.

Coffee shop add-ons are a relatively new development in the evolution of libraries, but they're one I heartily approve of. This particular library was trying to transform its massive medieval-looking lobby into a warm and welcoming place without much success—it was a bit like trying to make a tank look like a hippie van—but the little coffee shop and the smell of pastries helped. I got in line so I could hold Sig a place. The little green banner over the coffee stand had a quirky little independently owned business–type name, but the coffee smelled like Starbucks. I was wondering what that was about when I smelled something else odd. Something like fresh rain and new leather. Nix smell. Nikki. I mean, Nick. Had he been following me ever since the subway? No way. He must have made some connection to Kimi's hotel while he was trying to track the gorgon down and picked our trail up from there. All that flew through my head before Nick's voice said, very, very quietly, *John? Scratch your neck if you can hear me.*

I scratched my neck. None of the people in line around me seemed to hear anything unusual.

Listen, there are some Crusaders on their way to pick you up. I heard some guards arguing about it while I was trying to figure out a way to sneak up to the top floor. One of them Tasered the other one in the west stairwell. They think you're in really tight with the head of the Round Table and that you'll be able to tell them where he's hiding and what he's up to.

Was that possible? I'd noticed that there were different people at the front desk and a different guard at the metal detector in the lobby, but Sig and I had been upstairs for a couple of hours, and I'd just assumed that a shift had changed.

The plan is to set off a fire alarm and bag you in one of the stairwells when you leave or the place is empty. You need to get out of here. I'm already gone.

I didn't bolt or look around to try to identify Nick. Was Nick setting me up? Was he working with the banshee to trick me into isolating myself? Or was this real? If it was real, and the plan was to set off a fire alarm, they would wait and see if Sig and I went back and trapped ourselves on the top floor. The same waiting period applied if this was a trick to get me out of the building. So, I waited until it was my turn to order two small coffees and a thick-looking blueberry muffin with raisins.

Sig got wind that something was wrong the moment she saw the small coffees.

"I just thought of something I really want to check out in that folder upstairs," I explained before she could ask the question in her eyes. "Can we go back up there in a second? We can come back down and get lunch in just a little bit."

"You've figured something important out?" she said.

"Maybe," I said, splitting the muffin and putting my half on a napkin. "I want to check it out."

Sig definitely knew something was up when I took the laminated map that was taped to the stairwell wall. It was a blueprint of the library with clearly indicated emergency exit routes. I made a cross with my fingers and smacked them against my forehead. It was our personal sign for Crusaders.

Sig didn't say anything.

On the third floor landing, I asked, "Hey, do you mind if we stop at the third floor and see if we can find a book by Leon Uris, first? It's about Ireland."

Sig flashed me another look. "Sure."

We moved on to the third floor, and after a brief canvassing suggested there were only three people on this level, I found the fire alarm next to a single elevator and a water fountain. There was nobody looking, and I pulled it.

"What's going on?" Sig shouted in my ear as I took her by the hand and threaded through some bookshelves.

"Crusaders may be doing something messed-up," I yelled back. There's a time to be subtle, and a time not to be subtle. This was no time to be subtle. I wasn't going to find an unguarded back entrance in this library, and the place wasn't crowded enough to slip out in a herd of people, so I motioned for Sig to go ahead and crouched down. The person shadowing us in the parallel aisle kept following her, and I swept the books separating us off the shelf with my left hand and leaned forward and punched him in the crotch with my right. He bent over, and I grabbed him by the campus security jacket and pulled him through the second shelf, scattering books everywhere while Sig steadied the bookrack. He was too big to go through the shelf gracefully, so when he was halfway through, I used my full weight to smack his head against the floor while his gun was still clearing its holster. He went limp.

In a perfect world, it would have been the guard from the stairwell, but it was some man I hadn't seen before.

I tossed Sig the guard's gun and plugged his earpiece into my ear. According to the map, the two-story wing adjacent to this part of the library was to our left, and we found a number of windows in a narrow aisle at the terminus of the bookshelves.

I could see a roof roughly fifteen feet below us, but the windows were barred. Of course they were barred. Heavily barred too, and fuck me if the metal didn't look like some kind of harder than steel alloy underneath a spot where some paint had flaked off. But there was a series of long narrow reading tables shoved against the walls between the windows, and Sig was already pulling one of them out. We had to shove the ends of two bookracks sideways to make some charging room, but we were strong enough between us, and then we used the table like a battering ram. If we couldn't bend the bars, we'd attack the stone around them.

The bars were anchored to a metal frame that was built into the wall surrounding the window, and the whole thing tore loose in an explosion of shattered brick and wood and plaster. It all landed on the roof below us at roughly the same time that I permanently got over my hang-up about misbehaving in libraries. We jumped down and made our way across the roof to a small courtyard heavily shielded from the outside world by some scenic trees and thick hedges. Fortunately, it wasn't a designated fire safety area, and there must have been a lot of confusion going on in the building behind us. If there were Crusaders, they were still in the process of taking over the library and now dealing with evacuating it before they were ready too.

Sig and I jumped down into the courtyard and ran so that we could build enough momentum to smash through the hedges. We wound up on a side street separating the library from a large duck pond. There was only one car on the street, a Honda driven by a co-ed who slowed and rolled the window down as we walked across the lawn. The fire alarm was still ringing behind us. I imagine someone was debating whether to turn it off so that they could communicate more clearly, or leave it on so that they could make a lot of noise when they found me. But somebody had to have heard or noticed that window or the sound on the roof.

The co-ed came to a stop. "What's going on?" the student asked. She seemed very excitable and sociable and animated. "Is there really a fire?"

Sig approached her on the theory that the co-ed would find another female less threatening, smiling in an open, friendly fashion as she pointed up at the library behind us. "Do you see where that window exploded?"

"Omigod, yes!" The student began reaching for the cell phone on her shotgun seat, I'm guessing to post a photo to her friends. "What happened?!"

"This," Sig said, and punched her in the jaw. Sig can actually do that kind of a thing without a stunt double or a broken hand. Her bones are harder than most people's. She opened the door and shoved the co-ed to the passenger side before the car drifted too far, and I got into the backseat.

My earpiece was silent, and in an odd way, this was reassuring. It wouldn't have been if Sig and I had done all that for no reason. At a guess, there really were Crusaders back there taking over the library, and they were using a different radio frequency. That also meant that the guard I'd knocked out wasn't a Crusader. He had nominally been on my side. Oops.

I tossed the earpiece out of the car and was already calling Virgil as Sig drove away.

I hope it goes without saying that we dropped the co-ed and the car someplace safe.

ᘓ40ᘐ

BUT HUSH, I SMELL A RAT CLOSE BY

Oddly enough, the incident at the library helped Simon and me communicate more effectively. This was partly because it was abundantly clear that we couldn't afford to dick around, and partly because he no longer wanted me to come in and stay close at hand where he could keep an eye on me. Werewolf–knight relations were even more tense and dicey, and Emil Lamplighter must have been busy dealing with the fallout with the Crusaders. Now Simon actually *wanted* me to stay out of sight and report on my activities as little as possible.

"I hope you know that those Crusaders were operating on their own," Simon said over the phone.

"I actually do," I said. "Have they officially seceded from the Order?"

"Of course not," Simon said bitterly. "As far as they're concerned, they're trying to save it."

"Ah," I said inadequately.

"That police officer you reached out to talked to her contact within the Order," he informed me. "And then he talked to me. Why are you interested in hematologists and bioengineers?"

Well, I'd known Officer Terry reporting me to the knights was a possibility, but I still felt mildly betrayed. Dammit, Jean. We could have had something beautiful. "Glimpse is being made from gorgon blood."

"We were looking into that," he mused. "We don't have blood from every supernatural species on hand for analysis. We should probably do something about that if our geas will let us."

"You should," I agreed. "So what else did Officer Terry tell you?"

Simon met me halfway. "She didn't come up with anything useful. That's why you should have gone through us. I kept looking just to see what you were up to and found out that a research scientist on blood-transmitted pathogens named Evan Stark is on indefinite leave to take care of a mother who has cancer."

"You're right," I admitted. "That wouldn't have shown up on a police report."

"Something is up with this Evan Stark whether it has anything to do with us or not," Simon said. "He was allowed to take some highly specialized lab equipment with him so that he could work from his mother's home. But when we sent someone dressed as a UPS man by the address, there wasn't anyone there. The knight broke into the house, and not only was there no lab equipment there, it didn't look like anyone had been by in weeks. It turns out that Evan owns the place, but his mother died years ago."

"Was this in Boston?" I asked.

"No," Simon said. "The family house is on Nauset. Evan really flew there and had the equipment shipped there too. We have security footage of him getting off a plane at the airport. I think he's still on the island too. Somebody's been sending e-mails to the school from a library there. And the lab reports that Evan has been sending to his college are postmarked from the mother's address."

"Huh." I was still recovering from having to admit that Simon was right.

"Do you know anything about Nauset?" Simon asked.

Again, I grew up in Boston. "I know it's the name of a Native American tribe that used to live in this area. It's also the name of an island and a beach and a county and probably a lot of summer camps and streets and high schools around here," I said. "Other than that, not much."

"Start learning," Simon advised. "I want you and Virgil to be one of the teams on point on this. We need werewolves to be involved in a big win. I want to send you two paladins too."

"Paladin" is a slang term for a small group of Knights Templar who are half priests and half Navy SEALs. They can sanctify ground, perform exorcisms, and then pull a machete or a shotgun from behind their back and start smiting. The paladins are kind of like a modern-day version of the Benedictines, except that paladins are supposed to be beyond politics or chapter disputes. Any knight from any branch or chapter can try to join them, but very few make it.

Since we were dealing with an unholy spirit, I saw the sense in what Simon was saying. My objection was on different grounds. "We don't have Templars spreading out over Nauset to foul up their visions of the future," I protested. "It'll be just like all the previous attempts here in Boston."

"No, it won't. Operation Blindside doesn't start for another thirty-eight hours." Simon sounded tense. "I have that long to round up another few thousand geas-born, figure out a plausible lie to mislead them about where they're going until the last minute in spite of the fact that everyone is suspicious of everyone else right now, find enough boats to transport them because there's no ferry to Nauset for some reason, work out multiple plausible excuses for that many strangers to be roving around the island all day without drawing attention to themselves—"

"Okay, okay, I get it," I said.

"I'm not sure you do," Simon grumbled. "I can only delegate so much of this until I find out who contacted the Crusaders and told them where to find you. It's got me stuck playing bureaucrat and diplomat and office manager while you get to run around." I wondered if Simon realized that Emil was using that need for secrecy as an excuse to force him into more and more administrative duties. "It's a monumental pain in the ass," he added.

"And you figured I'm already a monumental pain in the ass, so you might as well use me," I said.

"Something like that," he said.

Sig and I met the two paladins in the airport parking lot. They were both in their late twenties or early thirties, and their eyes and teeth gleamed with pure thoughts and good hygiene. Both men dressed neatly and simply and with everything clean and tucked and unwrinkled. They weren't particularly friendly or unfriendly, and I actually appreciated that. They did offer hands, and I took them.

"Matt Petrucelli," the big one said. He didn't look like a body builder, but he was a pale-eyed ton of hard muscle just the same. He didn't smell hostile, but his face didn't give away much.

"Luke Pritchett." His partner was much warmer, hard-muscled but not bulging from every tendon. He was my height but a lot of it was torso. His legs were a little shorter, his chest a little wider, and he didn't quite have my reach. His brown eyes were open in every sense of the word, both giving and receiving.

"I'm John Charming." I paused for a moment. "Hold on. Are we really Matthew, Luke, and John?"

Luke smiled, low-key but sincere. "We wondered about that too. Maybe the Grandmaster is having a little joke."

"Well, unless I change my name to Mark or there's a book in the Bible called Sigourney that I don't know about, I wouldn't make too much of it," Sig said dryly.

I looked at Sig sideways while she and the paladins shook hands. I'd been trying to get Sig to tell me her full name since I'd met her. Sigourney. Aha!

Sig noticed my glance but refused to give me the satisfaction of acknowledging it. "I just found out about your group tonight. What is the paladins' stance on werewolves and Valkyries?"

Luke cleared his throat. I guess he was the de facto spokesman for the two. "We don't have an official stance. There has been a lot of lively discussion on the subject." That was probably an understatement. "I'm really looking forward to talking to you two on the plane."

I wasn't sure if an airplane in flight was the best or the worst place to have a theological discussion, but at least Boston to Nauset was a short trip.

"I understand you can use a cross to ward against the undead," Matt addressed me. "I would like to see that."

"Well, the odds are pretty good that you'll get a chance," I said mildly.

Like most of the small islands near Boston, Nantucket being the most well known, Nauset has a tourist-driven economy. As near as we could estimate, there were between seven and eight thousand people there at that point in time. In a month, that number would double, and in two months, there would be four to five times that many. The relatively small local population was a mixed blessing. It would make it easier to find strangers who had been hiding out among the permanent residents during off months, but it would make it harder to do so discreetly.

We took two different rental cars from the small airport, just to give us more flexibility. Sig wanted to look through the brochures she'd picked up, and I wanted to look at the town, so I was driving. As we went down Nauset's main street, I saw a lot of tall, narrow brick buildings and light-colored slatted ones built closely together, and most of them seemed to be local shops and restaurants. If an upscale beach resort like Hilton Head Island and a historical landmark like colonial Williamsburg ever somehow managed to get together and have sex, Nauset is probably what their love child would look like. It was nice.

"Look, honey," Sig said while she continued to flip through brochures. "We're getting to take that beach vacation after all."

I smiled wryly. "I kind of like this place, but I wouldn't call this a beach trip. It's off season. And this is a New England seaport."

"Same thing," Sig said absently.

"It's really not," I assured her. "Besides, there's already a Nauset Beach, and it's not on Nauset Island."

"Whatever. Hey, maybe we can visit the whaling museum while we're here."

I laughed.

Sig grew serious then. "We've come to the right place."

"How do you know?" I asked.

Sig looked out the window. "This place should be full of ghosts. And it's not."

Some kind of coastal weather variant was making Nauset warmer than Boston, but I have to admit that Sig's comment gave me a chill. What could make even ghosts lie low?

Virgil and five werewolves were already waiting in the very large, very grey, very expensive property that I had rented on short notice. They had been dropped off on the beach by a boat during the wee hours and had gone straight up to the house, dressed up and carrying gear as if they'd been night fishing. Fishing was, in fact, our excuse for renting the house in the first place—I'd even rented a charter boat for the week, starting two days from then. If our real business here took us longer than that, I'd just cancel.

"Why does this place have a swimming pool right next to the beach?" Sig wondered as we were walking in the back door. "Why didn't they just put a big sandbox in the backyard while they were at it?"

"You really don't get the beach, do you?" I asked.

"All I know is, you've brought me to another mostly white neighborhood that you expect me to blend in at," Virgil butted in. He had set up a sort of command center in the game room on the lower level, probably because it didn't have any windows except for the ones in the back door. The pool table was being used as a place to set printed-off sheets and steaming coffee mugs and glowing laptops that were opened up like plundered oysters. "Maybe next time, we should go to a mostly black neighborhood, and you can show me how you blend in there. Let me learn from the expert."

"You're making way too big a deal out of this, Virgil," I said. "We're on an upscale island in Massachusetts. Most of these people are educated and vote Democrat. I doubt anyone even notices skin color."

Just for the record, I was being sarcastic.

Virgil laughed. "Shows how much you know. I went out to get groceries and locals kept asking if they could have their picture taken with me."

"Forget all that," I said. "Did you bring it?"

Virgil shook his head and brought me my katana. I hadn't felt like trying to sneak it past airport security.

The two paladins came in at that point, and we made cautious introductions. It seemed to be okay. The two warrior priests were confident men. They weren't scared, trying to prove anything, or dominating any conversations, and they weren't looking for us to give them answers either. These two had probably been handpicked because they were both mentally flexible and tough. Or maybe all paladins were. What did I know?

I went ahead and looked at the maps that Virgil had laid out on the pool table. The other wolves in the house were all Round Table elite; I only knew one of them specifically, but they all gave off a lot of the signs. Two of them had some kind of military tattoos visible, and all of them were short-haired and clean-shaven, as if in reaction to werewolf stereotypes.

"Hey, John," the one I knew, Rob O'Keefe, greeted. Rob was short and very muscular, particularly from the waist up. I used to call him Muscles because he looked like he should have been part of that old He-Man action figure line, but I cut that out when I got to know him better. Rob had been one of Bernard Wright's most important lieutenants, but I didn't hold that against him; for a while there, so had I. "Want to hear what Virgil's come up with?"

"Always," I said.

"Tell me if this makes sense," Virgil said. "Occupied space on this island is sewed up pretty tight. Not a lot of abandoned buildings or places with a lot of space around them. So, I tried something different. I figured that all that equipment this Evan dude was using had to take a lot of energy—the refrigeration units, the centrifuge, the stuff I don't even know how to pronounce...."

"I'm with you," I assured him.

"Well, I had a friend of a friend of mine search power company records, looking for places that had unusual power bill spikes. And I didn't find anything that way, either."

"Okay," I agreed.

"So, I'm thinking either they're using a lot of gas generators, which means they'd have to be someplace private, or they're in the middle of a lot of buildings, sucking off power from a bunch of different neighbors so they won't draw any attention from anybody in particular. But if they were doing that, why wouldn't they just use this scientist dude's mother's house? It'd be perfect for that."

"They're holding a gorgon prisoner," I said. "They'll want some space."

"Which takes us back to someplace private that isn't stealing electricity and isn't getting a big power bill," Virgil said. "And then I thought, this bitch used an abandoned building in Boston. So, I started looking around, thinking, where are you going to find a big private stretch with some abandoned places on this island?"

"Still with you," I said slowly. Something was almost forming, right there on the edge of my consciousness.

"So, we ran a cross search of abandoned buildings and Nauset Island and images," Virgil said proudly. "And we found some old photos of railway houses and stations. Turns out this island has had two abandoned railroads. One of them went around the island, close to the shore, and the second one went through the middle where there's some undeveloped woods and swamp land. The second one went down in 1917."

Sig and I exchanged glances. That was the same time period we'd recently been reading a lot about. That might not mean anything, but if this banshee really was Aine, could she still be using places that she was familiar with and that nobody else was? There would be a kind of power in that.

"It's a good place to start," I said.

Ultimately, we wound up parking our cars and just following abandoned railroad tracks, spread out so that we wouldn't make one big target. We had to wait until six a.m. to do this, because that's when Simon was launching "Blindside," and that meant there was no way to conceal ourselves for long, open stretches and areas that wound behind or through or beside developed land. It was looking like it was going to be a sunny day too, with a cool coastal breeze. It figured. The one time I would have liked an overcast, rainy day in New England. But we had yellow hardhats that Virgil had taken from the construction site around the factory, and cameras and some clipboards to go with our satchels and backpacks, so it was doubtful anyone but a cop would give us a hard time, and the cops were going to be busy.

The local police force had to be noticing all of the new joggers, pamphleteers, tourists, surveyors, cyclists, power walkers, and similar entities besieging Nauset Island. Too many to round up or corner and no one breaking any laws, but still, if I were a cop, I'd be making some calls and keeping a wary eye out trying to figure out what it all meant and how these people had gotten there. Maybe the police were even getting a few reports of burglars or strange people hiding on rooftops or lurking in alleys.

We were walking beside an unoccupied marshy area. I'm guessing the land wasn't developed because of water tables and some kind of wildlife-preservation legislation, but I don't really know—and I began to notice something strange. Some of the lengths of rail on the railroad were much newer than others. Oh, they'd been smeared with dirt and grease, but the stages of rust were clearly different. Stranger still, when I pointed this out to the others, Matt and Luke were the only two who could see it, though the wolves could smell Fae stink.

The sections of rail had been glamoured.

"I hate it when you knights pull this," Virgil stated. "If I can't trust my own eyes, what am I supposed to do?"

Sig had more immediate concerns. "So, someone's using the railway for something? Like what? I don't think anyone could hide a whole train."

The best answer seemed to be to keep going. A little farther on, we all heard the sounds of a vehicle, but Rob was the first one to notice the rails vibrating. There wasn't a lot of tree cover, but we scattered and lay down among the high grass, which isn't as simple as it sounds. High grass isn't as bad as snow when you want to avoid leaving tracks, but it's close. Fortunately, the visitors that followed didn't seem to be skilled trackers, and we found out how the rails were being used in the bargain.

A white pickup truck drove by on the rails. It looked like it had some kind of undercarriage fixed to its bottom that dropped smaller wheels like an airplane's landing gear, wheels perfectly fitted to the rails. I didn't get a good look at the passengers because I was lying on my back, my gun held below my navel. I got a better look when the vehicle passed. The pickup truck's tailgate was down and the bed was empty.

I was better prepared when the second pickup truck came along about three hundred feet behind the first one. This one was tan, and its bed was also empty, but that's not what got my attention. Her hair was a plain sandy brown, but the person riding in the passenger side was Dawn.

After the trucks were out of sight, we pulled into a little group huddle. The sight of Dawn had flash-fried my brain, but I was in charge, unfortunately, and I had to act like it. So, I verified that phones and radios weren't working, and of course they weren't. Then I verified that someone else had seen Dawn. Sig and Virgil looked stunned. Well, so was I.

"It was the witch," Matt confirmed, and his anger held an undercurrent of satisfaction.

I had a brief mental flash of a cunning woman, Sarah White, and her opinion of knights in general, but I decided to save any conversations with the paladin about witches and merlins for later. Through the process of elimination, we determined that everyone had seen at least one of the people who'd passed us, and none of them looked like Steven Hunter, Dawn's assigned guardian.

"So, this Dawn is the traitor the knights have been looking for?" Rob asked. Most of the wolves weren't having as hard a time dealing with this sudden turn of events. Dawn meant nothing to them.

I was about to respond when Sig suddenly exclaimed, "Walking in the shadow of the dead, my ass!"

"Sig?" I asked.

"I knew I smelled some weird death trace I'd never sensed before on that bitch! It's because she's both living and dead! John, Dawn is the banshee!"

ᔰ41ᔱ

GIVING TREE, MY ASS

My own thoughts had been circling that possibility and refusing to land on it.

"No, wait, that can't be right," Sig said a few seconds later. "You smelled her in that subway tunnel."

"No, I didn't," I said reluctantly. This was no time for a town hall meeting, but if we could pin down Dawn's status as prisoner, traitor, double, mastermind, or Simon's secret plan quickly, it would be helpful. "The airflow was behind me, and my nose was broken and clogged up with blood. And she collapsed the tunnel behind her."

"Yeah, but wasn't Dawn the one who figured out how to get to that other world?" Virgil asked.

I thought about that. "Not really. I figured out everything but the runes. And Sig was the one who realized that Dawn ought to be able to read Austin's possessions. Once that psychic trance came over Dawn, I'm not even sure she knew what she was doing when she drew those marks."

"And Dawn only went along because Simon kept talking

about how he couldn't believe a psychic as powerful as she was hadn't found anything." Sig looked sick.

"Right," I agreed. "Simon was about to bring in another merlin. If he had, and it turned out there were psychic impressions all over the place, Dawn would have been in trouble. Remember how she made such a big deal out of how her thinking Austin was a knight had blocked her? She could have been covering her ass."

"So, why didn't she just have you all killed?" Rob wanted to know.

"Maybe she tried," I said. "We barely survived that ambush on the way to the house. Then she was stuck in the middle of a bunch of paranoid people watching everything. Maybe she was only pretending to be so upset about Nathan so I wouldn't think anything about the frustration and anger I was smelling."

"But wasn't she the one who killed the skinwalker?" Virgil asked.

"Well, yeah, but that actually hurt us. We were about to take it prisoner," I said. "It was choking, and knights and werewolves were running down the stairs. Before that, Dawn was about to do a spell when she caught a ricochet in the ass. I just assumed the spell was to help us."

"But she could have tore us up—" Virgil halted and corrected himself. "Or, I guess, maybe not. Simon had everybody paired up."

"Sure, to keep anybody from being jumped and taken over by a skinwalker," I said. "It would have been hard for Dawn to do a lot of sabotage with Steven Hunter around."

Where was Steven, anyway? And how had Dawn gotten away from him the night I first met the banshee, if we were right?

"That voice-broadcasting stunt Dawn did in the castle

worked both ways too," Sig contributed. "She acted like she was trying to save human lives and start a revolution, but it told Mistress Malea who was coming and to get the hell out of there."

"But her geas," Luke protested. "She couldn't be possessed."

That was actually the sticking point for me too. It wasn't something we were going to figure out anytime soon, and we couldn't talk about a lot of things openly, anyhow. "We'll have to do this later," I said tersely. "Virgil, do you still have that map?"

Dammit. I had liked Dawn. As soon as I thought that, I wondered if she had really been joking about smothering me with that pillow when Virgil stopped her in the storage silo.

But Virgil had the map, so I shook it off and tried to focus. It turned out that there had been an old railway station about two and half miles away. It was inside an overgrown wooded area, past a lake about a mile ahead.

I told Rob and the paladin, Luke, to keep traveling up the railway, stopping about half a mile from the station. "Rob, you're carrying the C-4, right? See if you can figure out something to derail those trucks if they try to leave, but don't use the C-4 unless you have to."

"What are you going to be doing?" Rob asked.

I indicated the wooded area on the map. "The rest of us are going to get sneaky. If we don't find anything at this railway house, we'll come get you. If we do, we'll entrench and wait for reinforcements as long as we can."

"Is there a time limit?" Luke wasn't pleased, but knights generally don't argue in the field. Of course, off the field, arguments can wind up involving medics.

"Those trucks were empty," I said. A wolf named Ed looked confused, so I spelled it out. "They aren't taking supplies from town to someplace else. They're picking stuff up."

"You think Dawn is bugging out," Sig said.

"If she's a traitor, yeah," I said. "As soon as Dawn found out Templars were coming here, she would have known we'd found something. Then she would have had to start making arrangements to get rid of Steven, book a flight—"

"Warn the people up ahead that we might be coming..." Sig finished.

"We have to be prepared for that," I affirmed.

And then...I didn't want to do it, but I used a signal mirror and got an answering flash from back at the cars. "I want you to go with Tracy and Gar when they drive up, Virgil," I said. "Drive until you can get a signal and tell Ben what we found here so he can tell Emil. And have someone check on Steven."

Virgil wasn't a knight, and he did argue directly. But Virgil was a known commodity, and using back channels and sending a dependable messenger seemed important. If the rest of us all died, I wanted someone to know what we'd just seen.

Ed and another were, Chris, got detailed to make a wide circle of the area, looking for hikers or any kind of wildlife-preserve types. We had some fallback story about clearing the area because of pockets of methane gas being released from the swamp. If that didn't work, Ed and Chris would flash fake ID and admit that the DEA was raiding a meth lab hidden in the woods. And if that didn't work, there were going to be some pain-in-the-ass civilians getting knocked out and zip-tied and dragged somewhere safe with a hell of story to tell their grandkids.

That left four of us. Me, Sig, Matt the paladin, and a wolf named Gustavo. It also left me with a critical decision. I could try to form a very wide perimeter around the suspected target to contain it, or I could try to sneak in a little closer and scope it out. I couldn't see an obvious right choice. There were reasons to try to scout the place out: We didn't have enough people to form any kind of containment grid, and we weren't even sure the old railway house was where those trucks had been headed. If the trucks had kept going, every second we stood around with our hands in our pants was time wasted. And even if the railway house was our target, we didn't know if they really were leaving or in what direction or how soon. There were too many unknowns, and I really, really wanted to get some eyes on that house.

On the other hand, because of Operation Blindside, the whole island of Nauset had become a containment grid. If our targets were leaving, at least some of them were leaving via the train rails, and we did have enough people to cover those. And if Aine was Dawn, or even if Dawn was just a traitor, she'd had a long time to study knight tactics. Sneaking up on her would be doubly hard, triply if any Redcaps with sensitive noses and hearing were around. And the banshee had demonstrated a real tendency to unleash all kinds of unholy havoc and destruction when cornered. If Aine would use zombie hordes and factory explosions when she wasn't even directly threatened, what would she do if enemies were actually closing in on her? And how the hell could four people hope to deal with it? The problem with being advance scouts was that communications were down and we were too far in advance. If we set off any defenses—and that seemed like it was more than fifty percent probable to me—we'd wind up giving the enemy a heads-up and time to bail out or prepare before our side got there.

"Let's get some cover and wait for reinforcements," I said reluctantly.

Sig stared at me.

"What?" I said. "It's the smart play."

"*That's* what," she responded. "This is usually the part where you explain how it's strategically necessary for you to go in there alone and naked with nothing but a pair of fingernail clippers."

"I don't have to try to impress you anymore," I explained. "We're already having sex."

"Don't make me undermine you in front of your troops," Sig advised me.

I took the warning seriously.

Angel Solis also seemed surprised by my sudden attack of caution. "I bet Simon a bottle of Glengoyne scotch that you would leave as soon as you heard us coming so that you could do what you'd already decided to do." He and fifteen other knights had arrived roughly thirty minutes after we did, emerging from the woods southwest of us in knight field armor that was colored like camouflage suits rather than matte-black. They were armed well enough to begin an insurgency in a small country.

"I wouldn't be here if Simon hadn't told me about this island," I said. "I'd have to be a complete shithead to pay him back by cutting you out of the loop."

His answering silence was thoughtful and mildly unflattering. I decided to change the subject before I got irritated. "I'm kind of surprised Simon didn't show up personally."

"He's dealing with all kinds of heavy shit that we don't have to worry about right now," Angel replied, and I took the hint.

"Something weird is going on with sounds. There are birds all around us, but I don't hear any calls coming from the railway house." I pointed in that direction. "I can smell breakfast smells, but I don't hear any doors slamming or chairs scraping or electronic sounds either. I can see tree limbs moving in the breeze a ways off, but I can't hear limbs rustling. And I don't understand why."

Angel wasn't listening any longer, or at least not completely. He was staring at a set of windmill blades peeking above the thinning trees where there must have been a clearing. They weren't traditional windmill blades. They were metal and sleeker. Like those turbines for windmills that generate electricity. Angel nodded at Gustavo. "Can the wolves see the windmill?"

"No," I told him. "Neither can Sig. All they see is an old, swaying tree a little taller than the others. That thing is glamoured."

"Well, I guess we've found their lab, then," Angel said. "And its power source. Are you willing to be our advance scout?"

"Sure." I began pulling off my clothes. "Do you have any fingernail clippers?"

Sig punched me in the shoulder.

"Private joke," I explained to Angel as I pulled my shirt back on.

"Yeah, funny," he said impatiently.

"Are there other knight squads out there?" I asked.

"Three," he said. "The one to the north will join in if they hear any shooting. The ones on the south and east are farther out and finding cover."

I nodded. The east and south squads would be there to catch the Redcaps if they tried to flee, but we wouldn't have to worry about hitting them in a crossfire.

I looked at Matt the Paladin. "You follow me at about fifteen yards. Sig, you and Gustavo follow him at about twenty." I wasn't wearing a field suit, but I had body armor on beneath my clothes. I left the submachine gun with my pack but strapped on my katana and a holster with two weapons in it. One was my Ruger Blackhawk. The other was a trank gun. Spare magazines with some very specialized ammo for both guns hooked to my belt. My knife went on a forearm sheath, and a garrote made out of braided mistletoe vines went into a sheath around my ankle. I already felt loaded down, but I went ahead and added a spray canister with compressed liquid nitrogen belted beneath the small of my back in case we met up with any more skinwalkers. It was only good for one shot up close, but it was better than nothing. Well, unless a lucky shot exploded it and gave me the worst case of frostbite ever in the history of ever.

The real surprise, though, came from Matt the Paladin. Matt was wearing more crosses than a tic-tac-toe tournament, a lot of them stickers that he had briefly blessed before peeling off and putting on his weapons. He also had an MP5 slung over his back instead of a sword. But when Matt the Paladin pulled out two pair of brass knuckles from his satchel—actually titanium knuckles—he offered them to me. "Take these."

My fingers fit through some thin metal rings, but the weapon wasn't as bulky and unwieldy as normal knucks, and there was a thin layer of foam padding beneath the metal plate that went over the outside of my fist. There was also a sharp protrusion shaped like a plus sign carved into the metal. If I punched someone hard, I would leave a cross shape cut into their skin. I experimented holding my katana handle and the butts of my guns with the knucks on. The reaction time moving my index finger around triggers was maybe a little slower, and that might get worse after I'd punched something a few times, but it wasn't too bad. "Can I keep these?"

I couldn't see his face behind the helmet, but it sounded like he was smiling for the first time since I'd met him. "If that works for you."

Sig had the same gear as I did, but instead of a katana, she had a straight sword with a weighted tip. She also had a spear that actually came in two halves. Sig didn't like the spear—she claimed the metal joinings threw the balance off—but with her eyesight and aim, that just meant she couldn't split insects in half from any farther than fifteen yards away. There were runes carved into the spear that Sig had never thoroughly explained to me, but I knew that they had something to do with exorcism. She was currently using it like a walking stick.

Gustavo was the most loaded-down of all of us. He had an LWRC rifle in his hands, a double-barreled shotgun and a machete on his back, a flare pistol on one hip, a Magnum revolver on the other, a bandolier of ammo across his chest, and a very mean look on his face.

I went in.

I wasn't consciously thinking about Dawn—I was paying attention to my environment, eyes mostly low and on the ground, ears and nose practically quivering. The earth wasn't a complete swamp this close to the edge. It was more like normal ground after a couple days of hard rain, which was good. Swamplike areas are hard to move quietly in and can be hard to track on or hard to conceal tracks in, depending on the weather.

Still, clues that I'd missed kept surfacing and appearing in the middle of my thoughts at random moments. Dawn's Celtic tattoos. The fact that Aine meant *radiance*, and so did Dawn, kind of. The way Dawn had been nearby when the banshee's wail had helped summon the *jötunn*, but she hadn't directly appeared until afterwards. Damn it! I had to pause twice and pull myself back into my body. Then the sounds of the woods suddenly weren't muted anymore. A wave of noise swelled over me, and my katana was in my hands before I even realized it. I could still hear sounds from behind, but now I could hear everything in front of me too: leaves rustling, the slight grinding sound of the windmill blades, the impact of something heavy being tossed on a hard surface, and most of all, wind chimes. Lots and lots of wind chimes. I couldn't see them, but they sounded like big wind chimes. I took half a step backward just to check, and those sounds disappeared again. Then I stepped forward. The sounds came back.

Huh. Somebody had designed a ward that trapped or converted sound waves. I'd never come across that before. I recalled an old TV comedy from the sixties or seventies called *Get Smart* about a bumbling spy. The secret agency on that show had this glass dome called the Cone of Silence that lowered from the ceiling to cover the spies when they wanted to talk privately. Somebody had lowered a big Cone of Silence over the railway house, and this one actually worked. All energy has to go somewhere, though, even with magic, so where was the sound going?

Well, at least no one would hear me scream. Oh, wait. That was a bad thing.

I saw an odd ripple in the mud in front of me, then another. I tried to dart to the side, but I was only partially successful; the roots that burst out of the wet soil still managed to wrap around my ankles. I did a crazy thing instinctively, rolled into a somersault and swung my katana behind me coming up. The can of liquid nitrogen I'd forgotten about dug into my back and threw me off balance a little, and if my rolling weight hadn't managed to unearth the roots slightly, I would have cut my toes off. I severed the roots instead, but it only bought me a few seconds. Several vines from nearby bushes came lashing out as I finished rolling to my feet, and by the time I finished slicing and tearing them, the roots had caught up with me again.

The wind chimes were going off like town bells by this point. I don't know what was worse, the noise or the suspicion that the wind chimes were jangling so loudly because the trees they were attached to were moving unnaturally.

I had seen some possessed trees in Wisconsin, but those had been individual trees. This was possessed...everything. The bushes and roots and vines and branches didn't seem to be working separately, either. The curling vines mirrored each other from different directions as if guided by a single intellect.

"Don't cut me!" Matt the Paladin yelled from behind me. As if I could. Roots had already wrapped up my legs and wrists. Then Matt put a hand on the roots and they recoiled away from him, pulling me off my feet but unwrapping and writhing around my legs in the process.

"Stay close to me!" Matt ordered, and I didn't make any smartass cracks. I just scrambled to my feet and did what he said. Positioning myself so that I could gaze past Matt's shoulder, I saw muddy roots and branches and tendrils and shoots reach out and then hesitate and bend away as Matt drew near. It would have made a great deodorant or breath freshener commercial in other circumstances.

For a moment, I thought we were safe. Then I saw a big rock emerging from the ground like a giant egg being laid from below, pushed out of the soil by God only knows what sort of contractions. The tall tree behind the rock bent slowly with a series of sharp cracks—for all the world like an old man with a bad back—and then the tree swung a branch. The ends of the tree limb spread out into a network of smaller branches, and that network of webbed fingers scooped up the small boulder and flung it forward.

I shoved Matt violently to the side, using the motion to push myself in the opposite direction, and the rock flew between us. Unfortunately, this meant I was no longer in the protection of Matt's priestly radius effect, and roots erupted from the soil and wrapped around me almost immediately. Before Matt was even back on his feet, I was being dragged along the forest floor. It was rocky soil too, beneath the puddles and mud. The tip of my katana got embedded in the earth and was torn out of my bound hands.

I tried to grab on to something, anything, but exposed roots withdrew into the mud, and bush branches parted, forming a clear pathway between me and the tree whose roots were pulling me along. The tree had a large knothole, and that hole was opening and closing like a maw while the tree's trunk swayed and bent. I was actually spun around crazily while roots beneath the soil played some kind of tag team, positioning me so that my head was facing the knothole while I jerked and thrashed.

But it wasn't my skull that went into that maw. It was Sig's spear. The weapon flew straight over me like a harpoon and punched into that tree and half through it with a splintering crack. The runes along the spear's length flared to life, but the effect on the tree was the opposite. It went still. So did all of the surrounding vegetation, thank God.

For the first time, I got a good look at and a good whiff of the tree. It was a Japanese maple tree. Again with the magical eastern trees? And then I understood. Somebody had transplanted a Jubokko tree here. It was the kind of thing Akihiko Watanabe would have done, the kind of thing not many other people could have. I recalled the banshee...was it really Dawn? Shit. I recalled the banshee mentioning New York and the Crucible, but she had never explained what Redcaps were doing there. I had assumed that she was interested in Akihiko's Asian door magic just like she was in the dalaketnons', and then I had assumed she was scouting out the gorgon. But maybe she and Akihiko had actually made some trades while they were negotiating, just like she had wanted to do with Parth.

Jubokko trees are unholy aberrations. It has been proven that talking to plants affects their growth, and that plants respond to positive emotions better than negative ones. Jubokko trees are an extreme case of an opposite reaction. Jubokko trees grow on the edge of battlefields or other places where a lot of violently killed bodies have been dumped without being buried properly, and their roots feed on human blood that has soaked into the soil, while the trees' life force absorbs the rage and despair and hatred of restless souls. The trees literally become bloodthirsty, and as their sentience grows, so does their ability to exert control over the surrounding vegetation.

I'd never heard of anyone using a Jubokko tree as a guard dog before. It would be like putting a hive full of killer bees behind your house. But then, I was having a lot of first times. I'm still waiting for the "Everything goes smoothly" first time.

The roots around me had loosened, but I was still thrashing and contorting to free my knife when I heard the wail. I saw a strange bubble pop up in a puddle of water about ten feet away from me, then saw mud slither aside around its edges. A bony hand wearing a glove of tattered flesh and mud emerged from the water.

Draugr.

∼42∼

A VOICE TO DIE FOR

I thought I knew what thrashing wildly was. I was wrong. Compared to the movements I made while trying to tear off those roots snarled around me, every other jerk, yank, lunge, and twitch I had ever made was leisurely and civilized. The noise alerted the draugr, and it continued to emerge from the ground like the tip of an obscene tongue. I got my right hand free, but the draugr was already crawling toward me on its hands and knees, the inside of its mouth shockingly red beneath all that mud and bluish-grey flesh. The remaining teeth in those black gums were rotten but still jagged, and they were gnashing. There was no way I was going to free my knife and my legs before it got to me, so I rolled to my side and punched the thing in the forehead with all of the leverage and momentum and arm strength I could muster.

The cross-shaped razors on the titanium knucks cracked into skull, and the draugr stopped yelling and started screaming. I wasn't used to hearing draugar scream like that. Draugar are dead; they just happen to be extremely bad at it. I couldn't see the imprint of the cross beneath the mud and the draugr's panicked movements, but it reeled back and clawed at its forehead, then scrambled away and rolled around on the ground. It was acting as if it wanted to get away from its own body, and finally it did. The spirit animating the draugr fled, and its body dropped wetly to the earth.

Not that I was lying around watching the spectacle slack-jawed. By the time that fuck bucket kicked, I was running to find my katana. The banshee's wail was still going, high and piercing, and I could see why no one had come to help me; draugar were coming out of the ground everywhere, and Angel Solis was leading his team into the fray. The knights were firing shotguns whose shells were loaded with small silver prayer beads, and the draugar they hit flew apart and collapsed. Nobody shot the one who was running to get me as I crouched beside my sword, though.

There wasn't a dry place on my body to wipe my hands, but parts of the handkerchief in my pocket were salvageable, and I rubbed it over my palms and the katana's hilt frantically while the dead bastard came charging. Then I took the hilt of my sword in my hands and the world slowed. My fear numbed. I crouched to bring the draugr's hands down when it lunged for me, and when I came up swinging over the draugr's arms, its head went flying. My katana is a blessed blade. I whirled aside as the draugr's body continued to move, but it wasn't going anywhere but past me and down.

"Form around me!" Matt the Paladin yelled, and we took his advice. Sig got behind his left shoulder, I got behind his right, and after a little direction, Gustavo walked sideways behind the paladin, watching our backs. Matt basically formed a running wedge. Draugar charged us only to peel away from Matt at the last moment, and then Sig and I finished them off with our respective swords, or at least made it a lot harder for them to run after us.

Then we crossed another ward, and the presence or pressure of draugar abruptly dropped off. No more draugar appeared in front of us, and the ones behind us stopped and turned around. We must have passed some picket line of hidden holy symbols or buried ward stones. I suppose if I'd arranged for an undead orgy to take place behind my house, I would have put up some No Trespassing signs too. The railway house in question finally came into sight as we broke through the wooded area, only twenty feet away.

The wooden building was grey, as much from decay as from the original paint. It was actually three different square buildings of varying height that seemed to have grown into each other. All of the sections were covered by triangular roofs that had recently had work done on them. No efforts had been made to paint or pressure-spray the building, but the grass around it was short, and there was actually glass in the windowpanes and no gaping holes in the walls. One of the two specially fitted trucks we'd seen was visible on the rails next to the house, and its bed was full of lab and industrial equipment.

I didn't get a chance to examine the house very closely. The banshee screamed again, this time Gaelic words instead of a wail, and a Redcap came running around the corner of the house, firing an Uzi. There was an impact sound and Matt the Paladin went down with a new dent in his helmet. Fortunately, for me, Matt the Paladin fell sideways, and I think his body armor continued to absorb hits that were meant for me. Even more fortunately, the Redcap's weapon jammed. That sounds really convenient, but it wasn't all that surprising. Uzis have a reputation for being dependable, but they need to be maintained. This one had probably come from a black market, and the Redcap was jerking the weapon up and down while running supernaturally fast through mud in heavy steel-toed hiking boots. That kind of jarring isn't enough to cause a misfeed all by itself, but it would contribute to all kinds of factors that might, especially if the weapon had an old coil spring or a loose barrel nut.

Sig launched her spear so fast that it disappeared, but the

Redcap still tossed his Uzi aside and plucked the spear out of the air like a magician performing a trick. His grin wasn't professional and friendly, though. The pointed teeth made him look like a shark on legs. I had one brief glance at that nasty smile, and then the Redcap was on Sig with the spear held out in front of him. Did I mention how fast these assclowns were? I didn't actually see what happened next, but Sig wasn't fast enough to grab the haft of the spear before the Redcap rammed the point into her stomach. It was her body armor and the mud that saved her. Sig's body skidded backward at the point of impact, and the spear only punched through her body armor a quarter of an inch or so before she got her hands on the haft. The unexpected halt made the Redcap slip in the mud himself, and even though Sig had gotten the wind knocked out of her, she managed to stomp on the Redcap's shin sideways and break it while pinning him to the ground.

The reason I didn't see this was because another Redcap came hurtling off the top of the railway house, the section that was only one story high. He was apparently running from all the shooting happening at the front of the building, and he'd jumped onto the railway house and used the triangular roof like a ramp. It was dramatic as all hell. Impressive-looking or not, though, I like it when opponents leave the ground. The dumbass wasn't wearing anything but a wife-beater and some grey sweatpants, and he couldn't dodge or turn while he was airborne. I fast-drew the dart gun and shot him twice before he landed behind me. It wasn't a trank dart—the dart injected hydrogen cyanide that had been extracted and condensed from dozens of packets of elderberry seeds, one of the plants that the Fae introduced to earth from their own realm.

The Redcap landed somewhere behind me, and then Gustavo was on him.

Unfortunately, Mr. Jumphappy had drawn my attention when the last Redcap—or at least the last real Redcap, not one of the human gangbangers they'd recruited—came through a window. Several bullets hit me hard and fast in my center mass and knocked me stumbling back, and for a moment, I lost it. I just lost it. It was some kind of PTSD thing from getting shot in the chest by a silver bullet. I don't know if these bullets were silver or not. The body armor stopped them. All I know is that for the first time since I was a page, I totally freaked out for a few seconds in the middle of a fight. Somewhere in there, I dropped the dart gun. I flailed. I screamed. I scrambled while backing up and swinging my katana wildly and one-handed with no art to it.

I should have died, really. I deserved to die. I dishonored my sword. Instead, the Redcap's forward momentum and the slippery mud drove him closer to me than he wanted, and my wildly swinging katana sent his pistol and two fingers flying through the air. The Redcap snarled and drew a knife with his other hand, and he was faster and using more skill than I was at the moment, but I had a longer blade and my instincts and reflexes weren't completely useless. In fact, they were so erratic that they were hard to predict. The flashing blades between us probably looked like a Cuisinart. But he slipped, I didn't, and he lost his hand, and then a large part of his throat.

Maybe Iceland wasn't such a bad idea after all.

But not right then. The Redcap who had leaped over me was weaponless and covered in blood and limping, but he still managed to run past me and dive through the window frame his partner had just cleared. I didn't run back to where Gustavo and the Redcap had been fighting. The headless body I glanced at back there wasn't going to heal. Sig was still standing even if no one else was, so I pulled myself together and went into the railway house.

PART THE FOURTH

Scry Hard

~43~

AINE THAT A SHAME

It looked like the poison darts were finally taking effect. I wound up walking behind the Redcap while he staggered mindlessly through the railway house, shooting around and over his shoulders. Sig was trailing behind both of us, firing around corners, and four dead human gangbangers later, I was moving behind the Redcap when he collapsed into the main greeting room and began crawling forward. There were only three gangbangers left that I could see, one firing out the front window while two turned to face me. Dawn, or the thing pretending to be her, was pressed against the wall alongside the front door, and there was a bound figure with a bag over its head lying at Dawn's feet. Dawn had been shot in several places, but she didn't seem to notice; she threw a black eggshell through the broken windowpane next to her, and I saw a serpent made of dark smoke rise up from the ground and slither through the air, toward the woods.

A knight from outside shot one of the men who'd turned to look at me, and Dawn whirled while I was shooting the other two. Her face was tight and white and really didn't look like Dawn's at all as she pushed off the wall with a shriek. It wasn't a normal shriek, but it wasn't a magical one either. Just a plain old *I want to rip your guts out and sprinkle a little oregano on them and eat them in front of you while you die slowly in agony* kind of a shriek. The banshee didn't make it very far. Sig's spear flew past me and caught the thing in the shoulder, knocking her back and pinning her against the wall.

The runes flared to life, but Dawn just snarled and reached out with her free hand and yanked the spear out. I shot her in the other shoulder, right in her parietal nerve cluster. She didn't seem to feel pain, or she was able to cut her pain receptors off at will—but the bullet had been soaked in the holy herb verbena and had a cross carved in the casing by Molly Newman, and the banshee's other arm went limp.

"If you start wailing, I'll cut your head off," I said, drawing my katana and continuing to walk forward. I had to maneuver slightly to keep the bound figure on the floor next to Dawn in my line of sight. "Fair warning."

Dawn leaned back against the wall and slid down it until she was sitting. "Well, now." It was the banshee's voice coming out of Dawn's mouth, Dawn's horribly grinning mouth, and I'm going to stop calling her Dawn now, because she wasn't, not in any sense of the word. Aine shook her torso so that her arms swung limply at her side. "Sure, and I hope you're not going to tell me to raise my hands."

Normally, I might have made some joke about her being disarmed, but I just holstered my Ruger so I could put both hands on the katana's hilt. Sig was pulling her gun out anyway, and I felt a lot safer with a blessed blade at the ready. The Redcap had almost reached Dawn now, and I kicked him in the back of the head and he went limp. He didn't look like he was faking dying, but I didn't look like I was faking not caring either, so maybe it balanced out.

"All I want to hear from you is who's been helping you,

Aine," I said. "And maybe how you possessed a host with Templar blood in her veins."

"So, we're just friends having a nice talk now, are we? Give us a kiss, then." She arched her crotch upward, her lips peeled back from her front top teeth. "That's what you Charmings are on about, isn't it? Plant one right on my pissflaps."

Well, she had a point. What was I going to threaten her with? Death? Sig could probably exorcise the banshee, eventually, or I could cut her head off, but then what?

Sig kept her gun leveled at the banshee, looking fascinated and repelled. "I can't see where you end and Dawn begins."

"We don't," the banshee taunted.

"You really aren't one thing or the other, are you?" Sig squinted, though as far as I know, she wasn't looking with her physical eyes. "Not a ghost. Not alive."

"Well, there you are," Aine went on with that grating false cheeriness. "Death is a cold asshole, life is a hot pussy, and I'm the stinker's bridge in the middle. You and me could be sisters."

Well, I guess expecting her to explain her master plan had been a little optimistic. I kicked her in the face, hoping to knock her unconscious. Blood spurted out of her nose and her head bounced off the wall, but she didn't stop grinning. My next kick caught her under her chin. She made a sound that was half a cackle and half a sigh of pleasure and snapped her teeth at my boot playfully. It was like trying to turn a car's engine off by kicking the doors and bumpers.

"Sig?" I asked.

"If you don't want to just kill her, I think we should get the paladins," Sig said. "This is outside my experience."

"Just watch her a second." I sheathed my katana and pulled the sack off the gorgon's head just to make sure it was really her and not some kind of trick. That's the kind of thing I would have done to stack the deck a little. But the prisoner smelled like scared gorgon. Her hair was bristling around a blindfold as if the strands were alive. Then I pulled Aine from the wall and threw the banshee down on the ground. Her arms still weren't moving when I forced them behind her back and zip-tied them. Three times.

"Scared, Johnny boy?" the banshee taunted.

"Freaked out," I admitted, then knelt down beside the gorgon and undid her gag. If the banshee was just going to spout freaky filth and nonsense, maybe the gorgon would know something useful.

The gorgon didn't gasp out any warnings, though. She just started yelling for me to free her. I told her I wanted to gag the banshee first, and that actually seemed to calm her down. It had the opposite effect on Aine. For the first time, the banshee got serious. "You're making a mistake, Johnny boy."

"Then there's nothing to worry about," I said. "I'm really good at making mistakes."

"If I leave this body, I'll come back," the banshee spat. "It's yourself I'll be hunting, you and anyone you love, and you'll never know when I'm back or who I'll be. I'll make your suffering my art, you cheeky little snot."

"Last time I checked, it took you almost a century to come back," I said conversationally. "People totally willing to give their body over to some psychotic skank from their family tree must not come along all that often."

"And if it's dead you're being, I'll hunt your family," she hissed.

"I don't have a family," I said absently, pulling her head up so that I could slip the gag under her face.

She made a harsh, gargling cackle. "The knights don't tell you everything. You think you're one of them? A real knight at last? You're not the only Charming by a long shot." That almost made me pause, but since she still seemed to be stalling for some reason, I just kept on. The banshee yelled, "Wait! This is your last chance. Let me go now! Just walk away, and I will leave you and yours alone for the rest of eternity. I swear it. But if you don't, I will hunt you and hound you until you would do anything to change this moment, and it will be too late. It will always be too late."

"Careful there, Aine," I said. "That kind of promise goes both ways." And I forced the gag into her mouth and bound it tightly. I wasn't hearing any more signs of fighting outside, and one of the windows gave me a view of a knight cautiously emerging from the woods. I waved at him and addressed Sig. "Want to check outside and see if you can wake up the paladin?"

"All right," she acceded, but she didn't take her gun off the banshee.

"Shout out if we have a clear line of retreat too," I said. "I want to get this wackjob out of here. I don't like the way she was playing for time."

"Roger that." Sig walked out rapidly.

At some point during this brief exchange, the gorgon had rolled over, gotten ahold of the Redcap's knife, pulled her bottom and legs between the arms tied behind her back so that they were in front of her now, and was sawing at the zip tie binding her ankles. Gorgons' bodies are very sinuous. It's that snake thing.

"Drop the knife and leave your arms bound," I commanded. Just because I wanted to save the gorgon didn't mean I trusted her. "Scooch back against that far wall and stop distracting me."

I didn't have any zip ties left, so I put my knee on the back of Aine's calves to keep her from thrashing around so much and unholstered my Ruger and trained it on the back of her head, though I don't know what I expected her to do. When the front door to the railway house opened, I pulled Aine's head up and put her between me and the door, keeping the weapon trained on her. Even before I glanced up, I knew something was wrong with the quality of air and the background sounds and smells. The door wasn't opening to reveal Nauset Island. It was opening to reveal some kind of storage room full of wooden crates. And Mistress Malea was standing right in the middle of them.

My Ruger was ripped out of my hands and I was picked up and hurled across the room by some force I couldn't see or smell, bounced off the ceiling and the wall before I wound up skipping across the floor like a rock above the surface of a lake, and eventually I sank down into dark welcoming waters.

"Wake up, you shit biscuit!"

Something hit me in the face. My eyes didn't quite have a chance to focus when something hit me again. Hard. I tried to move my arms and couldn't. There was a cutting pain in my stomach. I wanted to collapse, but that just moved the pain to new and excruciating places. I tried to say something and my mouth filled with blood. Finally, I opened my eyes—well, one of them anyway; the other seemed to be swollen shut—and I saw Aine pulling back to hit me again. I tried to change into a wolf but nothing happened. My body was already overtaxed trying to repair itself.

"Wake up! I want you to see this."

"Hi," I managed. There was a hilt sticking out of my lower torso. The hilt of my katana. It must have been pinning me to one of the wooden crates. I was in the storage room I'd seen, with no sign of the railway house anywhere. There were wooden crates all around me, and the shattered remains of a door. Ever seen those doors on display in department and furniture stores? Sometimes, they have them just standing alone in midair in wooden frames that are braced on big wooden bases sticking out from the bottom like flippers. The shattered door had been in a frame like that. I knew this because there was a second door intact and standing upright in a display frame of its own. The light illuminating the room came from old-fashioned gas lights like they used to use during the Victorian era. There wasn't an electronic device in sight.

Mistress Malea was watching me. She was wearing a red faux leather jacket with tassels and designer jeans, her dark eyes shining. The bitch was wearing my guns holstered at her side too. The most bizarre thing, though, was that she was standing next to a picnic basket. It seemed so out of place. No, wait, this wasn't Mistress Malea. It was one of her slimmer doubles. Or maybe the original's weight gain had been some kind of complicated ruse so that she could trade places with one of her duplicates? Or maybe this was a double who had survived the death of her maker? Somebody—I couldn't remember who—had said that it was taboo for a dalaketnon to make too many doubles or spend too much time on other worlds, because they could lose control of their mind or their creations. Could this be an ultimate expression of split personality? A double surviving the death of its maker?

Sig had been the one talking about dalaketnons. Where was Sig? What was she doing? Was there a way for anyone to figure out where I was?

Beside Malea 2.0 stood a completely hairless and gaunt man, naked except for a bronze amulet and the symbols he was smearing on his chest in blood. I didn't have to see the trail along the floor to know the blood was mine. I didn't have to recognize the style of symbols to know that he was a skin-walker either. The only surprising thing was . . . he smelled like a half-elf. But then, a lot of cunning folk and psychics have a Fae ancestor somewhere back in the family woodpile. The

Redcap was there too, propped in the west corner of the room and looking like I felt, his lips blue and flecks of foam in the corners of his mouth while his chest heaved up and down rapidly. The banshee was standing in front of me and over me. She was down to a sports bra and black panties, four bandages taped to her body.

I looked down at my arms to see why I couldn't move them. They were dislocated from my shoulders. Someone had tied my shoes together too, and not just by tying the top knots. The entire shoelaces had been taken out and then the shoes retied with some kind of wire, the new metal laces crisscrossing between shoes. There were two teeth on the floor next to my shoes too. With a bit of a jolt, I realized that they were mine. I spit more blood onto the hilt of the sword, looked up, and croaked, "So, do you give up?"

The banshee laughed. "It's too late to make me like you, Johnny. You almost ruined everything."

"Like what?" I gasped. I was in shock, freezing, and having a hard time putting thoughts together while my body shut down all but its most vital systems.

Aine crouched down so that she was facing me. "Here, now, do you really think I'm going to blab away all my plans and wrap all my mystery up in a neat little bow and give it to you? You can die with your questions unanswered, you wolfshite. The gorgon jumped through a window in the front of the station house and got away because of you."

I couldn't respond, so she nodded at the two people behind her. "Watching you and the Valkyrie die slowly is part of Malea's price for joining us. She didn't like it much when Sig killed her maker. And Conor needs you alive when he eats part of you if he's going to make a John Charming skin suit. If it weren't for that, you'd be dead already."

I spat a mouthful of blood in her face.

Aine wiped her hand over her cheeks, then slowly licked my blood off of her fingers and grinned and kissed me. I didn't even have enough wherewithal to bite her lips in time. "Mmnnn. Ta, Johnny." She stood up and turned to walk out of the room, but paused and spoke to Malea. "I'll be at the vault, but I'll check back with you in a few hours whether he's finished or no."

The vault?

Malea didn't answer. She hadn't taken her eyes off of me since I'd woken up. I don't think I'd ever once heard the dalaketnon or any of her doubles speak, come to think of it. The guard, Dan, had said that Malea had grown up with a domineering mother and liked to watch while other people had sex or suffered. Maybe she only crawled out of her shell when she had to. Aine turned to me one last time. "I'll tell Sig you died crying."

I didn't react, and then the banshee was gone.

The skinwalker smiled, and I realized that he had filed his incisors into points. "Now, which part should I eat, then? I usually like to do hands, but Malea here wants me to fry up your testicles."

Malea laughed. Then she didn't. In fact, she stopped and fell to the floor. The Redcap was standing behind her, and the very long and sharp nails on his right hand were covered in her blood. The skinwalker whirled and reached for his skinning knife, but the Redcap almost casually slapped it out of his hands. "Do you know what would be really scary?" he asked the skinwalker. "If you fought with somebody who could fight back."

"Leave him alive," I croaked.

"No! Stop!" The skinwalker babbled. "Stop! Stop! St—"

The Redcap didn't stop, but he didn't kill the skinwalker either. "You knights are crazy," Nick said, and he reached down and pulled my katana out of my abdomen.

~44~

JUST THE TOO OF US

Okay, here's the deal. I got sick of our enemies planting doubles and traitors on me, so I thought it might be advantageous to do the same to them. Gustavo, the werewolf who had been part of my scouting team, wasn't Gustavo. Gustavo was Nick. The wolves knew about the switch, of course, but not the paladins. Nick's condition for cooperating had been that the knights not know who he was or how he was involved, if at all possible. Honestly, I think the idea of pulling one over on the Templars was as much a part of the attraction for the nix as revenge.

When Nick as "Gustavo" killed the Redcap, he covered its body in mud and took its place. Nixies don't just change into another person's shape; they can alter the shape and size of their vocal cords to imitate another person's voice. They can change the way their skin reflects light to alter color. That same skin can assume the texture and shape of a person's clothes, although nixies only do this as a last resort. Nixies like to retain the option of taking their clothes off. The whole ruse where Nick staggered into the railway house and pretended to be almost dead was just so that Aine would take him with her if she somehow escaped or turned the tables on us. We had killed the other Redcaps who would smell any difference in Nick, and the banshee would want to see if her last enforcer revived. It had been easy enough for Nick to change the color of his lips to blue, and his apparent near-comatose status had kept the banshee from asking him questions.

I know, I know, I skipped the whole part where I tracked Mama Lenke back down to the sewers. She knew how to get in contact with Nick, and for whatever reason, she was capable of shaming him into going along. I think he really wanted to help me deep down, though. Nixies don't just assume new shapes and genders and skin colors and ages periodically; they try on new personalities and approaches to life. The core personality seems to remain, but the channels it travels through go in different directions, if that makes any sense. I don't know if this practice is the result of boredom or some spiritual quest or a survival instinct that preserves their sanity and improves their chances of staying undetected from generation to generation or what. Whatever, the awkward truth is, I don't think that the fact that Nick's newest primary form looked a little like me was a coincidence. I think I had made some kind of impression on the nix when we'd met, maybe not even a good impression, but a distinct one. When the nix shed her last old life like a snakeskin and tried a new male perspective on for size, she'd decided to see what it would be like to be me.

If I'd been around, I could have explained to the nix that this was a bad idea. I'm pretty sure one of me is enough. Hell, I'd just be happy if one of me wasn't one too many.

But Nick was my hole card.

∾45∾

OUT, OUT, DAMNED PLOT

Nick shoved my arms back in their sockets, and I lay heroically on my side, gasping out of my blowhole and passing in and out of consciousness. While the nix was securing the skinwalker, I also picked up my teeth and shoved them back into my gums at some point, which at least had the benefit of waking me up again. The injury was recent enough that the roots would regrow and reattach. Then Nick dragged Malea's body behind some crates and assumed Malea's form. At least we wouldn't have to explain the blood to anyone. The banshee had said she would come get Malea in a few hours, and Nick and I decided to take her up on that. It would be a lot easier to isolate and ambush the banshee if she came to us. We would eliminate our most dangerous opponent, and Nick could impersonate Aine, which ought to make it a lot easier to escape wherever we were.

Of course, the real reason we waited was that I needed to heal. But finding strategic reasons to justify it makes it sound better. There was nothing for it, though. I began forcing myself to eat some of the roast chicken and fruit and cheese from the picnic basket, washing it down with swallows of wine and mineral water. For some reason, eating made me even more out of it. My body was working overtime.

"Good night," I mumbled.

Nick seemed surprised. "You're going to sleep *now*?"

"My stomach has to mend." I could barely keep my eye open. "Kill Aine if she shows up. Wake me up in two hours."

"Wake up," he replied.

I groaned. "I said give me two hours."

Nick sounded like his patience was getting strained. "It's been two hours."

I hate it when that happens.

I managed to pull myself up and checked my stomach. It seemed to be in one piece again, though I didn't feel like cranking out sit-ups to make sure. I could see out of both eyes again too. The biggest aftereffect of my injuries was sheer physical exhaustion.

"I'm going to scout outside a bit," Nick said. "I didn't want to leave you while you were out of it, but I want to have an escape route figured out after we kill the banshee."

"Hold on," I protested.

"I need to see more people I can impersonate too, John," Nick said impatiently. "I want to figure out who's where and who's alone and who obeys who. I'll be fine. Even sadists need to use the bathroom."

"I'm not arguing." I nodded at the skinwalker, who was bound and lying on his side. "Take his amulet. And check both their clothes for any other kind of ID or badge."

Nick gave me a slightly pitying look and pulled a bronze amulet from his jacket pocket. Or I guess he pulled it from a pouch made out of his own flesh. I decided not to think about that too much.

I studied the amulet thoughtfully. "You'd better put it on."

"Malea wore it under her shirt," Nick said impatiently. "I can't do that." I decided not to think about that too much, either.

"Hold on." I went over and removed the amulet the skinwalker was wearing and studied it more closely. As near as I could tell, it was identical to the one Nick had. "You definitely need to wear it."

"Why?" he said suspiciously.

"Because these amulets are either a guest pass or a protective device or some kind of fraternity pin on steroids," I said. "And either way, we don't want to get caught without them."

Nick slipped on the amulet and slipped out of the room, and I put the second amulet on and looked around a bit more alertly. Nick had amused himself while I was asleep by looking through the wooden crates whose lids had been pried off. One crate was full of some kind of sharp, bitter herb I'd never smelled before. Another held several pressure-sealed containers with scroll tubes in them. But when I saw that the third crate held a chest with multiple locks on it, I got distinctly uneasy. The chest had a Seal of Solomon scratched on it. Something nasty was bound inside that container.

After Aine's comment about a vault, I was beginning to think that we were in one of the Knights Templar's secret archives. Hell, the Order's central US archive is in Boston. When Simon was telling me about all of the chaos that had erupted within the Templars, one of the things he'd mentioned was an attack on the Loremaster too. Simon had said the knights involved had honestly been misled into believing that the Loremaster was a skinwalker. But what if it was a double fake and the knights hadn't been misled? Or only partially so? No, that didn't make sense. Aine or her allies wouldn't have drawn attention to the archives if they owned them. But what if the attack had been a distraction or a way of weakening the archives' defenses so that someone could take over or sneak in?

Too many *ifs* and *maybes*. It was time to get some answers. When I woke the skinwalker up, I wasn't gentle about it. He came to in a world where my knife was under his chin and already drawing blood. "I don't have a lot of time. You're useful or you're dead," I informed him. "There are no other choices."

He believed me. He should have. The only nice thing about dealing with narcissists and sociopaths is that they'll betray anyone, under a real threat of death. They all know deep in their heart of hearts that their continued existence is the only important thing in the universe.

"Where are we?" I asked. "And don't even think of lying. I'll smell it. I'll hear it in your heartbeat." That wasn't necessarily true. Sociopaths don't have normal physiological responses when they lie. It's one of the reasons lie detectors aren't admissible in court.

"The knights' central archives," he gasped.

"How the hell did a banshee possess a Templar?" I asked. It was self-indulgent. I should have asked what Aine's plan was first. But I was still a little groggy, and it had been eating at me.

The dumbass laughed derisively. He was such a prick that he couldn't hold it in even under knifepoint. "Your Dawn was never one of you geas-born. Dawn's great-grandmother Siobhan seduced a knight and married him. Then Siobhan cheated on him and had children with another man outside of the bloodline. She poisoned her husband and raised the children to be traitors."

"You're saying this Siobhan's kids became fake knights?"

The skinwalker laughed again. "All of Siobhan's children and her children's children pretended to be knights who married outside the bloodline. For the last three generations, Dawn's family has been a secret society within your secret society. Not a geas-born among them."

"Bullshit." I pressed the knife in more firmly. "The knights tested for that even before DNA came along."

He sneered. "Your haunted-brooch test was worthless."

"Explain," I demanded.

"The quartermaster in charge of the brooch substituted a counterfeit for Siobhan's children's ceremony." The skinwalker bared his teeth. "He was a skinwalker like me. You should know. You killed him later. And one of Siobhan's children grew up to be another quartermaster before it became an issue again."

"Why?" I asked. "Why would skinwalkers care about any of this?"

This time, his laugh was real. "We aren't just skinwalkers. We're half-Fae."

I tried to think back. Had the skinwalker I'd killed in 1965 been a half-Fae? I hadn't had my expanded senses very long, and some half-Fae smell more human than anything else, depending on how strong the elf strain is. There had been a lot of burnt flesh and blood and magic in the air too, and I hadn't been thinking too clearly at the time. What about the skinwalker Dawn—Aine—had killed? Or the one Sig had liquefied? Would Simon have told me if examination revealed that they were half-elves?

Probably not.

But all I said was "So what?"

"We're tired of being castoffs and rejects!" he snarled. His attitude really was a little strange for someone who was determined to live at all costs, but fear does weird things to people, especially ones who weren't all that emotionally stable to begin with. "The Fae had sex with our human mothers and fathers and then blamed us, their children, for our parents' perversions! As if we had a choice!"

"What's that got to do with the Knights Templar?" I asked.

"You're the Faes' slaves!" he jeered. "We're going to take back what's ours! We're going to gather the rejects and castoffs of this world and raise an army strong enough to claim our own!"

A cult or colony or tribe of half-elves who had declared jihad on the Fae? So fanatical that some of them were willing to become skinwalkers to pursue their goals, so full of hate that part of it survived even past the rituals that were supposed to kill every loyalty or emotional tie to their former life? Put a pin in that one too. "Okay, so why would a banshee care?"

"Aine wants vengeance even more than we do! She was full-blooded Fae when she was alive!" the skinwalker babbled. "All banshees were. They were Unseelie nobles who got killed in the war between the Seelie and Unseelie courts. It's why some call the banshees bean sidhe."

"Bullshit," I repeated. "Banshees have human descendants in the five families."

The skinwalker bared his teeth. "The magic binds banshees to a human family that has a trace of their Fae blood in them. It wasn't a gift to humans. It was a punishment for the banshees."

"Aine seems to be...enjoying herself," I said.

"She's not!" the skinwalker assured me. "When the Fae left this world, they abandoned the banshees to it, just like they abandoned all of us bastards and mongrels."

"Half-elves," I repeated.

"Yah. Like we're somehow less than elves. How would you like being called half-human your entire life?" he demanded.

I just looked at him. Did he know who he was talking to?

Conor closed his eyes. "You have no idea what it's like. I can hear a piece of the most beautiful song in all the worlds in my head. Just enough to know it's not enough. And I'll never hear all of it."

If half-elves had some kind of strong racial memory, maybe that explained how some part of their old life or value system hung on even after they became skinwalkers. Humans wouldn't have that intense a bond to cling to. But all that was a little too complex and vague for me to respond to in my condition. What I said instead was, "Malea's magic. You want that door to Faerie, don't you?"

"When we're ready," he agreed. "When the School of Night has enough power to—" The words choked off as his mouth contorted and his eyes bulged. His skin began to cave in as if his muscles were melting, his bones turning to dust. Sores began to emerge from that skin, and the liquid that oozed from them dissolved the flesh it touched.

I backed away fast. My immune system can handle almost any contagion, but I wasn't taking any chances with whatever this was. It wasn't a geas. In retrospect, I think that at some point, the skinwalker had been forced to go through some arcane ritual, create some elaborate spell and then not quite finish it. I think the verbal component for the spell—all that was needed to complete it—must have been the phrase *School of Night*. Saying those words aloud had doomed him.

Yeah, well, sucked to be him. I was shaken and stared at the skinwalker's body longer than I should have, half just to make sure that nothing else oozed out of it, but I didn't stand there and ruminate on the cruelty of existence or compose any funeral dirges. I didn't rail at myself for not finding out about Aine's immediate plans first, either, even though that was an obvious mistake in hindsight. It was blood under the bridge.

All I can say in my defense is, the need to survive has a way of focusing priorities.

Speaking of focus: We were in the central archives. The Templars' enemies were hiding beneath one of the most secure Templar strongholds in Boston while knights scoured the city all around looking for them. That took some serious cojones. What could I do about it? And how did Aine hope to escape? Oh. Right.

I walked up to the dalaketnon door in the display frame and stared at it until I found the small runes etched into the balete wood. The style was familiar, but I didn't recognize the rune pattern from any of the other doors I'd seen. Finally, I took my knife and began carving some extra lines into the door's surface, altering the runes and sigils but not obviously so. I smelled Nick as the door opened and explained the skinwalker.

"We're in the basement of some kind of bank," he informed me. "But it's not just like any basement. I got into a stairwell, and we're the fourth basement level down. There's a gold robot walking the halls, and weird guys in robes. I heard chanting too."

I frowned. "A robot?"

"Maybe it's a gold golem." Nick suddenly realized that I was cutting marks into the magic door. "What are you doing?"

"It's a new strategy," I grunted. "I'm carving the words *John hearts Aine.* Think she'll buy it?"

He came up closer and peered over my shoulder. When he spoke, it was with a very obvious effort not to yell. "You realize that you just ruined a door that could have been our escape route, right?"

I was too tired for this. I leaned my forehead against the panel and rested. "You're looking at this all wrong, Nick."

"How is that?" he asked acidly.

"I just ruined the door that could have been *her* escape route," I said.

All I meant was that I was willing to do whatever it took to throw a monkey wrench in their plans, but Nick thought I meant that I was trapping the banshee and her minions in with me instead of the other way around. "That's big talk for someone who just got tired from carving out a few lines on some wood," Nick retorted. "How are you going to back it up?"

"This isn't about logic, Nick," I said, putting away my knife. "This is about choice."

"What choice?" he demanded.

"Exactly," I said.

"Oh for...the only reason we don't have a choice," Nick replied, not quite evenly, "is because you just destroyed our emergency exit!"

"Who says Aine's emergency exit didn't go straight to a place crawling with more of her henchmen or allies?" I shot back. "Or that this door doesn't lead to whatever big, nasty surprise she has lined up next? She likes those."

"How do we know that door didn't lead to a nice cabin in Colorado?" Nick countered.

I tried a different approach. "Surprise is the biggest advantage you and I have going for us, Nick. Would you really have opened that door and risked throwing that away on a maybe?"

Nick got a stubborn expression on his face. "Maybe. That's why they call it *maybe*."

I sighed raggedly. This wasn't accomplishing anything, and I didn't want to waste what energy I had. "We have to work together, Nick. Okay? Right now. So, if it makes you feel any better, I'm sorry. I should have talked to you and given you a chance to be a complete dumbass."

"You gave me a chance to be a complete dumbass when you asked me to work with you!" Nick snapped back. "And for some reason, I took it."

That was fair.

"Thanks for saving my life, Nick," I said. "Seriously. I'm sorry."

That shut him up.

It wasn't Aine who came to get us. The sound of heavy clanking feet announced the arrival of some asshat who smelled like a half-elf and his apparent bodyguard, a type of bronze golem called a Talos. Talos were supposedly invented by Hephaestus, and they come in different shapes and sizes. This one was eight and a half feet tall and hammered into the form of a Spartan soldier. There were six-inch spikes built into the Talos's left knuckles, and the steel sword it was carrying was as long as my leg. The Talos also gleamed like gold except for the heavy steel boots that it was wearing. A Talos runs on some kind of fuel whose secret is more closely guarded than the formula for Coca-Cola, and the fuel plug is in its ankle. In Greek myth, the plug used to be made of wax and was a Talos's only vulnerable point,[1] but I guess some Templar security chief hadn't approved of this design flaw.

As for the half-elf, the only odd thing about him was that most half-elves I've met have tended to be very fashion-conscious, and this one was dressed in a dark red robe with a hood pulled over his face. He looked like something out of a fraternity hazing or an Italian horror film. "The knights are coming!" he yelled as he opened the door. "Aine says to get the door!"

---

[1] Oddly enough, Achilles was an invulnerable warrior from Greek myth who dressed in shining golden armor that covered him so completely that the Trojans couldn't tell when it was being worn by other people, like his friend and/or lover Patroclus. And Achilles' only vulnerable point was in his heel. Personally, I think there's something suspicious about that.

"How close are they?" I asked.

Apparently, skinwalkers *can* make a magic skin suit within four hours if they've already made preparations, because the half-elf assumed I was the skinwalker and that I now looked like John Charming. Considering the Talos in the doorway and how few reserves I had, I was pretty glad about that.

"They're on the main floor," the half-elf babbled. "We have to hold them in the stairwells until we get through the last vault. The bastards don't care about the hostages we've taken at all." Then the half-elf paused and wrinkled his nose as a whiff of the skinwalker's putrid remains reached him. He stiffened perceptibly. "What's that sm—"

The fist Nick hit him with was considerably larger than Malea's should have been. I tensed, but the Talos didn't react, and the half-elf collapsed to the floor with a broken jaw. "The robot won't bother us," Nick assured me, seeing my expression. "I walked right past it when I was scouting out the floor."

I was sort of getting the impression that Nick was impulsive.

The half-elf's feet were visible to the hallway outside our storage room, so I stepped up and grabbed him by the shoulders and pulled him into the room, watching the Talos the whole time. It didn't seem to have an opinion on the subject one way or another. Then I went ahead and grabbed the red robe by the hemline and pulled it over the half-elf's head. I had some vague idea about securing his wrists with the steel wire that Aine had used to re-lace my shoes, and I wanted to search him first. But when I tugged the robe completely over his head, the Talos moved surprisingly fast for such a heavy object. Its steel sword...well...I won't describe what that steel sword—presumably a magic sword—did to the half-elf's body. The image still occasionally pops up in my mind in random nightmare flashes that shrivel my testicles.

Nick jumped back and pressed himself against a far wall. I think if the Talos's action had caught him while he was inhaling instead of exhaling, Nick would have shrieked. I was crouching down, and I didn't move at all. I just watched the Talos very, very carefully. When it resumed a stance that looked something like a ready position, I very slowly finished sifting through the red robe I was holding until a bronze amulet clanked to the floor. The half-elf must have been wearing it under the robe, and it had gotten bunched up and pulled off. I picked up the amulet and showed it to Nick.

"Well," I said. "At least we know what the amulets are for now."

"What?!?" Nick refused to peel himself off the wall. "Who owns a magic robot that will kill them if they don't wear a damn amulet twenty-four hours a day?!? That's insane! And what was all that about knights coming?"

"The Talos doesn't belong to the banshee. It belongs to the Knights Templar," I said.

"How do you know that?" Nick demanded.

"We're in one of the Knights Templar storage facilities, and nobody makes a nine-foot golem for sneaking into a place," I explained. "The amulets are some kind of magical bypass Aine came up with to get around this thing."

"Why...." Nick began.

"Nick," I said. "I think we're in the middle of a heist."

∾46∾

DEUS EX MACHINA

A lot of unnecessary conversation followed where I had to say the words "I don't know" about two hundred times, but when Nick was finally convinced that a metaphorical meteor swarm was about to come raining down on us, he was mostly relieved. "This is awesome! All we have to do is hide until the knights get here."

I didn't agree happily.

Nick saw my expression and stared at me as if I were insane. He gestured at the remaining dalaketnon door. "John. You already knocked out their getaway car! You were right about the damned door, okay? I admit it. They're screwed and they don't even know it. Mission accomplished."

"Nick," I said. "Death is just a vacation for this crazy bitch. She likes to cover her tracks in a big way. I'm talking Old Testament big way. Floods. Explosions. The dead rising. There is no way she doesn't have something seriously messed up and huge planned for when she's got that vault open."

"Then let's start looking for a way to get out of here," Nick said. "I'll be guard A when I'm with guard B and guard B when

I'm with guard C, and we'll leapfrog our way out of this place. I'll set them up; you knock them down."

I tried again, pointing at the ceiling. "Nick, listen to me. You heard that half-elf. The banshee's people are concentrating on holding the knights off up there. Everything she wants to keep them away from is down here. We're inside her defensive perimeter."

Nick started to get angry. "You know what's crazy? You start talking all tactics and strategy and it actually sounds like you know what you're doing! But this isn't numbers and logic to me, asshole! You're talking about my life! And this knight bullshit? It isn't even my fight."

"What do you want me to do, Nick?" I asked. "For all I know, Sig is up there. And if she's not, people other people love are. This banshee kidnapped my goddaughter."

That at least quieted him down. "I have somebody too."

We were out of time. Aine would be wondering where her messenger went. I grabbed the red robe and pulled it over my head. "Do what you have to do, Nick. If something happens to me, would you find Sig and tell her the sex was incredible?"

He frowned.

"She doesn't seem to like it when I tell her I love her when I think I'm going to die," I explained.

"John . . ." Nick protested.

I picked up my katana and the canister of liquid nitrogen and the holstered guns and carried them in my arms as if they were a load of laundry. They would show up under the robe, and I figured there was at least a chance it would look as if I was delivering them somewhere. It would give me an excuse to keep my head lowered too. "Go fuck off and be safe, Nick."

That wasn't really fair. He was right. It wasn't his fight.

*   *   *

I could tell immediately that I wasn't in the vault proper. I was in some kind of support wing with two long and empty windowless hallways that held the kinds of facilities that would enable people to barricade themselves underground for months. I passed by a laundry room, some kind of communal bathroom with showers, a common room with a wind-up phonograph and a lot of books and magazines, and finally a closed door that I didn't mess with. I was following the banshee's scent, and the Talos came clanking along right behind me. The lack of bodies was disconcerting. I could smell human blood in the air, and half-elf scents that were so fresh, it was almost like the owners were still there. A stream of dust fell off the ceiling, though I didn't feel the floor shake.

Three voices were muttering in the distance, and beyond them, there was chanting. I only caught fragments because the voices were speaking low and the Talos's metal boots were providing their own percussion section to the background, but there seemed to be some talking about the independent air supply for the basement level going on. The knights must be using gas or smoke somewhere on the upper levels. I thought about a place like this, four floors underground, and all the ways that knights would design it so that it could be defended by a small number of people. Then I imagined some of those people being skinwalkers who were virtually invulnerable and half-elves who wouldn't be hurt by most natural elements, and my sphincter tightened.

I could see the vault proper now. It was a solid metal wall with a door that looked like a battleship hatch, though fortunately the door was swinging open. At a guess, they were getting ready for a quick exit stage left. I could only see one of the men who'd been talking, a short, intense-looking guy in body armor holding an assault rifle I didn't recognize. The gun looked Chinese, but I have no idea how to explain why. "Where's the door?" he called.

Oh, that's what the messenger had meant about getting the door. He'd wanted us to carry the door and its display stand to Aine so she could leave directly from the vault if things went tits up. I really wasn't functioning on all cylinders. "They're bringing it," I called. "Aine wanted the prisoner's gear." The messenger had had a high reedy voice, and I'm a pretty good mimic, at least with male voices. Nothing like Nick or a skin-walker, but the noise the Talos was making behind me helped.

Really, it came back down to how the mind sees and hears what it expects to see and hear. These weren't trained guards. They were killers, sure, but they weren't soldiers. They had just seen a hooded someone like me go down the hall followed by a Talos, and they'd known he was on an errand and coming back, and now here came the hooded man they were waiting for back up the hall, followed by the same Talos. They were jumpy, but that's not the same thing as alert. Their nerves actually worked against them because they were straining their senses for what they couldn't see and hear, not what was slowly and confidently walking up to them right in front of their faces.

As soon as I stepped through the door, I drew the katana. The blade wasn't in the proper position, and I had to drop everything else and there was nothing pretty about it, but I was fast. My initial motion flung the scabbard and its harness off the blade and into the face of the farthest guard on my left. The bared blade cut the throat of the closest guard in front of me, and when I kept going with the motion, I cut the throat of the guard to my right. The full turn I kept moving into brought both of my hands on the hilt and centered my body weight behind the blade—the first really proper strike I executed. To give you an idea of how quickly this went, the first guard still hadn't cleared the harness out of his face when I took his head off. Half-Fae are immune to a lot of things. My katana isn't one of them.

One of the throat-slit guards tried to raise his rifle directly at me, and I cut it out of his hands. The other one was too focused on the inconvenient fact that he was dying to worry about doing his job. He stumbled away as if he could leave his cut throat behind him. The guard who I had decapitated had at least managed to get a lot of blood on my robe, though. You would think blood would blend with a red robe—especially one worn by the kind of people who presumably liked to sacrifice living beings—but that wasn't the case. It left dark and very visible stains all over my torso.

Fine. I took the robe off, being very, very careful not to dislodge the amulet I was wearing underneath it. The wave of adrenaline receded and left me stranded there, weak and dizzy. Not good. But with all due respect to Robert Frost, I had promises to keep, and miles to go before I got my head ripped off, so I strapped on my weapons and kept going. Hopefully, I would have at least a second where anybody who saw me would assume I was the skinwalker that Nick had killed.

The Talos kept clanking after.

Fortunately—sort of—the defenses I passed through had been disabled. I went through a stone passageway with square tiles on the floor, and someone had thoughtfully spray-painted specific tiles. I had a bad moment where I wondered if that meant I was supposed to step on them or avoid them, but when I stepped on them, nothing happened. Then I had another bad moment when the Talos kept following me, but when I looked back, it was stepping on the painted tiles too.

Another corridor had square patches on the walls where

pictures had been removed. I didn't even want to know what kind of pictures. One of the many things Templars do is create forgeries of haunted paintings, quietly replacing the paranormal landscapes and portraits so that the pictures' notoriety will fade into urban legend status. I don't know if the Templars have gotten *The Anguished Man* or *The Hands Resist Him* yet or not, but whatever canvases had been here recently, they were presumably the supernatural equivalent of radioactive to anyone not protected by a geas.

I have no idea what the next room would have done to me under normal circumstances. Or normal abnormal circumstances.

The last obstacle was a maze. Seriously. The walls were made of overlapping writhing tentacles. I don't even want to know how that was possible or what ancient bargain had been made to arrange it. This was primal dark Fae magic. I would be willing to bet, though, that the walls moved and rearranged their patterns daily or weekly, and that making a wrong turn was instantly fatal. Fortunately, the correct pattern had once again been spray-painted on the floor, and I came into a large metal room where five men and women in red robes were at the forefront. Three of them were standing in a line, maintaining a chant whose language was unknown to me, while the other two waited to spell them when their voices got weak. At the back of the room was a vault, which opened and led to another vault, which had been opened and led to another vault, which had been opened and led to another vault, which...well, you get the idea. There were four open vaults in all, and all of them contained curious items, sarcophagi and necklaces and rings and coins and books. I even saw a spinning wheel. The foremost vault door was the only one I could see clearly, and it was titanium and massive. A series of runes had eaten through it like acid, leaving their shapes permanently seared through the metal.

Speaking of Aine, she was in front of the last vault door, along with two other people. She was playing a xylophone. Well, not really playing it. She was just standing in front of it with whatever you call xylophone sticks. A tall white-bearded man in a grey business suit was next to her with his hands poised to press into openings that I couldn't actually see. I later found out that each of his fingers had a ring with a different gemstone, the rings arranged in a specific sequence. And a third man, dark-haired, fit-looking, and fortyish in a knight field suit with the helmet off was giving them directions. "No, we'll die if you try that one."

Well, at least now I knew why the banshee hadn't been willing to just leave Boston entirely. The central archive and its defenses and guards had been her primary objective all along. That had really been bothering me.

I shot one of the chanters in the face with my Ruger. Not point-blank, but close enough. I was using my last magazine, bullets made out of a high-entropy alloy so new that it didn't have a name yet, produced in some lab that the Templars financed. The alloy was aluminum-light and titanium-hard and insanely expensive. Each bullet cost as much as a midsized luxury car, which is why researchers were still trying to find new ways to produce the same results before marketing it. But all I really cared about was that no ward or pact or spell had ever been formed against the alloy. I had intended to use the bullets to kill Redcaps, but I wasn't going to discriminate. The chanter stopped chanting forever, half-Fae or not.

The truly bizarre thing was that neither the remaining chanters nor the two half-elves standing by tried to stop me. One of the watchers immediately began chanting to replace the half-elf

I'd killed and keep the cycle unbroken. That was so strange that I shot another chanter just to see if it would happen again. It did. But there were no backup singers left. Maybe that's why Aine screamed so loud when I was about to shoot a third time.

The scream staggered me. Her wailing thinned the barrier between our dimension and some energy-parched place that wanted to suck all life down to the rind. Light and heat and something else got drained out of the room like water swirling down a hole. I was already weak, and I almost passed out. Fortunately, that wail staggered the chanters too, and Aine quickly realized that she had to stop or end the very recitation she was trying to sustain.

"JOHN!" she called as she and her two companions ran back through the series of vaults, and I tried to pull myself together enough to function. "DON'T! WE'RE TRYING TO END THE KNIGHTS' GEAS!"

What? That paralyzed me for a moment in an entirely different way.

"It's true!" she said earnestly, continuing to move forward. "Claimh Solais is in that vault! We already have the Spear and the Cauldron! We've located the stone! All we need is the sword and we can undo the spell of binding!"

She was referring to the four great treasures of the Tuatha De Danann. The four great Fae artifacts that the Knights Templar had sworn their oath on when they pledged to maintain the Pax Arcana almost a millennium ago. It was too much to take in. My geas was kicking in and trying to take control of my body to stop her. My brain was seizing up under this latest assault of shocking news and intense emotional responses. My body was confused. Was it supposed to fight, flee, or faint?

I desperately wanted to be free of the geas, that foreign presence that gave me migraines and nightmares and made me sleepwalk and pass out and freeze up when I resisted it too much or too often. That slave yoke that so many Templars had been bound to for so long. I wanted it so badly that for a moment, I was tempted to try to shoot myself in the stomach just so that I couldn't stop her.

"That's what this has all been about?" I gasped. Pieces began falling into place fast and powerfully as if from some great height. She wasn't just playing games with my head; she was playing Tetris. Without the geas, the Order would fall apart. Thousands and thousands of Templars would leave, or talk, or refuse to raise their children to be anything but children. Some Templars would stay in the Order out of stubbornness, or habit, or fear. Some would try to use the vast resources the Order had acquired—the corporations and networks and political influence and dossiers with sensitive personal information and magic artifacts—for purely personal gain.

It would be a whole new world. Maybe better, maybe worse, maybe just different, but I could tell that world to go to hell whenever I felt like it. I wanted that. I wanted that with all my heart.

But there were other factors to consider.

Like the fact that Aine might be lying.

Like the realization that the scheme probably wouldn't work because Aine no longer had the safe exit out of the archives that she thought she did.

Like the fact that the Round Table's fate was linked to the Templars now, Crusaders or no Crusaders.

Like the way Aine thought I didn't notice how she was using my moment of hesitation to creep closer and closer.

And no matter what else I was, I was a Charming. The evil witch had kidnapped a goddaughter. My goddaughter. What did she think was going to happen?

I didn't shoot another chanter. I shot Aine in the throat. She staggered back, and even if she could make that body she was wearing like a torn-up suit keep moving, she wasn't going to be wailing again anytime soon. Then I shot another chanter. The guy in the knight armor was already charging me at this point, and I'd thought I had more time, but I was moving slower than I realized. I managed to shoot him once in the face, but I might as well have shot a blank. I watched the bullet actually drop off when it hit him. It didn't even bounce. He was a skinwalker. That was my last coherent thought before we went down into a tangle of limbs. He was only moving at normal human speeds, but I was so weak and slow that it didn't matter.

I managed to lower my chin when he went for my throat. I brought a knee up into his crotch, and the impact died as his skin suit's aura transferred the kinetic energy somewhere else. I shook my head when the skinwalker tried to gouge my left eye out, and then Nick was on top of him. I don't know where Nick came from or what had changed his mind. All I know is that Nick reached around the skinwalker's throat and shoved his fist into the skinwalker's mouth, and that fist went all the way in and kept going. I guess that's another advantage of having malleable flesh. Nick's arm was buried in the skinwalker's mouth all the way up to the elbow when the skinwalker thrashed off of me, eyes bulging. Somewhere under that magic disguise, there was a body that still needed to breathe. Hell, for all I know, Nick had his fingers on the skinwalker's tonsils.

I dragged myself to my feet and was fumbling for my katana when Aine hit me. Once. Twice. Going. Going. The katana was gone and Aine was gargling. Her face was contorted into a rictus of raw hate, and her blows had maniacal strength behind them, but I wasn't quite unconscious when the banshee lowered her head to hammer another shot into my breadbasket. I collapsed forward and grabbed onto her head in a headlock, forcing her skull down under my shoulder. It was as much to keep myself from falling as anything else. She hammered a punch into the place below my navel and above my crotch, and I threw my legs back so that my body was almost a straight line, letting my weight and her lack of leverage do what my fading strength couldn't, pressing her head down farther.

Bent way over, Aine rammed into me and reached behind my thighs to lift my legs up, and I let her, tucking my knees in so that all my weight and all of her upper torso and motion pulled her down on top of me with her head still locked in my arms. I wrapped my legs up around her ribs and over her back, and that's when she somehow managed to grab my testicles. Game over. I released her and threw myself backward, and she slid forward and slammed her knee into me, then hit me in the stomach, then the throat. She didn't even have to put her whole body into it. I was done. I tried to make my body move, but that was it. I had nothing left. Nothing.

Well. Nothing except her bronze amulet. It was in my left hand. The Talos's sword came swinging, and if Aine hadn't sensed something, the blade would have torn her in half. As it was, she turned just enough that some of the flat of the sword caught her before the massive blade's edge did. She was knocked violently through the air, her left arm a stump at her shoulder.

The white-bearded man tried to pull Aine to her feet where she landed, but as soon as she was on her knees, she reached up with her remaining hand and took the man's bronze amulet off of his throat while the Talos was clanking forward. Aine draped the amulet over her head and fell back to the ground. Her ally gaped at her, and then he died. The Talos's sword didn't even slow down when it passed through him.

What followed was one of the stranger races I've been in during my long life. Nick was out of it. He had killed the

skinwalker and the two remaining chanters, but the last one
had somehow managed to set Nick on fire before dying, and
he wasn't getting up again anytime soon. I lay on my side,
watching Aine. She lay on her side watching me, her shoulder
stump unbound and uncauterized. How much control over her
mortal frame could that unearthly will exert when she had lost
so much blood and was still bleeding? Aine's eyes were wide
and crazy and full of burst blood vessels. I don't know what
mine were like. We both just stayed down, trying to gather up
enough will or energy to be the first one to start moving again.

Aine won. To be fair, Aine's spirit wasn't quite as linked to
her body's physical well-being as mine was. She looked like a
meat puppet with invisible strings when she yanked herself jerk-
ily back up to her feet and staggered back into the vaults. The
vaults? Aine came back with a brass canister in her remaining
hand. It looked a bit like one of the clockwork bombs Templars
use in areas where the magic is high, but beneath the clock in
the canister's side, there was a combination lock.

Aine sat down so that she could steady the device with her
knees and set the timer. Then she turned the canister so that I
couldn't see what numbers she was using and turned the combination once, twice, three times. She was no lady. A clock
started ticking. Satisfied that her work was complete, Aine
straightened, almost fell over, then began staggering off. She
didn't have anything else to gargle at me and didn't try to finish
killing me personally with her hands. That's right. You don't
want any part of this, bitch. I'll drag myself over there with my
chin muscles and bite your toes off.

Aine didn't even wave good-bye. Being a sociopath means
never having to say you're sorry.

Hurhrgh. So. A bomb. A combination I didn't know. Huh.
I lay there staring at it. Clockwork. I was about to run out of

time. Hah. Wait a minute. I managed to throw one of my arms up over my side and flopped my hand around the small of my back. The canister of liquid nitrogen was gone. It took another burst of will, but I yanked my head to the side. There it was. On the floor over there. How did that happen? Oh, right, the skinwalker. *Okay, you can do this, John. Curl the body up into a fetal position. That's right. Palm on the floor and push. Try again, dumbass. Rock a little first. There you go. Stay on your knees. No, don't. Leg up, come on. Leg up. You got this. That's a boy. Houston, we have a foot on the floor. Countdown to lift-off. 1...2... 3...2...okay. That's okay. Let's try that again. 1...2...3...*

Eventually, I managed to shuffle over and get the canister of liquid nitrogen. Eventualater, I dragged it and my body back to the brass canister. I sprayed the bomb with liquid nitrogen, and it froze. Fortunately, it didn't shatter, and neither did my hopes and dreams. Finally, I lay back down to heal.

I wasn't worried about Aine coming back when she discovered that I had messed with the dalaketnon's door. You see, I didn't just render that door useless. I'd been studying runes lately, and I have a good memory. I'd gotten a pretty good look at that scary-ass door in the dalaketnon castle too. So, I'd sent Aine to the Faerie realm.

I didn't know much about the Fae. I knew they'd punished Aine and that they were notoriously unforgiving. I knew that Aine had been making long-range plans to undo the Fae's geas, defy their banishment, and invade their land. And I was pretty sure that if anyone could keep Aine from coming back to a new mortal host so that she could just try, try again, it was the Fae.

Take that.

~47~

AND THEY LIVED HAPPILY FOR AN INDETERMINATE PERIOD OF TIME AFTERWARD

So, that brass canister? It wasn't a bomb. It actually contained a bunch of tiny magical organisms called gigelorum that are basically microscopic. They're so small that they can live like fleas on the bodies of fleas, drifting on air currents with dust motes when they need a host. These gigelorum had somehow been infected with a virus, and the brass canister had magically put them in stasis. All the combination mechanism had been designed to do was pop the top of the canister off, but if that had happened, the gigelorum would have dispersed into the air, looking for new hosts. Basically they would have become a mobile sentient plague, though a finite one. The virus wasn't airborne; it was gigelorum-borne, and the disease had sterilized them. Gigelorum don't have long life-spans, either. They would have all died off after an entire city or two.

I knew this because Emil Lamplighter told me so himself, after a search-and-destroy team of knights discovered me. And

Emil knew this because Aine hadn't created the brass canister mechanism or the magical virus—she had just known that the gigelorum were in the second-to-last vault. That archivist who had been with her turned out to be Dawn's uncle, a member of the family tree of traitors the skinwalker had told me about. The family that was currently being hunted down and run to ground.

On the plus side, the Templar Loremaster had turned up alive in one of the closed-off rooms I hadn't investigated. He was a valuable treasure trove of information that Aine had hoped to delve into once she had undone the knights' geas. Even if the Loremaster didn't prove cooperative, without the geas to ward him from enchantments, or choke the words in his throat, or shut his heart down if he tried to abandon his duty, Aine would have been able to have fun spelling or torturing information out of him.

I won't say this is ironic, because a lot of people toss that word around without actually understanding what it means, but what I'm about to say is something anyhow—it turned out that the whole mess had been set into motion when the Loremaster started implementing werewolves from the Round Table as Central Archive guards. Not in the lower levels, but in the upper levels that archivists would have to pass through in order to get to the lower levels.

This was a problem for Aine because two skinwalkers had already replaced Templar guard dogs, and three others had been studying and training to replace carefully selected staff members of the Central Archives, and the new addition of werewolf guards who hung out with other werewolves off duty would have ruined everything. Constance had been kidnapped to help create a climate where those werewolves would leave, be dismissed, or be removed without creating any undue suspicion that the archives themselves were being targeted. And it had worked. When those werewolves didn't show up, the Loremaster had just assumed that they had gone into hiding, like so many of the Round Table werewolves were going into hiding, and, given the climate of distrust, he hadn't hurried to replace them.

It was a bit like setting off a bomb that would kill a thousand people just to kill one. So much collateral death and damage would make it very hard for anyone to find one specific motive in that kind of maelstrom, and again, overkill wasn't something Aine shied away from. She was playing for very big stakes. She had been willing to expose herself or the skinwalkers because she was ready to initiate an endgame before the Templars even realized that they were playing.

And speaking of the resulting climate of distrust, I also found out where Simon had disappeared to. Thomas Cassibury and four of his most trusted lieutenants were captured. Not only that, Cassibury and his inner council had been proven to be skinwalkers in front of other Crusaders who had been captured. Word was being spread that Cassibury had done so much to spur on conflict between knights and werewolves—both in recent events and during the original war between knights and werewolves that had drawn me back into the Templars' orbit to begin with—because Cassibury wanted to destroy the Order and was afraid that werewolves would prove to be too strong a strategic asset.

And you can believe as much of that as you want to. I didn't believe much of it. It was too convenient. This was pretty much the only scenario that could have healed—or at least bandaged—the rift in the Order that Cassibury had caused. In one incident, the Crusader issue was defused, or at least as decisively settled as possible for the time being. I'm not saying

I know how Cassibury and his subordinates could have been framed so convincingly. Was it possible that the raid had killed some of the Crusaders who could have contradicted this version of events, while leaving a few other Crusaders who were actually Emil Lamplighter's agents in place? Could there have been some sleight of hand involved to make it look like Cassibury and his cohorts were invincible skinwalkers? Shooting Cassibury and his council with blanks, stabbing them with stage knives in front of witnesses, maybe even setting them on fire with that liquid that burns out so quickly that it doesn't damage the skin?

For that matter, Simon never had told me about how all those efforts to track down and expose skinwalkers were going. Somebody the Templars had trusted had installed that door in Constance's home. Somebody had to have helped the skinwalkers pretending to be Austin and Bob when they first began their impersonations. Was it possible that Simon had captured five skinwalkers and done something really convoluted? Like capturing Cassibury and friends and then putting them in cages with skinwalkers, torturing the skinwalkers until they were willing to make suits out of their fellow captives and put on those suits just to stop the pain, then putting the skinwalkers in some circumstance where they could be visibly killed in front of witnesses? Hard to imagine.

I honestly have no idea what happened. But I find it very suspicious that Emil's number-one fixer just happened to disappear at such a crucial time shortly before this Order-shaking revelation went down. I don't know what to do with my suspicions, though. Am I morally bound to search for a truth here? I would inevitably do a lot of harm looking for a truth that I'm not a hundred percent sure exists, and also wind up hurting my pack's chances of survival in the process. For now, I just want to live, learn, and keep my eyes open and my opinions to myself.

But I don't want to keep myself to myself. The weather had finally turned, and Sig and I were at a small private party at a beach house that we'd rented on Nauset Island. The vodyanoi Mama Lenke was catering the event while waiting to reopen the Buried Treasure—we'd boated her in at night and she seemed to be enjoying the company. And there was a lot of company, at least by my standards. Molly Newman had healed from her burns enough to be out and about and would soon be returning to Clayburg. It was really good to see her looking lively again, though I didn't get much of a chance to talk to her. Molly spent most of the evening out on the shore in earnest conversation with Babette, the rusalka. I'd checked in on them a few times, and I'd never seen the rusalka looking so animated and friendly and excited before, and then at the end of the evening, she was just gone. I kind of had a feeling that Babette wasn't coming back either.

Choo and the ex that Choo was trying to win back were there too. Her name was Chantelle and she was currently a paralegal in Roanoke while she put herself though law school. She didn't open up much, mostly just sat back and took everything in and radiated tension, at least until Choo brought a Scrabble game out. Apparently, Scrabble was Chantelle's passion and her curse. She started trash-talking and getting competitive despite herself, which made her much more likable and more aggravating at the same time. When I was ready to meet her, I would challenge her to a game, but that evening, I stayed out of it and fed my geas scraps of information.

Sarah White and Ben Lafontaine and Virgil and Tula and Constance were all there too. Kevin Kichida, Sarah White's apprentice, and the woman very pregnant with Kevin's child,

Leanne Collins, were there as well, though they weren't a couple. Leanne was ten years older than Kevin and had gotten Kevin's sperm from a clinic, not knowing that the donor was a psychic with a troubled family history. Now Leanne was living with Sarah, learning the baking trade. It was good. Leanne would need guidance if her child developed the sight. She and Kevin seemed to have a wary respect for each other, though they did spend most of the evening arguing about the gestating baby's name. Kevin wanted Leanne to name the baby after his father. Leanne was determined to name the kid Sidney.

Parth and Kimi showed up. We had mended fences, Sig actually a bit more grudgingly than me. I didn't feel betrayed by Parth. I actually felt more comfortable around him now that the fact that his cooperation was conditional and motivated by self-interest was out in the open. Parth and I didn't have to pretend to be friends, which actually made us better friends. Maybe that only makes sense to a paranoid person. Although, are you really paranoid if people actually do keep trying to deceive you and kill you?

Nick and his girlfriend, Adriana, who I really liked, were there too. Nick hadn't been around when the knights found me, by the way. You can add how Nick got out of the Central Archives unobserved to the list of all of the other things I don't know. Maybe he went into chameleon mode. Maybe his semisolid body is really good at squeezing through vents. Maybe he just took turns being different people in all the confusion until he hopped, skipped, or jumped out of there. I never told anyone under a geas about how Nick had helped me. That was the least I could do. I didn't offer to let him have my share of the bounty Mama Lenke paid out, though. A deal is a deal.

Maybe, someday, I would be able to invite some knights to something like this. Steven Hunter, for example, was alive and well. It turned out that Aine had been drugging him to make sure he slept deeply at nights, and she'd left Steven alive on the off chance that she might be able to come back and pretend to be Dawn Jenkins a little while longer. Steven was just lucky he'd been spending so much time hanging around werewolves familiar with his scent. Otherwise, Aine probably would have had a skinwalker wearing her guard's face in a heartbeat. Or under four hours, anyhow. But I couldn't invite Steven or Angel or the paladins. Mama Lenke and Sarah White and Parth and Nick never would have come if any other geas-born were on site.

It was a nice evening. Everybody avoided shop talk—or, more accurately, chop talk—because everyone in the room had at least one mutual friend with someone else, but nobody knew everybody. At some point, I was going to have to look into the organization that the skinwalker had mentioned. I was going out on a limb and assuming that "The School of Night" wasn't a name for a community college with evening classes, but I wasn't convinced that all of the half-elves in the world were about to rise up in revolution, either. Most of the half-elves I'd met in recent years weren't likely to be involved in any kind of jihad. They just wanted what most people want—to live their lives and be left alone. No, this School of Night, assuming the banshee hadn't just fed the skinwalker a line of bull, was probably some kind of secret society or terrorist group within the larger population, just like all terrorist groups. The only reference I'd found to the name was an occult secret society that had existed in England in the Elizabethan era. In an era where secret passages, spies, poisonings, and political intrigue were the norm, the group had done a very good job of keeping its goings-ons secret. The only thing anybody seemed to know about it was that John Dee, Walter Raleigh, and Christopher Marlowe, the author of *Dr. Faustus*, were all rumored to be members.

Shakespeare had mentioned the group once, just once, in *Love's Labor's Lost*. "Black is the badge of hell, the hue of dungeons, and the School of Night." That sounded encouraging. But I wasn't getting pulled back into any more quests anytime soon. I had some stuff to work on, and stuff to work out, and stuff to work around. Sig and I were planning to take that trip to Iceland, though we hadn't told anyone and wouldn't make any reservations until we showed up at the airport counter.

Toward the end of the evening, I was sitting in a comfortable armchair, and Sig was nestled in my lap, her scent in my nostrils, her body in my arms, her cheek and neck next to my lips. "I owe all of this to you, you know," I whispered in her ear.

She tilted her head and kissed me, ardently if awkwardly, and then settled back into my shoulder. We half sat and half lay there for a time, listening to Virgil and Tula tell Adriana about the similarities between being members of a police force and an army and a werewolf pack. No surprise attacks. No detailed planning. No big, emotionally intense discussions. No high-stakes decisions. I could use at least a couple of months of this. Then Sig turned her head and murmured, "So. It seems to me that that back when all this started, you said something about loving me?"

ACKNOWLEDGMENTS

Thanks to Colleen Oefelein for doing her best to drag me kicking and screaming into the social media age. Thanks a lot, Colleen! No, seriously, thanks a lot, Colleen. I'm sure it's been a pain in the ass, but I don't want it to seem like an entirely thankless task. Best of love, life, and luck.

The story continues in...

Legend Has It
Book 5 of the Pax Arcana

Keep reading for a sneak peek!

extras

orbit

meet the author

An army brat and gypsy scholar, ELLIOTT JAMES is currently living in the Blue Ridge Mountains of southwest Virginia. An avid reader since the age of three (or that's what his family swears, anyhow), he has an abiding interest in mythology, martial arts, live music, hiking, and used bookstores.

introducing

**If you enjoyed
IN SHINING ARMOR,
look out for**

LEGEND HAS IT

Book 5 of the Pax Arcana

by Elliott James

CHAPTER ONE

JEEPERS CREEPERS, WHERE'D YOU GET THOSE PEEPERS?

Once Upon a Time, I was being stalked. It wasn't a mercilessly hot afternoon in the twisty stinking backstreets of Calcutta, and I wasn't hurriedly making my way through the dimly lit compartments of a rollicking train headed for Istanbul—it was actually a quite pleasant summer evening in Clayburg, Virginia, on the campus of Stillwater University. The grass was freshly cut, the warm air was cooling, and the sun was a soft

433

lingering glance...and I was being stalked anyhow. It seemed a little unfair. I didn't see or smell whoever (or whatever) was trailing me, but you know that feeling you get when you can feel someone's eyes on you, and when you turn around, you see them? I didn't turn around, but it wasn't because I dismissed the feeling—it was because I trusted it completely. I'm part wolf and all paranoid.

Casually reaching into my pocket, I took out that week's burner phone and stared at it for a while as if I were getting a message instead of making one. Then I texted Molly Newman that I wasn't going to be meeting her after all. Molly was the holy person in my Monster-Hunters-R-Us club, and she had gotten badly burned while performing an impromptu exorcism. She was off her pain meds, but Molly still wasn't driving because it made her tense, and having to lift her shoulders and keep them in the same position while steering hurt. I was supposed to be picking Molly up from some kind of philosophy seminar whose title was a full sentence and contained a lot of suffixes. I had sat in on some of the first session out of curiosity and whispered to Molly that this was no time to stop taking pain medication, but she had just shushed me and kept taking notes.

Somebody's watching me. I texted. *Have Choo pick u up & tell Sig I'm heading 4 library.*

Molly couldn't have been too into the class because she responded immediately. *By the texting of your thumb, something wicked this way comes?*

I smiled in spite of the situation but didn't have anything substantial to add, so I tapped out *Unsure. Be careful* and put my cell away. Molly would tell me if she couldn't get in touch with Sig or Choo or if everything wasn't okay with them, so in a way I had just killed two birds with one phone.

extras

There weren't a lot of students on Stillwater's campus in July, and the commons had a lot of wide open space for Frisbee throwing and outdoor graduation ceremonies and public displays of affection and such, so I didn't pull any of that overt pretending-to-tie-my-shoe-so-I-can-look-behind-me nonsense, not while I was that exposed. I just turned left and headed for the university library.

There was no sign of anyone reflected behind me in the library's double glass doors, but I hadn't really been expecting to get that lucky. The library's lobby had metal detectors that had been installed after the Virginia Tech shooting not too many miles or years ago, and I had a silver steel knife and a Ruger Blackhawk in my knapsack. Well, it was more like I had a knapsack around my silver steel knife and Ruger Blackhawk, but either way, it could be a problem. There were small wooden cubicles against the wall where students could put their possessions before passing into the library proper, but I decided to just put my knapsack on the small wooden table next to the metal detectors, then put my keys and phone in the small wicker basket setting on it.

As soon as I passed through the metal detectors, I reached around and grabbed the knapsack again. There was no campus security guard around to call me on it—I'm guessing the university cut the funding for that about three months after the devices were installed. The bored student on some kind of work program behind the front desk hadn't looked up from his texting when I came in, and the only two other people in the lobby were sitting in the plush comfy chairs in the west corner having an animated discussion about the upcoming parking issues that would arrive with the fall semester. They smelled like adjunct faculty (coffee, pizza, and desperation).

I decided to hang out in the front lobby for a little while. If I was being followed by a single competent individual, he, she, or it would have to come in after me quickly to make sure I wasn't threading through the library to find another exit. A team would send someone after me too, but they could afford to give me a little more lead time while they spread out around the building, and whoever they sent would have to remove any ear buds or concealed weapons before going through the metal detector. That was a show that I wanted to see. Either way, staying still for a few moments would tell me something, so I grabbed some book called *The Devil's Grin* off the recent arrivals shelf and sat down at a wooden table facing the entrance. When I set my backpack down by my chair, I unzipped the top.

The book looked pretty interesting.

My stalker walked in before two minutes had passed. The library took a deep breath when she opened the door, and that made two of us. I caught a whiff of dhampir, which just meant that whatever ceremony had tried to turn her into a vampire had been interrupted or bungled somehow, and at the very least she still retained enough humanity to walk around in faint daylight. Her build was slim and feminine and athletic, and I could tell from the way she moved that she had martial arts training. A lot of it. It was the way she kept her weight centered and feet balanced so automatically that it seemed natural. Her skin was pale but not waxy looking and her red hair so dark that it was almost brown. She wore both her hair and her dress short. The latter was black and high on her upper thighs, tight but comfortable looking as it hung around almost a foot above knee-high boots. A purse on very long straps was slung casually by her right hip at about the same place that a gun would be holstered, and her hand was resting against it. She looked like she was auditioning for a video game.

Intent eyes narrowed in on me immediately, then took in the metal detector. Her slender mouth quirked, but she walked over to the wooden storage rack and somehow managed to crouch elegantly in that short dress. I'm pretty sure she transferred something that wouldn't fit in her purse from her right boot to the back of one of the small cubicles, using her body as a screen.

She didn't waste any time coming over to my table, moving her purse around the metal detector the same way I'd negotiated my knapsack. This time everyone in the library was watching, but no one protested. When she got closer, she greeted me in a low voice that sounded like she had smoked before her body stopped getting damaged by such things. "You're not as stupid as you dress."

I was wearing running shoes, faded jeans, and a dark green tee shirt. "I look like I belong here," I told her. "You fit in about as well as a porcupine in a petting zoo. What do you want?"

She didn't flash anything but a tight smile as she drew a chair and sat across from me in one smooth motion. She was sex on legs. Long legs, though I studied them dispassionately. "I'm just satisfying my curiosity. I heard Stanislav Dvornik was dead. I wanted to see who had finally killed the old bastard."

So that's what that flat place where an accent should be was all about. She was probably East European. Stanislav Dvornik had been a kresnik, a Croatian vampire hunter, and kresniks weren't as uptight about working with werewolves and dhampirs as knights were. Stanislav Dvornik had also been a homicidal shitheel, and I was in a relationship with his former girlfriend. "Are you sad that I beat you to it or looking for revenge?" I asked.

Her eyes were hazel and sharp and had seen a lot of people die. "I haven't decided yet."

"I've had relationships like that," I admitted. "Are you going to let me know when you figure it out?"

That thin mouth made another slash of a grin. "Now where would the fun in that be?"

"Ah," I said. "You're one of those."

"One of what?" she asked without sounding like she cared too much.

"I'm not sure there's a word for it," I said. "But it's like ennui with sharp teeth. In my experience, very few things are as dangerous as predators who have long life spans and get bored easily."

She laughed softly. "Do *you* get bored easily?"

"I'm pretty sure I don't," I said. "I've tried really hard to find out, but people like you keep showing up and ruining the experiment."

"Ah," she mocked me. "You're one of those."

I played along. "One of what?"

"In *my* experience, very few things are as sad as killers who don't want to admit they're killers."

"Oh, I'm a killer all right," I said. "But I try to make a distinction between killing and murder if that's what you mean."

"That's part of it," she agreed. "The hypocrisy."

"Everybody's a hypocrite sometimes," I said. "It's the reasons we need to be a hypocrite that make us who we are."

"Maybe you should be the one taking a philosophy class instead of your friend," she observed.

At the mention of Molly, my body released some chemical into the air. It was a pheromone with fear and rage and more than a hint of homicide seasoning it. My stalker inhaled slightly through her nose as if smelling the bouquet of a delicate wine and smiled faintly. "Did I just make an enemy?"

"I haven't decided yet," I echoed. "But if I remove your head from your shoulders now, I won't consider it murder."

"Good," she told me. "You should keep that kind of thing clear cut."

"It will be," I promised. "So, how did you know good old Stan?"

Maybe she kept her smiles so tight because of fangs. Whatever the reason, the next grin she flicked my way was almost gone before I saw it, and she ignored my question. "He must have really hated you."

"It was loathe at first sight," I confirmed before trying again. "How did he react when he met you?"

"He wanted me," she said this without a trace of self-consciousness. "Stanislav was a hypocrite too. He was terrified of getting old, so any woman who represented immortality threatened and attracted him at the same time. Any male who didn't age just pissed him off."

"That doesn't make him a hypocrite," I pointed out.

"He was a hypocrite because he slept with the things he hated," she explained. "And killed the things he wanted to be."

That sounded about right. "You're Kasia," I guessed. I had only heard the name once, while Sig and Stanislav were arguing in the back of Choo's van years ago, but I have a good memory for such things.

She smiled that smile again, so minute that it almost wasn't, but at least she wasn't faking it. "Sigourney mentioned me?"

Sig hates being called *Sigourney*, and I suspected Kasia knew it. "Only once, and briefly," I said. "I don't think she likes talking about you."

"Guilty consciences will do that," Kasia asserted.

"Are you sure you're here about Stanislav?" I asked.

She made an amused sound and ignored my question again. "How did he die?"

"An asshole," I said.

She just waited.

"He tried to kill me," I elaborated. "I won't say it was unprovoked, but it was definitely an overreaction. A betrayal too. We were supposed to be on the same team at the time."

"So it was over Sigourney," she said.

"It was never about Sig," I disagreed. "He just made her his excuse for a lot of things. That's what self-destructive shitheads and narcissists do. They have this idea of what they need, like a cookie cutter mold, and they try to force other people to fit into it. And when people don't or can't, the asshats blame them for it."

She nodded, but I don't think she realized that she was doing it. "You aren't what I expected." It sounded like an accusation.

"That's the other way Stanislav died," I said.

"I believe it." She switched topics abruptly. "You smell like you're attracted to me. Do you want to have sex?"

"Sure," I said. "I'm into bondage though. I like to handcuff my partners and put them in a shark cage first. Is that okay?"

Kasia laughed. "I could be up for it, but somehow you don't seem like the type." She rose up from her chair then, scooping her purse off the floor by the top of its straps so that I wouldn't be alarmed, and smoothly shifting it onto her shoulder.

"Leaving so soon?" I asked.

"I'm guessing Sigourney will be here shortly," she explained. "I don't think it would be a good idea to be around both of you at the same time."

"It probably wouldn't," I agreed. "Speaking of good ideas, something needs to be said before you go."

She paused.

"I'm a wolf," I told her. "This is my territory."

"Better," she said approvingly.

"You sound like a judge with scorecards."

Kasia mimed holding something over her head. "Seven point five."

"After all that training and hard work," I said. "It comes down to politics."

"I think you might be funny." She studied me for a moment, then announced: "I've decided to tell you something."

"Okay," I said.

"The knights are going to be contacting you soon."

"Because of something you've done?" I asked carefully.

She dismissed that suggestion with a small puff of breath. I caught a whiff of nicotine so faint that it was almost a rumor. "I wish. No, something big is happening. I'm not sure what, but I keep my ear to the ground, and I've felt the tremors."

"So it's really big," I said. "Whatever it is."

"Somewhere between the *Titanic* and the apocalypse," she agreed.

"Which one of the four horsemen does that make you?" I wondered.

She gave me one more of those enigmatic smiles for the road. "I think you know the answer to that."

"You are awful pale," I said.

This time she didn't smile. "Careful."

"It's a little late for that," I told her.

"Hmmn," she said thoughtfully. "Maybe even an eight." I didn't respond, and she turned to leave then. "By the way, I'm driving a red Audi, but it's not mine. I can give you the license plate if you don't want to bother following me to my parking lot."

I waved that off. "It's no bother."

introducing

**If you enjoyed
IN SHINING ARMOR
look out for**

CHASING EMBERS

by James Bennett

ONE

East Village, New York

Once upon a time, there was a happy ever after. Or at least a shot at one.

Red Ben Garston sat at the bar, cradling his JD and Coke and trying to ignore the whispers of the past. The whiskey, however, was fanning the flames. Rain wept against the window, pouring down the large square of dirty glass that looked out on the blurred and hurrying pedestrians, the tall grey buildings and sleek yellow taxicabs. The TV in the corner, balanced on a shelf over the bar's few damp customers, was only a muffled drone. Ben watched the evening news to a background of murmured chatter and soft rock music. Economic slump to the Eagles. War in Iran to the Boss. The jukebox wasn't nearly loud enough, and that was part of the problem. Ben could still hear himself think.

Once upon a time, once upon a time…

He took a swig and placed the tumbler on the bar before him, calling out for another. The bartender arrived, a young man in apron and glasses. The man arched an evaluating eyebrow, then sighed, poured, and left the whole bottle. Ben could drink his weight in gold but Legends had yet to see him fall down drunk, so the staff were generally tolerant. Seven East Seventh Street was neither as well appointed nor as popular as some of the bars in the neighborhood, verging on the dive side of affairs, but it was quiet on weekdays around dusk, and Red Ben drank here for that very reason. He didn't like strangers. Didn't like attention. He just wanted somewhere to sit, drink, and forget about the past.

Still, Rose was on his mind, just as she always was.

The TV over the bar droned on. The drought in Africa limped across the screen, some report about worsening conditions and hijacked aid trucks. Strange storms that spat lightning but never any rain. What was up with the weather these days, anyway? Then the usual tableau of sand, flies, and starving children, their bellies bloated by hunger, their eyes dulled by need. Technicolor pixelated death.

Immunized by the ceaseless barrage of doom-laden media, Ben looked away, scanning the customers who shared the place with him. A man slouched farther along the bar, three sat in a gloomy booth, one *um*-ing and *ah*-ing over the jukebox at the back of the room, all of them nondescript in damp raincoats and washed-out faces. Ghosts of New York, drowning their sorrows. Ben wanted to belong among them, but he knew he would always stand out, a broad-shouldered beast of a man, the tumbler almost a thimble in his hand. His leather jacket was beaten and frayed. Red stubble covered his jaw, rising via scruffy sideburns to an unkempt pyre on his head. He liked to think there was a pinch of Josh Homme about him—Josh Homme on steroids—maybe a dash of Cagney. Who was he kidding? These days, he suspected he looked more like the other customers than he'd care to admit, let alone a rock star. Drink and despair had diluted his looks. No wonder Rose didn't want to see him. And in the end, his general appearance, a man in his early thirties, was only a clever lie. His true age travelled in his eyes, caves that glimmered green in their depths and held a thousand secrets....

That lie had always been the problem. Since returning to New York from a six-week assignment in Spain, his former lover wouldn't answer his calls or reply to his emails. When he called round her Brooklyn apartment, only silence answered the buzzer on the ground floor. Sure, he'd hardly been the mild-mannered Englishman, leaving her high and dry, dropping everything to run off on the De Luca job. And it wasn't as if he needed the money. A week back in the city and Rose was another ghost to him.

But once upon a time, once upon a time, when you didn't ask questions and I could pretend, we were madly in love.

Outside, the rain lashing the window, and inside, the rain lashing his heart. April in Insomniac City was a lonely place to be. Ben took another slug of Jack, swallowed another bittersweet memory.

A motorbike growled up outside the bar. The customers turned to look at the door. Exhaust fumes mingled with the scent of liquor as the door swung wide and the rain blew in— with it, a man. The door creaked shut. The man was dressed completely in black, his riding leathers shiny and wet. His boots pounded on the floorboards, then silenced as he stopped and surveyed the bar. His helmet visor was down, obscuring his face. A plume of feathers bristled along the top of the fibre-glass dome, trailing down between his bullish shoulders. The bizarre duds marked him out as a Hell's Angel or a member of some other freeway cult. The long narrow object strapped to his back, its cross end poking up at the cobwebbed fans, prom-ised a pointed challenge.

As the other customers lost interest, turning back to their chatter, peanuts and music, Ben was putting down his tumbler of Jack, swivelling on his stool, and groaning wearily under his breath.

The man in the helmet saw him, shooting out a leather-gloved finger.

"Ben Garston! This game of hide-and-seek is over. I have some unfinished business with you."

Ben felt the eyes in the place twist back to him, a furtive pressure on his spine. He placed a hand on his chest, a faux yielding gesture.

"What can I say, Fulk? You found me."

The newcomer removed his helmet and thumped it down on the end of the bar. It rested there like a charred turkey, loose feathers fluttering to the floor. The man called Fulk grinned, a self-satisfied leer breaking through his shaggy black beard. Coupled with the curls falling to his shoulders, his head resem-bled a small, savage dog, ready to pounce from a pedestal of beef.

"London. Paris. LA." Fulk named the cities of his search, each one a wasp flying from his mouth. Like Ben, his accent was British, but where Ben's held the clipped tones of a Londoner, the man in black's was faintly Welsh, a gruff, rural, borderland burr. Ben would have recognised it anywhere. "Where've you been hiding, snake?"

Ben shrugged. "Seems I've been wherever you're not."

Fulk indicated the half-empty glass on the bar. "Surprised you're not drinking milk. I know you have a taste for it. Milk, maidens, and malt, eh? And other people's property."

"Ah, the Fitzwarren family wit." Through the soft blur of alcohol, Ben looked up at the six-and-a-half-foot hulk before him, openly sizing him up. What Fulk lacked in brains, he made up for in brawn. Win or lose, this was going to hurt.

The whiskey softened his tongue as well. He made a half-hearted stab at diplomacy. "You shouldn't be here, you know. The Pact—"

"Fuck the Pact. What's it to me?"

"It's the Lore, Fulk. Kill me, and the Guild'll make sure you never see that pile of moss-bound rubble you and your family call home again."

But Ben wasn't so sure about that. Whittington Castle, the crumbling ruins of a keep near Oswestry in Shropshire, England, was in the ancestral care of a trust. The same trust set up in 1201 by the then-presiding King John, signed and sealed by Lackland and later bestowed to the Guild of the Broken Lance for safekeeping. The deeds to the castle would only pass back to the Fitzwarren estate when a certain provision was met, that being the death of Red Ben Garston, the last of his troublesome kind. The last *waking* one, anyway. Of course, the Lore superseded that ancient clause. Technically, Ben was protected like all Remnants, but he knew that didn't matter to Fulk, the same way he knew that the man before him was far from the first to go by that name. Like the others before him, this latest Fulk would stop at nothing to get his hands on Whittington and reclaim the family honour, whether he risked the ire of the Guild or not. Vengeance ran in Fulk's bloodline, and his parents would have readied him for it since the day he was born.

"The Lore was made to be broken," Fulk Fitzwarren CDXII said. "Besides, don't you read the news? The Pact is null and void, Garston. You're not the only one anymore."

"What the hell are you talking about?"

Before he could enquire further, the man in black unzipped his jacket, reached inside, and retrieved a scrunched-up newspaper. He threw it on the bar, next to Ben's elbow.

It was a copy of *The New York Times*. Today's evening edition. Warily lowering his eyes, Ben snatched it up and read the headline.

STAR OF EEBE STOLEN

Police baffled by exhibition theft

Last night, person or persons unknown broke into the Nubian Footprints exhibition at the Javits Center. The thieves made off with the priceless diamond the Star of Eebe, currently on loan from the Museum of Antiquities, Cairo. Archaeologists claim that the fist-sized and uncut gem came from a meteor that struck the African continent over three thousand years ago. Legend has it that the Star fell into the possession of a sub-Saharan queen.

According to a source in the NYPD, the thieves were almost certainly a gang using high-tech equipment, improvised explosive devices, and some kind of ultralight airborne craft, a gyrocopter or delta plane. Around midnight last night, an explosion shook the Javits Center and the thieves managed to navigate the craft into Level 3, smashing through the famous 150-foot "Crystal Palace" lobby, alighting in the exhibition hall, and evading several alarm systems to make off with the gem. The police believe the thieves took flight by way of another controlled explosion, fleeing through the Javits Center's western facade, out over 12th Avenue and the Hudson River, where police suspect they rendezvoused with a small ship headed out into the Bay, across to Weehawken, or upriver to...

God knows where. Ben scanned the story, plucking the meat off printed bones. The details were sketchy at best. Between the lines, he summed them up. No fingerprints. No leads. No fucking clue.

The bar held its breath as Ben slapped the *Times* back down. No one spoke, no one chewed peanuts, no one selected songs on the jukebox. The rain drummed against the window. Four-wheeled fish swam past outside.

"Clever," Ben said. "But what does this have to do with me?"

"More than you'd like." Fulk grinned again, yellow dominoes lost in a rug. "You're reading your own death warrant."

"If this is a joke, I don't get it."

"No, you don't, do you?" The man in black shook his head. "I've travelled halfway around the world to face my nemesis and all I find is a washed-up worm feeling sorry for himself in a bar. Is it because of your woman? Is that why you returned? She won't take you back, you know. Your kind and hers never mix well."

"You came here to advise me on my love life?"

Fulk laughed. "You're asleep, Red Ben. You've been asleep for *centuries*. The world holds no place for you now. You're a relic. You're trash. I only came here to sweep up the pieces."

"Yeah, your glorious quest." Ben rolled his eyes at their audience, the men in the booth, the guy holding peanuts frozen before his mouth, the one shuffling slowly away from the jukebox. "You need to get over it. Mordiford was a very long time ago."

A storm rumbled up over Fulk's brow, his deep-set eyes sinking even farther into his head. Obviously, it was the wrong thing to say. The ages-long river of bad blood that ran between Ben and House Fitzwarren was clearly as fresh to the man in black as it had been to his predecessors, perhaps even to the original Fulk, way back in the Middle Ages.

Muscles tense, Ben sighed and stood up, his stool scraping the floorboards. Despite his height, rivalling the slayer's, he still felt horribly slight in Fulk's shadow. The whiskey could make you small too.

He didn't need this. Not now. He wanted to get back to the Jack and his heartbreak.

"It was yesterday to us," Fulk said, the claim escaping through gaps in his teeth. "We want our keep back. And Pact or no Pact, when we have it, your head will hang on our dining room wall."

The bartender, cringing behind the bar, guarded by bottles and plastic cocktail sticks, chose this moment to pipe up.

"Look, fellas, nobody wants any trouble. I suggest you take your beef outside, or do I have to call the—"

The sword Fulk drew from the scabbard on his back was a guillotine on the barman's words. The youth scuttled backwards, bottles and cocktail sticks crashing to the floor, panic greasing his heels. He joined the customers in a scrambling knot as they squeezed their bellies out of the booths, tangling with the other guys pushing past the jukebox to the fire exit at the back of the bar. In a shower of peanuts and dropped glasses, they were gone, the fire exit clanking open, a drunken stampede out into the rain.

Ben watched them leave in peripheral envy. He grimaced

and rubbed his neck, a habit of his that betrayed his nerves. Then his whole attention focused on Fulk. Fulk and the ancient sword in his face. There was nothing friendly about that sword. They had met before, many times. Ben was on intimate terms with all fifty-five inches of the old family claymore. Back in the Middle Ages, the Scots had favoured the two-handed weapon in their border clashes with the English, and while this one's saw-toothed edge revealed its tremendous age, the blade held an anomalous sheen, the subtle glow informing Ben that more than a whetstone had sharpened the steel.

"Who're you having lunch with these days? The CROWS? That witchy business has a nasty habit of coming back to bite you on the arse." Ben measured these words with a long step backwards, creating some distance between the end of his nose and the tip of the sword. "House Fitzwarren must be getting desperate."

"We are honour-bound to slay our Enemy."

"Yeah, yeah. You're delusional, Fulk—or Pete or Steve or whatever your real name is. Your family hasn't owned Whittington Castle since the time of the Fourth Crusade, but you dog my heels from Westminster to Manhattan, hoping to win a big gold star where hundreds of others have only won gravestones. And as for this"—Ben nodded at the gleaming blade—"tut tut. Whatever would the Guild say?"

"I told you, snake. The Lore is broken. The Guild is over. And now, so are you."

The sword swung towards him, signalling the end of the conversation. The step Ben had taken came in handy; he leaned back to avoid an unplanned haircut. The blade snapped over the bar, licking up the tumbler and bottle of Jack, whiskey and glass spraying the floorboards.

Fulk grunted, recovering his balance. The weight of the claymore showed in his face. His leathers creaked as he lunged forward for another blow, the blade biting into beer-stained wood. Only air occupied the space where Ben had stood moments before, his quick grace belying his size as he lifted his barstool and broke it over the man in black's head.

Cracked wood made a brief halo around Fulk's shoulders. His strap-on boots did a little tango and then steadied, his shaggy mane shaking off the splinters. He grimaced, his teeth clenched with dull yellow effort. The sword came up, came down, scoring a line through shadow and sawdust, the heavy blade lodging in the floorboards.

The stroke dodged, Ben rushed through his own dance steps and elbowed Fulk in the neck. As the man choked and went down on one knee, Ben leapt for the bar, grabbing the plumed helmet and swinging it around, aiming for that wheezing, brutish head.

Metal kissed fibreglass, the sword knocking the helmet from Ben's grip. Sweat ran into his eyes as Fulk came up, roaring, and smacked Ben with the flat of the blade. If this had been an ordinary duel, Fulk might as well have hit a bear with a tooth-pick. The Fitzwarrens' attempts to slay their Enemy had always remained unfairly balanced in Ben's favour, and over the years, he had grown complacent, the attacks an annoyance rather than a threat. Now his complacency caught him off guard. This was no ordinary duel. Resistant to magic as he was, bewitched steel was bewitched steel and the ground blurred under his feet moments before his spine met the jukebox. The air flew out of his lungs even as it flew into Jimi Hendrix's, a scratchy version of "Fire" stuttering into the gloomy space.

The song was one of Ben's favourites, but he found it hard to appreciate under the circumstances. He groaned, trying to pull himself up. Stilettos marched up and down his back. His buttocks ached under his jeans. He tasted blood in his mouth, along with a sour, sulphurous tang, a quiet belch that helped him onto his feet, his eyes flaring.

Across the bar, Fulk's eyebrows were arcs of amusement.

"Finally waking up, are we? It's too late, Garston." The man in black stomped over to where Ben stood, swaying like a bulrush in a breeze. "Seems like my granny was wrong. She always said to let sleeping dogs lie."

Fulk shrugged, dismissing the matter. Then he brought the sword down on Ben's skull.

Or tried to. Ben raised an arm, shielding his head, and the blade sliced into his jacket, cutting through leather, flesh, and down to the bone, where it stuck like a knife in frozen butter. Blood wove a pattern across the floorboards, speckling his jeans and Doc Martens. They weren't cheap, those shoes, and Ben wasn't happy about it.

When he exhaled, a long-suffering, pained snort, the air grew a little hot, a little smoky. He met Fulk's gaze, waiting for the first glimmers of doubt to douse the man's burgeoning triumph. As Fulk's beard parted in a question, Ben reached up with his free hand and gripped the blade protruding from his flesh. The rip in his jacket grew wider, the seams straining and popping, the muscle bulging underneath. The exposed flesh rippled around the wound, shining with the hint of some tougher substance, hard, crimson, and sleek, plated neatly in heart-shaped rows, one over the over. The sight lasted only a second, long enough for Ben to wrench the claymore out of his forearm.

Hendrix climaxed in a roll of drums and a whine of feedback. The blood stopped dripping random patterns on the floor. The lips of Ben's wound resealed like a kiss, and his arm was just an arm again, human, healed, and held before his chest.

"Your antique can hurt me, but have you got all day?" Ben

forced a smile, a humourless rictus. "That's what you'll need, because I'm charmed too, remember? And as for my head, I'm kind of attached to it."

Flummoxed, Fulk opened his mouth to speak. Ben's fist forced the words down his throat before he had the chance. The slayer's face crumpled and then he was flying backwards, over the bloody floor, past the bar with its broken bottles, out through the dirty square window that guarded Legends from the daylight.

Silvery spears flashed through the rain. Teeth and glass tinkled on asphalt. Tyres screeched. Horns honked. East 7th Street slowed to a crawl as a man dressed head to toe in black leather landed in the road.

Somewhere in the distance, sirens wailed. Ben retrieved the rag from the bar, thinking now was perhaps a good time to leave. As he stepped through the shattered window, he could tell that the cops were heading this way, the bartender making good on his threat. Who could blame him? Thanks to this lump sprawled in the road, the month's takings would probably go on repairs.

Stuffing the *Times* into his jacket, the rain hissing off his still-hot shoulders, Ben crunched over to where Fulk lay, a giant groaning on a bed of crystal. He bent down, rummaging in the dazed man's pockets. Then he clutched the slayer's beard and pulled his face towards his own.

"And by the way, it isn't sleeping dogs, Fulk," he told him. "It's *dragons*."

454